For Solly,
Happy re
James M...

Mademoiselle Maupin

~ A Blood Opera: Book One ~

James Frost

Clink
Street

Published by Clink Street Publishing 2022

ISBN:

Acknowledgements

This book is dedicated to Amanda, whose boundless support and encouragement have made it possible.

My gratitude also goes to the members of the Clink Street Publishing team, for all of their help at every stage of the process, and to Louis for his illustrative work.

Author's Note

Julie d'Aubigny existed in history, though she is depicted here in a fictitious manner, as are other historical characters, events and locations. The life of the real Julie d'Aubigny is surrounded by much scandal and conjecture, but there is little doubt regarding her willingness to disregard the social mores of her time, or to engage in behaviours not typically expected of ladies in the 17th and 18th Centuries. She never allowed herself to be defined by the imposed strictures of social hierarchy.

Part I

~ Arnold ~

Monday September 13th, 1756

The Gin Trap, was what they called it nowadays. London, the sprawling capital of the British Empire and the industrial capital of the age, was a city heated by coal fires and cloaked in smog. Narrow, stinking streets consisted of houses built atop houses, where the overflowing gutters played host to the carcasses of rats, of dogs, of the occasional abandoned horse, and all too often of men and women. This century had brought industry and scientific enlightenment to this mightiest of cities, filling its avenues with the endless clanking cacophony of workshops and factories, and turning the metropolis itself into a diabolical machine whose air scratched at the lungs with every breath.

Babies born here were lucky to survive beyond their first two years; more than half perished in that time. Disease was as rampant as poverty. Comfort and luxury were the preserve of aristocrats and industrialists, who looked with public disdain and private envy towards their French and Prussian rivals. For the teeming multitude who lived their lives in hardship, respite from this misery lay in the welcome embrace of intoxication.

The gin craze had found its way into London's very soul,

and while Parliament sought to fight it with the passing of the Gin Act five years ago, the pestilence of alcoholism was one from which the city's common classes would be slow to recover. For so many human beings, London the Great was very much the Gin Trap.

For Arnold Brennan, it felt like there was no clearer evidence of the Devil at work upon British soil. Born out of wedlock to a barmaid in Whitechapel, drunkenness and deprivation had been all around him from the time of his very earliest memories. His reaction to the vices that surrounded his upbringing had been to adopt an ascetic life of faith and piety, joining the ranks of the Church of England in hopes of bringing the light of God upon this place of darkness.

Although there had been ample opportunity to move on from this notoriously filthy district of London, to seek a quiet parish in less troubled surroundings, he had chosen to stay in Whitechapel and serve as a curate to the vicar of St Mary Matfelon Church, hoping to bring as many despairing souls as he could into the Lord's salvation. In the war against evil, every soul saved was a victory; but as the district continued to mire itself in violence, vice and a lack of hope that bordered on nihilism, Arnold could not help but feel that his success as a crusader for the Word of God was proving rather limited. When the day came that he stood to face judgement for his life's deeds, would he honestly be able to look upon the face of the Lord and claim that he had done all that was in his power?

While Arnold's decision to join the priesthood was certainly rooted in his childhood, it was perhaps not something that either of his parents would have anticipated. Lisa Brennan worked in the Queen Anne Stuart, a drinking establishment which Arnold considered to be a wretched hovel of iniquity at the best of times, and she had raised him by herself in the upstairs room where she lived.

Of course she needed money to survive, and in a place of such desperate poverty she considered herself lucky to have stable employment, but Arnold could never quite rid himself of the view that his own mother was a part of the fabric of this city's sins, for she made her living serving that very gin which ensnared and poisoned so many lives. She had dared hope that the brief affair between herself and Arnold's father would offer her a route to a better life, but that hope had proven to be a vain one. Sean Musgrave, at the time a young physician with good connections and a promising future, would not lower himself to supporting – much less marrying – a public house wench, even if she were carrying his child.

After Arnold's birth Sean had disavowed any further contact with her, and it was only when Arnold was a grown man of sixteen years that he had first spoken with his own father. All too often he had prayed for God's forgiveness for the fury that he felt towards that man, recalling Jesus' teaching that to look upon a person with anger was to have committed murder in one's heart. But now Sean Musgrave was gone, his life seemingly one more casualty of time and tide, and Arnold was on his way to the offices of K. Whitfield & Son Attorneys at Law, in response to the letter which they had sent him. Much to Arnold's surprise, it seemed that the late physician's will had made some mention of his bastard son's name.

For the life of him, he could not fathom what inheritance his father would leave to a son whom he had never wanted and never sought to include in his life. Arnold suspected that Sean had never viewed him as anything other than a walking reminder of his own sexual immorality, which given the chance he would much rather forget.

The Whitfield & Son legal practice was tucked away in a rather shabby building on Houndsditch, but as Arnold made his way in through the front business entrance, he was at least grateful to be out of the afternoon's rain. The office itself was spartan, orderly and lacking in undue grandeur, something of which Arnold's personal tastes could approve. It was also, thankfully, considerably better-maintained than the building's exterior, though the bitter aroma of pipe tobacco clung to the room. Behind the office's main desk, a grey-haired gentleman of older years peered over his spectacles from the papers in front of him, taking stock of his new visitor.

By appearance Arnold was of tall and slender build, with a sallow-skinned face that looked a little older than his twenty-two years. He kept his hair short and beard neatly trimmed, though as with many Londoners, there were the red scars of eczema at the corners of his mouth and around the collar of his throat. His clothing habitually leaned towards the austere: a simple grey raincoat and brimmed hat over black jacket and breeches, with a stiff-collared white shirt. A small, plain wooden crucifix hung about his neck, habitually worn whether he was in church or not. The man at the desk put aside his papers and writing pen before addressing him.

"May I be of help to you, Sir?"

"Since you summoned me here, I expect you can," Arnold replied, reaching beneath his coat to retrieve the letter which had brought him here. "My name is Arnold Brennan, I have an appointment with you concerning matters of my father, Doctor Sean Musgrave."

"I see. Please do take a seat, Mister Brennan."

"I take it that I am speaking with Mister Whitfield, then?"

"Kenneth Whitfield, yes. I served as your father's legal

counsel, and now I am the executor of his will. I do of course offer my condolences regarding his passing."

Whitfield stood in order to shake Arnold's hand, his grip surprisingly firm for such aged fingers. The lawyer returned to his chair, and the clergyman took the seat across from him, after removing his hat and coat.

"Thank you," Arnold told the older man. "You are so far the only one to do so, given that your letter was the first news I received of his death. But I'm sure you are aware that my father and I were never terribly close with one another. I cannot claim to know his widow nor his other children closely, and for the most part I doubt that they want much of anything to do with me. They didn't take the trouble to inform me of any of this. And quite honestly I'm surprised that my father made any provision for myself or my mother at all, given how far he had distanced himself from us."

Whitfield offered no comment on those of Musgrave's living family who actually carried his name, but instead stated matter-of-factly; "Oh, I'm afraid that your father's wishes do not concern Miss Lisa Brennan. This meeting pertains to items which were left specifically to yourself. However, if my correspondence was the first that you heard of his passing, then I must assume that you do not know how your father died?"

"I do not."

"Then I am deeply sorry to tell you that it was not of natural causes. Sean Musgrave was murdered, not far from the London Hospital on Prescot Street. I do believe that the Bow Street Magistrates' Office are investigating the case, though it seems probable that it was a violent robbery."

Arnold fell silent for a time as he absorbed what the lawyer had just told him. He was no stranger to the rate at which this city's inhabitants ended one another's lives, be it by accident or intent. Bloodshed was a routine occurrence in Whitechapel; there were plenty of occasions when he had assisted the Reverend Lowther with the funerals of victims, and plenty more when he'd had to console members of his parish who had lost friends and family to violence.

Knowing that his father had died from one such act of malice did not provoke the same stabbing feeling of personal loss that he had experienced from the deaths within his own congregation, but nonetheless it kindled a spark of deeper grief which had not been there until now. Or perhaps not truly grief, but simply compounded guilt for all those times that his thoughts of Sean Musgrave had been blackened with anger. Negligent parent or not, he never truly meant to wish the man dead.

"I see," he finally mustered. "I shall pray further for him. At least now his soul is at God's mercy. And I pray that the Bow Street Runners are successful in apprehending his killer."

In truth, Arnold did not hold the Bow Street Runners in terribly high regard. He could admire the sentiment behind their creation, the desire for a regulated and official public body to carry out the work of law enforcement, rather than relying on private individuals and hired guns. But he had heard too many stories of the brutality of some of their methods, their disregard for the wellbeing of innocents, and all too often their neglect of duty and their outright corruption. Sometimes it seemed that there was little to differentiate the Runners from any of the criminal gangs that plied their ugly business on Whitechapel's streets.

"Of course, may he rest in peace. He did mention to me when he last amended his will that you had chosen to join the clergy. Perhaps that was why he decided to bequeath certain possessions of his to yourself, feeling that you would likely have more interest in them than any of his more immediate family."

"Which possessions, exactly?"

"A number of written documents and items from his natural philosophy collection. He placed them in my custody a little over two years ago, when he made the amendments to the will. I'm given to understand that many of the items were themselves only recently acquired by him, inherited from a friend of his who had themselves become deceased not long prior."

That statement was enough to draw Arnold's curiosity. His mother may have been poor her whole life, but he knew that his father hailed from a relatively well-to-do family in Killyleagh, and that another, somewhat older and wealthier Irishman from that same town had likewise been a practitioner of medicine. A rather renowned one, at that.

"Inherited from a friend? Are you perchance talking about Sir Hans Sloane? I'm given to understand that my father was a student of his in his younger days, and they remained in contact for a long time afterwards, even during Sir Hans' tenure as the Physician Royal. I recall that he died in January, three years ago. I'm sure I read that he donated his entire natural philosophy collection to the crown. Has it not been on public display in Montagu House since then?"

"Quite so, Mister Brennan. Some 71,000 curiosities were purchased by His Majesty King George II from Sir Hans' estate, in accordance with his dying wishes, for public exhibition. The 1753 British Museum Act was passed to establish them as a permanent display. But Sir Hans did also leave some specific manuscripts and items to Sean Musgrave, who made it clear to me that he wished them to be passed to yourself in the event of his death. Whatever those items were, he did not see fit to keep them on display in his own house. They have been sitting in a locked chest in your father's bank vault for the past two years. But legal ownership of them now passes to you. I should like to arrange for the chest to be transported to a place of your choosing."

How very like my father, the words coursed through Arnold's mind before he immediately chastised himself for thinking ill of the dead. Never had Sean taken the time to actually know his illegitimate son, yet he assumed that because Arnold was a clergyman, he would have use for a collection of pressed flowers and trophies of dead animals. Granted, natural philosophy was a common pursuit among many country vicars in the Church of England, but Arnold's ministerial obligations here in Whitechapel seldom afforded him time or opportunity for such things.

Of course he could think of one immediate use for them; he could pass them on to the museum collection at Montagu House, perhaps in return for a modest donation to St Mary Matfelon Church, which would be of considerable help to the poor and needy of the parish. That, at least, would be a fitting legacy for his father's inheritance.

"Very well, Mister Whitfield. I would be grateful if you could arrange for the delivery to St Mary's Church. Whatever is in this chest, I am certain that myself and Vicar Lowther will find appropriate use for them. Are you able to tell me where and when my father's funeral will be held? I would never presume to attend without invitation from the family, but I should like to be able to visit his grave in future."

"If you wish to discuss the funeral, then you shall do best to reach out to either Missus Musgrave or your half-siblings, as I would not wish to betray their confidence. But I do believe he is to be interred at St Benet Gracechurch, should you wish to pay your respects in your own time."

Shortly after that, the appointment came to its close. The young clergyman came away from the meeting with uncertainties knotting inside him, unsure about whether to seek contact with his father's true, legal family. There was a bond in shared mourning after all, and since Sean had seen fit to not entirely neglect his bastard from his will, maybe it would be within the bounds of propriety to ask them if he may attend the funeral. Perhaps they would be understanding, maybe even welcoming. But there was also every chance that his attempts to speak with them would be akin to poking a finger into a healing wound, and he had no wish to be the source of further undue distress for a grieving family.

He continued to contemplate the issue as he made his way eastwards from Houndsditch, through the tangled warren of streets which made up Whitechapel. His route did not take him directly back to St Mary's; as much as he would have preferred to return to the church and his daily duties, there was somewhere that he felt obliged to visit first. Some forty years ago the Queen Anne Stuart had been the site of the Ponies Inn, until an unfortunate lightning strike during a late-summer storm had resulted in that establishment being burned to the ground. A retired ship's captain named Fulton Darby had then bought the land and built his new drinking house there, naming it in honour of the monarch under whose reign he had been born. His son Robert Darby was now the landlord, and the Anne remained one of the worst hives of drunkenness and criminality in the city. As he approached the entrance, Arnold steeled himself to enter the very place which he had once worked so hard to escape.

Stepping in through the front door, his nose met the all too familiar scents that were soaked into the sawdust on the pub floor; the scents of cheap liquor, human vomit, urine and worse. The hour was getting close to midday, not exactly the busiest time in the Anne's open hours, but nonetheless the pub was host to a number of its unemployed and ungovernable clientele. Bloodshot eyes and sour expressions glanced in Arnold's way as he entered, but his arrival did not hold attention for long.

Even the worst of the scoundrels who frequented this place knew the curate's face, and didn't question why this particular man of the cloth would set foot here. Behind the public bar, a stout-bodied, brown-haired Irishwoman with a face toughened by a lifetime's hardships looked up towards her son. It was fair to say that Arnold's looks took far more after his father than his mother. Her blue-grey eyes were not devoid of love, but it would be foolish to pretend that there was no strain between the pair.

"Good day to you, Mother," Arnold began, moving to a spot towards the end of the bar, away from the collection of patrons who sat nursing drinks, in varying states of consciousness. He chose to remain standing rather than take a stool, though he did remove his hat and place it down on the bar.

"So how did it go?" she replied, never one to waste time on pleasantries. Lisa Brennan had long since abandoned any sense of attachment to her one-time lover, and she had been just as surprised by the news of Sean Musgrave's death as Arnold had. He had in fact been the one to inform her of it after receiving Whitfield's letter, since he was certain that none of Musgrave's family would have gone out of their way to tell her. She had perhaps been even more surprised than Arnold was that he had been included in the will at all. It was only natural for her to wonder what share of wealth might have been left for herself.

"There was some deeply unfortunate news. Mister Whitfield informed me that the cause of Father's death was in fact murder. His body was found near the hospital, not far from here at all. Given that he was a man of good standing, I'm told that the Bow Street Runners are investigating. Someone's likely to hang for his death."

For a moment Arnold could have sworn there was a flicker of sadness in Lisa's gaze, a feeling of loss and injustice for the man who had cast her off so many years ago, but that flicker was swiftly smothered.

"The Runners know they're not welcome around here. They won't find anyone answering their bloody questions if they come knocking. And I don't doubt that some poor bastard will end up on the end of a rope for what happened to Sean, but I'll be damn surprised if the man they hang is the man who killed him."

"I know that, Mother. I just wanted to tell you what Whitfield told me."

"Aye. And what else did this lawyer have to say?"

"Father hasn't left anything to your name, I'm sorry. The effects that he's given to me are going to be moved to St Mary's soon. It's nothing much… bits and pieces from his natural philosophy collection, things that for whatever reason he didn't donate to the museum. He probably thought a clergyman would have use for it."

Lisa's fingers tapped idly on the bar as she absorbed what Arnold had to say. Given Sean's abandonment of her twenty-two years ago, could she truly have expected him to have a change of heart now, when he had a wife and legitimate children to think about? But after Arnold had mentioned the letter, maybe she had let herself feel a sliver of hope that he would have provided her some small measure of security.

"Whatever's in this collection, I don't plan to keep it," Arnold told her, "I'll either donate it to Montagu House or I'll find a private buyer. Its value will be donated to St Mary's, but I promise I'll put aside some provision out of it for you, Mother. If the money's enough… then maybe you won't have to work here anymore."

He couldn't stop himself from saying it, but he knew that it was a mistake even as the words left his lips. Arnold despised the life that the Anne represented, but he knew that Lisa was all too attached to it. Her wages may be a pittance, but the job had kept a roof over her head for as long as she'd lived in London.

"This again, boy?" she snapped. "I'm happy where I am. You can look down on me, and count as many of my sins as you please, but this is a living to me and it's the reason you didn't starve as a babe. I don't need a bloody rescue."

Arnold stiffened. He didn't want this argument and he knew this exchange was futile, but he couldn't help himself. What he wanted was to get her away from this den of vice, more than anything. Surely, if the opportunity for a more virtuous life were there, she would take it?

"With a bit of money to fall back on you could afford to look elsewhere. You could find work somewhere better, maybe even find a husband. You could live a respectable life."

The look that she gave him for that remark caused his words to catch in his throat. Since joining the priesthood Arnold had tried to persuade his mother on several occasions that marriage to a responsible man would be a right and proper thing for her to pursue, but she remained steadfast as ever in her opposition to the idea. Far from a path to happiness, it was clear that Lisa Brennan viewed the prospect of marriage as a chain. While she'd certainly had her share of lovers in the past two decades, her views on the subject of lifelong vows had only hardened ever since Sean's rejection.

"A husband? *Really?*"

Arnold looked away, unwilling to meet her gaze.

"I just think that—"

"Your father left us alone, Arnold. Left me alone after I told him I had you in my belly. And you stand here now that he's gone and you tell me that I should put that trust in someone again? You must think your mother's a bloody fool."

"I don't think that at all."

"Enough. He abandoned me, but I raised you, so you're damn right that you'll put some provision aside for me, however much you sell that bloody collection for. All that time you spend preaching about God's justice, it shouldn't hurt you to give a bit of consideration to man's justice while we're alive."

At this, Arnold's expression darkened. He could have scolded her for blaspheming, for what little good that would have done. He could have reminded her that while Sean's murder was the work of man's sin, this inheritance was surely a sign of God's benevolence, an olive branch that Lisa would do well to grasp and not to selfishly squander. But he'd spoken similar words to her so many times before now. As a girl in Londonderry she had been raised as a humble Protestant, but her faith in the goodness of God had long been extinguished by life in this city. Resigned, Arnold picked up his hat.

"Goodbye for now, Mother. I'll be in touch."

It was later that afternoon when the delivery was made to St Mary Matfelon Church. A wagon arrived with two men and a large chest of oak and iron, with a very sturdy-looking lock upon its lid. The workmen had been paid in advance for the delivery by Mr Whitfield, so Arnold could only assume that the cost of the transportation was likewise covered by the will. He had the two men move the heavy box to his room in the rectory, after which they handed him the key and went about their business. What surprised Arnold as he examined the hefty iron key was the tiny cruciform symbol engraved upon its handle, and he wondered why anyone would see fit to mark a simple key with the emblem of the

Lord. Further examination of the chest revealed identical markings chiselled into the lock and hinges, along with the words of Psalm 23 carved in very fine script along the edge of the lid.

"The Lord is my shepherd," Arnold read quietly to himself, following the letters that encircled the box, "I shall not want. He maketh me to lie down in green pastures: He leadeth me beside the still waters. He restoreth my soul: He leadeth me in the paths of righteousness for His name's sake. Yea, though I walk through the valley of the shadow of death, I will fear no evil: for Thou art with me; Thy rod and Thy staff they comfort me. Thou preparest a table before me in the presence of mine enemies: Thou anointest my head with oil; my cup runneth over. Surely goodness and mercy shall follow me all the days of my life: and I will dwell in the house of the Lord for ever."

Of course he knew the words of the Psalm by heart, but he couldn't fathom why they would be written upon a box containing artefacts and curiosities of the natural world. It was upon a growing tide of intrigue and anticipation that Arnold finally inserted the key into the lock, turning it with a dull clunk of metal before easing the lid up and back. The chest was filled with papers, some loose, but mostly organised together in a collection of leather folds. Beneath those neatly-curated papers he could see what appeared to be a collection of small wooden boxes, or perhaps frames. A single note, written on vellum, sat atop the rest, as if inviting him to read it first. Gingerly, Arnold picked it up and looked it over.

S,

This is all of it that has not been lost, stolen or destroyed. Every correspondence, every study, every sketch and every piece of research which we have deemed to be both authentic

*and useful. You might wonder why I have chosen to entrust
these things to you when I have had ample time to induct my
own daughters into the truth of our endeavours, but the fact
is that I could not bear to see my dearest children burdened
by these revelations. No, I would rather that they live full
and happy lives, blessedly free of the darkness which you and
I have explored. I can think of no more fitting custodian
than yourself for these effects. Guard them well. Should you
find a worthy successor to continue our crusade, I suggest
that you first refer them to the final correspondences sent to
me by La Maupin.*
    Yours,
        H.

Was this all some absurd game? It seemed obvious enough
that the two parties identified by singular letters were Sean
Musgrave and Hans Sloane respectively, but this note was
hardly what Arnold would expect to accompany works of
science and scholarship. The letter's talk of darkness and
a crusade, and a desire to leave Sir Hans' children 'unbur-
dened', all sounded like the workings of some clandestine
occult society. Had this all been some gentlemen's joke, a
kind of eccentric pastime that his father had been involved
in with no lesser a man than the Physician Royal of Great
Britain? And who exactly was La Maupin?

Looking upon the collected bundles of documents, he
immediately noticed that one of those leather folds was
marked with the letters *Mlle. Maupin*, and Arnold immediately wondered at its contents, if Sir Hans deemed them
to be a suitable starting point for whoever was intended to
inherit this mystery.

Opening up the fold and looking through the assembled papers did nothing to assuage his curiosity, however,
for absolutely none of them were legible to him. The young

clergyman could recognise the French language when he saw it written down, but he had not the faintest knowledge of how to read it himself. He opened up another fold of parchments, likewise marked with that same curious name, but found only more documents – all correspondences by the looks of them – written in French. Perhaps his father had been fluent enough to read these, but to Arnold they were of no use.

Another fold, this time containing not letters but a treatise of some kind, perhaps medical in nature, but equally impossible to understand for it being written in Latin. Unlike Arnold's contemporaries in the Catholic Church, the priesthood of the Church of England had little use for the language of the long-gone Roman Empire, viewing it as a needless barrier between the common people and the Word of God. Since Arnold possessed no medical education and no particular academic learning beyond that of his station in the Church, the Latin text was just as indecipherable to him as the French.

His attention was most definitely caught by an anatomical drawing, however, one which depicted a creature that was as loathsome to his eyes as it was impossible. It was drawn standing upright like a man, with a lean, hard body of corded muscle. Its hands and feet were clawed, and its posture was hunched, leaning forward. Its arms were proportionally longer than those of a human, and seemed partially joined to the beast's flanks by membranes of skin, labelled '*Patagium*' on the diagram. Most disturbing of all was the creature's head, which bore little in the way of human features, but was rather more like that of some grotesque bat grown to a man's size. Above this impossible anatomical study, written in the same handwriting as Sir Hans Sloane's note, there was a title: *Strigoi*.

Well this was most definitely a work of fiction. Arnold

may not have been a scholar of science, but he was quite confident that no such grotesquery as this existed in nature. Upright beasts with the combined features of bats and men were a fabrication of myth, surely no more real than dragons and unicorns. Arnold had known his father to be a serious physician, not a charlatan or a peddler of medieval superstitions, so it was clear that this whole collection was simply the product of an elaborate game of make-believe, some eccentric fantasy which Sean and Sir Hans had concocted to entertain themselves. Why Sean would bequeath this to Arnold was a mystery in its own right; did he honestly believe that the bastard son who had dedicated his life to piety and duty would be interested in such nonsense as this?

Arnold gave a sigh of disbelief and looked down at the rest of the chest's contents, those which were tucked away beneath the folds of papers. There were indeed a series of wooden frames, glass-fronted, of the sort that entomologists and butterfly-collectors would use to preserve their specimens. Yet mounted within these frames were not the tiny corpses of invertebrates, but rather arrangements of teeth. All manner of teeth, of different shapes and sizes, clearly from all manner of wild animals. While the teeth bore a myriad of different forms, they were clearly all pulled from the skulls of carnivorous beasts, for despite their variations in details they were all sharply pointed, made for the piercing and cutting of flesh.

Within each frame, beneath each mounted arrangement of predatory fangs, a small label appeared to detail the name of the creature to whom the teeth belonged, and the country in which these specimens had each been harvested, with the locations' names being given in French. Tentatively Arnold picked up one of the frames, looking upon the two sharply-pointed canines displayed within, and the label that accompanied them. '*Strigoi, Roumanie.*' An elaborate fake, surely? Those teeth could just as easily have come from a large fox, or some kind of wild feline. His eyes caught another one of the frames, and he held it up for inspection: '*Vetala, Inde.*'

Another: '*Aswang, Philippines.*'

'*Soucouyant, Caraïbes.*'

'*Sasabonsam, Empire Ashanti.*'

'*Jikininki, Japon.*'

'*Yee Naaldloshii, Haute Californie.*'

'*Camazotz, Mexique.*'

This was insane. Clearly these were just forgeries, the teeth of wild dogs and cats and other meat-eating beasts which had been carved, polished and refashioned into more exotic forms, and then mounted and labelled with these bizarre folkloric titles. Obviously a lot of work had gone into the creation of these artefacts of wild fancy, but if this was some amusing pastime between two men of science, then Arnold certainly did not condone it. It suggested altogether too feverish an obsession with pagan myths and the campfire stories of foreign heathens, and surely it would have been most unseemly – scandalous, even – for a man of Sir Hans Sloane's social standing to be openly involved in this sort of thing.

But of course he had not been *openly* involved in any such activity. Sir Hans had been known as an avid collector of curiosities with an intense fascination for nature, but also very much a rational man, not someone to go chasing fairy-tale monsters or forging elaborate 'proofs' for the existence of nonsensical things. But that was simply what was known of him publicly. Arnold could not claim to be familiar with the workings of so-called secret societies, but he had heard the same rumours as anyone in this city that hidden fraternities did exist. It was in the nature of men to plot and conspire with one another, after all, and there would always be those who chose to gather in secret to do things which wider society found decadent or objectionable.

He could perhaps believe that this was how a couple of respected physicians and scholars would entertain themselves in private, by concocting these works of superstition dressed as science. But none of that explained why Sean would want his illegitimate son to inherit any of this. Arnold had never been a party to any such games as these, so why try to involve him now that both of the original participants were deceased? He was at a loss.

It did of course leave him wondering whether any of this would be of interest to a buyer. Somehow he doubted that the serious curators of Montagu House would want anything to do with these forgeries, and Arnold would not feel at ease selling them on to one of the many travelling freak shows, which he considered to be a grossly immoral form of entertainment. His gaze did linger upon the last of the framed specimens which he inspected, to the pair of teeth which bore the label of *'Camazotz, Mexique'*. Mexico; a land about which he knew very little, save that it was a wild territory in the Viceroyalty of New Spain, far across the Atlantic Ocean. The frontier of the New World had a reputation for being a brutal place, full of dangerous diseases, savage animals and equally savage native-men.

Sir Hans was widely known to be a well-travelled adventurer, and through marriage he had acquired a lucrative plantation in Jamaica, which he had sailed to on various occasions. It wasn't unreasonable to think that he may have visited the 'Green Hell' of the Central American jungles, where he had shot some ferocious beast whose teeth now sat within this frame. And these two great fangs must have come from a ferocious animal, for they were larger and more fearsome-looking than any of the other specimens here.

Something about them left Arnold feeling distinctly unsettled, and he found himself not wanting to look at them for long. He would find time to properly assess this collection at a later, more appropriate date. For now he placed the specimens and the papers back in the chest and promptly closed the lid. He turned the key, locking the wretched artefacts away within their box, and walked out of his room feeling rather more at ease.

~ Julie ~

Thursday September 16th, 1756

There were many reasons why Julie d'Aubigny had not grown tired of travelling with her present companions, not least of which was Aida N'Dour's exquisite taste in accommodations. Their current lodgings were in a small but well-appointed inn located in Constantinople's Old City, surrounded by the architectural splendour of the Ottoman capital, and the cornucopia of spicy scents from the market in the street below. Behind the window drapes the evening sun was ebbing, disappearing beyond the city's western skyline. With each moment that the light grew fainter, Julie could feel an oppressive weight lifting from her muscles. By day she was weaker, diminished, but the night was *her* time.

Of course, the obligation towards a nocturnal lifestyle did not prevent her finding agreeable ways to pass the daylight hours. At this moment Julie and Aida lay entwined with one another atop the bedsheets, basking in the afterglow of their lovemaking. In appearance it would have been difficult for the two women to be more of a contrast. Where Julie was petite and lean of build, with the firm muscles of a dancer and more than a handful of old battle-scars, Aida's form was one of more ample feminine curves, largely unblemished save for the marks of a long-healed wound behind her left shoulder. Julie had always been fair-skinned, her complexion having only grown in pallor during the decades since her mortal life ended. Aida's body was as intensely dark as Julie's was pale, for she was a child of the Senegambia, a daughter of Wolof nobility.

Rolling free of her lover's post coital embrace, Julie stretched like a cat, enjoying the renewed sense of vigour that crept through her limbs as the sun retreated. Pulling herself upright, she sat and glanced down at Aida with eyes full of predatory yearning. Her pupils were heavily dilated, and in the fading light they appeared to reflect blood-red, not at all like the black of a human. And yet, it took far more than the sight of a vampire's hungry eyes to frighten Aida N'Dour. She had been Julie's lover for four years now, and the two had become quite accustomed to one another. Aida's fingertips trailed lazily through the black tresses of Julie's hair, her eyes watching the loose strands which stuck to her skin with sweat. As if to herself, she quietly mused;

"You are always like this, when we are about to embark on a hunt."

Julie smiled and lowered herself towards her lover, planting a delicate kiss upon her lips.

"Like what, my love?"

But of course she knew the answer to that.

"The way you make love to me like it is the last chance we shall ever get. Like you expect we will never do this again."

"We're in the heart of House Laskaris' territory. If we succeed tonight, there's still every chance that we won't make it out of this city before retribution finds us."

"You have led us on dozens of hunts, my darling. We have yet to find an enemy that can best the three of us. We will kill Eşref tonight and be gone before anyone knows to pursue us."

Such confidence, such unwavering faith that Aida had in her. But this air of assurance was far from unfounded. Julie could not have asked for a more capable and resolute pair of companions than Aida and Saul. The N'Dour twins were gifted, and at Julie's side they did more than just survive in the hidden world of bloodthirsty immortals; they positively *thrived* on this absurdly perilous lifestyle. That was one more reason why after four years of their companionship, Julie had not tired of them.

She gave Aida one final kiss before climbing off the bed, making her way towards the trunk which held their belongings. Lifting the lid, she began to retrieve some clothes. She could feel her lover's salacious eyes upon her bare back, as if teasing her.

"Are *you* feeling strong enough?"

Aida's question caused Julie to glance back over her shoulder. Her ebon lover had fixed her in her dark-eyed gaze, and one hand had shifted towards her throat, a fingertip tracing the line of her jugular.

"You know I only fed last night," Julie told her, though there was little conviction in her words. She could already hear the rise in Aida's heartbeat, the sweet anticipation in her veins.

"Just a taste, lover. It's been weeks since you drank from me. There's not a mark left from your last bite."

She was right, it had been weeks. The punctures from the last time that Julie sank her fangs into Aida's flesh had faded entirely. Mortals were prone to suffer certain effects when a vampire fed upon them repeatedly, even if that vampire only took a trivial amount of blood. But if enough time had passed for the bite to completely heal, then the risk ought to have elapsed. Julie dropped the shirt she was holding and moved back to the bed, climbing atop her lover.

"I really shouldn't weaken you on the night of a hunt…"

"I did say just a taste."

"You just want to feel the bite."

"You know that I do."

Aida tilted her head back, eyelids drifting closed, her heart thundering behind her ribs. The sight of her, the smell and the feel of her desire, was enough to tear down what little resistance Julie might have felt. She planted a trail of kisses down Aida's throat, journeying along to the shoulder, wetting the skin with a lick of her tongue. The women's hands found one another and fingers entwined, gripping tightly as Julie's red lips pulled back, revealing the lengthened fangs of a predator. A gasp escaped Aida's throat as she felt the sharp pinch, the prick of penetration, and then Julie's mouth closing upon the wound, suckling hungrily as the sweet, warm nectar began to flow.

It was the curse of every vampire to live with a hunger that could never be sated. Even when full the urge to kill, to drink to excess and gorge upon the lives of the prey remained an ever-present whisper in the back of the mind. Julie knew full well that to go without feeding for more than a few nights would provoke that whisper to become a roar, a demand which must be fulfilled. Only in the act of feeding itself, in the moments when hot, vital blood was flowing into her mouth and coursing down her throat, only then did the demon within her fall truly silent. Such moments were a bliss that could not be described with any words that Julie knew of, in any tongue that she had learned.

Beneath her Aida writhed in sensual abandon, one hand slipping free of Julie's grip and reaching up to her back, fingertips grabbing tightly at toned muscle. The act of breaking the hunger's silence was almost painful, but the vampire forced herself to stop feeding, to lift her lips away from the bite. Her lover was gasping for breath, nerves afire with pleasure, but Julie could not afford for Aida's strength to be diminished if she were to be of use on tonight's hunt. Gently she licked at the wound, bringing the blood flow to a stop. Her muscles were thrumming, their fibres burning with stolen vitality. As ever, a vampire was at their strongest right after slaking their thirst. With her hunger sated, the redness of Julie's eyes faded as they returned to their natural, human green.

"We need to get out of bed. Your brother will be waiting for us."

To Julie's reckoning, Saul N'Dour was every bit as beautiful as his twin sister, his body honed by physical training from the age when he had first been able to pick up a weapon. As the eldest son and heir apparent of Amadou N'Dour, Saul's father had been keen to ensure that his successor would be very capable of keeping himself alive in the face of adversity. Regular practice with a range of expensive tutors had fashioned the boy into an exceptionally capable swordsman and athlete by the age of fifteen. When the twins were coming of age, their father had used his close connections with the French colonial authorities in Saint-Louis to have Saul and Aida sent to Paris to be educated.

In truth it still grated upon Saul that his family's wealth and influence were maintained through collaboration with the foreign power that had attached itself to their homeland, but that influence had brought them benefits and opportunities which he had not refused. And now, nine years later, it was his father's wealth which enabled he and his sister to travel Europe in the company of Julie d'Aubigny.

Upon hearing the knock at his door, Saul surmised that the two women had finally made themselves ready for this evening's agenda, and he opened the door to welcome them into his room. Aida looked focused and ready, her mind on the task at hand. Julie likewise seemed calm on the surface, but Saul had known her long enough to be keenly aware of the predator's instincts within her, like a caged animal yearning for the wild.

She had often told him how he and his sister provided her with an anchor, allowing her to hold on to simple human pleasures rather than give in to the merciless indulgence of the bloodthirst. But he had seen her in combat more times now than he bothered to count, and sometimes he wondered how much truth there was in her assurances. If he sought words to describe her behaviour during her feuds and vendettas against her own kind, 'human' would not be among them.

With the trio now gathered, Julie looked over her two companions. During their time in Paris the N'Dour twins had wholeheartedly embraced the city's fashions, dressing in finely-tailored clothing that left no doubt as to the wealth and quality of their origins, in a city where many who shared their skin colour were slaves. Since joining Julie in her travels the pair had toned down their more ostentatious leanings, although their outfits were still very much those of the gentry.

Saul wore a midnight-blue coat and tricorne hat above a fine silk waistcoat, with knee breeches, silk stockings and leather riding boots. His sister had opted for a grey riding habit along with a deep green kaftan worn in the local Ottoman style, buttoned to just beneath her bust. For her part Julie was long accustomed to dressing in men's clothing, and while her white linen shirt, brown leather coat and tricorne looked far less impressive than the attire of her companions, it had been many decades since she last had a taste for high fashion. And here in Constantinople, it would be obvious that the three were foreigners no matter how they dressed.

"Any change from last night's reconnaissance?" Julie enquired.

"None that I could see," Saul replied. "Eşref certainly has not left the house during the daytime. A slave trader did arrive there in the mid-afternoon to deliver his wares. Six live bodies that I saw. From that I think it is probable that our target will be dining at home this evening. Nothing to change our initial estimations on the number of guards. We know that a strigoi of his age is rarely alone."

"So, we're facing Eşref and at least four thralls that we know of. And in this city we cannot rule out the arrival of other strigoi, especially if we lose our element of surprise. Constantinople is where House Laskaris is at its strongest, we need to finish him quickly and then vanish before more of them come looking."

Julie's voice could not have been more different from the playful tenderness that she had shown in the bedroom with Aida not long before. Her demeanour now was pitiless and unyielding, caring only for the hunt to come. Her fixation became dangerously intense every time that she pursued another vampire, but there were some for whom her wrath was far more personal than others.

The twins both knew that Eşref of House Laskaris had been present in Paris fifty-one years ago, and that made him one of the vampires on Julie's list. They had no way of knowing for certain, but the mere possibility that he was Marie de Senneterre's killer meant that her vengeance would come for him.

"We can be gone swiftly," Aida reassured her, "The horses are fed and rested, the carriage is in good repair. We will be on the road to Thessalonica before sunrise."

"Good."

Saul gave a nod of assent and moved to unlock the large oaken trunk which housed the group's arsenal. From within he took a pair of long and exquisitely-crafted scimitars, blades forged at great expense by one of the most highly reputed smiths in Damascus. Although in function the two swords were of identical design, the pommel and scabbard of each bore their own distinctive decoration, and Saul handed one of them to Julie before fixing his own to his belt.

Very few weapons could endure for long under the forces that a vampire's strength could exert, but Julie had been wielding one of these masterworks for the past three years, and the blade's integrity still held. She had first mastered the art of the rapier when she was but a mortal girl in her teen-age years, but for clashes between inhuman blood-drinkers, a more durable weapon was a necessity. If a sword could not readily cleave right through a limb or a neck, then it was scarcely worth bringing to the fight.

Along with the two heavy scimitars, the arsenal held a variety of other tools of their grisly mission. There were a number of wooden stakes, three-foot lengths of Persian iron-wood whittled to a keen point and hardened in flame. Julie, Saul and Aida each took two of those, with Saul also taking a lump hammer, an iron chisel and a coil of rope. There was Aida's heavy crossbow and a quiver of bolts, though tonight she forsook that larger weapon in favour of her pistols. Aida was perfectly adept in handling a sword, but she would not claim to be as highly trained as her brother, and she had nothing close to the preternatural swiftness and bone-shattering strength of Julie.

Instead, her loose-fitting kaftan would serve to conceal six firearms strapped to her body: two modern French duelling flintlocks and four older pistols of last century's Lombard design, with tapering muzzles. The flintlocks she loaded with typical lead bullets, intended for use against thralls or other lesser minions of the vampire whom they hunted. When preparing the Lombard pistols she neglected bullets entirely, instead loading the barrels with finely-cut filaments of magnesium. Where Julie and Saul put their trust in steel, Aida preferred to face inhuman foes with fire.

With arms gathered and preparations made, the three companions set off into Constantinople's nighttime streets. The hunt was underway, and Julie's mind was racing with bloodthirsty anticipation.

For as long as a city had stood here, from the ancient founding of Lygos and the imperial power of Byzantium, this place had been a vital nexus between Europe and Asia. Once the centre of the Eastern Roman Empire and now capital of the Ottoman Empire, it had been a hub of trade, diplomacy and military conquest for more than twenty-four centuries. Humans had always gathered here in great numbers, and so too did those who preyed upon them.

Hidden covens of strigoi lurked within metropolises across the mainland of Europe, but there were few cities where they were as entrenched as Constantinople. For all of this city's art and architecture, all of its wealth and culture in this century, its shadows played host to an old and vicious society of predators.

The name of Laskaris once belonged to a Noble House in the time of Byzantium, rulers of the Empire of Nicaea during the thirteenth century. With the conquest of the city by the Ottomans their power among mortals came to an end, but by that time the House was already infested with vampirism. When the exiled human inheritors of the family sought refuge in Italy, the Laskaris strigoi remained in Constantinople, retreating into the shadows and observing, adapting to their new reality. A new flag and a new Sultan in place of the old Emperors mattered little to them; they cared only that their territory was full of oblivious mortals to exploit and to prey upon.

In the centuries since, they had worked their way into the

fabric of the city, gathering wealth and resources, cultivating human spies and sympathisers wherever they were needed. Gone were the days when House Laskaris could openly rule, but its members had nonetheless made the Ottoman capital their domain. The House's subservient covens and territories spread throughout much of Europe, and Constantinople served as the beating heart of their empire.

Eşref's lair lay in the district of Zeytinburnu, to the south of the walls of the Old City, on the shore of the Marmara Sea. Once this place had been home to the fortress of Kyklobion, built during the heyday of Emperor Justinian I to guard the approach to Constantinople, but that citadel had long lain in ruins. Although Zeytinburnu meant 'the cape of olive trees', in this century the district was known mainly for its slaughterhouses, butchers and tanneries. As Julie and her companions made their journey through the winding streets, the rancid odour of leather manufacture was all around them. When Mehmed the Conqueror had assigned the leather-workers to this district three centuries previous, not without reason had he put that industry outside of the city walls. Saul remarked on how easily one could hide rotting carcasses in this place without anyone being able to smell them.

It was not far westward of the stinking tanneries where a fortified villa stood, its stone walls enclosing a small grove of olive trees in front of the main house. Constantinople had a long relationship with the Italian city-states that was as tumultuous as it was lucrative, and the aesthetic influences of the Genoese and Venetians could be found here and there throughout the city. These touches were most obvious in the Pera district north of the Golden Horn, where the Venetian Palace and the great Galata Tower stood. When this particular villa was first built it had likely belonged to an Italian merchant, but now it was the nest to which the three hunters had tracked Eşref and his minions.

The walls surrounding the villa's grounds were tall and imposing, built to withstand attack in an age when banditry and unrest were rife. The trio avoided the front gate as they made their approach, circling around to the northwest side of the house. As they neared the outer wall, Saul took the coil of rope that he carried and handed it to Julie. Without a word she scrambled upwards, scaling the fortification with an effortlessness that was unnatural.

Saul and Aida had both taken the opportunity to read Sir Isaac Newton's *Principia Mathematica* during their time in Paris, and had an understanding of the laws of universal gravitation. Having that knowledge only made it all the more otherworldly when they watched how Julie so casually defied those laws. There was both fear and awe in witnessing a human form climb up sheer surfaces with a spider's ease, though it was but one among the impossible things that Julie and her ilk could do. Vampires, the twins knew all too well, were outside of nature.

Reaching the top of the wall, Julie took a moment to anchor the rope around the gnarled branch of an olive tree before throwing it down for the twins to follow her. As her companions climbed up she made her way down into the grove, crawling head-first down the stonework just as readily as she had scaled it moments before. Saul and Aida made their way down the rope behind her, and the three of them began their silent approach towards the house. Up ahead a servant's entrance beckoned, leading into the building's kitchen. The stink of the tanneries may not be far behind, but as the three drew closer to the doorway, Julie's nostrils could pick up on the unmistakable scent of raw human flesh. Not at all surprising, given what they knew of Eşref's company in this house.

A moustached young man in a household servant's uniform stood guard outside the door. Ordinarily there would have been little remarkable about his appearance, but there was an ashen and unhealthy quality to his skin which, coupled with the bloodshot redness around the edges of his eyes, marked him as a thrall: a human infected with vampirism, but not yet fully turned by it.

Even at a distance Julie recognised him as one of the four thralls whom the trio had counted on the previous night's reconnaissance run. Strigoi may exist on an exclusively sanguine diet, but thralls undergoing the transformation process tended to develop a craving for uncooked flesh, hence the smell from within the kitchen. If Eşref had fed upon a human to the point of death this evening, it would hardly surprise Julie that he had bestowed the exsanguinated body to sate his minions' hunger.

Beside her, the twins fell still in their advance, taking cover behind the trunks of two looming olive trees. There was a stretch of open ground between the edge of the grove and the door, and it would be extremely difficult for any human to cross that span without the thrall catching sight of them.

But not for a vampire.

From her hiding position Julie darted forward, her body little more than a blur in the darkness as she tackled the sentry. He barely knew what was happening before her hand grabbed onto his face, clamping tightly over his mouth.

His eyes widened in momentary surprise, soon giving way to instinctual fury as he tried to push her off of him. His hands grabbed and clawed at Julie's body with maddened strength, his muscles carrying the beginnings of a vampire's unnatural puissance, but this battle was already over. Julie's free hand grabbed the back of the thrall's head and she twisted hard, his neck vertebrae cracking apart as he was forced to his knees.

The feral hunger in the young man's eyes flickered and faded, and for a brief moment there was only a very human look of fear as his life was snuffed out. Carefully Julie lowered him to the ground, one hand closing his eyes for good. As Saul and Aida advanced behind her, she drew her scimitar and pressed the tip of it to the thrall's chest, sliding it between his ribs and feeling it pierce his heart. His muscles seized and his body spasmed once, twice, as the last remnants of the vampiric infection in his blood died. In truth it was unlikely that he would recover after his neck was shattered, but in Julie's experience it was best to make certain.

She slowly withdrew the blade and wiped it on her victim's clothing before returning it to its sheath. The twins had already proceeded inside, and thankfully it seemed that there were no other minions lurking in the kitchen to greet them. However, the smell of flesh was very strong here, and as Julie looked in towards her companions, she saw that there were enough butchered body parts in there to have belonged to several people.

Saul and Aida looked over their surroundings with grim resolve; Julie could sense the disgust that they felt at what they saw, but it was hardly their first encounter with the cruel excesses of which vampires were capable. Regardless of whether or not Eşref had killed Marie, putting an end to him would at least bring some vengeance for the poor bastards whose remains hung in here upon meat-hooks. Aida's voice remained level as she met Julie's gaze, but there was hot fury in her eyes as she stated plainly;

"I invite you in."

Julie gave a nod of thanks and stepped forward, crossing the threshold into the kitchen. When she had stood outside the doorway, the thought of entering was as uncomfortable as a chain about her neck, but that feeling evaporated with Aida's words of invitation. After three and a half decades among the immortals, Julie still did not understand why it was such a violation of her instincts to enter a living human's house – or the lair of another vampire – without first being asked in. If she steeled herself she could force her way across a threshold, but the effort left her disoriented, weakened and vulnerable. That was not something she could afford when going into combat, but fortunately she had found that the invitation did not have to come from the owner of the building. The word of a guest, or even an intruder, was enough.

And now that the leave to enter had been given, that invitation could not simply be revoked. To invite a vampire in once was to give them indefinite power to return. If all went to plan, however, setting foot in this house once would be all that was needed.

The outward appearance of the villa had been impressive enough, but the interior left little doubt as to the affluence of the one who dwelt here. Julie wondered if Eşref actually owned this place, or if it simply belonged to some unfortunate human who had fallen under his sway. Ultimately it made little difference to her mission tonight, but it was clear that Eşref was the kind of bloodsucker who liked to surround himself with finery. Through the decades Julie had found that her fellow immortals were a varied bunch of parasites, running the gamut from refined hedonists who revelled in luxury and decadence, through to maddened beasts who buried themselves in the dirt by day and rarely bothered to appear human by night.

The latter, it seemed, were increasingly a dying breed as the world progressed into the Enlightenment of this age. The bestial vukodlaks and mindless revenants who had terrorised villages in centuries past were on a march to extinction, losing the endless territorial battles to the more cunning strigoi. In this era, the greatest advantage belonged to those who could easily hide among their human prey.

For a vampire looking to afford themselves privacy among mortals, there were few assets as useful as wealth and aristocratic privilege, and Eşref had wholeheartedly embraced the trappings of such a life. This house was lavishly decorated, its furnishings clearly the work of expensive craftsmen. Each room and hallway that the three hunters crept through was adorned with artworks and tapestries, ornamental vases and sculptures, lit by the soft glow of oil lamps. The rank odour of the tanneries and the flesh-stink from the kitchen was still present in the air, but it was heavily masked beneath perfumes and incense. The overall result was enough to give the house an air of sickly sweetness, a sensation almost akin to biting into an overripe peach.

Julie and her companions moved with quiet, practised focus, but it soon became apparent that apart from the sentry at the kitchen door, the ground floor was empty of people. In the main hallway, Julie's eyes looked towards the staircase. If her target were here, he could only be up above. If he had already left for the evening on some business, then she would happily lurk here and ambush him when he returned. This house was hardly an uncomfortable place to wait, after all.

She could not help but notice one empty space upon the wall of the stairway, where something had clearly been taken down from a display. A painting that Eşref disliked? Or perhaps it had been a mirror which had hung in that space? All vampires had to grow accustomed to their lack of a reflection, but there were few who could stand to be confronted with that absence on a nightly basis.

A gentle tap on her arm from Saul drew Julie's attention back to the moment. Aida had opened the door to a small study off to the right of the staircase, and was beckoning with one hand for the other two to join her, indicating something that seemed to be of importance. Julie and Saul moved in to look, the three of them crowding around a writing desk where various papers lay. Julie might have guessed them to be letters, but while she spoke a smattering of the local language, the written alphabet of the Ottomans remained a mystery to her.

"You know I can't read Turkish," she whispered. "What do these papers mean?"

"They are letters to Eşref," Aida explained. "These messages are unsigned, but they are obviously from someone that he answers to, because they are giving him orders. This one is telling him to come to London as soon as he is able. There is mention of passage being arranged for him on a ship, the *Petra*."

"London?" remarked Saul. "There are no strigoi covens in London. Not in all of England. There have not been for decades."

"None that we know of," Julie mused. "Territorial expansion, perhaps? House Laskaris deciding to move in on unclaimed ground?"

"I think it is rather more personal than that," came Aida's reply, as her fingers gestured towards other letters. "These make mention of Sir Hans Sloane. They talk about his death three years ago. The author of these letters suspects his involvement in the deaths of several Laskaris vampires. Sevket, Hayal, Meryem, Nazarius, you have spoken to me of these names. These are vampires that you destroyed. Now House Laskaris thinks that he was connected to this, they are looking into his legacy, his family. You told me that you and he exchanged a lot of letters when you worked together. If he kept them somewhere, they could discover his connection to you."

Aida looked deeply concerned, and Julie was not about

to tell her that her worries were unfounded. When Julie and Sir Hans had known one another, back when Julie was still breathing, he had mentored her when she first began to dabble in the world of vampires. His knowledge and advice on matters occult had kept her alive when she first started to seek revenge for the death of her beloved Marie. He had financed her travels across Europe, Asia and Africa, and even to the Americas. When Julie had finally returned from the New World with the curse flowing in her own veins, she could not bring herself to re-establish contact with him. It was better, she thought, to let her old friend believe that she had met a mortal's death.

To this night, much of Julie's success in her struggles against her fellow vampires lay in keeping some degree of anonymity. Her correspondences with Sir Hans may be old, but they contained details and insights that she would never wish to fall into the hands of House Laskaris. If they recovered those letters, then they would learn of both who Julie was and the catalogue of vampires whom she had hunted during her collaboration with Sir Hans. House Laskaris would be searching for her, and once word spread among them she would be lucky to find a safe port anywhere in Europe.

"We're killing Eşref tonight," Julie reiterated, "and then, forget about Thessalonica. London is our next destination. If he has passage on the *Petra*, we'll travel in his place. Saul, you can use his name. Aida, take all of these papers. We'll go to London, hunt down and kill every strigoi that is looking into Hans, and if my letters to him still exist, we'll track them down and burn them. We leave nothing for the Laskaris to find."

A knowing look passed between the twins; they had seen Julie like this before, on occasions when something dear to her was under threat, and there was little sense in arguing with her course of action. If those letters contained anything that would expose her identity to House Laskaris, then that would endanger Saul and Aida just as much as Julie herself. Aida grabbed the letters, bundling them together and stuffing them into a pocket of her kaftan. It was then that all three of them found their attentions drawn upward, to the sound of a dull, heavy thud from the floor above. There was no mistaking the very particular sound of a human body dropping onto a floor.

"They're still here," Julie breathed.

Weapons drawn, moving cautiously, the three hunters ascended the main stairway. Until now, Julie's nose had been somewhat confounded by the powerful competing aromas of this place, but as she moved to the upper floor of the villa, the scent of fresh, living human blood was making itself inescapably known. Her nostrils gave an involuntary twitch as the smell invaded her senses, demanding her absolute attention. Her pupils were beginning to dilate once more, the red savagery creeping back into her eyes.

Fangs lengthened on instinct and she felt them prick against the inside of her lower lip, drawing the coppery taste of her own blood into her mouth. Within her breast the demon was twisting and straining to be unleashed, knowing that there were rivals to be fought, that vampires not of her own blood were close by. Her ears were already yearning for the sound of snapping bones, of tearing flesh.

Up ahead a bedchamber door stood slightly ajar, and from this close she could hear the sucking sounds of vampiric feeding taking place within. She could hear one human heart still beating on the far side of the door, but it was weak, failing as the blood was stolen from it. At least one human had been drained of life within the last few minutes; for another to be so close to death meant that there were either multiple strigoi gathered in that room, or one of them was truly feeding to excess, glutting itself on multiple victims. A vampire which had consumed so much blood would be strong, but if they were still lost in the sensory euphoria of feeding, they might not see Julie's blade coming until it had already found its mark.

The three hunters froze suddenly as the floor beneath Julie's foot let out an ominous squeak, instantly betraying their presence. Of course Eşref had been cunning enough to install a trick floorboard, fully expecting that enemies might seek to infiltrate his home, and Julie cursed herself for not having anticipated such a basic trap. From within the bedchamber came the sounds of feral snarls, more than one vampiric voice reacting to the intrusion. The door burst loudly open, a young woman dressed in peasants' rags charging out of the bedroom with fangs bared and lips stained in blood.

Julie lunged with her scimitar, thrusting for the oncoming vampire's heart, but the girl leaped at the last instant and took the blade in her gut, the tip of the sword bursting out of her back. Clawed hands grabbed onto Julie's shoulders and forced her backwards, the momentum of the strigoi's charge sending both of them crashing between Saul and Aida, past the twins and down the stairs.

The two vampiric women hit the floor, rolling apart from one another, the scimitar still lodged in the peasant girl's midsection. A vampire's alien physiology possessed tremendous resilience to harm, able to shrug off wounds which would kill a human several times over, but normally the creatures were not entirely oblivious to pain. When Julie looked upon her assailant, however, she instantly recognised what she was facing. Last night this girl had been a mere thrall, but now she was a newly-turned vampire, her veins hot with the incomparable rush of her first feeding, and she was experiencing the murderous power of the demon within her for the first time. Compared to that wild exultation, the pain of the sword in her gut was meaningless.

The girl charged her again, moving with a skittering, clumsy speed, still unaccustomed to the new capabilities of her muscles. Julie reacted with far greater skill, her fist lashing out in a blur and catching the side of the strigoi's face, knocking her off her feet with the loud crack of a breaking cheekbone. The fledgling vampire struck the ground and Julie followed up with a brutal kick to her ribcage, sending her rolling onto her back, enabling Julie to grab the hilt of her sword and pull it free. Undeterred, the strigoi scrambled back to her feet, her body warping and stretching as she did so. The need to blend in with one's prey obliged vampires to confine themselves to human form much of the time, but there were occasions when the inner demon would not be concealed.

As the girl pulled herself upright her entire visage became fluid, her flesh reshaping itself into the true form of a strigoi. Ragged clothes pulled and tore around a body that was no longer remotely human, but now a sinuous grey-black monstrosity of whipcord muscle and visceral hunger. Translucent wing-membranes stretched between the vampire's flanks and its long arms, which ended in lethally taloned hands. On the creature's nightmarish bat-like face, blood-red eyes stared out with burning fury. The strigoi's jaws gave an ear-splitting shriek, opening to reveal a mouthful of predatory fangs, and the creature leaped for Julie like a rabid animal.

From the landing above there came further snarling noises as more figures emerged from the bedchamber. Another newly-turned vampire, a man in a soldier's uniform with the same wild look upon his face as the girl, came barrelling towards the twins. Aida's head snapped in his direction as she raised the duelling pistol in her hand. Her finger tensed upon the trigger and the firearm barked loudly, a bullet smashing into the front of the bloodsucker's skull and knocking him backwards.

Saul followed up by charging forward, striking for the wounded fledgling's neck with his blade, but Julie had little time to watch her companions at work. She brought her own scimitar up to intercept the frenzied strigoi's attack, catching its forearm and sending a spray of dark blood across the rich carpet.

The strigoi did not slow for even a moment, striking out with its undamaged arm and slashing its claws across Julie's face, barely missing her left eye. The blow was enough to elicit a bestial response from Julie's own lips, a predatory growl that was every bit as inhuman as the monster before her. The demon within fed upon the pain, its rage howling through her limbs as she swept her scimitar into an upward arc.

Against a more skilled foe she may have sought to feint or misdirect her opponent, lure them into creating a gap in their defences, but a blood-maddened fledgling gave no thought to defence, fighting like a frenzied beast. Julie's sword sheared into the vampire's throat as it bore down upon her, the scimitar biting deep into flesh and hitting bone. Blood gushed from the wound in a torrent, and the sudden sense of mortal vulnerability was enough to give pause to the creature's manic assault.

The strigoi recoiled, a spark of newfound fear creeping into its furious eyes, and Julie pressed her advantage. The creature tried to dodge her next blow, but Julie anticipated its movements with ease and the tip of her sword struck left of her enemy's sternum, sinking into its ribcage and stabbing deep into the monster's heart. The vampire tried to scream, but all that came out was a strangled keening, the sound of air gurgling through a severed windpipe. Thrashing like a stabbed fish, the monster's flailing talons raked four deep gashes into Julie's chest. The muted agony that blossomed beneath those wounds only stoked her killer's instincts further, and she ceased to care that this particular bloodsucker could not possibly be the one that killed Marie. In instants like this, every death she inflicted was a singular act of vengeance.

With a cry she pulled the scimitar back, whirling on the spot and finishing what her earlier slash to its throat had begun. The strigoi fell silent as Julie delivered a decapitating blow, its monstrous head rolling away across the bloodstained carpet as its twitching, spasming body collapsed.

There was little time for Julie to enjoy her victory, as the sound of ongoing combat from the upper floor caught her ears. She leaped up the staircase, taking the steps four at a time as she went to the aid of her companions. The uniformed vampire whom she had glimpsed earlier was down, with one of Saul's ironwood stakes protruding from his chest and Aida standing mere feet away with the lump hammer in hand.

Two more strigoi were on the landing, one blood-crazed fledgling which had metamorphosed into its nightmare true form, and a strikingly handsome young man dressed in highly fashionable silks. Neither of them were Eşref, but the handsome boy was sufficiently composed that Julie could guess he was no newborn.

The bestial fledgling shrieked and hurled itself at Aida, swatting the hammer out of her grip and tackling her to the floor, jaws open for a killing bite. Julie darted forward and grabbed the strigoi in both hands, discarding her sword as she hauled the monster away from her lover and hurled it down the staircase with all her strength. A clash of steel echoed as Saul engaged with the finely-dressed strigoi, the strike of his scimitar being skilfully deflected by a long dagger that the vampire held.

In a flash of movement the bloodsucker grabbed Saul's wrist and wrenched his arm, drawing a cry of pain from the man as the sword was forced out of his grasp. In response Julie snatched up her own blade and re-joined the fight, moving in to engage the strigoi as he grappled with Saul. The handsome vampire brought up his dagger to parry Julie's blow, but failed to anticipate as she redirected her strike and slashed down into his leg, slicing through his calf and forcing him down to one knee.

Saul tried to pull his arm free, but as strong as he was for a mortal man, he couldn't break the vampire's iron grip. Instead he pulled a stake from his belt with his left hand and rammed the point into the strigoi's chest with all the force he could muster. Without the hammer it was all but impossible to fully impale his enemy's heart in a single blow, but it was definitely enough to get the vampire's attention.

The strigoi roared like a bull and threw Saul backwards, shoving him into the wall with bone-jarring force. Pain wracked Saul's body as he hit the stonework, but at least he was out of the monster's grasp. He looked up just in time to see Julie bring her sword down hard atop the vampire's shoulder, the blade biting deep into his thorax and almost cleaving him in two. With their enemy down, Julie pinned him beneath her boot and looked towards her companion.

"Your arm?" she enquired.

Saul flexed his fingers, wincing slightly.

"It will be fine. Nothing is broken," he assured her.

From the stairway there came the cry of the fledgling strigoi as it charged back up towards Aida, but this time she had one of her Lombard pistols drawn and cocked. As she squeezed the trigger a plume of white-hot fire exploded from the muzzle, a cloud of burning magnesium engulfing the oncoming vampire. A hellish scream filled the house as the strigoi's body erupted in flame, the monster tumbling back down the stairs and landing in a blazing heap at the bottom.

The creature shrieked and thrashed as it burned, its wild movements spreading the flames to the carpets and furnishings. Fire was one mortal weapon which vampires had every reason to fear, and this made Aida's choice weapons extremely effective, but there were definite drawbacks to using them indoors. She tucked the spent pistol into her belt and turned back towards Julie and Saul with a look that was only mildly apologetic.

"We shall want to leave, before this place burns down."

The handsome-faced strigoi was far from dead, but the blow which Julie had dealt him was a crippling one. She knew that his body had the capacity to heal in time, and with enough fresh blood, but for now he could put up little resistance as she dragged him to the bedroom window and unceremoniously tossed him out onto the villa's front lawn. The twins pulled the sheets from the bed and rapidly tied them together, anchoring one end to the bed before using the rest to aid their descent. They made a slow and careful climb down, especially Saul with his wounded wrist, while Julie simply scrambled down the wall in her unnatural fashion.

Before departing the villa, they could not help but notice the four bodies of exsanguinated slaves that had been left on the bedroom floor, though there was little chance to give dignity to the dead. As the twins made their way down the makeshift rope of sheets, Julie strode up to the broken vampire and crouched over him.

"Four thralls here last night," she said pointedly. "Tonight, one thrall and three new strigoi. Why create so many in one sitting?"

She wasn't terribly surprised when her inquiry was met with silence. Vampires of any breed were rarely cooperative in the face of questioning. This particular bloodsucker was no fledgling, but Julie could also guess that he was no elder either, and certainly not a Master. Like herself, he had maybe survived a few decades of vampiric existence. Even as he lay on the ground his eyes leered, as if daring to see what she would do next. She responded by shoving her hand into the gaping wound that ran down his torso, her steely fingers groping for his heart and curling around it. That was enough to bring a look of fear to his face.

"The Master's orders!" the strigoi choked out. "He wanted them turned!"

"Eşref's orders?"

"Yes!"

"Four dead slaves in there. One for you to feed on and three for the fledglings. Six were handed over here today. Where are the other two?"

Once again the vampire fell silent, as if his fear of Eşref's displeasure was more terrible than his fear of the one looming over him. To correct him of this assumption Julie loosened her grip on his heart for a second, then promptly tightened it again.

"He took them with him! For his journey!"

His journey. *Shit.*

"He set off tonight? Tell me where he's going."

"To England! London!"

Julie snarled in anger and pulled her hand out of the crippled bloodsucker, fighting down the urge to rip out his heart and put an end to his eternity. He might still have more information to give, and she had to admit that Aida was better at asking questions than she was. Julie rose to her feet as the twins approached behind her.

"You heard what he said?" she asked them.

"We should head to the docks," Saul replied, confirming that they had. "If the *Petra* has not yet sailed, we might still catch him."

They could not have missed Eşref by long. Saul had been watching the house most of the day, and had only left to rendezvous with Julie and Aida shortly before sundown. That left a very narrow window in which Eşref could have made his departure. The odds that he would leave Constantinople on the very night that they chose to attack seemed ridiculously slim, unless… *Unless they knew you were coming*, Julie thought.

When the trio came to scout out the area last night, they had been careful. They had kept their distance, and were confident that nobody had known they were here. But how certain could they be, really? Was it not probable that a predator as experienced as Eşref had dozens of eyes watching out for him, here in his own territory? Given the power that vampires possessed to manipulate mortal minds, the Petra's captain would sail early if Eşref commanded him to.

Aida was advancing towards the captive strigoi, a pistol in one hand and the bundle of papers from the study in the other. Behind her, the lower windows of the house were alight with growing fire.

"These letters to your Master," she began, "are unsigned. There is no name on them. But they are not making requests, they are giving orders, and they clearly expect to be obeyed. So who sent them? On whose command is Eşref travelling all the way to London?"

If the handsome-faced vampire had been reluctantly willing to answer the previous questions, it swiftly became clear that Aida was asking for information that he was not prepared to divulge, even in the face of imminent death. A look of hateful spite came over his features.

"Fuck your ancestors, blood-sack. You are *cattle*. I'm not answering cattle."

Rage flared within Julie at the insult to her lover, as hot as the magnesium fire from Aida's pistol. In an instant she was on him, her fists descending over and over in a barrage, each impact being rewarded with the cracking of bone. She may have doubted that there was much difference of years between her and this bloodsucker, but Julie was no mere strigoi. The curse in her veins stemmed from a far older and more primal bloodline, and her physical strength and power was commensurately greater than his. When her rain of blows came to an end, his once-beautiful face was a mess of broken, battered flesh, his eye sockets shattered, his lips torn and nose caved in.

"You will answer her," she spat. "You'll tell her everything she wants to know."

But any hope of further disclosure was swiftly interrupted. From the front gate of the villa's grounds the snorting of horses and the thunder of hooves cut through the night air. Julie looked up to see black-clad men inserting iron grapnel hooks through the bars of the gates, and then came the scream of tortured metal as the bolting horses ripped those gates from their hinges. Silhouettes began to advance through the breach, dressed in leather armour beneath black coats. There were maybe a dozen of them in total, and the first four wielded large, heavy crossbows.

"*Compagnie du Saint-Sacrement*," Aida gave voice to what her brother and Julie were thinking. She spoke the name of the Company of the Holy Sacrament as if it were a curse, and in Julie's eyes it was. For years now these men had hunted her, as doggedly as she had hunted for every vampire who might have killed Marie de Senneterre.

While this clandestine Catholic society operated primarily in nations where their Church held sway, it seemed at times as if no country in Europe were beyond their reach. And there was one among them in particular who seemed bent upon Julie's destruction above all else. Forever would she regret the night that she had approached them, thinking that these fanatics could be allies on even the most temporary basis.

"Go," she told the twins. "Head back to the rope. Get out of sight and back to the inn, I'll draw them off."

She did not need to tell them twice. Saul and Aida took off towards the olive grove, dashing for the cover of the trees. A crossbow bolt came tearing through the night in their direction, and Julie swatted it out of flight with a swipe of her hand. A second bolt was loosed for her and she moved just enough to take the impact in her shoulder rather than her heart. With a snarl she ripped the bolt out of her flesh and tossed it aside. The other two crossbowmen both unleashed their shots, but this time Julie was ready, and she dropped to the floor with preternatural speed as the twin bolts sailed over her and clattered against the wall of the burning villa.

She sprang to her feet, grabbing the brutalised strigoi who lay upon the lawn and throwing him with savage force at the four reloading crossbowmen. Two of them had the presence of mind to drop their weapons and dive to the ground, but Julie smiled in satisfaction as the other two were knocked sprawling by the hurled body. The other eight men were now advancing, however, two with axes and five with burning torches, and one in the lead with a broadsword in hand. Even if Julie were inclined to stand and fight, these were not good odds to face by herself. She started to make a dash for the outer wall, heading in the opposite direction from Saul and Aida, and the group of men followed, looking to corner her.

As they drew closer she could hear their chanted Latin prayers, a noise which scratched at her ears like the wailing of a cat. She could see the crucifixes that they wore about their necks, and even the sight of those icons was enough to draw a rasping hiss from her lips and force her to avert her eyes. Much like her deep disinclination to enter homes without invitation, exactly why Julie had such an instinctive aversion to displays of faith was not something she could fully explain.

Of course the Company of the Holy Sacrament had an answer for her in that regard: it was because she, like all vampires, was a creature of the Devil, unable to bear the sight of any representation of the Divine.

Reaching the wall, Julie leaped and began to scramble upwards, only to feel a stabbing pain as another crossbow bolt punched into the side of her thigh, impaling her leg. Forcing the sensation out of her mind, she made it to the top of the wall, turning back to look down at the cluster of grim, resolute men beneath her. She remembered men such as this from the first time she was sentenced to be burned at the stake, back when she was still human.

Their leader, the blonde-haired Frenchman with the scarred throat and broadsword in hand, was all too familiar to her. A bitter laugh escaped her as she met his eyes. When battling her own kind, Julie's behaviour tended towards the coldly stoic or brutally vengeful, but there was something about the sanctimony of the Catholic Church which drew out the playful vindictiveness that she had so often indulged during her mortal days.

"Michel," she addressed him with a mirth that was as false as it was condescending, "we really need to stop crossing paths like this. People will talk, you know."

"Do you never get tired of running from us, demon?" He spat back at her. "There is nowhere you can hide from me. The Company will put an end to you. You know this."

She smiled and raised one hand to blow him a mocking kiss.

"Did you know that your mother's quim could take my *entire* fist?"

The seasoned vampire-hunter was far too resolute a man for his composure to waver at her vulgar joke, but Julie did notice his fingers clench tighter upon the hilt of his sword, and that brought her some small pleasure. She began to laugh merrily as she vaulted backwards off the wall, disappearing from his sight.

"By God and all the saints, I will have your head," Michel swore, but even if he had enough men with him to surround the villa, he knew it was futile to give chase now.

From the far side of the wall there came the beating of vast leathery wings and then an immense chiropteran shape soaring upwards, black as pitch and with a wingspan more than twice the height of a man, but swiftly growing distant until it dwindled from view against the night sky.

~ Arnold ~

Saturday September 18th, 1756

The graveyard of St Benet Gracechurch was tranquil next to the din of city, perhaps hauntingly so. It was mid afternoon and a thick fog had rolled in from the Thames Estuary, blanketing London in one of the city's infamous 'pea-soup' smogs. Arnold could barely see ten feet in front of him, and he stood with a handkerchief clutched to his mouth and nose in vain hope of preserving his lungs from the soot and filth in the air. Today was the day he had chosen to visit his father's grave, and in spite of the all-encompassing fog, he had managed to locate the tombstone that marked Sean Musgrave's final resting place.

The carved slab of limestone was not especially ostentatious, but it would certainly weather the ages. The church building itself had endured more than its share of adversity; it was one of the fifty-two London churches which had been destroyed in the Great Fire of 1666, and then subsequently rebuilt. Of that, the young clergyman approved.

In keeping with his better judgement he had avoided the funeral on Wednesday, leaving his father's family to their grief, but nonetheless he had made up his mind to reach out to them. Or in the very least he wished to speak to

Nathaniel, the eldest of his half-siblings and the only one with whom he had any meaningful previous rapport. So yesterday he had left a message at Nathaniel's home asking for a meeting, and had received a reply later that evening inviting him to take coffee together on Saturday afternoon. But first, Arnold had resolved to visit the place where Sean was laid to rest.

In truth he was unsure exactly what manner of closure he hoped to attain from this visit, but now that he was here, his every thought was clouded with uncertainty. The old anger was definitely there, the bitter resentment for Sean's abandonment of Lisa, and of Arnold himself while still in her womb. Never once had Sean apologised, never once shown repentance to his unwanted son, but Arnold had to accept that such a thing was immaterial now. In the grand scheme it mattered not that Sean had never asked for Arnold's forgiveness, so long as he had sought God's forgiveness for all of his sins.

He had undoubtedly been alone and in terrible pain when he lay dying in the street. Arnold could merely hope that his father's final thoughts had turned towards the salvation of his soul, rather than vainly clinging to mortal life. How desperately he wished he could have been there in those last moments, just to be certain that Sean had met the hereafter in good faith.

Standing now over his grave, Arnold had no wish to imagine his father in Hell. He firmly believed that God was both just and merciful, and that absolution would always be given to those who asked for it with honest intent. Yet ever since reading John Calvin's *Institutes of the Christian Religion* some years ago, he had been haunted by the concept of predestination, and the idea that the salvation or damnation of all souls was decided by God from the moment of their creation. For how else could the Almighty be both omniscient and omnipotent, if the course of every life were not an immutable part of His plan?

All things that transpired were the will of God, but it was grim contemplation for Arnold, to consider that his father had been destined to never be saved and that he might now be forever cast out from the kingdom of Heaven. No, he had to believe that the man had found salvation. Eternal torment must surely be reserved for those who had truly earned it.

Gingerly, he reached out and placed one hand atop the gravestone, feeling its smooth, cold edge beneath his fingers.

"I… there's nothing I can say to make things right between us," he began. "A son is supposed to honour his father and mother, and I would have honoured you, had you permitted me to."

Arnold's voice wavered and he began to cough into his handkerchief, his mind telling itself that the smog was the blame, and not the leaden weight of sorrow and regret within his chest.

"I forgive you, for your negligence towards me. I don't think that Mother ever will. But I pray that God forgives you. I pray that you are with Him in Heaven now, Father."

He had to believe it. He had to believe that the divine plan was for the greatest good, even when the world brought so much pain. Had Sean never abandoned Lisa, then there was every likelihood that Arnold would never have sought a life in the Church. And while Sean's murder was a terrible thing, that did not mean that some good might not come out of it. The young clergyman's thoughts veered once again to his half-siblings, and how they would be coping with this loss. He knew that Nathaniel was strong, but could he say the same for the younger Conchobhar, or sweet and kind Imogen? He barely knew them, yet he felt for them nonetheless.

I could not bear to see my dearest children burdened by these revelations. No, I would rather that they live full and happy lives, blessedly free of the darkness which you and I have explored. The words of Sir Hans' note resurfaced in his mind, unbidden and unwanted. The past few days had not changed Arnold's opinion that his inheritance was nought but some kind of game or joke, but it felt like a rather sick joke given how Sean had met his end. Surely the note from Sir Hans had not been written in seriousness, and yet it felt to Arnold as though darkness had indeed claimed his father in the end. This was partly why he needed to see Nathaniel. Maybe the young man might know something about those letters and documents, and that absurd collection of teeth.

From somewhere up above, the bells of St Benet Gracechurch began to ring, their sonorous chimes announcing that it was three o'clock of the afternoon. For a few uncertain moments Arnold lingered, until finally deciding that he had said all he truly wanted to say. With that he turned away from his father's grave and sought to trace his steps back through the fog to the churchyard gate.

West of Whitechapel, towards the ancient centre of London, Lombard-street was where much of the city's thriving financial industry was headquartered. Commerce was the lifeblood of every empire in history, after all, and this place was the beating heart of the British Empire's international trade. A steady tide of coins and credit notes rolled back and forth between London's banking houses and its merchant venturers, the vast wealth of the colonies being funnelled here to fill the coffers of investors.

Charters for spice and silk from Asia; slaves and ore from Africa; sugar, coffee, cotton and tobacco from the Americas were all traded here on this street. Contracts were signed, payments were made and the international trade in lives and goods would continue, borne upon the waves by untold thousands of ships.

Lombard-street was also the home of Lloyd's Coffee House, an establishment popularly frequented by sea captains and merchants, and also a favoured drinking spot for Nathaniel Musgrave. The rich aroma of roasting coffee as Arnold stepped in through the front door was a welcome relief from the guttural stink of the city streets, and he gladly paid the one penny entrance fee before making his way to the counter and placing his order.

He waited for the cup and saucer to be handed to him before joining the table where his half-brother sat with a printed copy of the *Lloyd's List* news sheet in front of him. The sheet was open on an article about the recent loss of the Fort Oswego trading post to the French, and the likely impacts this would have on trade between Great Britain and its North American colonies.

"Good afternoon, Nathaniel," Arnold addressed him. "Thank you for replying to my missive."

Nathaniel looked up from his reading and offered his half-brother a welcoming smile. The expression was genuine in its warmth, even though his eyes betrayed a flicker of unease. Despite their ties of blood, these two men inhabited very different social strata, and Nathaniel had never been entirely at peace with that disparity. At twenty years old, he was two years Arnold's junior, and he had always unquestionably been Sean's favourite child. His youthful features were soft and well-groomed from his life of relative privilege. His hair was a shade or two darker than Arnold's, and unlike his sibling he kept himself clean shaven. He was typically a dandy dresser, fond of rich colours and fine fabrics, though on this occasion his sense of fashion played second fiddle to the requirements of mourning.

When last that the two half-brothers had met, Nathaniel

had sported a maroon jacket over a salmon-pink waistcoat and lace shirt which could not have been more at odds with the grey and black of Arnold's rough-spun priestly attire. This time around both men were dressed in black, although naturally Nathaniel's clothing was of a substantially finer quality, and he wore a green velvet neck tie as a concession to his more usual tastes.

"Good to see you, Arnold. Do sit down with me, will you?"

The older half-brother sank into the offered wooden arm-chair, returning Nathaniel's smile and placing his hat down on the table alongside his cup and saucer. Around them, the coffee house was alive with the sound of merriment, gossip and lively debate. The clientele of Lloyd's may be of a primarily mercantile bent, but London's coffee houses were also a haven for students and scholars, and given the many and free exchanges of ideas that occurred in these places, it was not without reason that the establishments had become known as 'penny universities'.

"Keeping up with foreign affairs?" Arnold enquired, nodding towards the news sheet.

"The pertinent ones, certainly," Nathaniel replied. "Though it seems everything in the world is pertinent when there is the good of the Empire to consider. I must admit, I wasn't overly keen on the French and Indian War when it broke out two years ago… I didn't think that our colonies in the Americas were sufficiently fortified for it. But after this year's diplomatic upheavals, all the powers of Europe are swept up in conflict, and we all do what we must. France has enjoyed some victories, but if you ask me, their position is tenuous. If Great Britain picks its battles carefully, I think that we could put a stop to French military dominance in Europe. The Empire could profit greatly from that."

"You seem to have given this some thought," said Arnold

with a raise of one eyebrow. "Are you a military strategist now?"

"Not quite," Nathaniel responded with a wry look, "Though I am involved at the logistical level. Last year I took a secretarial post at the Navy's Victualling Board. I work in the office down at Deptford. It's no easy task, keeping the men of the Royal Navy fed and watered, but it is essential work. And there is plenty of opportunity for advancement, for those with a keen sense of order."

"I have no doubt of that. I'm sure Father was immensely proud of you."

Arnold did not wish to sound bitter, but the words came out with an edge that was just a little harder than he had intended. There was a momentary shift in Nathaniel's expression, a look that might have been one of mild offence, though it vanished just as quickly as it had arisen. The younger half-brother was a patient man, quick to forgive, and he had always extended greater acceptance towards Arnold than the rest of the family, even if that acceptance was to some degree rooted in pity.

"He was proud. I think he'd realised that although neither I nor Conchobhar were going to follow him into medicine, we would still find our own accomplishments. He was glad that I'd chosen to serve the Empire, even in a bureaucratic capacity."

"And what of Conchobhar, and Imogen? I hope they're faring well, in spite of Father's passing."

A waitress arrived with a fresh pot of coffee. Arnold thanked her and offered to refresh Nathaniel's cup, before filling his own. He poured a little coffee from the cup to the saucer, letting it cool for a few moments on the shallow ceramic, before taking a sip. The liquid was rich and bitter, and most welcome. Nathaniel drank his directly from the cup, preferring it boiling hot.

"Conchobhar is not yet aware," he explained to Arnold. "The ship carrying the letter to inform him only set off two days ago. Of course you yourself won't have known that Conchobhar is currently living in the Massachusetts colony. He sailed to Boston in February. He manages an importing charter there for the East India Company."

"I see. So your interest in the French and Indian War is due to more than just your professional obligations?"

"I don't think he's in any danger. The French are very unlikely to commit sufficient forces to be a threat to Boston, when there are bigger targets closer to their territories. But all the same, I prefer to keep abreast of developments."

"He was brave to set off on his own. I shall pray for his safety, and for his prosperity in the colonies. How about our sister? Is she keeping well?"

The look on Nathaniel's face warmed somewhat. He was deeply fond of Imogen, and it showed whenever he spoke of her. Given the chance he would have liked for Imogen and Arnold to be closer family, but Imogen was also closely attached to her mother, and Sybil Musgrave would have preferred that her husband's bastard had never been born at all.

"She was distraught at first, when she learned what had happened. She loved Father, and you know how women can be, especially a girl of only fifteen. But bless her, she is strong. I think Mother should be suffering a great deal more, without Imogen by her side. You ought to be as fond of her as I am, I think. She's an avid reader, has plenty of books on religion and philosophy. I'm sure she would find much to talk about with a man of the cloth like you. And you should hear her play the violin, she has quite a talent. She says that she wishes to join an orchestra and play in concert someday."

"It sounds like she's growing into a most admirable

young woman. I am happy for her, and I'm glad that she's showing such endurance in the face of loss. May God watch over her."

"May He indeed."

The two men fell silent for a time as they drank their coffee. The talk had – for the most part – been rather pleasant thus far, but Nathaniel had surmised that there were more serious reasons why Arnold had asked for this meeting.

"Listen, Arnold, I was glad to receive your message," Nathaniel broke the silence, "but I'm also glad that you chose to wait until after the funeral. I don't think mother could have handled it, if you had asked to attend. She doesn't even like it when I mention you at all, so I… I am grateful for your discretion, and your consideration. If it were up to me I would have invited you, but I had to respect her wishes on this. I know that you understand."

"It's quite alright," Arnold told him, fighting down the bitterness that was creeping into the back of his throat. "I knew that Sybil would not be comfortable with my presence there. Since she is his lawful wife and I am not his lawful son, it should have been selfish of me to press the issue. I did visit the grave earlier today, to pay my final respects. He never wanted me to be a part of his life, but I am at peace with that fact. I simply pray that he too is at peace in the hereafter."

"I'm happy that you have done so. I'm sure that his soul is glad of your prayers."

"I had to visit, for myself as much as for his sake. But the reason why I wanted to meet with you was not to do with his burial. It rather pertains to the inheritance that he left me."

Arnold's words were enough to draw a look of confusion from Nathaniel. The younger half-brother was quick to regain his composure, but the momentary look was enough to suggest that he had been entirely unaware of what had transpired with Sean's will, and the objects which had been held in Kenneth Whitfield's custody.

"Do forgive me Arnold," he said gently, "but when I attended the reading of Father's will, there was no mention of yourself. As you said, you are not his lawful son. The lawyer who handled the matter is Mister Whitfield, his practice is not far from here, just over on Houndsditch. If you want to discuss any matters regarding the will, then he shall be the man to speak to. But if you have fallen on hard times and simply need some assistance, then perhaps I can help."

"I'm sorry Nathaniel, I should have said something earlier. I did speak to Mister Whitfield. I received a letter asking me to attend an appointment at his practice on Monday. He told me that Father had left some items in his care that were bequeathed to me, and he had those items delivered to me that same day. I just found the items to be… rather *strange*, to put it mildly, and I wondered if you might be able to shed some light on them."

"Well this is all sounding very unusual. Whitfield mentioned none of this to myself, nor Imogen nor Mother. He didn't tell us that Father had left anything with him for safekeeping, let alone that it should be passed on to you. Perhaps Father had instructed Whitfield to keep the matter secret, but why on Earth should he wish to conceal such action from his own family?"

"I wondered that myself, believe me. But perhaps he wished to avoid causing unnecessary duress to his wife? As you said, Sybil finds it distasteful enough to be reminded that I exist."

"Maybe, but this is a matter of family. The family should surely have been made aware. And what was so strange about these items that you now have? What are they exactly?"

"Documents, correspondence," Arnold explained,

wondering how best to describe this situation without sounding extremely foolish, "and a collection of animal teeth. With Father being a physician, I assumed he had some interest in natural philosophy, that he had simply collected a few relics of nature, beasts that he'd shot and whatnot. That would make sense, given his friendship with Sir Hans Sloane, and certainly some of the documents in there are written like scholarly treatises. But they're… I don't know, exactly. They must be works of fiction."

By this point Nathaniel's confusion was plain upon his face. He took another mouthful of coffee, but was quick to put the cup down when he realised that its contents had grown too cold for his liking.

"You're not being very clear, old chap. If you want me to help you in some fashion, you're going to have to be more succinct."

"Each set of the teeth in the collection is labelled, but not with the names of real animals. Instead it's as if they're presented as evidence of folkloric creatures. Vukodlak, soucouyant, vetala, these are monsters of myth and pagan superstition. And those scholarly papers I spoke of, they seem to depict beings which should not exist. Bizarre chimeras like nothing in nature that I've heard of. Many of the documents are signed by Sir Hans directly, the majority of them are in his handwriting. And there are a number of letters written in French, from someone that went by the alias *La Maupin*. I can't even read most of it, much less explain it. Obviously Sir Hans had gone to a great deal of trouble to create and assemble this collection, perhaps with Father's help. But I can't fathom a purpose to it, nor why he should leave it to me in his will."

"I have to say, this is quite a fantastical tale you're spinning me. I think many would find it wholly unbelievable, or a bit suspect to say the least."

In truth, Arnold had expected his half-brother's incredulity to be greater. Certainly Nathaniel's words were not encouraging, but there was something in the tone of his voice which suggested that he was not completely surprised by all of this. If anything, his tone had grown less sombre and little more energised, suggesting that Arnold's story had stirred his curiosity.

"I have no reason to fabricate such a story, Brother. The best explanation I can arrive at is that Father and Sir Hans were involved in some form of elaborate game, fabricating evidence and writing fictional studies of creatures from old wives' tales. As if they meant to write a novel that was never published. So what are you inclined to believe?"

Nathaniel leaned forward in his chair, and much to Arnold's surprise, there was a hint of a smile upon his lips, along with a look in his eye that suggested almost childlike mischief.

"I believe there *is* a game afoot," he confirmed. "This is all a little thrilling, if I do say so. I have no doubt that Father and Sir Hans were capable of concocting the things that you speak of, and I am wondering if he left them to you fully in the expectation that you should approach me about them. He may have anticipated a means to bring together his disparate children."

Now it was Arnold's turn to react with bewilderment. Sean Musgrave had never been anything but distant towards him, why go to the trouble of arranging some posthumous mystery to create common ground between Arnold and his half-siblings? That idea seemed every bit as unbelievable as the bat-faced monsters drawn in those documents.

"Are you sure about this? This hardly seems in keeping with his past behaviour towards me."

"Perhaps so, but with respect, you didn't know him as I do. Father kept a sombre and serious face in public, as any good physician should, but I happen to know that he and Sir Hans liked to socialise in private with some rather eccentric company. There are a few Oddfellows who were known to both of them, and whose acquaintance I happen to also keep. Give me a little time, Arnold. This sounds like the sort of game that some of them might play, and if I ask around I might be able to find out more. With a little more information we may be able to solve Father's last riddle together, what do you say?"

Arnold really was not sure of what to say. How quickly Nathaniel's mood had turned, as though this mystery had to some degree overshadowed the grief of Sean's death. Maybe that was exactly what Nathaniel wanted right now, some meaningful enigma to solve that would distract from his father being just one more victim of a random, senseless murder in London. Arnold wasn't sure if such an attitude should be indulged, and yet he couldn't simply dismiss Nathaniel's certainty that this was a game intended for them.

"Very well then, since you seem rather more confident about all of this than I am. Ask around among these odd fellows that Father knew, and see what you can find. I trust in your discretion of course. I'm not really accustomed to private social circles and *eccentric company*, as you put it."

"Have no worry, my brother. I shall let you know as soon as I have discovered anything of interest. We'll get to the truth of this matter, one way or another."

At least Nathaniel didn't take me for a madman or a charlatan, Arnold thought to himself when he departed Lloyd's and began his walk home. The last thing he wished to do was alienate the one member of the Musgrave family who would do him the courtesy of speaking with him. He was honestly quite thankful that his half-brother had taken such an interest in the matter of the inheritance, even if Arnold found the whole idea of his father arranging posthumous riddles and games for his children to be more than a little unseemly.

He recalled Whitfield saying that the collection had been entrusted to him two years ago, which meant that Sean must have planned this outcome for at least that length of time. But why set up some elaborate scenario like this at all? If Sean wanted Arnold to find common ground with the rest of his children, why not just accept him as a member of the family, even a distant one?

Perhaps he had simply lacked the courage to do so. Perhaps he couldn't bring himself to do such a thing while having to bear the prospect of his wife's relentless disapproval. Maybe in his mind this was a better way to accomplish it, a way which would not require his direct participation because it could only happen after his own death.

To Arnold that seemed both irresponsible and ludicrous, yet Nathaniel had seemed so convinced that it was his father's intent. Odd-fellows, he had said. Just how odd was the company that Sean and Sir Hans kept, that these men of science and learning would formulate a plan such as this? If he wanted to get to the truth of the matter, then he would have little option but to humour it.

I could not bear to see my dearest children burdened by these revelations. He could not shake those words from his thoughts. For some reason they chilled him greatly, but it was surely foolish to be afraid of such a warning, if it applied to something entirely fictitious. Some part of his mind could not shake off the notion that Sean Musgrave and Sir Hans Sloane had indeed peered into dark places, perhaps engaged in dealings which they would prefer to be kept secret from the world at large. Deeds worthy of gossip and scandal were practically a vocation among so many of England's well-to-do families, after all.

But again, it was nonsensical to think that Sir Hans Sloane, the man who had been physician to the king, would have gotten involved in anything so nefarious that it would pose a threat to his public reputation. *No*, Arnold thought to himself, *this is simply a game. A ridiculous and distasteful one, but a game nonetheless. Nothing to be concerned about.*

~ Julie ~

Wednesday September 29ᵗʰ, 1756

The azure waters of the Mediterranean Sea were calm as a millpond, glistening beneath the prow of the schooner *Agueda*. Up ahead the Strait of Gibraltar loomed, that immense natural gateway of sun-bleached rock which the ancients had called the Pillars of Herakles. The legends of old said that those gates would close upon unwary ships that sought to navigate between them, crushing the strongest hulls to splinters between the immense and unforgiving landmasses of Europe to the north and Africa to the south. Maybe there was a time when this place had felt like the very edge of the world, but in this century it was a busy shipping route, and one which Julie and her companions needed to pass through in order to reach London.

They had of course missed the *Petra* in Constantinople. Eşref had slipped through their grasp and had already set sail when the three hunters had made it to the port. They had immediately began searching for alternative travel arrangements to England, selling the carriage and horses to pay for their passage, and by the next night they had acquired two cabins aboard their current Portuguese vessel.

Its captain was a silver-haired old fellow by the name

of Erasmo Magalhães, whose attitude was as genial as his face was weather-beaten. He had intended to give his crew a few more days' shore leave in the Turkish capital before departing, but Julie had rapidly persuaded him to change his mind. Ultimately the poor man was just a bystander to her, his ship and his crew a means to an end, and under other circumstances she might not have been so quick to resort to dominating the mind of an innocent. But every day that Eşref remained ahead of the trio was a day for House Laskaris to pursue its goals, and that was time which they could ill afford.

The sun was high and dazzling bright over the Mediterranean, and its warm caress left Julie feeling utterly weak with exhaustion as she stood on deck. Above her head she held a parasol borrowed from Aida's belongings, one large enough that its shade would disguise the fact that her body cast no shadow of its own. A pair of smoked-lens spectacles further shielded her eyes from the hateful light. No trace remained of the claw-wound which had almost removed her eye in the battle at Eşref's lair. The scars that she had acquired during her mortal years would be with her forever, but most injuries that she suffered as a vampire were fleeting, temporary things. Those awful slashes upon her face had healed to mere scratches within a few hours, and had faded entirely by the next sundown.

In her free hand she held a slender pipe, which she raised to her lips and took a long drag. One thing she had learned early on about her inhuman condition was that intoxicants had a rather diminished effect upon her unless she absorbed them from the blood of her victims, but partaking of tobacco in the more publicly acceptable fashion could still confer a mildly pleasant sensation. She exhaled a stream of bittersweet smoke which was quickly swept away on the sea breeze, as behind her the approach of barely audible footsteps betrayed Saul's presence. She had to respect the man's capacity for stealth; to human ears, his movements would have been as silent as a cat.

Saul drew level with Julie, standing beside her as they gazed over the prow of the ship. Julie was not especially tall by any measure, and the muscular frame of her companion loomed a full head and shoulders above her. She glanced up towards him as he regarded her with a look of concern.

"Twelve days at sea, and for the past week you have barely slept," he remarked. "You only make yourself weaker by staying up here in the light. Weaker and hungrier. You will not be at your best when we reach London."

He was right about that much, and she knew it. So long as she remained on this ship, with a very limited pool of warm bodies on which to slake her thirst, she was being careful to consume only the minimal amount of blood that she needed. The situation would very quickly grow troublesome if the crew all started to realise that they were suffering from blackouts and anaemia, and things would get far worse indeed if she allowed her instincts to get the better of her, and she killed one of them.

With a crew of only nine, and very few passengers, a disappearance would swiftly give rise to a witch-hunt. Spending time out in the sunlight only worsened her hunger, causing her body to deplete its blood reserves faster than normal, and yet she still chose to be up here.

"I appreciate your concern, Saul, but I'll feed when we get there. There will be plenty of opportunity in England to recover my strength."

"My sister is worried about you."

"Your sister knows full well why I am doing this."

"So the visions have been bad."

Julie nodded silently.

"Worse than before?" Saul enquired.

"We don't usually spend this long on water," she muttered quietly. "Not without taking adequate preparations. Our pursuit of Eşref has left me more vulnerable than usual."

She turned to face him directly.

"The more time we spend at sea, the more *He* gets into my head. If I try to sleep, *He* is there in my dreams. I don't want to spend the daytime sleeping in Aida's cabin because of the chance that I'll wake up under *His* influence, and come to my senses drenched in her blood. She knows this, and so should you. I don't like standing here in the sunlight, but I do know that it makes it harder for *His* thoughts to connect with mine. That alone makes it worth the effort."

She took another deep drag from her pipe, before upending it and tapping out the ashes over the side of the ship. She watched Saul reach one large hand into his coat pocket, and knew immediately what he was reaching for. He withdrew the talisman that he had carried on every vampire-hunt for the past three years: a rough iron medallion engraved with a cruciform sigil at its centre, surrounded by two concentric circles of occult inscription in a language that was incomprehensible to Julie and Saul alike.

"You should take it," he told her.

"It's *your* protection," she replied, keenly aware of the irony that a vampire was being offered a talisman created to shield human minds against vampiric control.

"And the only danger on this boat is you. The best way to protect me from you is to protect you from *Him*."

Gingerly, she accepted his offer. The amulet felt cold and heavy in her hand, a testament to how feeble she had grown under the poisonous sunlight. She gave her companion a nod of thanks and slipped the item into the pocket of her breeches. She wondered briefly if wearing the talisman herself would inhibit her ability to influence the thoughts of others, just as she was inhibited from manipulating any human who wore it. She would keep it on her person if it offered any benefit in resisting *Him*, but it may be for the best if she left it behind when she next decided to feed.

"I will get it back from you when we next make port," Saul remarked, and went back to watching the Pillars of Herakles passing them by in the distance.

Drums beat in the darkness, an implacable rhythm that crawled along the skin and reverberated through the very bones. The humid air was alive with the myriad scents of the forest, and the crackling fires that adorned the stone steps of the temple. Its pyramidal structure rose above the neighbouring jungle, groping upwards for the sky and the fat, blood-red moon which hung overhead. Behind the thunderous beating of the drums there could be heard the wet tearing sounds of obsidian knives cutting into the chests of sacrificial victims. The night was rent with the screams of the dying.

With each agonised wail of a sacrifice, acolytes of the cult responded with shrieks and hollers of their devotion. Priests in ceremonial dress chanted their incantations as they went about their blood-soaked task. The consecration of the temple had to be renewed, and a temple of the Gods could only be made Holy through the sacrifice of lives. Through blood, all things.

From above there came the rush of wings, a great shadow briefly silhouetted against the crimson moon. The black form descended like a falling star, moving with a speed that was beyond all reason. Priests and acolytes fell silent, and even the captives, fearfully awaiting the ritual knife, ceased their protestations. There was only the crackling of the fires as the winged silhouette atop the pyramid blurred and shifted, its outline becoming briefly indistinguishable from the surrounding darkness before congealing, solidifying into the shape of a man.

Firelight danced upon golden skin, and two favoured priests ascended the pyramid, to adorn the figure with bright feathers and gleaming jewellery. As each sacred article was placed upon the body, a low chant began to echo among the faithful, soon rising like the roar of a summer thunderstorm. A name, repeated over and over.

Tloque Nahuaque.

The figure began to descend, and with each step he took down the pyramid his power rolled out before him in a miasma that was palpable. Men and women kneeled at the sight of him, some averting their eyes as he drew close while others stared in rapturous wonderment. Hairs stood on end, the skin of the faithful prickling with the lightning in the air. The figure's visage was obscured, the upper half of his face covered by a golden mask that was a part of his ornate head-dress.

Tloque Nahuaque.

Tloque Nahuaque.

Tloque Nahuaque.

Behind the mask, inhuman eyes burned a fierce red. Captives were pushed forth by the scrambling hands of the faithful, offering up flesh and blood to their God. Caught among the throng of priests and acolytes, Julie could only watch helplessly as the figure's mouth opened wide, devilish fangs revealed in the moonlight. Words formed, not spoken in the air like the voices of mortals, but rather a grasping, cloying sensation that crawled into the brain, a message knitted together out of millennia of blood and screams and darkness.

I am the Mouth of the Gods.

I am the Teeth of the Gods.

Through blood, all things.

Julie's eyes slammed open as she awoke. She lay upon the narrow bed of the cabin with Saul's amulet clutched in her hand, her fingers gripping it so tightly that the metal edge was biting into her palm. She had risked a few hours' sleep before sundown, but now she was regretting even that. She could feel Him in her veins, His hunger calling to her, barely abated by the talisman which Saul had hoped would shield her. Now that the sun had set and night had fallen, she was thirsty. She was *ravenous.*

Her ears detected a heartbeat approaching, her nostrils quivered at the scent of living flesh on the far side of the door. After twelve nights on this boat she knew the scent of every crewman and passenger, but this scent was more familiar than most. *Restrain yourself, Julie. You are not Him.*

The door handle turned and Aida stepped in, a canteen clutched in one hand. The scent emanating from it demanded Julie's attention, causing her eyes to redden with anticipation.

"I thought it better to leave you alone while you slept," her lover began. "I checked in on you earlier and you were restless. Saul, he… he thought that you would be feeling depleted. So he took the surgeon's kit and prepared this for you."

Aida held out the canteen and Julie grabbed it like a woman freshly recovered from the desert, her body aching with need. Her lips engulfed the neck of the canteen and she drank deeply, gulping down the precious fluid and feeling its vitality creep through her thirsting muscles. The blood was still warm, and could not have been out of Saul's body for long, but the refreshment it offered was nothing close to feeding straight from a vein. There was no pulsing heartbeat behind it, no exquisite blend of moment-by-moment fear and euphoria that came only with biting into a living vessel. It was an unsatisfying meal, but as she hungrily swallowed the last of Saul's offering, it was enough to take the edge off of her hunger and make restoring her composure just that bit easier.

"Thank you," she gasped, tossing the empty canteen

aside onto the bed. "Your brother was right. This journey is taking its toll. I'll be fine, but I do need to feed properly tonight."

"I know," Aida said, the concern in her voice quite apparent. In this moment she would happily have offered herself for her lover's sustenance, but when they had set out on this voyage, Julie had sworn that she would not sink her teeth into Aida for as long as the journey lasted. Not while she still bore the scars of her last feeding.

"Out at the stern, there is a young crewman mopping the deck," Aida continued, "Christiano, I think his name is. The handsome boy from Valencia. You have not tasted him yet. When I looked a few minutes ago, there was nobody else on that part of the ship. He's alone."

Julie stepped towards her lover and placed one tender hand upon Aida's shoulder. Briefly the two women stood, silent, foreheads tilted together as unspoken devotion passed between them. Finally Julie leaned in closer for a passing second, and kissed Aida with lips that still carried the trace of her brother's blood. Then she was gone, slipping past her and out of the cabin door, setting out on the hunt.

The *Agueda* was the first ship on which Christiano had ever sailed. He had grown up poor in the Spanish port of Valencia, living on the waterfront, never knowing much in the way of comfort or certainty through his sixteen years. His place aboard this ship had been acquired by sheer chance in the springtime, when he was selling shellfish on the docks where the *Agueda* was waiting to sail, and he overheard Captain Magalhães talking with the first mate about how a deckhand had failed to return.

Apparently the man could not be found in any of the nearby inns or brothels, and the ship needed another crewman. Christiano had approached and asked if he could take that job, perhaps embellishing his experience a little with regards to helping out on the local fishing boats. The captain and mate had debated among themselves for a couple of minutes in Portuguese, but when Magalhães had told Christiano to grab his things and get on board, for they would be leaving soon, the boy felt like this opportunity had been handed to him by God.

Compared to the poverty he had known, life aboard the *Agueda* was one of luxury. He had two meals every day, and the ship's cook was good at his job. The work of a deckhand was hard and often repetitive, but the sense of adventure was exciting, and in the past four months he had travelled further and seen more of the world than in his entire life before then. He had visited Algiers, Tunis, Malta, Tripoli, Catania, Piraeus and Constantinople, among others. They never stayed long in these places, but Christiano loved the feeling that wherever they sailed next would be somewhere new. He was always ready to find out what lay beyond the next horizon, and he gladly imagined that he would spend his whole life aboard sailing ships.

The crescent moon was razor-thin in the sky above, but the night was clear and countless stars shone like white diamonds. The boy gazed up at them as his mop swept back and forth on the deck. He had gone all his life with no education to speak of, knowing nothing about astronomy, but the first mate seemed to be quite versed in the stars and their constellations, and had taught Christiano how to identify a few of them. Cygnus, Pegasus, Draco, Orion… what marvels God had painted upon the sky. *Do angels sail among them as we mortals sail upon the sea?* he wondered to himself.

The young deckhand tensed as he suddenly realised that he was not, in fact, alone. He caught sight of Julie as she stood watching him, not more than ten feet away on the deck. How long she had been standing there, he had no idea. Christiano could not say that he knew much about this ship's passengers, but he recognised that Julie was the French woman who was travelling with the two Africans. He was not sure what connection there was between her and those mysterious twins, but from the way that they dressed, he would guess that they were not her slaves.

"I am sorry, Señorita," he uttered. "I did not see you there."

Too late he wondered if she would actually understand a word he said. The boy did not speak any French himself, though thankfully it seemed that she was quite proficient in Spanish.

"Not at all," Julie told him, dismissing his concern. "A beautiful night, is it not?"

"It is," he replied with a nervous laugh. Now that he was looking at her directly, the young deckhand could not help but feel slightly unnerved in her presence. Julie was a striking woman, there was no doubt of that, and certainly his teenaged imagination could be stoked in all kinds of ways by her appearance. She was without a doubt older than him, but beyond that he found it difficult to gauge what her age might be. Her face seemed oddly timeless, difficult to define, as if she could be anywhere from her mid-twenties to approaching fifty.

And yet if she was that old, age had not diminished her grace or vigour. She stood with perfect poise, eerily still even as the ship rocked gently beneath her. Moreso, there was something just indefinably *off* about the way the star-light cast itself about her.

Christiano knew that it was rude to stare at a woman, especially at a paying passenger, but he couldn't stop himself from looking her up and down as she drew closer to him. His prick was growing hard, as it often did when he was close to a woman, and his hands clutched tightly about the mop handle as he tried to fight down his embarrassment. He did his best to avert his eyes from hers, staring at the floor instead, but as he glanced downwards he noticed, in a rather distant and light-headed way, that where her boots touched the deck there was no shadow beneath her. How was it even possible for a person to not cast a shadow?

Julie could feel her prey's boyish arousal mingling with fear, as the primal part of his brain started to realise that he was in the presence of a predator. Her slender hand moved to his cheek, tilting his head back up so that his gaze met with hers, and the blackness of her growing pupils gave way to bloody crimson.

"It's quite alright," she whispered, "There's no need to be alarmed."

Her jaws opened, pearl-white fangs descending into view, and Christiano felt her fingers tug at the neckerchief about his throat. Moments later his eyes bulged wide as he felt the stabbing pain of her bite. He fought for breath and tried to cry out, but his voice would not obey. He attempted to struggle, but the woman was impossibly strong, and he soon found that she was pulling him downwards, pinning him upon the deck as her mouth nuzzled at his throat, drinking his blood. A whimper finally escaped his lips as he realised that he was going to die here, helpless in the grasp of this demon.

Don't kill him. Julie's rational mind warred with her instincts, telling her to slow down, to get a grip on her hunger. *You cannot afford to kill anyone on this ship. If the boy disappears nobody will believe that he just fell overboard, not in seas this calm. They'll know he's been murdered.* She knew that her reason was sound, she knew that if she lost her control even once there would be no way to cover her tracks. She knew this, and yet she continued to suckle, continued to feed her all-consuming addiction.

The captain, the crew, they'll suspect you, and Aida and Saul. They'll try to kill you. If you kill one member of the crew you'll end up having to kill them all. How much had she taken? She had only been drinking for a few seconds, she was certain of it. She could still feel the strength of the boy's heartbeat with each fresh mouthful, she could surely afford to take a little more.

You are not Him.

Julie snarled with the effort, forcibly pulling herself back from her bleeding prey. Freed from the sensation of her kiss, Christiano attempted a strangled cry for help, but she saw what he was doing and grabbed his jaw in her hand, clasping his mouth shut. She felt him shake with panic as she once again lowered herself to the wound, now licking and cleaning the bite, stimulating the punctures to begin healing. Carefully she pulled the neckerchief back up, concealing her handiwork as she licked the last of her meal from her lips.

"Stay quiet," she ordered the boy, her eyes locked onto his, her words speaking directly to the most submissive and obedient part of his mind. She knew that the vast majority of humans had an instinctual craving for hierarchy. Dominance and authority gave them a sense of structure in their chaotic world, and it was this craving which the vampiric power of mental manipulation exploited so effectively.

"You will sleep for a little while," she commanded. "And when you wake, you will recall nothing of this. You never spoke with me this night. You simply felt tired as you were working. So when you wake up you will finish your job, and then go to your hammock."

Christiano nodded weakly, his will no more capable of resisting her manipulation than of holding back the tide. Silently Julie rose to her feet, picking up the fallen mop and placing it back in the boy's hands. As she strode away, moving back towards her cabin she took a slow and deep breath, filling her lungs with cool air out of habit rather than necessity.

The scent of his blood was still fresh in her nostrils, but although her thirst cried out for more, she had placated the inner demon enough that it could not overpower her control. How easily she could have killed him. How easily she could have drunk her fill and left him a bloodless corpse. But to do so would have been to set the dominoes tumbling, and the *Agueda* would become a charnel ship by the time it reached England. Unlike the one who made her, Julie would not permit herself to become an unthinking murderer.

I am not Him.

~ Arnold ~

Sunday October 3ʳᵈ, 1756

The autumnal morning was bright and clear, the crisp sunlight streaming in through the stained-glass windows of St Mary Matfelon. Last night had been a stormy one, a night of fierce winds and hammering rain, but now in the aftermath, the pall of London's smog had been dispersed for a time. At times like this, Arnold was most in his element. The majority of the sermons at St Mary's were delivered by the Reverend Charles Lowther, but one week per month, the vicar led the congregation in hymns and prayer while allowing his curate to give the main lesson.

Arnold relished these moments, for they were a chance for him to connect with his people and do all he could to make them feel the light of God at work. Behind him, the stained-glass depiction of Christ crucified shone resplendent in the morning light. Usually Arnold worked hard to tailor and personalise his sermons, presenting the scripture in ways that his congregation would relate to in their lives, but on this particular occasion he had felt right in turning to a tried and true source, the First Book of Homilies published for the Anglican Church in 1562. In particular he was presenting its ninth sermon, An Exhortation Against the Fear of Death.

"It is not to be marvelled that worldly men fear to die," he addressed the church; *"For death depriveth them of all worldly honours, riches and possessions, in the fruition thereof, the worldly man counteth himself happy, so long as he may enjoy them at his own pleasure, and otherwise, if he be dispossessed of the same, without hope of recovery, then he can no otherwise think of himself, but that he is unhappy, for he hath lost his worldly joy and pleasure. Alas, thinketh this carnal man, shall I now depart forever from all my honours, from my treasure, from my country, friends, riches, possessions and worldly pleasures which are my joy and heart's delight? Alas that ever that day should come, when all these I must bid farewell at once, and never enjoy any of them after."*

The morbid beginning progressed into further exploration of mankind's reasons for fearing its own mortality, from the separation of oneself from material possessions and beloved people, to the fear of what lay beyond death's curtain. Fear of judgement, of accountability for the wrongdoings of one's life, and fear of eternal condemnation without comfort or hope. What greater fear was there for mortal man, than to be found unworthy of God's kingdom, and cast out to face endless existence with only the Devil's mercy to beg?

From there the sermon moved onto the promise of salvation; that by faith in God, repentance for one's sins and adherence to the teachings of Christ, the imperfect spirit of man could be made worthy to dwell in Heaven with life and joy everlasting. For the faithful, death was not a thing to be feared, Arnold told his congregation; for when death arrived at such an hour as God decided, it would be a release from the hardships and sufferings of this world made broken by sin. For those who lived as Christ instructed – in humility, piety and obedience to God – to meet an honest death should hold no dread.

There was a certain degree of catharsis for Arnold in delivering this lesson. Just shy of three weeks had passed since he learned of his father's murder, and he had decided that this sermon should mark the end of his mourning period. Nobody had been caught for the murder, and by this point Arnold fully expected that nobody would be. No credible witnesses had come forth, despite offers of a reward for any information leading to an arrest. Just as predicted, the magistrates' office had found little cooperation from the people of Whitechapel in hunting down the killer. The only thing which mildly surprised Arnold was that the Bow Street Runners had not found some random miscreant who loosely fitted the bill, and condemned them to the gallows for the crime.

The sermon was followed by several more hymns and the weekly rite of the Eucharist, followed by a closing address from the vicar. When the service came to its end, Arnold waited by the church door to shake hands with the departing members and wish them well. Lisa Brennan was far from a regular attendee at St Mary's, so it pleased Arnold that his mother had been present today for his sermon.

He hoped that the lesson had been as welcome for her to listen to as it had been for him to give, but when he thanked her for coming and wished her "God bless you," she leaned close to his ear and told him quietly, "There's been a copper around, asking a lot of questions these past few days. Calls himself Clayton. He knew about me and Sean, so I think he'll be looking for you too. Watch yourself, Son."

Of course it was not enough for her to simply attend her own son's church to hear him speak. When he had paid her a visit the previous week, to tell her that the items he'd inherited from Sean were nothing but worthless fabrications, her reaction had been predictably bitter. "Even from the grave, it's just like your dad to dangle a glimpse of a good thing and then snatch it away," she had told him. In the end she had not even mustered up much anger at this hollow outcome. Her reaction became one of pure cynicism, just one more confirmation that she had always known her place in the world, and that any hope of advancing beyond it was a lost cause.

Arnold had left her alone after that, sensing that she was in no mood for his ministrations, so he supposed that he should be thankful for her coming here to inform him of this much. If a visit from an officer of the law was indeed in Arnold's immediate future, then she would not want him to say anything that might cast her in a bad light. It would be all too easy for the magistrates to close the case by pinning Sean's murder on his disgruntled ex-lover, even this many years after their relationship had ended. But unless the detective in question had anything to definitely connect Lisa to the crime, then the testimony of her good character from a known clergyman should be enough to exonerate her.

If Arnold hoped that his mother had anything more to say to him at this juncture, he was naturally disappointed. Once the hand-shaking and well-wishing was done, he watched the last of the congregation leave. He turned as he felt the vicar's hand on his arm, the old man looking at him with a kindly smile.

Charles Lowther was what Arnold considered an exemplary priest and mentor, a man of immense patience and forbearance. His fire had dimmed a little with age, perhaps, but his soul and his mind were still bright beneath his body's frail exterior. Should Arnold be chosen to replace him as vicar of St Mary's when he finally passed on, the young curate could only hope to be good enough to fill his shoes.

"You did well today, my son," the vicar assured him. "It

has been some time since you last delivered a sermon that you had not written yourself. But while the words were not your own, your delivery was most powerful. I felt in my heart every word that you spoke."

"Thank you, Reverend. I chose that sermon because it has a great deal of personal meaning for me. With the awful murder of Doctor Musgrave just three weeks ago, and no killer having been yet exposed, I felt that our congregation should benefit from reassurance that death is conquered by our Lord Christ, and that they need not live in fear."

Of course Arnold had long ago told Reverend Lowther that Sean Musgrave was his father, but the vicar was never one to bring up the topic of his curate's parentage. The old man did not subscribe to the idea that a son should suffer for the sins of his father. Regardless of certain passages in the Old Testament, it was his firm belief that ever since the sacrifice and resurrection of Jesus, each human soul was accountable to God for their own sins, and theirs alone. They had of course conversed on the matter after the news of Sean's murder, but the conversation had been brief.

"Very astute of you to think so. I would venture that everyone who heard your sermon today is all the better for it. Now come, join me for some tea, and then we have work to do. I'll be offering Holy Communion to a number of sick parishioners in their homes today, and I'd like you to be with me."

The home visits took up much of the afternoon. There were only half a dozen of them, but the addresses were spaced out around Whitechapel, and the vicar's walking speed was rather slow these days. Arnold helped him as much as possible, carrying the blessed wafer and wine in his satchel, along with a Bible and other materials of the rite. For the Eucharist to be performed in a person's home was something that only happened by request, but it was a request that Vicar Lowther was all too willing to grant, wherever a parishioner was too enfeebled or unwell to attend at St Mary's. Arnold enjoyed these visits; each one felt deeply personal, a chance for the worshipper to connect with God in their heart, rather than a ritual being simply observed out of social expectation.

The first visit was to the home of David Jefferies, a carpenter whose leg had been badly injured in a collapse at a building site. Surgery at the London Hospital had saved his life, but he had since been discharged because his family could no longer afford to pay the fees for a recovery bed. The second was to Margaret Thomson, a very frail and elderly widow looked after by her unmarried son.

The third was to poor Edith Chambers, whose mind was heavily damaged by mercury poisoning from the felt factory where she used to work, and who was only barely coherent enough to take the Communion with the help of her family. Arnold always found her case to be uniquely poignant in its sadness, and he frequently prayed that the Lord would find it in his heart to heal her, even if such miracles seemed few and far between.

The fourth visit was to the home of Richard Sinclair, a regular attendee at St Mary's, who in the last few days had come down with some unknown illness. It was his wife Helen, who had asked that the vicar visit them in order to perform the Eucharist.

The Sinclair home was an impoverished place, as were most in this part of London. The walls were thin, and marked by rising damp. The furniture was likewise old, much of it in poor repair. Helen Sinclair made some earnings as a flower-seller, while her husband took whatever manual labour he could find. The pair did have a son, who had enlisted in the army and was currently serving overseas. None of their other children had survived beyond their earliest years, and the Sinclairs had precious little money to fall back on, so if Richard did not recover from his sickness swiftly, they would be relying on the kindness of the landlord to avoid becoming homeless. Arnold hoped that this visit would help to improve the man's morale and speed his healing.

"He was in a terrible state, when he came home on Thursday night," Helen explained as she guided the two clergymen up the bare, creaky stairs to the bedroom. "He'd been suffering since Monday, but Thursday he was at his worst. I've never seen my husband so weak. He's been bedbound since, but I swear he seems a bit stronger these past two days. He's started eating again. He'll be glad to see you two here, he's always been fond of church."

If this was him looking stronger, Arnold dreaded to think how bad Richard must have been on Thursday. The man looked emaciated and pale, anaemically so.

"Dick?" his wife enquired softly, a hand on his shoulder gently shaking him. "Dick, the vicar's here to see you, to give you Communion. The curate's here too."

Richard's eyes opened a little as he rolled over, and Arnold found himself concerned at just how bloodshot they looked. His pupils were wide, heavily dilated, and his eyelids soon screwed shut again as even the faint light from the window fell upon his face.

"It's too bright," he complained, his voice weak.

"The curtains are drawn, dear," Helen told him. "I can't make it any darker. But Vicar Lowther and Mister Brennan are both here. They've come to visit you."

Richard pulled himself upright, now sitting on the bed, and as he did so the loose collar of his nightshirt fell lower, exposing an odd-looking scar near the base of his throat. The marks didn't look fresh, Arnold was sure of that. He was no physician of course, but the two short, ragged lines of pink flesh looked like the remains of a wound which had healed over. Not a cut from a blade, he was certain. If anything it looked more like a bite, possibly from a rat?

Rats were a constant nuisance around here, especially to young children, but they would not hesitate to bite a grown man if they felt cornered. Arnold had in the past seen men turn feverish from such bites, but these scars looked clean, and the skin around them bore no obvious signs of inflammation or infection. He also thought that those punctures looked rather too far apart to have been made by the mouth of a single rat.

Reverend Lowther greeted Mr Sinclair warmly, assuring him that they would do all they could to make him feel better, and to attend to his spiritual wellbeing. Richard seemed only mildly responsive, his grip almost pathetically weak when the vicar took his hand, and for a moment he seemed to actively shrink back from the old man. When Arnold opened his satchel and took out the Bible and the book of common prayer, followed by the Eucharist wafer and wine, he could not help but notice how acutely Richard's gaze fixed upon those items one after the other, as if their presence were enough to cause him some personal discomfort. The man's eyes likewise lingered upon the little wooden crucifixes worn about the necks of his two visitors.

With the articles of the ceremony prepared, Reverend Lowther began the rite with an acclamation, invoking the name of the Father, the Son and the Holy Ghost. Richard looked ill at ease throughout, his sickness clearly making things difficult for him. When the vicar reached the end of his prayer and pronounced "Amen," Arnold and Helen both joined in the closing affirmation, though Richard only managed to mouth the word feebly.

In church the opening address would be followed by a hymn, with the *Gloria in Excelsis Deo* being the usual music of choice at St Mary's. For home visits such as this one the singing was typically omitted unless the parishioner in question felt well enough to request it. Next came the Proclamation of the Word, but as the vicar began his reading from the Gospel of Mark, Richard voiced his objection.

"Enough of this!" he spat, interrupting the priest mid-sentence and catching them all off guard with the level of spite in his voice. "Enough! I'm tired, and I don't want any of this! Just leave me in peace."

Perhaps it was just that the man's ill health had caused his gums to become withdrawn, but Arnold could not help but notice how his teeth seemed a little more pronounced than they ought to. His canines even appeared just a touch more pointed, enough so to catch his attention. Naturally the curate's thoughts steered towards those frames of mounted teeth which still sat in his room at the rectory, each one labelled with a different breed of mythical monster.

Internally he chastised himself for even having such thoughts. Richard's teeth may look a little odd, but they were most definitely human teeth, not the enlarged fangs of a predatory beast. Monsters only existed in superstitions and story books, he reminded himself, and dwelling on such nonsense would not help this poor afflicted man.

"Husband!" Helen was clearly quite upset at Richard's behaviour, and she moved to his bedside with an expression of worry. "The vicar's come here for you, because I asked him to."

"I didn't ask for it," he snapped back at her. "Make them go!"

"But you've always liked the church, you always–"

"I said make them go!"

Richard's hand grabbed onto Helen's arm when she reached for him, and despite his earlier show of weakness, his grip now seemed formidable. His fingers squeezed tightly around her forearm, his already pale knuckles turning white.

"Get. Them. Out."

"Dick, you're hurting me!"

"I said—"

"Please, let go of me!"

"Mister Sinclair, please calm yourself! What is the meaning of this?" Reverend Lowther interjected, clearly as shocked by Richard's outburst as Helen was. The pallid man in the bed looked sharply towards the old priest, his gaze now containing a look of such pain and hatred that Arnold would never have expected to see. Many times in his youth had he witnessed the capacity for evil in men, especially when the drink was in them, but rarely so unprovoked as this.

"Richard, let go of her!"

He stepped towards Sinclair, who tensed like a frightened animal, muscles locked on the edge between fight and flight. With a cry he hurled his wife away from him, shoving Helen back so forcefully that she struck the bedroom wall and caused the furniture to rattle. Horrified, Arnold moved to restrain the man, but no sooner had he drawn close than Richard seemed to grow frail again, his unexpected burst of strength evaporating, leaving him. Sinclair fell back onto the bed, limbs coiling into a foetal position.

The bedroom filled with the sound of coughing and crying, dry sobs racking the sick man's body. Arnold took a cautious step back, unsure what to make of this. In this moment he could scarcely imagine Richard being a threat to anyone – save perhaps himself – so where had he found the strength, mere moments ago, to manhandle his wife in such a fashion?

Thankfully, Helen did not seem to be badly hurt. Her shoulder had taken the brunt of the impact, and she had avoided hitting her head, but she was understandably very shaken. Arnold did not know how strict a husband Richard was, but he would have ventured that the man did not often physically discipline his wife, and nor had he seen any signs of undue cruelty from him in the past. For all appearances the Sinclairs had a loving, dutiful, Christian marriage, and it definitely appeared that Helen was not accustomed to this kind of treatment.

The vicar helped her back downstairs to the living room, while Arnold stayed a little longer to make sure that Richard was not going to have another outburst. When he leaned over the stricken man, he observed once again how Sinclair tried to shrink away from him, as if due to some awful, blind unwillingness to be near him. Whatever illness he had succumbed to, it was clearly hurting his mind as much as his body.

Downstairs, Arnold and Reverend Lowther did their best to comfort Mrs Sinclair, and shared in a pot of tea that she made. The vicar urged her to be strong, to look after her husband and pray for his recovery, but to inform him at the church if Richard's condition continued to worsen. In the event that he could not return to work and they found themselves unable to pay the rent, he promised that alms from St Mary's would be available to ensure that they had a roof under which to sleep. Arnold was troubled by what he had seen upstairs, but he kept his stoicism for the sake of Helen Sinclair. Before departing, he untied the cross from his neck and passed it to her, placing it in her hand.

"Please, I should be grateful if you kept this about your person," he told her. "Hold onto it for me when you pray."

Sunday afternoon's incident remained with Arnold through the rest of the day, though he did his best to put it out of his mind while assisting the reverend with the remaining two visits. The horrible look upon Richard Sinclair's face still nagged at his thoughts the following morning, when he was sweeping the floor in St Mary's. Unlike yesterday there had been no winds the previous night to clear the smog from above the city, and with the return of the autumn rain in abundance, the Monday morning was as grey as Sunday had been bright. The dull, thumping sound of three heavy knocks at the church door caused Arnold to look up from his sweeping, and he set the brush aside as he moved to answer.

Outside in the pouring rain stood a man very nearly as tall as Arnold himself, but far sturdier of build. He was dressed in navy blue, with a grey rain-cloak about his shoulders and a brown leather tricorne. Much like Arnold he kept an orderly beard and moustache, though his walnut-brown hair was shoulder-length and tied back in a ponytail. Somehow, the curate had a feeling as to who this man was.

"May I come inside?"

"Of course," Arnold replied. "All men are welcome in the House of God."

"My thanks."

The stranger stepped inside, the rainwater dripping from his cloak. He took a moment to wipe his feet as he entered, but his boots were wet and muddy enough to still leave some footprints as he walked into the church hall. As Arnold got a better look at the newcomer, he noticed how the man was clearly a seasoned professional of violence. His large, meaty hands bore the callouses of a fighter, his knuckles having clearly been broken and healed more than once. And as he took off his rain-cloak, the momentary glimpse of a flint-lock pistol could be seen holstered at his belt, beneath his blue jacket. Arnold would honestly not be surprised to learn that one of his boots also concealed a dagger.

"My name is Lawrence Clayton," he introduced himself.

"I'm a detective investigator for the Bow Street Magistrates' Office. I wanted to speak to Reverend Arnold Brennan about some recent occurrences here in Whitechapel."

Straight to business then, Arnold thought to himself, though he was in truth glad that the man was not making unnecessary pleasantries. His reason for being here was far from convivial, after all.

"It's just Mister Brennan, I'm afraid. I am merely a curate here, not the vicar."

"But you are Arnold Brennan?"

"I am indeed. Am I to assume that you are here to talk about the murder of my father, Sean Musgrave?"

"That would be correct, yes. Obviously at this juncture we have no cause for suspicion upon yourself, Mister Brennan, but given your mother Lisa Brennan's connection to the deceased, we cannot rule out her involvement."

"I thought that might be the case, Mister Clayton. I had been told by Mister Kenneth Whitfield, my late father's attorney, that the Bow Street Runners were investigating the killing. But whatever objectionable aspects there might be to my mother's life, I am quite certain that she is no murderess. Her... *unmarried relations* with my father ended before I was born. In fact, my conception was the very cause of that ending."

"We don't like to use that name, Sir."

"I'm sorry?"

"Bow Street Runners. A filthy bit of street slang, not one that we at the Magistrates' Office are fond of."

"Ah. I do apologise. No offence was intended."

Yet somehow, Arnold got the impression that offence had been taken on Clayton's part. The detective was being polite enough, but all the same the young clergyman was finding something intensely dislikeable about him. He got the impression that Clayton was one of nature's bullies, a fellow who was not at ease until he had established some manner of social dominance over everyone around him. Perhaps that was the very reason he made his living from catching criminals; he liked the sense of authority that came with his profession.

"Did you converse with Mister Whitfield on the matter recently?"

"I did," Arnold told him. "I met him at his office last month, on the thirteenth. We discussed matters of my father's will. Given my rather estranged situation with the rest of the Musgrave family, that was the first I learned of the fact that Father's death was not of accident or natural causes."

"I see. And have you spoken with him more recently than that?"

"No, I can't say I have. My business with him was concluded on that day."

"I see."

"Is my meeting with Mister Whitfield important, in some fashion?"

"Could you tell me specifically what matters you discussed with him? You mentioned that it pertained to the will."

"Yes, my father had left me some things. Mister Whitfield had them delivered to me within hours of our meeting, they're being kept in my lodgings here. I can show them to you if you wish it."

Arnold had the increasing suspicion that Clayton was hiding something from him, deliberately withholding information of import, in the hope that Arnold would reveal something unintended. He did not like this game at all.

"If you haven't spoken directly with him, did you receive any written correspondence from him or his legal practice, in the time since your meeting?"

"No, I haven't. May I ask why this is of such interest?"

"It would be because Kenneth Whitfield is dead. He was found floating face down in the Thames on Friday morning. His death, so soon after that of his client Sean Musgrave, is a little too much of a coincidence, do you not think so?"

The clergyman blinked in surprise, his disquiet evident upon his face. The revelation had completely blindsided him, and this news held the potential to change everything; it suggested that his father's murder may not have been the random act of greed or desperation, but rather a planned step in some criminal conspiracy. From the facts that were available so far, he could see why his own mother would fall squarely within the Runners' pool of suspected conspirators.

"I… I'm sorry, this is the first I have heard of it."

Arnold suddenly being on the back foot like this seemed to call out to Clayton, like blood in the water drawing in a shark. The detective was standing closer than he had realised, his physical presence suddenly occupying all of Arnold's attention.

"You now understand the cause for my interest, yes? Sean Musgrave is murdered, and to your surprise you receive some inheritance in his will. As a dutiful, pious son who honours the Fifth Commandment, I'm certain that you coming into money should have been of benefit to your mother, perhaps helping her to find a better life than the one she has in this neighbourhood. Except that from what I've learned, the inheritance that was left to you was not so terribly valuable after all. A person who has committed one cold-blooded murder might feel inclined to commit another upon learning that their scheme has failed."

The accusation was enough to stoke Arnold's ire. He could feel anger rising in him, boiling up like a tide, and he fought to keep his temper. *How dare this man come into this sacred place and suggest these things?*

"Are you honestly saying that I conspired to murder my own father for money, and that I then killed his lawyer out of nothing but anger?"

"No, Mister Brennan, I don't believe that you are a killer at all," While Arnold was struggling to maintain his composure, Clayton's voice was still maddeningly calm. "You're a man of the cloth after all, and a very devout one at that. Everything I've heard about you tells me that breaking any law of Man or God is simply beyond you. But I do think that you could have been used. I think that Lisa Brennan might have learned that your father had made provision for you in his will, and so she sought to speed up his passing so that she might benefit from it. And when you told her that you had nothing of value for her, I suspect she grew rather displeased."

"Not at all, if you must know," Arnold said through gritted teeth. "In fact anger ought to have been welcome, compared to the sheer lack of feeling that she showed when I gave her the news. She said that it was just like Father to dangle a glimpse of a good thing and then snatch it away."

No sooner had he uttered those words than he bitterly regretted it. The look upon Clayton's face was one of cool, self-assured satisfaction; he had called Lisa Brennan a cold-blooded murderer, and Arnold's own description of her 'sheer lack of feeling' aligned perfectly with that accusation. Of course this was not hard evidence. It was barely even circumstantial, but it was enough to give Lawrence Clayton the sense of vindication of his instincts. It told him that he was on the right trail. Lisa had warned Arnold about this man, if only so that he would not say something to inadvertently condemn her, and now it seemed he had done just that. Clayton would keep hounding his mother until he found something, however insubstantial, that would result in her hanging from a noose. The law would have little mercy for a woman like her.

"I shan't take up any more of your time today," the investigator assured him, "but I'll come by in the near future so that you can show me the items that you mentioned. Just so that I can be sure of all the facts, you understand."

Clayton turned away with a curt nod and made his way back out into the rain, leaving Arnold alone in the church, and feeling as though he had signed his own mother's death warrant.

~ Nathaniel ~

Wednesday October 6th, 1756

Less than half a mile from the Victualling Office in Deptford, south of the River Thames, Greenwich Park was a pleasant expanse of greenery amidst the narrow confines of London's urban sprawl. First enclosed as parkland by royal decree some three centuries previous, the area played host to certain features which were considerably more ancient, such as the Anglo-Saxon burial mounds on the park's western side, which had stood for a thousand years. North of those mounds lay the hill upon which the majestic Royal Observatory was constructed, built for the purpose of mapping the night sky to advance England's knowledge of maritime navigation.

Nathaniel Musgrave often liked to come here after work, to walk among the trees and fields, and enjoy the relative peace that this place offered. It was early evening now, the angry red halo of the sun creeping lower towards the horizon, and Nathaniel was making his way to the observatory's garden in order to make good on a promised meeting. As he stepped into the secluded Garden of the Astronomer Royal, a smile touched his lips as his nose confirmed the waiting presence of an old friend.

Thomas Ashford was a man who was all too often detected by scent before he was seen. The flamboyant thespian indulged a number of vices, including a passion for smoking a particular and rather distinctive blend of tobacco from Egypt. He often experimented with additional herbal aromas to flavour his habit, and the peculiar scents of the smoke stuck to his clothes even when he didn't have a pipe in hand.

His appearance was no less distinctive than his odour, however, for a long life lived in theatre had left old Tom with a marked tendency towards eccentricity. His lordly scarlet coat and breeches were finely made but rather worn, and his gold-embroidered waistcoat was verging on threadbare in places, noticeable especially where it stretched around his rather portly physique. A powdered wig sat atop his head, concealing the fact that he had scarcely any hair left. At seventy-three years of age he carried a walking cane in his hand and still wore a rapier upon his belt, but practised stage-fighter or not, Nathaniel rather suspected that Tom's duelling days were long behind him.

The two men smiled broadly and greeted one another with a firm handshake and a clap upon the shoulder. The velvet cuff of Tom's coat was embossed with a symbol of three interlinked rings, but Nathaniel had no need of such an image to know of this man's fraternity. The pair had known each other through the Order of Patriotic Oddfellows since Nathaniel's induction at age sixteen.

"How fares, Tom? It's awfully good to see you again, I must say. I have been hoping to speak to you for the past couple of weeks, but Sir George told me that you were away on business in Edinburgh. A pleasant trip for you, I hope."

"It certainly was," the jovial old dandy replied. "Just offering a little patronage to a friend who has started up a new theatre company in that fine city. I knew he would be most grateful for my efforts and my advice, and I do jump at any excuse to visit Caledonia. The air up north always does me good, I think."

The two men fell into step together, strolling at a leisurely pace. A quick glance around the garden confirmed that nobody else was in earshot, though their conversation continued at a rather more modest volume.

"While you were up there, did you happen to pay a visit to any of our friends on the opposing side of the Jacobite divide? It's a shame that so many of them are still so bitter over the Young Pretender's failure, even after these past eleven years."

"The 'Young Pretender', you call him? My boy, you were but a child when the uprising happened. Had you not barely reached your eighth birthday before the Battle of Culloden?"

"I was nine, Tom, as you well know. And since the people called him by that title, so do I. The prince was never more than a pretender, after all."

"Such impudence! *As I well know*, ha! Well it might please *you* to know that I did make one or two diplomatic overtures to some of our northern former brethren, but my proffered olive branch was roundly repudiated. 'Tis a shame that competing claims upon the throne should carve so deep a cleft, between we who once called one another brothers, but ever is that the way of mortal men. I suppose that divide will endure so long as Prince Charlie keeps the Jacobite cause alive, even in exile. But of course a young buck like yourself has no memory of our Order being a united whole."

"You're right, I do not. But I can nonetheless dream that someday it may be so."

"And our dreams are what we live for, are they not?"

Tom stopped mid-stride, his bonhomie suddenly giving

way to a look of profound sadness. Nathaniel had often wondered if his friend's capacity for rapid changes of emotion were a product of his career on stage, or vice versa.

"Oh, my dear boy. I was so sorry to learn of what happened to your father. It was only when I returned home from Edinburgh that I found your invitation to the funeral. Rest assured I would have been there, had I known. Sean was such a dear friend to me, to everyone in The Order."

"I know that he was," Nathaniel nodded, keeping a stiff upper lip. "Most of his friends from the fraternity were there, and the ceremony was very moving. I think he would have approved."

There was great sympathy in Tom's grey eyes, and great sorrow, but he seemed at ease with not pressing Nathaniel any further on the matter. Doubtless he knew that Sean's end had been a violent one, and there was nothing he could do to erase it. But it was the ripples of consequence from that very death which Nathaniel had asked him here to discuss.

"You know, Tom, it is a matter connected to Father which I wanted to talk to you about this evening."

"Is that so? Do tell me, my boy, I shall listen to anything you have to say of him."

"It concerns him and another deceased affiliate of our fair brotherhood, the former Physician Royal."

"Sir Hans? Well, he and Sean were always close associates, far more than mere student and teacher. I cannot claim to have intimate knowledge of every scheme and plot which they wove between them, but if you have questions, I shall endeavour to answer."

Nathaniel took another look about his surroundings, just to be certain that they were alone and would not be overheard.

"It also concerns my half-brother, Arnold. I know that

you are aware of Father's indiscretion in his earlier years with that tavern wench, Miss Brennan. She bore him a son, whom Father always kept at a great distance. Mother despises Arnold, my siblings are indifferent, and I am the only one among us who actually seems to think of him as kin. But last month we met to speak with one another at Lloyd's, and he revealed to me something rather surprising. It seems that Father left him an inheritance, in the form of letters, documents and artefacts of natural science, a collection of animal teeth to be exact. He told me that some of the documents bore Sir Hans' signature, and most of them appeared to be written in his hand. Latin and Greek, I think, languages with which neither I nor Arnold have any great fluency.

"But the oddest thing Arnold said to me is that all of those things seemed to pertain not to medicine or science, but to superstition and folklore. Even the teeth were labelled with the names of mythical monsters. It seemed most bizarre at first, but then it struck me that Father might have prepared this inheritance for Arnold as some kind of game. A riddle that should require him to work with at least myself in order to solve, and in so doing perhaps create some commonality between Arnold and the rest of us. It is all rather strange I know, but from stories that others in the fraternity have told me, I don't think it beyond the bounds of Father's thinking."

Tom was quiet as he digested everything that Nathaniel said to him. Only the rhythmic tapping of the old man's cane upon the ground created an almost metronomic break in the silence.

"What a delightfully curious notion," he finally gave voice to his thoughts. "Sir Hans was always a peculiar chap, an obsessive collector of all kinds of strange paraphernalia. An admirable scientist to be sure, but ultimately as avid a student of the esoteric as the rational. Such is not unusual among our company, of course, but it does seem that his more occult leanings might have rubbed off upon Sean in some fashion."

"That's the very thing that I was thinking. Their shared delvings into esoteric matters could have inspired Father to concoct this little game for his progeny. It all seems a trifle morbid to orchestrate such a thing from beyond the grave, but I can imagine him planning it all long before his passing."

"A fascinating notion, my boy. Given the circumstances, I would be honoured to help you and your half-brother to solve this little mystery. In fact I would consider it my last fraternal tribute to my dear Sean."

Arnold smiled at the sentiment, glad of Tom's desire to be involved. Maybe at the end of this, there could be the consideration of a place for Arnold among the Oddfellows, provided his very Christian sensibilities would permit him to take membership in a secretive society.

"That's excellent to hear. Excellent! I must be honest, old boy, you are rather my last hope on the matter. None of the other fellows that I asked had any idea about such a collaboration between Father and Sir Hans, though naturally my discussions with each of them were taken under gentleman's word of confidence. But I know that you were closer to Father than anyone these past three years, so I thought you might at least have some light to shed."

"Well, I don't wish to disappoint you my boy, but as I said, I can't claim intimate knowledge of this scheme."

"Perhaps not, but I do know of a definitive way you could assist us. Arnold told me that some of the letters in his collection were in French. You've told me before that when you were a young travelling thespian you spent some years in France, and I know quite well that you never lost practice of the language. How about you do us the very great favour of translating those letters, and we shall proceed from there?"

"My dear boy, I should be delighted to. What a marvellous little mystery this shall be! I'll tell you what, I shall happen to say that this very next week, on Thursday the fourteenth, the Minories theatre is hosting a special performance of *Twelfth Night*. What do you say that I acquire a couple of the expensive seats for yourself and Arnold, and after the show we can take a look at these letters together? Perhaps offer to bring your dear sister along too? I cannot think of a more splendid way for me to meet another member of your family."

"Splendid indeed, Tom. I thank you greatly for your assistance."

A playfully sly look came upon the old man's face. It was an expression that Nathaniel had seen many times before.

"You know, since I am aiding you in this game that Sean has left you, perhaps you could answer a question that has been weighing upon my mind?"

"Oh? Do tell, old boy."

"Since you brought up the matter of the exiled Bonnie Prince Charlie earlier, maybe you could settle for me whether there is any veracity in the rumours that his charming Scottish mistress, Miss Clementina Walkinshaw, is in fact a spy for His Majesty the King? I thought a man in your profession might be privy to such knowledge."

Nathaniel laughed heartily, enjoying the joke.

"I work in victuals, my friend, not in espionage. But for what my opinion is worth, I should venture that she most certainly is. The House of Hanover has eyes and ears everywhere."

As the last of the day's light disappeared and night set in, Tom dug into his pocket for a tinder box, and lit up a lantern to illuminate their path as they continued their walk through Greenwich Park. When they made it back to the park gates and returned to London's streets, the old man decided that he'd had quite enough exercise for one day, and Nathaniel flagged down a Hackney carriage to transport Tom back home.

The two friends said their farewells and went their separate ways, and in the darkened streets Nathaniel only caught passing notice of the finely-dressed Turkish man walking at a discreet distance behind him. He did not give the stranger's presence any particular thought, though undoubtedly he would have done, if he knew that the man had been following the pair of Oddfellows ever since they left the observatory garden.

~ Aida ~

Thursday October 7th, 1756

The *Agueda* had arrived in London a little ahead of the captain's initial predictions, thanks to a favourable tailwind in the latter days of the journey. Unfortunately that meant the *Petra* would have likely enjoyed similar conditions, and the three hunters had no idea how fast a ship it was, relative to the *Agueda*. Julie's instinct was that their quarry had gotten here before them, and Aida N'Dour had learned from experience that her lover's intuitions often rang true where other vampires were concerned. For all they knew, Eşref had been in this city for several days now. Depending on how many more of House Laskaris' strigoi had come here, he could by now be just one among a formidable nest of bloodsuckers in London.

None of that changed their objective here. Julie was still quite adamant about keeping Sir Hans' writings out of Laskaris hands, and the twins did not debate her reasoning. Their past four years as her companions had been an adventure that was as thrilling as it was perilous, but that peril would increase immeasurably if Europe's largest and most powerful strigoi coven began actively hunting them. Far better to make sure that the enemy never laid eyes upon those documents.

Sailing into the Howland Great Dock on the River Thames, Aida had witnessed London for the first time. It was not as beautiful as Paris, to her eyes, though very few cities in the north of Europe were. She definitely knew that she had never visited a city whose air was so choked with the scent of smoke and soot. Her throat was already tickling uncomfortably when she made her way down the *Agueda*'s gangplank with Julie and Saul, and that alone left her doubting that she would enjoy her time here.

She knew that Saul, unlike herself, had travelled to this city once before. When her brother was still a boy he had come here with Father on one of his business ventures, to give him a glimpse of the mercantile operation which he would one day inherit. The wealth of the N'Dour family – like that of many elites among the Wolof people – was rooted in gold and in slaves, and England was just one more country which had plenty of buyers for both.

It was around two o'clock in the afternoon when the ship had docked, and although it was still broad daylight, Julie was clearly relieved to be standing once more upon dry land. Accustomed as Aida was to her lover's boundless strength and force of spirit, it had pained her to see Julie grow steadily weaker, more listless and irritable through the course of the voyage. More than once she had feared that Julie's resolve might break, but even in the face of exhaustion and recurring hellish visions, the immortal woman had kept her nerve.

She had fed upon the *Agueda*'s crew to sustain herself, but she had not indulged beyond necessity. She had not killed, no matter the temptation, and that alone was enough to maintain Aida's belief in her. Of course, their arrival in London brought with it a new set of problems.

"We shall need to be careful here," Aida began as the trio assembled on the dockside with their luggage. "England

and France are at war, so there is the chance that we will face suspicion here for our accents alone. We are clearly not invaders of this country, but–"

"But the English could mistake us for spies," Saul finished her sentence. "It would be a shame to have come all this way, just to be arrested and put on trial for espionage."

"So we shall be civil where we need to be, and not ask too many questions," Julie remarked. "I don't think I have ever travelled anywhere that the locals took kindly to strangers asking questions. So we shall be here on business, nothing more."

"We have some money left over from the sale of our horses, but it is all Ottoman piastre," Aida continued. "We shall need guineas and shillings to spend here, so a visit to the Grasshopper will be required for us to obtain funds. Then we look for lodgings."

Given their family's long list of trading contacts, it was normally Aida's preference to send letters ahead of their arrival in any major port in order to arrange accommodations. With their decision to come here being rather impromptu, that had not been an option. However, they did travel with an extensive collection of credit notes for various European banking houses, including some based here in London.

"We shall find no want of inns in this city," Saul assured her. *Even ones that will not look askance at a pair of masterless Negroes*, being the unspoken subtext. Travelling in countries where people of their colour were not typically free, the twins had grown accustomed to the fact that locals would often view them as no different to slaves at first glance. Insults, harassment and denial of service were common obstacles. Nonetheless, it was a rare landlord who would refuse them lodgings once it became evident how much coin they could offer.

The sign of the Grasshopper had been used as a trading crest in London for nearly two centuries, when it had initially belonged to Thomas Gresham's goldsmith shop on Lombard-street. Little over a decade ago that freehold was purchased by the financier John Martin, and the site had begun trading as one of the new breed of merchant banks which were cropping up in London. Martins Bank now provided services to numerous mercantile operations, and was the N'Dour family's facility of choice for depositing wealth or acquiring credit in the isles of Great Britain.

Since neither of them had personally set foot in the building before, however, the arrival of the twins at Martins was met with initial reservation from the clerk whom they approached, as well as more than a few raised eyebrows from other clientele. Hasty apologies were offered once their identity as representatives of the family was made clear, and Aida's credit note was handed over in return for a substantial withdrawal of money. The clerk was keen to resolve their business quickly, and as the twins departed, they could scarcely fail to notice his relief that were leaving. Aida bristled at the disrespect from a lowly cashier, but like her brother, she refrained from causing a scene.

A short while later they had reconvened with Julie on the north bank of the Thames at Wapping, near to the Execution Dock where prisoners convicted of piracy and smuggling were routinely hanged. Not far away from those grim scaffolds stood a three-storey inn which, ironically, had garnered quite a reputation as a nest of thieves and brigands. Originally named The Pelican, locals now referred to the place as the Devil's Tavern, and it was there that the three hunters paid for a couple of rooms to see them through their stay.

Once they had carried their luggage upstairs, Aida looked over their new surroundings. She was unsure if this place would be any more comfortable than their cabin aboard the ship had been.

"I'm sure we could have found somewhere better than this," she remarked to her lover. "The clientele downstairs did not look terribly friendly, did they? I wonder if they will try to rob us."

"Let them," Julie replied with a playful grin. "I should find that most entertaining."

"Rob us, rape us… this Devil's Tavern would hardly have earned its name if was not a nest of cut-throats."

Julie's hands grabbed Aida's waist, pulling her close.

"Nobody lays hands on you but me, *ma cheri*."

Aida's arms rose to wrap Julie in their embrace, and she met her lover's lips with her own, all thoughts of the hunt and the mission slipping away for a time as they enjoyed a sweet, languid kiss.

"Well," Aida finally whispered, "I am confident that at least *you* will make this stay pleasant for me."

Julie took a step back, fingers still entwined with Aida's, her expression relaxed and playful, though there was still a hint of seriousness in her voice.

"Don't get too comfortable, my darling. With any luck our stay here won't be a long one."

"It might be longer than we first hoped," Aida ventured. "Eşref may have come here, but we cannot be certain how easily we will pick up his trail. And while Saul has been here before, even he does not know this city well. We are going to be hunting blind, for a time."

"His scent won't elude me for long. If we can find living associates of Sir Hans, we'll soon find House Laskaris."

"Is that your plan? We begin by observing Sir Hans' old properties?"

"Properties, family, and friends who might still be alive. I know that his wife died long before he did, but his daughters, Eliza and Sarah, they are still alive. I should be surprised if the Laskaris are not already watching them. Beyond that there is the Royal Society to consider. Sir Hans was its president for a good number of years, so there ought to be some living members who were on close terms with him. If I remember rightly, one of the last letters he sent to me mentioned that he had also become involved with a secret brotherhood, some order of philanthropists. I don't recall their name, but I remember his illustration of their symbol, three rings linked together like a chain."

Aida absorbed what Julie had to say. In truth she did not share her lover's confidence that any of those things would connect them directly to the vampire that they were seeking, but it was good to have some starting points, however vague they may be.

"We have some leads to investigate, then. Enough that it may be worth dividing our efforts at first? The more ground we can cover, the better."

"I was thinking much the same," Julie replied. "Where do you wish to start?"

"Saul and I had some written correspondence of our own with members of the Royal Society when he studied at the Sorbonne. It was even Sir Hans who fostered and encouraged communication between French and English scholars for the pursuit of scientific knowledge. I could write to some of those old contacts, let them know that Saul and myself are in England and shall like to meet in person. It will give us a chance to find out who among them remained close friends with Sir Hans until the end of his life."

Julie nodded in agreement.

"A good start."

Aida could sense, however, that her lover was looking to take a more direct and hands-on approach for her own part.

"What do you intend to do?"

"It's very nearly sundown. I plan to head into the lowest, filthiest districts of this city and see if I can catch any vampires hunting. If I come across agents of House Laskaris, then so much the better. If all I find is some local upyr or vukodlak scraping out a living in this city, then they still might be able to tell me something worthwhile. Eşref is a powerful strigoi, and someone even more powerful sent him here. If there were any vampires in London before he arrived, some of them are bound to have noticed his presence."

"Would you like Saul and I to come with you?"

Julie gave a gentle smile at her words. The expression was doubtless intended as one of kindness, but Aida could not help but feel it was just a little condescending. This was one of those instances where Julie simply would not require the help of mere mortals, and while Aida had nothing but awe for her lover's preternatural capabilities, it was never comfortable when those very capabilities left her feeling superfluous. How often she had pondered over how much more she could contribute to these hunts, if only Julie would consent to turn her. If she would do that, Aida could then turn Saul and the three of them would be unstoppable. If Julie would make her into an immortal, then their love really could last forever.

"No, I'll embark on this first hunt alone," Julie said, her gentle words stoking the bitter spark of disappointment in Aida's gut. "But you and Saul should take a few hours this evening to explore the city. Familiarise yourself with its streets. The more ground we can cover, the better."

"If you must," Aida finally conceded. "But after the rigours of our journey, I do insist that we take some time to acquaint ourselves with these lodgings. I have been missing the comfort of a proper bed."

She stepped towards her lover and kissed her once again, tenderly at first, coaxing and tempting, driving Julie to return it with fierce passion. Amorous hands moved to hastily unfasten clothing, and for a time all other plans, concerns and objectives faded from Aida's thoughts, rendered distant and insignificant as the two women fell upon the sheets.

It was a while after Julie departed that Aida washed and dressed herself, and knocked on the door of her brother's room. Saul was busying himself with the group's arsenal, checking over and cleaning the firearms after their three weeks at sea. His scimitar likewise was laid out upon the bed, though to Aida's eyes its blade scarcely seemed to be in need of cleaning, having not touched blood since the skirmish in Constantinople. Lamplight flickered and danced upon the intricate Damascene metalwork.

Julie's sword was absent of course, having been taken with her on her reconnaissance run. Saul picked up one of the freshly cleaned pistols – the very pistol which had been responsible for burning down Eşref's previous home – and presented it to his sister. He addressed her in the Wolof tongue with just a smattering of French vocabulary thrown in, the way that the twins always spoke to one another when alone.

"I doubt that you will get many more shots out of this one," he told her. "I don't question that your magnesium filaments are good at burning flesh, but they burn so hot that the gun barrels begin to deform. One of these days, you will try that trick and your pistol is going to blow up in your hand."

"You have told me this before, Brother."

"And I will keep telling you, until you decide to change your tactics."

"Or I will just keep on buying new guns. Consider yourself lucky that one shot of magnesium is usually enough."

"Enough to destroy the target, and anything nearby that can burn."

"Better that, than fail to kill my target and find my throat ripped out before my next shot."

Saul laughed, a rich and genial sound. While some might consider him an intimidating figure, there was something about her brother's voice which always brought comfort and reassurance to Aida. She imagined that if he were a commander on a battlefield, his troops would find him to be an inspiring presence.

"You should buy some new guns while we are here," he remarked. "London has some of the best weaponsmiths in the world. Even your Parisian duelling pistols are built upon a copy of the mechanisms that were invented here."

"Maybe tomorrow I shall do just that. But for this evening Julie has suggested that we explore the city a little."

Picking up his sword and a cloth, Saul sat down on the bed and carefully began to polish the blade. He glanced towards Aida, reading his sister's mood with a practised eye.

"You are disappointed that she is away by herself tonight?"

"I would have preferred to go with her," she admitted.

"You think you can scout a city the way she can? Scaling walls and rooftops? Come, Sister, if we went with her we would only be slowing her down. Let her find a target, then we will join her in killing it."

"We could keep up with her, if she would just–"

"Are you really saying this?" Saul cut her off abruptly. A look of regret crossed Aida's face for a moment, but her resolve soon reasserted itself.

"I don't see why not. Four years now we have aided her. I love her more than anyone. Why should she not share her power with us?"

"Because her power is a curse. We have seen the way she suffers with it. Is that really what you want, to find sustenance only in blood, and only pain in the touch of the sun?"

"In return for having her strength, for being able to do the things that she can do? I could consider that a fair trade. What I want is to be *with* her, Brother. I want to be with her forever, not to grow old and die while she stays the same. You have slept with her as well. Do you not share that desire?"

Saul's fingers tensed around the cloth that he held, and for a moment Aida feared that she had gone too far with her words. He did not meet her eye, but slowly resumed polishing the sword on his lap.

"She chose you, Aida. She may have had us both at first, but *you* are her lover. I have told you before, I do not begrudge it. Travelling with her, living this life, I am never bored. With her I am always learning more about this world, secrets that few men ever learn. But I do not plan to be this way forever. When Father is gone, our family will be mine to protect. I plan to run the business, take a wife and have children to carry on our name. I am not going to sacrifice all of that to become one of the monsters that we hunt."

Aida understood what her brother meant. Marriage, children, the future of the family, all of that mattered to him. The N'Dour dynasty was his to inherit, after all, and she would not dispute that. But for her part, Aida was less enamoured with the idea of going home. Her future must inevitably lead to a political marriage for the benefit of Father's interests, and she did not relish the thought of being any man's obedient wife. Julie was her chance to escape such a path.

"Julie is not a monster," Aida stated firmly.

"She is," Saul replied without hesitation. "She is not human, but we help her to act like one, which is exactly why she keeps us the way that we are. She may say that it is because she has never created Progeny before, that the process may fail and that it might kill us, but we know that is just an excuse. The truth is that if she made us into creatures like her, then we would no longer provide her the anchor that she seeks. We would become just a trio of predators, pushing each other to greater and greater excesses, caring nothing for our prey. We have seen exactly how vile and monstrous vampires can be, and within a few years that would be the three of us. She keeps *us* human so that we can keep *her* human, and that is the fact of it."

Aida could not bring herself to share her brother's belief. She *couldn't*. Julie's sense of humanity had persisted through her transformation into an immortal, and had endured for decades before she met the twins. Aida had to believe that she too would be capable of retaining her higher conscience, resisting the inner demon and not devolving over time into a craven killer. Of course Aida had never brought herself to ask if there had been other companions beforehand.

Julie had told her many wild stories of her mortal life, but details about her time as a vampire before they met had always been nebulous at best. But Aida remained convinced, it had to be possible to face eternity without succumbing to evil.

"Do you want to go exploring tonight?" she finally asked, letting the unwelcome conversation come to an end.

"Yes," Saul replied, seemingly more than grateful for the change of topic. "Let us see what London's streets have to offer us."

~ Lawrence ~

Thursday October 7th, 1756

The air in the crowded cellar was ringing with the cheers of onlookers and the meaty thuds of two men beating each other senseless. The odour of gin and sweat pervaded the place. Lawrence Clayton had no memory of a time when violence had not been a routine part of his life. His earliest years had been spent among thieves, whores, beggars and brawlers, and sheer necessity had taught him to fight as dirty as the worst of them, be it with his fists, a knife or a billy-club. Now that he was a man working on the legitimate side of the law, he felt a certain degree of superiority over those with whom he had grown up, but he felt no shame in rubbing shoulders with the unwashed masses when he came to watch a spot of bare-knuckle pugilism. Lawrence had an eye for a good fighter, and he won a bet far more often than he lost.

While he did enjoy the brutal entertainment on offer, there were other reasons for him to visit a place like this. The wages of a parish constable or a Bow Street Runner were far from grand, so much of his living was predicated upon state or private bounties for the apprehending of law-breakers. Tracking down criminals was a hell of a lot easier with the help of a few contacts in the kinds of circles where criminals moved, so Clayton frequented establishments such as this one in order to meet with and maintain his connections among London's disreputable underbelly. The line between a crook and a copper, he knew all too well, could be a very blurry one indeed.

Lawrence firmly believed, however, that a man was at his most honest during a fight. Stripped to the waist, with his back against the wall and only his opponent in front of him, that was when all pretences fell away, and the world got to see what that man was really made of. Out of the two fighters in the ring right now, Lawrence had bet on Billy Sullivan to win this bout. The young dock-worker was the less experienced of the two, but there was a hunger and a viciousness in him that Clayton was quick to recognise.

His opponent, a baker named Charles Warren, was easily the larger and stronger man, with far more wins to his name, but he was also getting old. Warren might have won more than a dozen fights prior to this one, but those bouts had taken their toll on him, and his current adversary was proving far too quick and far too tenacious for him to match.

Sullivan danced around the larger man, deftly avoiding blow after blow, darting in to deliver ferocious jabs to Warren's midsection before once more ducking out of reach. Lawrence smiled as his instincts were being proven right, watching the more veteran fighter beginning to slow and tire. Just one or two solid punches from Warren should have been enough to knock the fight right out of Sullivan, but the big man's fists could at best manage glancing blows to his opponent's shoulders or forearms.

Every attempt to grab or kick the young docker only met with empty air, and every time Sullivan struck back, Warren's response became just a little wilder, a little less coordinated. The baker's winning streak was at an end, and the crowd knew it.

The anticipation of victory suddenly turned sour, as a savage haymaker from Warren caught Sullivan right on the jaw. The younger man staggered back, just barely keeping his balance, bringing his arms up to deflect another shot to the face, but instead Warren's fist barrelled into the side of Sullivan's ribcage with a noise like a shovel smacking into wet cement. Finally Charles managed to grapple his dazed opponent, hefting Sullivan into the air before throwing him down like a ragdoll.

The countdown began; the rules gave Sullivan thirty seconds to recuperate, during which time it was forbidden to hit a downed opponent. He then had eight more seconds to get back to his feet and show that he was ready to continue the fight. As the crowd shouted the countdown, however, it was clear that Sullivan was not going to recover. By the thirty-eighth second he had weakly gotten to his knees, but there was no way that he was still in fighting shape.

"*Bollocks.*"

Lawrence cursed and crumpled the receipt for his bet, tossing the unwanted paper aside. With the fight having been called he watched Warren offer Sullivan a hand up, helping the younger man back to his feet. Why the fuck had Sullivan not dodged that blow to the jaw, when he'd had no trouble avoiding them up to that point? Had the boy grown overconfident in that moment, or had Warren simply gotten lucky?

Glancing about the crowd, Clayton could see many similar disgusted expressions, and it seemed evident that more than half of the spectators here had followed the same hunch about Sullivan that he had. Betting against the more experienced fighter was always risky, but word had gotten around about Sullivan being a capable up-and-comer, while

Warren's winning days were surely numbered. Lawrence was increasingly sure that the boy must have been paid to take a fall.

For a minute he considered having a personal word with the bookmaker, making clear his displeasure at what was evidently a rigged fight. If he could get the measly little man away from the crowd, he was quite certain that he could be persuaded to see the merit of returning Clayton's money. After all, Lawrence did have a pistol on his belt, and he had seen none of the fight's promoters wearing a firearm.

The notion quickly went out of his head, however, as the crowd was becoming increasingly rowdy. Angry shouts were beginning to fill the cellar, accusing the match of being a fix, and in several places there were cudgels already being drawn. It would not be long before this place erupted into a riot, and Lawrence had no wish to be here when it did. As the bookmaker's bodyguards closed in around him, squaring off against angry punters, Lawrence decided to cut his losses and head for the staircase.

His mood did not improve as he made his way through Whitechapel's squalid nighttime streets, bitter at having lost the day's earnings that he had bet on that fight. At some point he would have to track down the organisers – however many of them were left once the dust had settled – and extract some form of restitution. There were precious few benefits to being an officer of the law in this city, but surely one of them was convincing the promoters of a rigged boxing match to not push their fucking luck with a man like him.

Fumbling in his jacket with one hand, he fished out his pocket watch and checked the time of night. His chronometer was of the cheaper sort, a wooden-cased device of the type made primarily for sailors, a far cry from the intricately crafted silver or golden watches that the aristocrats wore to showcase their wealth. Its mechanism was not terribly accurate, but its hands currently told him that it was getting near to eight o'clock. Snapping the lid down, Lawrence decided that it was high time to pay a visit to one of his informants and find out if there was any new information regarding Lisa Brennan. The bitch had motive to commit the murder of her former lover, he was sure of that, and he did not doubt that she had the capability. All he was lacking was something to tie her directly to the killing, either of Sean Musgrave or his lawyer, Whitfield.

At the intersection of Ayliff Street and Lemon Street, on the north-east corner of Goodman's Fields, various ladies of the night had congregated in order to offer the tricks of their trade to passers-by. Lawrence knew many of these women by name; it was hardly uncommon for him to make use of their professional services, but it was just as frequent that he would seek them out for information.

Streetwalkers tended to see and hear a lot of what went on in the rougher districts of London, and usually their discretion – much like their physical affection – came at a negotiable price. A familiar trio of young women in low-cut dresses and excessive amounts of cheap blusher were clustered beneath a lamp post, and as Clayton approached his eyes fixed upon the middle one of the three.

"Good evening, Janice."

"Good evening to yourself, Mister Clayton," she responded, though her tone carried more resignation than enthusiasm. "Looking for some company, are you?"

"I'm looking for Rebecca. Is she around here somewhere?"

"She's busy at the moment. You sure one of us can't be of service instead?"

"Just tell me where she is."

Janice rolled her eyes, not willing to get into an argument

with a man like Lawrence just to protect the privacy of a fellow whore.

"In that alley over there," she gestured. "She is with a gentleman, you know."

He brushed off her objections with a dismissive wave of his hand, heading away in the direction that Janice had indicated. He didn't have to venture far into the filthy side-street before he could hear the muffled grunts of a man's fumbling exertion. Among the shadows of the unlit alleyway Rebecca Grey had her back pressed to the wall, her skirts hiked up and her customer's breeches down as he sought his release within her. Her breaths were shallow, rapid, but were hardly the sounds of genuine and heartfelt passion. Presumably, one had to pay more for that.

"Got a moment, Becca?"

The customer – a man in his late thirties by the look of him, well dressed enough to be of the middle classes – turned his head towards the source of the interruption, his expression becoming rather irate.

"What is this? Just who the hell do you think you are?" he snapped, but the indignation drained from his face the moment that Lawrence drew his flintlock and pointed it squarely at the man's chest. The customer's expression became one of sudden and unexpected mortal peril.

"Go. Now," Lawrence told him, and the man swiftly turned and hurried away, scrambling to get his breeches back up as he made his departure. Rebecca, for her part, did look rather angry, quite unfazed by the firearm in Clayton's hand. One of her breasts had been pulled free of her bodice while she was providing her service, and she fumed at Lawrence as she tucked it back into her dress.

"What the fuck is all this about, Clayton? You couldn't have waited for a few minutes longer, rather than scare off my customer? I have a living to make, you know!"

"I've waited almost all week," he replied sternly. "It's Thursday. You'd better have some news for me about Lisa Brennan."

"I do have something," she told him, "and we had an agreement about what it's worth for me to watch the Queen Anne for you."

Straight to the matter of payment, naturally. Lawrence reached down to the pouch at his belt, pouring out a few shillings which he had not lost on the boxing match. He tossed the coins across to Rebecca, who snatched them out of the air as though her life depended on them. She checked each one in her hands, making sure that they were not brass or iron, before tucking them away.

"Alright, so I've been keeping an eye on the place like you said," she began. "Though a girl can't be too careful. It's one thing for me to drink there, but the landlord, that Darby fellow, he knows what I am. If he gets the idea that I'm doing business there, he'll want to charge me a fee."

"I really don't give a damn. I'm only interested in Brennan."

"Aye, well, you mentioned that she might be conspiring with someone, and she has had a strange visitor these past few nights, some new fancy-man. Ever since Monday there's been a foreigner showing up to see her. A swarthy type, though he's obviously got a bit of money, dresses like an aristo. I heard him give his name as Ezref, or something like that. I don't know where it's from, but I'm not the only one who's noticed him. That Gypsy lad, Manfri, says that it's a Turkish name. He says that a bunch of Turks turned up in London a few weeks ago, and they've been poking their noses into all sorts of places."

Clayton's brow furrowed, his curiosity certainly drawn to this new piece of information. A pack of Turks newly arrived in London, one of them seemingly wealthy, and having nightly meetings with a bar wench like Lisa Brennan?

"Turkish, eh? And you trust this Gypsy's word, do you?"

"Aye. Manfri's a shifty type, but he's never done me any wrong."

Lawrence was convinced that Lisa's involvement in Musgrave's murder was due to some plan she had to steal his money, but he could not see any serious way for her to pull off such a scheme by herself, even if she could manipulate her hopeless idealist of a son. But what if Lisa was not the instigator here, but merely a pawn? Lawrence had already determined that Sean Musgrave had a few well-to-do friends, even some connections among the aristocracy, and his widow Sybil came from a good family herself. But did that mean that he had made some serious enemies along the way? Whatever the case, Lawrence needed to find out more about this 'Ezref' and his friends.

"That's interesting, Becca. Most interesting. Anything else you can tell me about this fancy-man of hers?"

"He's been there the past three nights, so there's every chance he'll be there tonight. I didn't see him earlier this evening, but there's plenty time yet."

She was correct, there were plenty of hours left in the night. Whoever this man was, Lawrence needed to find him. Something in his gut was telling him that this Turk was deeply important. He began to turn away.

"Thanks, Miss Grey. I'll be in touch next time I need a favour."

"Whatever you say, Copper. You keep interrupting me while I'm working and the price of the next favour will be a fair bit higher."

Clayton knew better than to expect that he would find willing answers at the Queen Anne Stuart. He had paid several visits to that stinking dive at this point, and not one among its staff or clientele had been forthcoming. *Thick as thieves,* went the saying, and that was certainly true of the people who drank there. The only difference between the customers of the Queen Anne and the pirates who drank down at the Devil's Tavern on the waterfront was that the pirates had a little more class and distinction.

Lawrence kept a healthy distance from the pub's front door as he observed the place, watching a steady trickle of ne'er-do-wells and ruffians making their way in, and penniless drunkards stumbling out. Occasionally he would get close enough to catch a glimpse in through the filthy windows, although it was hard to make out any detail of the faces inside.

As his nocturnal vigil progressed, Lawrence became increasingly aware of the biting autumnal cold, and he wrapped his rain-cloak tightly about his shoulders as he leaned against the wall of a butcher's shop. His pocket watch told him that it was nearing eleven o'clock when his luck finally changed, and he caught sight of an approaching man who looked very far removed from the Anne's usual occupants. This man was of tall and statuesque build, his hair dark as midnight, and his short beard and moustache immaculately groomed.

By looks alone Lawrence would suspect he was the type of man to employ a private barber. He was dressed in a fine black coat and matching tricorne hat, with leather gloves upon his hands. Although a man of such appearance would surely be a target for robbers in this part of town, there was no sign of flintlock or rapier anywhere on his person; evidently he felt confident travelling unarmed even in a neighbourhood such as Whitechapel. Clayton wondered if perhaps there were bodyguards close at hand, yet the stranger seemed to be entirely unaccompanied, and he moved with the kind of absolute self-assurance that was reminiscent of a lion; the confidence of one who had nothing at all to fear.

Let's see how long he keeps that up, Lawrence thought as he started on his way towards the pub, crossing the street and peering in through one window. If this foreigner had come to London looking to rob and murder its citizens, he was bloody well in for a shock. If Lawrence Clayton found anything to suggest that this man was a killer, that shock would come at the end of a hangman's rope.

Through the grime on the window and the sickly yellow light inside, he saw that the stranger had not taken any drink at the bar, but was already at the stairs and making his way up to the floor above. Cursing to himself, Lawrence decided that he had to go inside, and he shoved a hopeless, stumbling drunk out of the way as he stepped in through the door.

He was not expecting a welcome, and neither was he deterred when the pub fell silent as he made his entrance. His face was known here now, after all. He looked straight towards the bar and saw that Lisa Brennan was not there, but a younger blonde-haired barmaid – a slender little thing called Bethany, if he recalled her name correctly – was on duty. She met him with a distinctly unhappy gaze as he made his way towards her.

"The landlord's had words with us about you, after your last visit," she made clear. "He's of half a mind to tell us to refuse you service."

"I'm not here to drink and I really couldn't care less what your landlord has to say, unless he's offering to testify before the magistrates' court," Lawrence said bluntly. "Now tell me, who was that foreign man who just went upstairs?"

"Why should I tell you that? Under suspicion for some crime, is he?"

"He may well be. Now who is he?"

"He's a guest, that's all. He's been staying here the past few days, paid for his room for the whole week if you must know."

"What's his name? Is he Ezref?"

"Yeah, that's the name he gave."

"And what about Lisa Brennan? Friend of hers, is he?"

It was clear that Bethany was becoming increasingly unsettled by this line of questioning, and even Clayton only now realised just how much raw aggression had crept into his voice. Nobody in the pub was moving to interrupt him, but he noticed that some of the drinkers were giving him looks that suggested they were readying for a fight. Normally it took more than a handful of gin-soaked vermin to scare him off, but the Queen Anne was rather full tonight, and if a brawl ensued he would be badly outnumbered.

"Look, just tell me where Miss Brennan is," he asked, aiming to be somewhat more polite.

"She's not working tonight," Bethany told him. "What she does on her own time is her business. If you want to speak to her, come see her in the morning. The same goes for Mister Eşref."

Lawrence stalked back outside, infuriated with himself as much as the wretched skinny barmaid or the miserable clientele. Why had he allowed his temper to get the better of him, when he could have just said that he needed to go upstairs and question the Turk about a crime? He knew that he could be a little hot-headed at times, but he was still a professional investigator, quite accustomed to getting information out of people. Yet something about this situation had managed to crawl under his skin, and was prickling at him in a way that few cases ever did. He could have told Bethany that he was going upstairs and that was the end of it, but if she stuck to her guns and refused to let him, then a ruckus would certainly break out and a serious beating would be the more optimistic outcome.

He could just come back in the morning. If the Turk was

renting a room here, then Clayton could simply drop by at first light, before the man was likely to have left. But even from the brief glimpse that he had seen of Eşref as the man walked down the street and into the pub, there was something about him which struck Lawrence as being far more dangerous than the run-of-the-mill villains that he dealt with in this part of town. The way he had walked, alone and unarmed yet so very unafraid, as if he knew that he was the biggest, nastiest predator in these woods... somehow, Lawrence doubted that he would be able to frighten or bait such a man into giving away his guilt through mere conversation.

An idea struck him, and he began to make his way around to the back of the pub. The building was only two storeys tall, and while the stonework was hardly old, it was rather rough, and Lawrence imagined it would be climbable. More than that, he knew exactly which of the upstairs rooms was rented by Lisa Brennan, and as he glanced upward, he saw that the flickering light of a candle was present in the window. If he could clamber up there quietly, he might be able to catch a glimpse of what she was up to. Rebecca had said that Eşref had been visiting her, so merely seeing the pair of them talking together would confirm that connection.

Tentatively at first, his hands felt their way around the stonework of the back wall until he could locate a couple of handholds secure enough to climb. Lawrence was a strong man, more athletic than most, and once his fingers had tightened their grip, he began to pull himself upwards. Carefully he jammed the toe of his boot into a gap between a couple of stones, and his hands reached out to find their next grip. One step at a time he managed to ascend the wall, clinging on by his fingertips, not looking down.

Ever so quietly, he drew level with Lisa's window and

grabbed onto the wooden sill, bringing his head up to gaze into the room. His muscles tensed as he struggled to keep his grip, and his eyes tried to make out what was going on in the meagre light of the lone candle.

After a few moments he could discern two figures in the gloom, who appeared to be leaning against the bedroom wall, locked in a close embrace. *So he is her lover*, Lawrence noted, glad to know that his prime suspect and this unnerving foreigner were indeed in close cahoots. At first it looked as though the two were kissing, though he soon realised that Lisa's head was actually tilted backwards, leaning away from the man in such a fashion as to bare her throat. And his lips... his lips were fixed upon her neck, but not in the way of a lover's kiss.

What in Hell?

Clayton caught sight of Lisa's eyes, and he could see that they were glazed and unresponsive. Her whole body was likewise not moving, and he realised that she was not even standing under her own strength; she was limp as a marionette, being held upright by her lover's arms alone. And where the Turk's mouth was pressed onto her throat, his motion was that of gently suckling, drinking and swallowing. The merest trickle of blood had escaped his thirst, a couple of red lines coursing their way down Lisa's pale skin and staining her open collar.

Lawrence's eyes widened, scarcely comprehending what he was seeing. Lisa Brennan was hanging, feeble and unconscious in this man's grasp, *and he was sucking her blood*. His lips pressed harder upon her jugular, feeding upon the woman like some gigantic, awful leech, and for several minutes all that Clayton could do was stare upon the scene in pure horrified fascination. When Eşref – or this monstrous creature which called itself Eşref – finally lifted his mouth away from the wound on Lisa's throat, Lawrence caught a momentary glimpse of fangs, long and sharp like those of a wild beast, and eyes with immense pupils as red as the setting sun.

In that moment fear drove him to act, and he desperately wanted to be down from this window before that *demon* could catch sight of him. He barely made it a couple of feet down before his boot slipped from the narrow ridge on which he tried to balance, and his grip on the wall was lost. Lawrence plummeted downwards, landing hard, feeling the impact shudder through his body. The pain would kick in sooner or later, but for now he was in such a grip of fear and adrenaline that any damage to his back felt like a distant thing. Thankfully, he had avoided hitting his head when he landed. Scrambling desperately to his feet, he sprinted away from the Queen Anne Stuart as fast as his legs would carry him.

He did not know what to do. He wanted get home, to shelter, to the safety of four walls and a roof, but how could he ever feel safe after what he had witnessed? As an officer of the law, Lawrence Clayton had seen the evil of men. He had chased, fought, arrested and sometimes even killed evil men. But what he had seen tonight was not a man. What he had seen in that room was a devil, without any shadow of doubt.

Bloodsucking devils were real, and they were at large in London.

Part II

~ Arnold ~

Saturday October 9th, 1756

Amid the noise and bustle of Lloyd's on a Saturday afternoon, Arnold's coffee was sitting, untouched, on the table
in front of him. Nathaniel sipped at his own cup, but while
he appeared typically genial, his usual cheer was somewhat
dimmed. Arnold's fingernails drummed nervously on the
tabletop, and while he did his best to maintain a calm
demeanour, there were storms of panic evident in the depths
of his eyes. Recent events had left him desperately uneasy,
and he found it somewhat maddening that his half-brother
did not appear to share the full extent of his troubles. At this
point, he was still unsure just how much Nathaniel knew of
what had happened in the past week.

"Have you heard of what happened to Kenneth
Whitfield?" he enquired, hoping that his voice did not
betray too much of the nervousness that he felt.

"I received a letter from his son Marcus just yesterday,"
Nathaniel replied, between sips of coffee. "All very tragic,
I must say. Marcus has taken over the running of the legal
practice now, of course."

"My mother is a suspect, you know. A Bow Street Runner
by the name of Lawrence Clayton has set his sights upon

her. He seems convinced of her guilt, both in Whitfield's death and Father's. If he gets his way, she'll be facing the gallows."

"Do you think he has any definitive evidence?"

"Of course not. Whatever my mother's sins, she is not a killer. But given her situation, I don't think that her word will be of much weight against his."

"Don't worry, Arnold. If Lisa is brought to trial we can both testify to her character. You are a clergyman and I am a man of good standing. If you say that she's no murderer and I say that in twenty years she's shown not an ounce of malice towards our family, then that's got to be enough to absolve her, if there's no meaningful evidence linking her to the crime."

There was some assurance in Nathaniel's words, and Arnold was nothing if not grateful for his half-brother's willingness to defend Lisa Brennan before the magistrates. But that was only half of the reason why he had wanted to see him today. Fumbling slightly, he poured some coffee into his saucer and took a swift mouthful.

"I am thankful to you for that, Brother. But of course I'm still rather concerned about who may be next. Father is found murdered, and then mere weeks later his attorney's body is pulled out of the river? God rest them both, but I do not for one moment believe these events to be coincidence."

Something in Nathaniel's eyes told Arnold that his half-brother did at least share that sentiment. It strained credibility to think that random happenstance would result in the two men being killed in such a narrow frame of time. The trouble was, of course, that neither Arnold nor Nathaniel could claim to know anything solid of the killer's goals or motives.

"I don't know, Arnold. It does rather feel like there is a conspiracy afoot, but I'm damned if I know who is involved, or why. Father had a few academic rivals, to be sure, what man of science doesn't? But I never knew of him having *enemies*. I could never imagine him associating with the kind of people who would resort to murder. And why go after poor Whitfield? I just can't make any sense of it."

"When Mister Clayton came to see me at St Mary's, his theory was that Mother somehow learned of Father including me in his will, and then killed him in order to ensure that I received my inheritance as swiftly as possible, presuming that I would parcel some of it to her. When my inheritance turned out to be nothing of monetary value, she killed Whitfield out of spite, or feelings of revenge. Mother should never be capable of such a thing, but what if Whitfield had broken confidence and spoken to someone about Father's personal affairs, and they sought to profit from his death? I don't know how these criminal schemes work, but I know for certain that some men will do desperately immoral things for money. And if they have killed twice, they may not hesitate to do so again."

"You may be right. When I got the letter, I did immediately warn Mother and Imogen to be careful. I can't stomach the thought of anything happening to them, but thankfully they would never leave the house without a chaperone. And I bought myself a new pistol just this morning. It's been a few years since Father taught me to shoot, but I'll soon get back into practice. Are you taking any measures for your own safety?"

"I have faith that God is watching over me, and I shall be quite safe at St Mary's. My main concerns are yourself, your family and my mother."

"Arnold, you're the most pious man I know, but please do have a care for yourself. I'm not sure that prayer alone will stop a killer if he comes after you."

"If the killer is after Father's money, then I expect that I am rather low on the list of potential victims."

Where Nathaniel had been quite calm at the beginning of this conversation, a look of increasing concern now tugged at his youthful features. He was worried for Arnold, clearly concerned at his half-brother's apparent disregard for his own safety.

"You are most welcome to come and stay with me, you know. There's room in my place on Thames Street."

The offer was touching, but Arnold already knew that he felt far more secure in the St Mary's rectory than he would in his half-brother's rented rooms. If anything, he felt that he should be the one offering Nathaniel sanctuary.

"It's kind of you to say so, but I assure you I'm quite fine. Though, are you not tempted to move back to your family home for a time? It should enable you to keep a better eye on Sybil and Imogen."

"They have Wilson to look after them," Nathaniel referred to his mother's valet. "He's a far better bodyguard for them than I would be. And anyway, I'll still be at work the great majority of the time."

A few minutes passed in which the two men drank in silence. Given that Sybil Musgrave was hardly short of money at the moment, Arnold did consider asking Nathaniel if his mother would be making any efforts of her own to uncover the killer. He may not have much faith in the Bow Street Runners to apprehend the real culprit, but he knew that there were men about London who were skilled in the realms of investigation, and who offered their services for an appropriate fee. He was sure that their costs would be well within the Musgrave family's ability to afford. He was thinking of bringing up the subject, when Nathaniel raised a different matter.

"Oh, I should tell you, I did speak to a friend who may be of help in translating those documents of yours; or at least the French ones at any rate, he's rather fluent in that. I think he has some familiarity with Latin as well."

The thought of making progress in his father's macabre game did little to lighten Arnold's mood. No sooner did he think of that collection of papers and those dreadful framed pairs of teeth, than his thoughts flashed back to the sight of the emaciated Richard Sinclair in his bed, snarling like an animal as he flung his wife away from him. All the same, if there was some glimmer of understanding to be had, he would do well to grasp it.

"I see. Please tell me more."

"His name is Thomas Ashford, he's an old acquaintance of Father. A rather flamboyant old fellow, he manages the Minories theatre, you might know of him."

"I cannot say I do. I know of the building, but I've never been fond of stage performance."

"Well, regardless, I know that he spent a good deal of time in France in his younger years, and he has no shortage of friends in Soho to keep him in good practice. Father trusted him, and so do I. I can think of no one better to translate those letters for us. His theatre will be showing a production of Shakespeare's *Twelfth Night* this coming Thursday, which he has invited me to attend. There shall be a seat for yourself as well."

Arnold could not say that he was thrilled with that idea. Actors and singers were not people that he held in high regard, and he considered theatres to be almost as sinful as drinking holes like the Queen Anne. The kinds of farce and pantomime that were all too popular among the viewing public were not, in his opinion, conducive towards moral virtue. Still, he would attend if it was necessary.

"Very well, I shall come along. I hope this Mister Ashford will be as much help to us as you say. The sooner I find out what is in those letters, the better."

"The sooner the better, eh? And where has this sense of urgency come from? Last time we spoke, I rather thought that you were none too enthused about it."

"There was… something happened," Arnold explained, once more wondering if his half-brother was about to think him an idiot. He felt sure that he ought to keep the matter to himself, but it was also something to which he very much needed to give voice. "There was a strange incident involving one of my parishioners. He was sick, you see. His wife invited Vicar Lowther and I to come and perform Communion for him at their home. When I saw him, he looked gaunt, frail, I thought some form of rat-bite fever was to blame. But there was a fierce strength in him, and an aggression that I cannot understand. I don't know what malady he was suffering, but it drove him to lash out against his own wife, and against me. And then in a matter of moments he seemed to grow weak again, and I'm at a loss to explain it. His face… the look in his eye was more that of a starved animal than a man."

"I'm at a loss here too, Arnold," Nathaniel said, softly. "This all sounds very tragic, but I can't see what it has to do with our conversation."

"I had another look at those papers, later that night. After Clayton had visited me that the church, I felt compelled to go back to them. Some of the drawings in the medical treatises, they showed human skulls with… *alterations*, I suppose, lengthened teeth and that sort of thing. And I did see a word among some of the writings; '*vampyre*', that's a Slavic term, isn't it? Or Prussian? I'm sure that I've heard it before. Stories from the continent about the dead that crawl out of the earth to feed upon the living. Mobs of angry villagers digging up graves and desecrating corpses. I don't want such barbaric superstitions creeping into this city, into our lives."

"Brother, calm yourself down. Whatever the old wives' tales of Slavs and Prussians, this is still London, the heart of modern civilisation. This is all just morbid fiction and fable, you know."

Nathaniel's tone was intended to be reassuring, but that prickling undercurrent of pity was there, and Arnold did not want to hear it. He was not a fool, and he was quite sure that he was not going mad. There was simply something about those damned papers which did not sit well with him, after all of the recent happenings.

"Listen, I feel bad for this poor man you speak of," Nathaniel continued. "Let me make a donation to St Mary's in the coming days, and I hope the money will provide he and his wife some alms. But I expect that he is simply suffering some fever that has affected his brain, like so many others. I'm quite sure it's nothing to do with the fairytale monsters in Father's documents. Come to the Minories with me on Thursday, and we'll soon find out what's really in those letters, I promise you."

The walk back to St Mary's did little to abate Arnold's sense of unease. The sky above London was thick with smog and the rain fell in a light but persistent drizzle. The young clergyman's fears scratched and gnawed at the edges of his thoughts, drawing his eyes towards each street corner and alleyway, as if searching for some unseen danger. No demons or phantoms met his gaze... just more of the city's desperate and downtrodden people, hiding from the rain as the world passed them by. *What need does the Devil have for mythical monsters to torment us*, he thought to himself, *when the Gin Trap has ensnared so many lives?* Upon his return to the church he found Reverend Lowther waiting for him, though the kindly old man was looking uncharacteristically dour.

"Everything quite alright, Vicar?" Arnold asked as he stepped inside and saw the elderly priest approaching. Lowther gave him a look which was intended to be reassuring, but there was a sorrow in his eyes which would not be concealed. The young curate recognised that look all too well, for he had seen his superior relaying unfortunate news to people on a multitude of past occasions. Unconsciously, he began to brace himself for whatever came next.

"I was just at prayer," the vicar told him, "for your mother. I had a visit from Mister Darby, the proprietor of the Queen Anne, while you were out. He tells me that Miss Brennan has taken rather gravely ill. She is at present too weak to leave her bed, and she cannot afford to have a physician summoned. I was going to ask for your assistance in preparing for tomorrow's service, but in light of this news I thought it best if you go to visit her, my dear boy. Seeing you should be of great aid to her, I would think."

Those words were enough to provoke a growing sense of fear that coiled tightly about Arnold's gut. He knew that there were a multitude of reasons why his mother could be ill. Sickness was extremely widespread in a city such as this, where so many people lived in cramped and filthy conditions. After his prior conversation with Nathaniel, however, all he could imagine right now was his mother in the same condition as Richard Sinclair; pale and emaciated, teeth prominent against withdrawn gums, and with eyes full of bitterness and spite. He hoped dearly that it was not so. Even now, some awful selfish part of him would have preferred not to see her, simply to not find out.

"I… thank you for telling me," Arnold finally found his voice. "I shall go and see her right away. I can help you prepare for tomorrow when I get back."

"Take as long as you need," Lowther assured him, one aged hand grasping Arnold's shoulder. "I will be quite alright on my own. You have told me many times how dearly you wish for your mother to find our Lord's salvation. Go to her now, my son. It is important that she knows you are there for her."

Darkness had fallen by the time that Arnold arrived at the Queen Anne. Strictly there was still more than an hour to go until sunset, but given the time of year and the thick pall of smog above the city, there was precious little daylight to be had. The smoky yellow light of the lampposts flickered upon the cobblestones as Arnold made his way down the street towards the pub, and he spied a grimy-looking lamplighter moving towards an unlit post with oil and taper in hand. For reasons that were surely not rational, he found himself fearing for that man's safety. London's shadows somehow seemed deeper tonight, deeper than he had ever previously noticed, and while Arnold told himself that what he was experiencing was nothing more than a fever of the imagination, he could not escape the feeling that those shadows concealed worse evils than mere robbers and cut-throats.

The smell of sawdust, vomit and cheap gin that pervaded the Queen Anne was almost a welcome relief compared to the cold night outside. The landlord was standing behind the bar this evening, currently pouring liquor for one of his customers, a young woman with dirty blonde hair whose manner of dress and make-up left little doubt as to her profession. As Arnold drew near she gave him a bemused glance, apparently not expecting to see a man of the cloth in a place such as this. Arnold ignored her and looked towards the tall, burly man behind the bar; unlike this pub's founder, Fulton Darby, Robert had never spent a day at sea in his life, yet he still had his father's broad shoulders and powerful build. Having grown up here, the young curate had known the landlord all his life.

"Arnold," Robert greeted him, "I was hoping to catch you at the church earlier. I take it the old vicar told you about your mum, then?"

"Yes, he did. I thank you for bringing the news."

"Aye, well it's not exactly good news, is it? Look, I hope she makes a quick recovery, but she's in a bad way, Son. Can't afford a bloody quack, so the only medicine she's had is what's behind the bar here. Go up and see her. And whatever she's got had better not be anything catching."

"I'm sure she's glad of any care you have afforded her, Robert."

The leaden weight in the pit of Arnold's stomach seemed to grow heavier with each step that he took up the creaky wooden stairs. The upstairs rooms at the Anne were scarcely in a better condition than the bar down below; the walls were marked with rot and rising damp, and no fresh paint had been applied here since the pub was first built. Arnold's lodgings at the St Mary's rectory may have been spartan and humble, but at least they were clean, and he considered them infinitely preferable to this.

At the top of the stairs he continued on his course to Lisa's room, the room where he had been born and where he had lived the earliest years of his life. For all the times that he had visited her here since joining the Church, he felt not one shred of childhood attachment to this place. Each time that he returned here felt less like a homecoming and more like picking the scab off of a cut.

Gently he knocked at the door, waiting for a stifled grunt of acknowledgement from the other side before he opened it. Inside the cramped bedroom, Lisa Brennan lay huddled beneath a stained blanket, looking every bit as dreadful as Arnold had feared. Her skin was as pale as a sheet, her body anaemic and diminished, and yet as soon her son stepped into the room and spoke the word "Mother," Lisa sat bolt upright and stared at him with cold, red-rimmed eyes. Her appearance left no doubt that she was unwell, yet in this moment there was a vitality about her that seemed almost feral. The similarity between her case and that of Richard

Sinclair was frightening. But while Dick had complained about the light in his room, Lisa now seemed all too comfortable in the dark.

"Son," she responded with a strained voice, and an awful smile that lacked any hint of mirth, "come to see me, have you?"

"I have," he told her. "Robert came to St Mary's. He told Reverend Lowther that you'd fallen gravely ill, that you didn't have the strength to get out of bed."

"I've felt weak, these past couple days. But I'm getting stronger now, my boy, so much stronger. Soon I'll be up and about again, I promise you that."

"I'm glad to know that you're recovering."

That was a lie, and he knew it. Something in his mother's voice, the manner in which she spoke of her growing strength filled him more with dread than reassurance. He took a few nervous steps towards the bed, his unease being further stoked by his mother's sharp, unblinking gaze. Her breathing seemed so weak and shallow, as though even sitting up ought to be a great effort for her, but Arnold remembered the horrible force with which Richard had thrown his wife against the bedroom wall, and the thought of it sent a cold shudder down his spine.

His eyes glanced towards Lisa's neck, to the flesh that looked so very pale against the loose brown curls of her hair, and right above her jugular there were the same scars that he had seen on Sinclair: a couple of recently healed shallow punctures, as might come from the bite of a rat, but sufficiently wide apart to have been made by a human-sized mouth. Suddenly Arnold was keenly aware of the absence of his crucifix from around his neck.

"Are you alright, Son?" he could have sworn that there was an edge of mockery in his mother's tone. "You're not looking well yourself, you know."

"I'm quite fine," he promised her, before a thought occurred to him. "Do you still have that cross that I gave you? Two years ago, I brought you one as a gift."

Lisa's expression soured, her false smile vanishing in an instant.

"I never wear it," she snapped.

"I know you don't, Mother. But I thought you might find comfort in it, if you were ever going through a bad time."

"I don't need it."

Arnold moved to the bedside cabinet, aware now that he was well within his mother's reach. She had not shown the kind of aggression that Sinclair had demonstrated – at least not yet – but Arnold knew that he would feel a good deal safer once he had that token in his hand. He pulled open the cabinet's drawer, rifling through the various cheap knick-knacks inside, and felt a great swell of relief when he saw the plain wooden crucifix lying there, dusty and unused, but nonetheless present.

A sharp pain erupted in his wrist as Lisa's hand grabbed onto him, gripping with such tightness of which she would never have been capable before now. The ragged edges of her fingernails bit into his skin, drawing blood.

"Mother, enough!"

With his free hand he pulled the crucifix from the drawer, and at the sight of it Lisa's unnatural strength seemed to ebb, her fingers growing weak. Arnold yanked his arm out of her grip and she shrunk away from him, scrambling off the far side of the bed, rising to her feet. However frail she had been for the past two days, it was obvious that she had the strength to stand now. Her bloodshot eyes fixed upon her own son, holding nothing but venom in their gaze.

"Put that thing away, Arnold. I want nothing of it."

"This is the symbol of our Lord's loving sacrifice, Mother. He died for our sins and was risen to life everlasting."

"I said put it away, *Bastard*."

Her mouth had twisted into a hateful snarl, her stained teeth prominent behind her lips. They were not lengthened and bestial like the fangs in those frames, but nonetheless they looked sharper than Arnold had ever seen them. But it was the way her eyes looked at him that unnerved him the most; in all the years he had known his mother, even during their most bitter of arguments and disputes, he had never doubted that she loved her son. However troubled her life, however misguided her decisions, she had always cared for him. But the way she looked at him now carried not an ounce of care; she looked at him as if he were a complete stranger, and a dangerous one at that. The expression upon her face reminded him of a cornered animal, with nowhere to flee and no option but to leap for its attacker's throat. Not wishing to provoke her to rash action, he began to step backwards, but he did not dare lower the crucifix.

"This needs to stop. This isn't you. Whatever illness you're suffering, it's making you mad."

With a little more distance between them, she started to emerge from behind the bed. Her movements were wary, but her muscles were coiled tight with the promise of violence.

"Am I mad, for seeing things clearly?"

"Wha– what do you mean by that?" Arnold stuttered, suddenly feeling as though he were talking to a woman possessed.

"My new man showed me the truth, you know. He came to me and made me tell him about Sean. About those things you inherited. I told him all about what you told me. Papers, and teeth."

A cold swell of fear arose within Arnold's belly. Whoever this man was, he was clearly responsible for what had happened to Lisa. Maybe he was responsible for Richard Sinclair's condition too.

"Mother, who is he? Tell me what's going on."

"He wants what you've got, Son. There's something in those papers that's valuable to him. He was pleased with me for telling him of them. That's why he shared his gift with me."

"Gift? What *gift?* This is madness. That Bow Street Runner, Clayton, he suspects that you were involved in Father's killing, and in Mister Whitfield's. He'll see you hang if–" Arnold stopped cold. "By God. By God, did this man you speak of murder my father?"

"Don't worry about Clayton. If he comes for me, my man will take care of him. Or *I* will. He'll give me all of the gift, soon. I feel it getting closer every night."

Arnold felt the door against his back, only now realising now how far he had retreated from his own mother. Even the crucifix no longer seemed to hold her off, as if his own fear were lessening its effect. Lisa had become involved with someone deeply dangerous, and she had put this dangerous man on Arnold's trail. He had done something to her, changed her, and now he could no longer recognise his own mother. Searching for his resolve, the clergyman brandished the wooden cross towards the predatory woman in front of him, and felt a rush of vindication when she stopped in her advance.

"Enough of this! Enough, I say. I'm leaving now, Mother. Go back to your bed. I will pray for you, and with God's guidance I will be back. Whatever darkness this man has brought upon you, I will help you find your way to the light."

Lisa winced, drawing breath through her teeth in a sharp hiss, but she did not come any closer. Arnold's fingers groped for the door handle behind him and he stepped out of the room, not daring to turn his back while his mother was still in view. As soon as the door was closed in front of him, he made for the stairs with all possible haste.

This was either devilry or insanity, he was sure of it. The only explanations Arnold could fathom were that either he had taken leave of his own senses, or that *creature* he had spoken to was not Lisa Brennan, even if it did wear her face. He believed in miracles, of course, for he was a man of the cloth and he understood that there were times when God saw fit to intervene in the lives of mortals. He also grasped that if one believed in God's miracles then one must also allow for the possibility of Satan's. It was the Devil's role to tempt and deceive, after all, to test people's faith so that through repentance and piety they would make themselves worthy of God's love.

But until now the only power of the Devil that Arnold had truly believed in was his power to whisper in people's ears and in their hearts, to lead them astray with sinful thoughts and urges. It was another thing entirely to believe that Satan could affect mortals directly, to twist their nature and perhaps even override free will. He understood the concept of demonic possession, but it was not something that was widely regarded within his theology. Rites of exorcism were never something that was embraced by the Church of England.

But now he had to contend with the possibility that his own mother was possessed by some unholy spiritual force. He left the pub in a hurry, heading out into Whitechapel's maze of darkened streets, and as he walked on rain-slicked cobbles he recalled the account from the Gospel of Mark, of the exorcism of Legion. The possessed man in that story had lived in a cave and wandered the hillsides by day and night, crying out blasphemies and cutting himself with sharp rocks. The people had tried to bind him but he was too strong to be captured, even breaking iron chains with his bare hands.

Arnold looked down at his wrist, scratched and bruised

from Lisa's fingers, and he knew that if she had not backed away from the sight of the cross, he would have had little hope of breaking her grip by force alone. In the Biblical story, Jesus Christ had saved the benighted man from Legion's possession by sending the vile spirits into a herd of pigs, who ran into the sea and drowned. Arnold thought of himself trying to drive out whatever demon held sway over his mother, and he almost laughed at the absurd presumption. Even with the sign of the cross in his hand, he could scarcely muster the courage to stay in the same room as her, let alone confront the demon head-on.

Perhaps the vicar would know what to do. Reverend Lowther had never spoken with Arnold of such topics as possession and exorcism, and the curate doubted that the old man had ever performed such a rite. Surely if he had experience of those things, he would have made mention of it after the incident at the Sinclair household?

But even if the vicar himself did not possess that knowledge, maybe he knew people who did. He had served the Church for a great many years, after all, and was on friendly terms with the bishop. Maybe he would be able to find someone in the Church's ranks with a more specialised understanding of these things. Arnold felt a stab of shame. For years now he had considered himself a soldier of God, but when the time came for him to look the Lord's enemy in the eye, his resolve had failed him. He had to do better than this.

An unpleasant prickling on the back of his neck, and a momentary glance over his shoulder, made him realise that he was being followed. A man's dark silhouette, little more than just another shadow in the night, was keeping pace at a distance behind him. For a moment he thought – or more precisely, *hoped* – that it might be Lawrence Clayton, as if even that odious man's presence might lend some comforting reality to the situation. But this figure carried himself quite differently, his lithe movements showing none of the bullish vigour that Clayton had been so quick to throw around. No, this figure moved with all the silent grace of a cat, and Arnold was sure that if instinct or chance had not led him to look back at that exact instant, he would never have known that the man was there.

For a moment he considered that perhaps the stranger was not following him, but rather simply walking in the same direction, although that notion was quickly dismissed. The night was dark and wet, the working day was over, and most sensible people were by now at home. He was alone in the street, apart from his mysterious pursuer.

Or rather, *pursuers*. A second figure had come to a stop on the far side of the street up ahead, and was now crossing over to block his path. As the man passed beneath a lamp-post Arnold caught a look at him, and saw that while his mode of dress was typical of London, his features looked decidedly swarthy and foreign. An *Arab, perhaps?* More than just foreign, there was something deeply *wrong* about the man under the streetlight, though in that moment Arnold could not say exactly from where that sense of wrongness stemmed. Whoever these men were, he did not expect for one second that their intent was wholesome.

Again he looked back, seeing that his first pursuer was now a good deal closer, and as primitive instinct took him, Arnold ducked into a side alley and broke into a run. In this moment there was no doubt in his mind about how the lives of Sean Musgrave and Kenneth Whitfield had come to an end, and if these men caught him, he was sure to be next. But Arnold knew Whitechapel well, and terror lent him speed as he sprinted desperately through the side-streets, hurrying for the safety of St Mary Matfelon Church.

The panicked clergyman skidded to a halt as he heard

a bestial growl from up ahead, a deep-throated, doglike sound that no human mouth should be able to make. Somehow one of the men had gotten in front of him, cutting off the route ahead. The dark figure was drawing closer, and for a moment Arnold was sure that he saw a scarlet gleam reflecting from the man's eyes. To the left a corner beckoned, and Arnold charged away into the mouth of the alley, determined to put some distance between himself and his pursuers.

Some part of his brain already suspected that they were herding him into a trap, but what was he to do? He was not a soldier or a street-fighter, to stand his ground against them would only mean a swift journey to martyrdom. He picked up his pace, cornering right and then left again, hoping to come out onto a larger street where maybe, just maybe, there would be some people out on legitimate business who could offer him safety.

Up ahead, a third silhouette came into view, a human form detaching itself from a rooftop above and dropping into the alleyway as casually as stepping off a porch. Arnold stopped dead, his blood running cold. *This was impossible.* This latest arrival was a girl, not yet out of her teens by the look of her, and like the two men, her features appeared distinctly Eastern to Arnold's eyes. By rights there should have been nothing remotely threatening about her, and yet he had just watched her leap from a rooftop and land upon her feet in a way that was plainly inhuman. She advanced towards him, the pupils of her eyes enlarging and reddening, and when her lips parted in a murderous grimace, Arnold saw curved fangs glinting in the dim light.

A *vampyre.*

He was looking at an actual vampyre. This ungodly abomination was what his mother was transforming into, a demon in human skin. From behind him there came the sound of his pursuers' footsteps, the two men blocking one end of the alleyway, trapping him between them and the monstrous girl. Glancing in their direction, Arnold saw that all three of his assailants had the same crimson eyes, the same predatory fangs.

They had him outnumbered, and there was no escape. His back was pressed against the wall, his knees about to buckle in fear as this pack of inhuman horrors moved to surround him. Only distantly, he felt himself lose control of his bladder. *Please, God, let it not end like this.*

His trembling hand brushed against his coat pocket, feeling the shape of Lisa's crucifix within. Seized by a will that did not feel entirely his own, Arnold grabbed the cross from his jacket and thrust it into view, its sudden appearance causing the monsters to recoil in a chorus of livid snarls. They only took a few steps back, giving Arnold room to breathe, but not to escape. He tried to inch along with his back to the wall, but even then the demons moved with him, keeping him surrounded.

He brandished the crucifix towards the girl and she backed off a little further, only for the two men to begin closing in again, prompting Arnold to face the cross towards them. He couldn't make a break for it without turning his back on at least one of them, but knowing that they feared the symbol of the Lord, he was confident of other weapons in his arsenal.

"Our Father," he began, the fear now gone from his voice as he spoke the Lord's Prayer with burning conviction, "Who art in Heaven, hallowed be Thy name. Thy kingdom come, Thy will be done, on Earth as it is in Heaven."

The vampyres retreated further, backing away from him with sheer blind unwillingness, as though the words of his prayer struck them like a whip. Never before in his life had he felt such righteousness, such absolute fervour. Here he stood with the Devil's own soldiers before him, and by his faith and God's will, they were being driven back.

"Give us this day our daily bread, and forgive us our trespasses, as we forgive those who trespass against us. Lead us not into temptation, but deliver us from evil!"

"Enough, Priest!"

The click of a cocking flintlock interrupted Arnold's recitation, as he found himself staring down the barrel of a pistol. One of the male vampyres had drawn the weapon, and was pointing it squarely at Arnold's face. The monster's eyes were still averted from the cross, but at this close range he did not need to see with accuracy. It would be harder for him to pull the trigger and miss.

"Lower your talisman, now! You are coming with us."

In some absurd way, Arnold felt cheated. God had given him the tools to drive out three vicious demons, but now he was facing defeat at the hands of mortal gunpowder and metal. He wanted to repudiate the monster by continuing his prayer, trying to muster up 'For Thine is the kingdom,' but the words caught in his throat, knowing that one click of that trigger would paint the wall behind him with blood and brain matter. Surely, if the vampyre shot him, would God not intervene? The gun could misfire, the powder could fail to ignite. Surely all he needed was faith in the Lord's infinite protection.

"*Now*, Priest."

The monster's accent was as foreign as his looks, but his words were clear. That great and terrible zeal which had filled Arnold's body only moments before now felt like nothing but a memory, and the cross trembled in his hand. He felt the other two vampyres drawing nearer, their fear of him diminishing as his conviction wavered, and in that moment he resolved that he would not die in submission to Satan's forces. His grip tightened upon the cross.

"For Thine is the—"

It was not the thunderclap of a firing pistol which cut through the night air, but the smacking sound of something hard impacting on flesh, followed by a choked cry of pain. The flintlock fell from the vampyre's hand, clattering away as Arnold saw a sharp wooden tip, wet with blood, slowly pushing its way out of the creature's chest. The impaled demon began to spasm, muscles thrashing as his body was hefted off the ground from behind, before an upward sweep of a blade relieved him of his head.

The curate watched in stunned silence as the headless body was dropped to the ground, revealing the shaft of the long stake which had been driven into its back. Standing above the slain monster, clutching a great curving sword in one hand as though it were a mere knife, was a slender fair-skinned woman, dressed in a man's clothing and scarcely larger in build than the girl-vampyre.

Arnold's two remaining assailants rounded upon the newcomer in rage, fangs bared and clawed fingers raised. The woman spun her sword and took a practised fighting stance, before revealing her own razor fangs and inhuman eyes. *She was one of them.* The male vampyre pounced at her with outstretched talons and she cut him down mid-leap, a slash of her blade sending him reeling into the mud.

In a blur of motion the girl had joined the fray, but the newcomer reacted with lightning speed, dodging clear of her attacker's swipes before landing a sweeping blow to the girl's ribcage, eliciting a tormented howl from her lips. The male demon did not stay down long, scrambling back to his feet, his shape seeming to warp and malform as he moved. By the time he stood upright he was no longer a man at all, but one of the impossible semi-chiropteran monstrosities whose visage Arnold instantly recognised: a strigoi.

The girl, too, was changing, her human likeness

unravelling as her body twisted to reflect the demon that she truly was. The two strigoi descended upon the unknown woman, slashing at her with claws and teeth, drawing rents in her flesh wherever they struck.

And yet if those injuries caused her pain, it did not slow her, for she deftly avoided the worst of the blows that came her way, dancing between her enemies with fluid agility. The demons tried to grab onto her, but at every attempt she threw them off or slipped just beyond their reach, allowing their vicious talons to inflict only glancing cuts. Wherever she struck back her sword found its mark, cleaving the flesh of the monsters and spilling more of their dark ichor, bleeding them out.

Finally she landed a telling blow, her scimitar catching one of the unholy beasts just below the shoulder and slicing through its left arm with a nauseating wet *thud*. The strigoi screamed and leaped away, its severed limb twitching upon the ground. The second monster – the one wearing the tattered remains of the girl's dress – immediately went into full retreat, scrambling up the wall of the alley like some colossal insect, making for the rooftop. Incredibly, the surviving male did the same, ascending the wall at breakneck speed with only one arm to pull him up.

The swordswoman looked briefly in Arnold's direction, her fierce, hellish eyes pinning him beneath their gaze. For a moment he was certain that she meant to kill him; whatever quarrel she had with those who had accosted him moments ago, she too was a demon like them. But then she was gone, also scuttling up the wall to chase after her prey, seemingly unconcerned with the speechless clergyman. The bloody skirmish had lasted mere seconds, and yet for Arnold it might have been an eternity as each savage blow replayed itself in his head.

Suddenly conscious of the fact that he had stopped

breathing, he forcibly willed himself to exhale and inhale, filling his lungs with cold, soot-ridden air. The corpse of a man lay a scant few feet away from him, its head removed and a wooden stake right through its chest. A horrible claw-handed arm lay not far beyond that, fingers still faintly spasming as though death would not claim it. The stink of blood filled his nostrils, and he became distantly aware of the warmth in his trousers where he had pissed himself in his moment of terror. Demons had come to claim him, and had been thwarted by one of their own kind, yet Arnold was still alive.

He was *alive*, and by God he intended to stay that way. He saw the pistol dropped by the dead strigoi, and he lunged to grab it, snatching up the weapon and pointing it before him as his other hand still clutched the wooden crucifix in a white-knuckled grip. For a few moments all he could do was force himself to catch his breath, and calm his nerves. And then, tucking the pistol inside his jacket, he bolted for St Mary's.

~ Saul ~

Sunday October 10th, 1756

Dawn was not far away when Saul and Aida left their lodgings to convene with their mentor on the north bank of the Thames. It was no surprise that Eşref still eluded them after a mere two days of reconnaissance and searching, but Julie's patrols of London's more poverty-ridden boroughs had paid off with an early stroke of luck. The three hunters now stood upon a small wooden jetty not far along the river from the dock where they had arrived the previous afternoon. Laid out before them were the mutilated spoils of Julie's hunt.

"And you say there was a third one?" Saul remarked as he looked over the two corpses. Both were bereft of heads, each one apparently severed by a single clean blow, and both had been impaled through their hearts with lengths of iron-wood. One of the bodies had been brought here with only its right arm still attached.

"The girl got away from me while I was finishing off her friend," Julie responded, clearly frustrated at this turn of events. "That bastard put up quite a fight, even with just one arm. Afterwards I followed her scent as far as the river, but it ended there. She must have dived into the water to break her trail."

"But you are confident that their lair is in Whitechapel?"

"As I can be. And even if they're hiding in some other district, I'm willing to bet that Eşref will return there eventually."

"What makes you so certain?"

"When I found their trail they were close to a tavern, the Queen Anne Stuart. I took a quick look at the place in case that was where they were staying, but it didn't look to me like a strigoi nest. Still, in one of the upstairs rooms there was a thrall, heavily infected and close to death, and Eşref's scent was all over her. He must have fed on her half a dozen times, by my guess, and he might be planning to turn her fully. I reckon that he'll go back there, either to kill her, or to give her his blood and finish the process. I'll be keeping watch on that place for when he does."

"What about the man they were hunting?" Aida interjected. "You said that there was a priest?"

"Yes," Julie affirmed, "he was a young one, no older than you two I should venture, but there was some fire in him. I saw him hold off the three of them with nothing but a cross and a prayer. Impressive, to do that by himself, especially since I don't think he had a clue what he was really facing. When I doubled back to collect that one" – she gestured to the corpse which still had both arms attached – "he had gone. I followed his scent as far as a church, *St Mary Matfelon*, the sign called it. From the look of it I should guess it's the 'white chapel' that the district is named after. The two of you should probably keep an eye on him. I expect he's rather shaken by what happened, and Eşref's jackals must have been pursuing him for a reason."

Saul was not thrilled by the idea of playing guardian angel to an English priest. Back in Saint-Louis the N'Dour family were Catholic – in public at least – because converting to the ways of the Mother Church had been an effective way to curry favour with the French, but Saul had long considered priests to be the most sanctimonious of hypocrites. Still, if this particular priest was a target for House Laskaris, then he would at least serve as bait for them. Saul's eyes scanned the mutilated forms of the two dead strigoi, before he looked back to Julie.

"Have you searched these bodies?" he asked her.

"Not yet."

Sinking into a crouch, he began to run his hands over each one in turn, checking through pockets, looking for anything that might shed further light on where they had been hiding. His questing fingers unearthed a pouch of gunpowder, a handful of bullets, a coin purse, a brass key with nothing to identify it... the lack of anything useful caused him to expel a frustrated sigh.

His gaze was soon drawn towards his own fingertips, however; the dead vampires' clothing was faintly stained with soot, like everything in this city, but in among the grey-black patches that marked his skin there were just the faintest traces of green. Curious, he brushed his fingers against the seams and wrinkles of the corpse's jacket, discovering that a fine greenish residue clung to the fabric in places. Rising to his feet, Saul held out his hand for Julie and Aida to inspect.

"What do you make of this?"

Julie leaned closer and took a sniff, nostrils flaring as she focused her senses. "Smells like copper," she told him. "When I was tracking them I could smell traces of vinegar, or something like it, on their clothes as well."

"Then I shall wager that it is verdigris," Aida remarked a moment later, after taking a look for herself. "If there is verdigris dust on his clothing, then he has probably been hiding somewhere that it is manufactured. That requires copper plates and heated vinegar or wine. It certainly narrows our search, if we look for places in Whitechapel that are known to sell this compound."

"It gives us a starting point," Saul agreed, "but from what we know of Eşref, I do not see him contenting himself with sleeping in some chemist's workshop. He likes to surround himself with luxury."

Of which there is precious little to be found in Whitechapel, he thought to himself.

"Eşref does," Julie stated, "but he is not the Master here. He came to London because he was ordered to. These others will have done the same, and if House Laskaris has gathered here in numbers, it is certain that they have established more than one nest in the city. We will have to find and purge all of them. If one of those nests is in a place where verdigris is produced, then we can look for that one first."

"Sunrise will be here soon. You should head back to the inn. My sister and I will handle daytime reconnaissance."

Saul's words caused Julie to glance towards the eastern skyline, where a smudge of unhealthy-looking pink on the morning smog heralded the first rays of dawn. She was willing to bet that under a sky this polluted, the weak sunlight would not trouble her nearly so much as in most places, but nonetheless Saul was right. By day the twins were better suited for this kind of work than she was.

"See what the two of you can track down."

With little further to discuss, they weighed the bodies down with stones and heaved them into the turgid water of the Thames. As much as Saul would have chosen to cremate the remains if they had the means to do so, he was also quite certain that neither of those two strigoi would be rising from their watery grave. Julie had at times related to him tales of very ancient and potent members of her kind, bloodsuckers whose grip upon their unnatural life was so tenacious that their bodies could reconstitute themselves even after being hacked into pieces, but such individuals were vanishingly rare. These two were evidently not that powerful, and like most vampires that Saul had encountered, he doubted that either of them had lived beyond their first century.

As the bodies were swallowed up by the darkness of the river, he briefly wondered if they still had any family among the living, and what events had led to these people being snatched away and transformed into Eşref's footsoldiers. Some vampires would spend years observing a human, carefully deciding whether they were a worthy candidate for immortality, while others were coldly arbitrary in their choice of Progeny. Eşref had shown more than once that he had no qualms about turning people into disposable servants; in his estimations, the lives of mortals were weightless.

The gloom of night was giving way to a murky autumnal sunrise when Saul and Aida took to London's streets in pursuit of the strigoi nest. Verdigris – so called 'copper rust' – was a material with two primary uses, those being the burnishing of metal and the production of green paint. Since the substance formed as a natural patina on copper fixtures exposed to the weather, the market for manufactured verdigris was primarily in oil paints. Given the chance, Aida could have spoken at length about its use in the vibrant artworks of Jan van Eyck, though Saul could not claim to share her fascination with the subject.

The twins combed the streets and marketplaces of Whitechapel for every paint vendor they could find, enquiring about local suppliers of the pigment. Some of those whom they spoke to were forthcoming. Others met the twins and their questions with suspicion or outright hostility, although the offer of coin for information was generally enough to loosen recalcitrant tongues. After several hours of investigation, they had compiled a shortlist of houses in

Whitechapel from which the various paint sellers bought the material.

By midday they were hungry, so they took lunch at The Green Man inn before resuming their work. Over the past two days the pair had acquainted themselves with the food in London, and neither Saul nor Aida could fathom the apparent love affair between English tongues and bland flavours. For all of this country's influence in the spice trade, it seemed that any but the most basic forms of seasoning were a rarity here. With fuller stomachs they returned to their hunt, visiting each of the suppliers on their list. It was at the second address, tucked away among the tangle of alleyways that branched off of Brick Lane, where their instincts told them that they had found what they were looking for.

The building in question played host to a vinegar merchant, and the small shop was surrounded by the pungent odour of the stuff. During their journey Aida had remarked that if verdigris production was the same here as in France, then it was likely the shop's cellar would hold clay pots filled with vinegar, in which copper plates would be stacked for the patina to form upon them. As nesting places went, cellars did of course hold a certain appeal for creatures who loathed the touch of daylight.

The front door of the shop was locked, and a sign in the window declared that it was currently closed for business. On the upstairs windows, the curtains were pulled tight. Although dubious of announcing his presence at a potential vampire lair, Saul did give a knock at the door just in case anyone should answer. After a few minutes of waiting, it was clear that nobody was going to. A glance in his sister's direction was met with a single nod from Aida, confirming that she shared his intuitions. Having investigated many such nests during their time with Julie, the twins had developed a finely-honed set of instincts about these places, and both of them were feeling that indefinable prickling on the back of the neck that told them a bloodsucker dwelt here.

The street may have been quiet, but it was not devoid of passers-by, and if the twins were going to gain entry to this place, they had no intention of breaking through the front door in plain view. Instead the pair made their way around to the back of the shop, deftly climbing over the wall into the small yard. The back door was closed, and had been secured with a screw-key padlock, but a single blow from Saul's hammer and chisel was enough to break that apart.

The interior of the building was cramped and narrow, enough to make the use of a sword impractical, so Saul reached inside his coat and retrieved one of his stakes instead. Aida drew one of her duelling pistols, thumbing back the hammer in readiness for any attack. If there was a strigoi lurking here, then at the height of the day the creature should be at its weakest, and the twins would have the advantage. If there was still a whole pack of them, they would have to hope to all of the Gods that the creatures were not awake.

While the smell of vinegar had certainly been noticeable from the outside, the shop's interior was absolutely permeated by it. As the twins silently made their way through the ground floor, Saul peered through a storeroom that was filled with great glass bottles of the brown liquid, along with several sacks of malted barley for fermentation. The store front appeared to be largely in order, with no sign of neglect or abandonment, and it seemed that if this place had served as a vampire nest, then either it had only been used as such for a short period of time, or the resident bloodsuckers had taken some measures to keep up the pretence of legitimacy.

In either case, it soon became evident that there were no monsters present on this floor. It would be worth checking on the rooms upstairs, but the cellar presented the greater interest. A wordless look passed between the twins as they found the door to the stairs leading down. Aida grabbed a lantern from the store room and lit it, before the twins proceeded into the dark with weapons at the ready.

The only natural light in the cellar was the narrow shaft which filtered in through the ventilation grate, and its touch scarcely illuminated a single grimy wall. Saul and Aida relied upon the oily yellow glow of the lantern to push back the surrounding shadows as they made their way into the downstairs room. A couple of large baths occupied the middle of the cellar, and the smell of fermentation that poured from them was almost overpowering. As expected, a series of large clay pots were arrayed along the wall furthest from the stairs, along with a bucket and scraping tools for collecting newly-formed verdigris.

Cautiously the pair advanced, casting the lantern's light about them, making certain that no hidden vampiric forms awaited on the floor or clung to the ceiling. As they drew nearer to the fermentation vats, however, the twins shared a horrible feeling about what they may discover inside.

Saul had witnessed enough death and bloodshed over the last four years that the sight of a corpse rarely startled him, even when it was the mutilated victim of an enraged or sadistic vampire. But something about the pallid body submerged in the bath of vinegar was enough to make his stomach tighten in revulsion, and he fought down the urge to retch. The corpse was that of a middle-aged man still wearing a leather apron, almost certainly the owner of this business.

His flesh was white enough to suggest complete exsanguination, and as Aida held the lantern closer to illuminate him, the row of faint puncture scars upon his throat were made evident. The twins exchanged a glance, a silent affirmation that closer investigation was needed, and so they reached into the bath and hauled the dead man out onto the cold floor. Placing the lantern down, they crouched around the body.

"A thrall," Saul confirmed, pulling back the man's lips to examine the state of his teeth. His canines were not greatly lengthened, but they had begun to develop into sharp points. "I should wager that the strigoi infected him when they moved in here. Told him to keep the business running, make things look normal. Maybe they had planned to turn him, eventually."

"It looks like he has only been dead for a few hours," Aida replied. "If he had been sitting in vinegar for longer, I should have expected more desiccation of the flesh. I think it probable that after that third strigoi escaped Julie's pursuit this morning, the fight and the chase had depleted her. She came back here and drank from her own thrall, then hurried on to some other bolthole before sunrise. She clearly did not think him useful enough to keep."

"A pity that she did not choose to rest here. We could have ended her. Maybe we could have caught and questioned her first."

"Maybe. I do wonder how many lairs the Laskaris have established in this city. I do not think that finding all of them will be simple."

Saul was about to respond, but he fell silent as the sound of newly-arrived footsteps filtered down from the floor above. The twins both glanced towards the door at the top of the stairs, then back to each other. Quietly they moved to take position either side of the staircase, ready to intercept whoever should come wandering down here. Aida doused her lantern, plunging the room into darkness. At this time of day the new arrival was unlikely to be a vampire, but they could not rule out the possibility. And if the footsteps belonged to one of House Laskaris' thralls or mortal minions, then there was at least the potential for an interrogation.

They kept their silence as the unknown arrival moved about upstairs, methodically visiting one room after another. That pattern of movement suggested a search, leading Saul to suspect that this was no vampire's servant on an errand. But if someone else had cause to be investigating this place, did that person know exactly what they were dealing with?

The possibility that they did was enough to make Saul nervous. He could not rule out the chance that the Company of the Holy Sacrament was close on their heels, and getting caught down here by those fanatics would be almost as bad as facing a pack of strigoi. Saul had ended the lives of men before, in defence of himself, his sister and of Julie, but killing humans was something he preferred to avoid if at all possible.

The cellar door had been left slightly ajar, and although the new arrival nudged it open quietly, the increased light flooding through it announced their presence. Saul braced himself, stake in hand, muscles coiled like a spring. The mysterious individual was now making their way down the stairs, moving warily, as if expecting an attack.

The newcomer was not a vampire, Saul was certain of that much, and thralls tended to be more erratic in their movements. The silhouette of a heavy-set man in a cloak and tricorne came into view, his back to the staircase as he surveyed the cellar. With no lantern or candle, he could only rely on the light from the grate and from the top of the stairs. Even with that, however, he was bound to see the twins the moment he turned around.

Saul took a step forward, one hand reaching out to grasp the newcomer's shoulder. The burly man reacted seemingly on instinct, whirling on the spot and delivering a substantial blow to Saul's cheek, knocking him backwards and sending a jolt of pain through his jawbone. He rushed forward like a bull, arms raised in a tackle, but Saul braced himself and met his assailant head-on, blocking his charge and bringing up one leg to deliver a sharp kick to the gut. That was enough to throw the stranger off-balance, but only briefly.

Saul used his forearm to block an oncoming punch to the face, but the man followed up by slamming his shoulder hard into Saul's chest, knocking the wind out of him and very nearly sending him sprawling. Saul made ready to retaliate, instinct telling him to dodge the next blow and then break the man's nose with a jab, but he saw that his opponent had stopped advancing and was now reaching for something on his belt. The barrel of a pistol glinted in the meagre light, but Aida already had her weapon readied, and she appeared behind the stranger with the firearm pointed directly at his head. Wisely, she kept herself out of his arm's reach.

"Stop," she ordered him, causing his hand to pause with gun half-raised.

"Put that down, girl," he replied after a few tense seconds, the accent of his voice confirming that he was a local. Saul took the opportunity to dart in, one hand gripping the stranger's wrist while the other pressed the point of a stake to his throat.

"No. You put yours down."

Realising that he had little room to negotiate, the newcomer loosened his grip upon the weapon, and Saul quickly relieved him of it. Although disarmed, the man did not seem to have lost any sense of bravado.

"So what's a couple of wogs doing here? Armed wogs, at that. And what's your accent, French? You working with those damned Turks?"

So he is investigating, Saul confirmed. The Turks that he

spoke of had to be House Laskaris, almost certainly. *But how much did he really know about what he was looking for?*

"I think we will be the ones to ask the questions," Aida retorted, making it clear that she had no time for games. "You will start by telling us who you are and why you are in this place."

"I'm Clayton," he spat. "I catch criminals. Magistrates know I'm here, so if anything happens to me, there won't be anywhere in London for you to hide."

"A magistrate knows what you are looking for here?" Saul asked, curious as to what the man would say. Of all the people who may blunder upon the hidden machinations of vampires, an officer of the law was among the more likely candidates. But if this Clayton actually knew what kind of creatures he was hunting, Saul doubted that he would be able to convince a magistrate of it, without sounding like a madman.

"Of course they do."

Saul gave his sister a look that simply said: *he's lying.*

"Tell us exactly what you know about these Turks you mention," Aida continued, keeping her finger firmly on the trigger.

"They're savages," Clayton told her, his voice thick with anger and just a hint of sheer terror. "They're in London, and they're killing people. I saw their leader kill a woman myself. I need to stop him."

"If you saw him kill, then why did you not arrest him?"

"Because… because he's something dangerous. Because I don't think I could take him alone, that's why."

"Some*thing*? Please elaborate."

Clayton's face looked pained, frustrated, as though he wanted to convey the gravitas of his business, but was struggling to find the right words. Saul could guess as to what was going through his mind. The man was being held at gunpoint by foreign strangers, and while he had the opportunity to give voice to a dreadful truth, he did not wish to sound like a lunatic or a simpleton.

"He's something other than a man. I swear he's a devil."

"Why do you say that, Mister Clayton?"

"Because of how I saw him kill. He didn't use a blade or a gun or a bludgeon. I saw him drinking his victim's blood, do you hear me? Right from her throat, he was. And the whole time he was holding her off the ground like she weighed nothing. I swear it's true."

"You do not want to arrest this man, do you? You want to kill him."

"What do you think, woman? I can't arrest a bloody devil. Yes, I want to kill him. I can't put a stop to him any other way."

"If you want to kill a devil," Saul stated, holding up Clayton's pistol, "you will need something more than this."

He handed the gun back to the burly detective, who looked from Saul to Aida as if properly seeing the twins for the first time. There was confusion upon his face, and still no small amount of hostility, but in the man's gaze there was also a desperate hope that he might just have found some allies.

"You know something about all this, don't you?"

"This man that you witnessed drinking," Aida asked, "do you have a name for him?"

"Yeah. Yeah, I do. He's going by Eşref."

"Then we are hunting the same devil," Saul told him. "You shall do well to stay out of our way, Mister Clayton. We know his like. You obviously do not. You will only get yourself killed, or worse."

"What? Like Hell am I just going to stay out of this! That monster's been killing people in my city and you expect me to sit on my arse while a couple of bloody Negroes do my job for me? Not a chance! Whoever the fuck you are, this is London. *I* enforce the law here."

In his moment of outrage, Clayton did not see Saul's rising fist until it collided at full force with his mouth. The detective staggered away from the blow with bloodied lips, his feet tripping and sending him crashing into the staircase. Saul kicked away the pistol which he had given back only moments earlier.

"You think yourself in charge here?" he snarled at the downed man. "You do not know what you are hunting. If you find Eşref you will be lucky if all he does is rip the heart out of your chest. More likely he will make you his newest slave. You have not a hope of killing him. And if he takes you, I will have to kill you myself. So stay out of it."

Aida sighed, tucking her pistol back into her belt. She would have preferred that her brother's temper not get the better of him, but she was hardly going to blame him for punching Clayton. The self-righteous fool had brought it upon himself. Saul began to climb the stairs, with Aida following close behind. This shop was a dead end for now, but they may find other clues to the location of strigoi nests in the city.

"Wait…" Clayton called after them as he pulled himself back to his feet, spitting a mouthful of blood onto the floor, "Wait. I don't know what that man is. I don't know how to kill a devil. But it's not going to stop me trying. I've been chasing thieves and killers my whole life. You two seem to know what you're up against, so let me help. If monsters are real, then I have to fight them. Just show me how."

Saul's fist clenched once again. He could cheerfully have told Clayton to fuck himself. Perhaps dealing him some serious injury would guarantee that he kept out of action and out of their way. Saul certainly had no desire to work with this insufferable man, but he had only to look at his sister to know that she had other ideas. Whatever Clayton's shortcomings, he was a man who had discovered the truth of vampires and was intent on doing something about it. Four years ago, the twins were in that exact same position.

"You do not honestly want to get him involved?" he asked her, slipping into their mixed tongue of Wolof and French.

"He could be of use, Brother. He is clearly a fighter, and he knows that he is out of his depth. If we guide him, he can fight for us. I think we should take him to Julie and let her decide."

"He is an arse."

"Undoubtedly. But if we leave him alone, he will end up serving House Laskaris sooner rather than later. Better that he is fighting in the same direction as us."

"Let him find them. When they have turned him, I will enjoy hammering a stake through his heart."

"Brother, I am serious."

"Am I not?"

Saul did not hide the fact that he was unhappy, but Aida was not wrong. If this man was intent on his course of action, it was better that they give him some knowledge of what he was doing, some chance of retaining his humanity. As loathsome as Saul found the man to be, keeping him under their watch was still a better option than allowing him to run around half-cocked and throw himself into the clutches of their enemy.

"You will come with us," Saul finally addressed Clayton. "We are not working alone. There is someone that you must be introduced to."

~ Arnold ~

Wednesday October 13th, 1756

In Arnold's shaken consciousness the last several days had blurred together, becoming something only barely coherent. He recalled how he had returned to St Mary's on Saturday night, filthy and bedraggled, with images of fanged demons with infernal crimson eyes scorched into the fabric of his mind. Reverend Lowther rarely stayed up late, especially on the night before a service, and the young curate was immensely thankful that his superior had taken himself off to bed by the time he arrived. Arnold was unsure if he had slept at all that night, and he had been sure of very little since.

The vicar had insisted that Arnold take that Sunday off, for he was clearly in no fit state to be ministering to the congregation. Afterwards they had spoken in private. Arnold, trembling and stuttering throughout, did his best to explain that he had encountered the forces of Satan on Whitechapel's streets. The elderly reverend had listened calmly and without judgement, taking in Arnold's words. He did not scoff when Arnold tried to convey that the creatures he had witnessed were the same demons that were depicted in his late father's belongings, or that he feared for his mother's soul. In the end, the old man had looked Arnold in the eye and told him succinctly;

"I don't doubt that a terrible thing has happened to you, my boy. But you are here, alive. God has seen you through this test, and He will continue to do so, by His power and His love. Take some time to rest and pray. I have faith that God will show you the path you must walk."

And so, Arnold had prayed. For days he had barely eaten. He had performed what menial duties he could about the church, desperate not to feel useless, but so much of his time had been spent at prayer. He prayed for his mother, prayed that Lisa could be saved from the demon that plagued her, and he prayed desperately for guidance and understanding. His recollection of the incident was a nightmare, but the one thing he could remember so very clearly was that moment of absolute righteousness, the sensation that overwhelmed him when he raised his cross to the monsters and they backed away in fear. How dearly he wanted to replicate that feeling.

Ultimately, he feared that he already knew the path he must walk. Reverend Lowther had spoken as though those demons had been sent to test Arnold personally, but he was certain that there were greater designs at work. He had not spoken of the fourth demon, that mysterious woman who had fought against the others and saved his life. Even now, Arnold was unsure about how he would explain such a thing. It had to be a trick, surely? The Devil's forces were seeking to lure him into false security by appearing divided.

He knew that he must find those demons and confront them again, not simply to repel them but to drive them back to whatever black abyss they had come from. Yet the thought of facing them again filled him with dread; he longed to summon up that unstoppable conviction, but try as he may, it eluded him.

The Wednesday morning was cold and unusually clear, but the sunlight coming in through the stained-glass window brought him little joy that day. Arnold sat alone in a front-row pew of the church hall, hands clasped in his lap as he hoped that maybe today, God would grant him the courage he had been seeking. The sound of the front door opening drew him out of his reverie, and his head turned, gut tightening at the prospect that the Devil's minions were invading this Holy sanctuary. Three figures had entered, stony-faced men dressed in black coats, walking with a grim purpose that made Arnold think of executioners approaching the block.

One of them walked a little way ahead of the other two, who flanked him as if they were bodyguards. The lead man was a striking individual, with golden-blonde hair and keenly piercing eyes, but as he drew nearer, Arnold could not help but glance towards the man's throat, where the collar of his jacket only barely concealed the scar of what must have once been a dreadful wound. The man came to a halt, looked towards the church altar and – with a moment's hesitation – raised his right hand to cross himself. *A Catholic?* Arnold realised, caught a little by surprise. Nervously, the curate rose to his feet.

"Good morning, gentlemen. Can I be of help?"

The blonde-haired visitor looked him up and down. It was a cold look, one which left Arnold feeling rather like an insect pinned to a collector's table. There was something unnerving about this man, a presence that was hard as iron and just as unfeeling. Arnold might have compared this stranger in some ways to the brutish detective who came to this place the previous week, but on some instinctive level he felt that this man was far, far more dangerous than the likes of Lawrence Clayton.

"Good day to you, Father."

The man's accent was French, and his voice carried not an ounce of warmth.

"Actually, I am just the curate," Arnold replied. "St Mary Matfelon belongs to the Church of England. I'm afraid that if you gentlemen have come to debate the finer points of doctrine between our faiths, then you may not have caught me at the best of times."

He gave a faint smile, which the Frenchman did not return. It was a feeble attempt at humour, but it was all that he could muster, and somehow he doubted that this man smiled very often. Instead, he watched the stranger reach into his coat pocket and retrieve something, which he presented to Arnold: a plain wooden crucifix. Recognising it instantly, Arnold felt the bottom of his stomach tumble into a pit.

"I am sorry, *Monsieur*. Perhaps you were not yet aware, but one of your parishioners was found dead on Monday. The body of a woman named Helen Sinclair was discovered in her home, beaten to death. Her husband is missing, and is presumed to be responsible for her murder. This cross was not far from her body. After making some enquiries, I learned that she had been visited by priests from this church, and that the cross likely belongs here."

It took all of Arnold's willpower not to retch. In his mind's eye he saw Richard Sinclair, first pale and emaciated as he had been in that bed, and then standing upright, with bloody eyes and lengthened teeth, his fists laying into his poor wife with a mad, sick strength that was not human. Had Arnold known then what he knew now, he would have told Helen to get out of that house. He would have told her to take sanctuary at the church and go nowhere near her ailing husband. But he did not, and now she was dead. Helen was dead, and the sickness within Richard had surely made him a demon too.

"I…" he reached out slowly, taking the offered item, feeling its weight in his grip. "Oh, God. God, please no."

"You have my condolences," the Frenchman told him. "I suggest you stay vigilant and keep watch of your flock. There is a sickness taking hold in London. Men of faith will be needed to fight it."

The three visitors moved away, beginning to make for the exit, but amidst the horror that gripped Arnold, he found a spark of his courage and grabbed onto it tightly.

"I've seen it!"

He all but shouted the words, causing the departing men to stop and look back his way. The blonde-haired Frenchman turned to face him, clearly intent on what Arnold might have to say.

"I've seen the sickness you speak of. I have seen a demon in London. Three of them came for me on Saturday night. I showed them my cross, and I spoke the Lord's prayer, and they recoiled from me. But I have seen their sickness spread. They infect people, and make men and women into more demons like them."

The three men kept the same stony expressions as they listened to Arnold's words. Their eyes appraised him, as if only now taking him seriously. Whatever they might be thinking, it was clear they were not about to dismiss his story out of hand.

"Describe these demons."

"They looked like people, at first. Two men and a woman. But their eyes became red, like blood. They had fangs like wild beasts. And then I saw them become… monsters, tall and lean, with claws and bat-faces. *Strigoi*."

The Frenchman shared a glance with his two companions. From the look in their eyes, Arnold did not doubt that they believed his testimony.

"Strigoi," the Frenchman replied, "Upyr, vukodlak,

nosferatu. All permutations of the same devilry. And you say that you turned away three of them by your faith alone?"

"God was with me," Arnold said, and he truly did believe it. "They could not bear the sight of the cross, nor the words of the prayer. I held them at bay, but then a fourth one, a woman, arrived. They fought, she cut the head off one of them and the arm off another. Then they fled, with her in pursuit. You seem to know what these demons are? Tell me of them."

"I can tell you," said the Frenchman, and it seemed to Arnold as though some small degree of respect had crept into his voice, "but it is better if I show you."

"My name is Father Michel Renard," the stranger finally introduced himself, once Arnold had agreed to accompany him and his two companions into a carriage. "As you are aware, I work for the Catholic Church. The hierarchies of our respective faiths may have their differences, but we are both men of God, and at this time we have a common enemy."

Within Arnold there was a growing sense of relief, and perhaps even hope. His predicament had not abated in the slightest, but there was such tremendous reprieve in the simple knowledge that he was not alone in this fight. More than that, these men who had come to him held vital information, an understanding that he was eager to share in. Sean Musgrave's documents were a mystery of foreign languages, but these men could speak to him plainly.

"What are they, exactly? What manner of demons does God allow to walk the Earth?"

"They are the undead," Renard told him. "Vampires. Blood-drinkers. They are devils in dead flesh, inhabiting human corpses and resurrecting them to an unholy semblance of life. They sustain their evil existence by feeding upon the blood of the living, and so long as they are able to feed, they cannot die a natural death. They are a plague which has haunted mankind since time immemorial. Some scholars of my order believe that they originated before the Great Flood, and that in their tenacity, some of them survived when the waters cleansed the Earth of all Semjâzâ's other creatures. Given the way that they grow their ranks through infection, so long as even one of them endures, they are legion."

"Semjâzâ? I don't recognise that word."

"The Prince of the Fallen. The Adversary."

"You're speaking of the Devil?"

"I prefer to call a thing by its true name. But yes, the Devil."

"So, if vampires can spread so easily, why have they not over-run the world?"

"Because just as they have their strengths, they also have their weaknesses. In the night they are strong, but under daylight they are lesser than mortals. They cannot abide the signs and words of our Lord, as you yourself have seen. God has marked them as beasts of the wild, and so they cannot enter a civilised home without invitation. Though they hide in mortal guise, they can be identified by the fact that they cast neither reflection nor shadow. And although their bodies are hard to kill, they are not invulnerable. Lastly, when they grow too numerous, they are prone to betrayal, turning upon each other like dogs fighting over scraps. With these limitations they know that they cannot rise against mankind openly, so they must hide themselves. They prey upon us from the shadows, and like shadows, they vanish when the light shines upon them."

They cast neither reflection nor shadow. Arnold realised, in that moment, why he felt that sense of indefinable *wrongness* when he had witnessed a strigoi passing beneath a streetlamp on Saturday night. The creature looked like a man at that point, but he had cast no shadow.

"I see. And these monsters exist in numerous different forms?" he asked. "The strigoi are just one kind among many?"

"Tell me, where did you learn that word? I should not expect an English priest to know much about Romanian folklore."

"I… I only learned it recently. My father died, just a few weeks ago. In fact, I'm quite sure that vampires were involved in his death. He was Sean Musgrave, a friend of Sir Hans Sloane. He left me some papers in his will, researches that he and Sir Hans had been conducting. I thought they were just fanciful tales, but it now seems they were true. I'm thinking that he left them to me, because maybe he wanted a man of faith to take up the fight."

"Tell me about them."

"There's not much I can say. Most of them are in Latin, which I cannot read. You should probably have more luck with them. But some of them had sketches, diagrams, and a collection of preserved teeth. That was how I recognised a strigoi when I saw one."

Renard fell quiet; he looked pensive, as if digesting what Arnold had told him.

"Do you wish to see those documents?" Arnold ventured. "There may well be information that you could make use of."

"In time, yes," Renard told him, "but myself and my men are hunters, not scholars. I will send word to my order for someone who can make good use of them. For now, keep them close. You have them at your church?"

"Yes, I do."

"Good. A church is a sanctuary; very few vampires should be bold enough to come looking on consecrated ground, even if someone were foolish enough to invite them in."

"I had been hoping that was the case."

Knowing that the grounds of the church were indeed sacrosanct was heartening, as though a burden had been lifted from his spirit. It did, however, bring to mind a question which had been nagging him.

"If I may ask, we know that these monsters are repelled by signs of God. But if so, how was Helen Sinclair's husband able to kill her? When last I saw Richard Sinclair he was heavily infected, though I did not understand it at the time. I gave her that cross to comfort her and, in some way I suppose, I hoped it would protect her. Why did it not?"

"Against the undead, a cross is only as good as the faith of the one who holds it. Without the sincere belief that God is protecting you, it is just a piece of wood. Perhaps she did not believe strongly enough. Or… more likely, in my experience, she felt pity for her husband which caused her to lower her guard. Vampires are fast. Her vigilance should only have to waver for a moment, for him to take advantage."

Arnold could certainly believe that, though it pained him to imagine that all it took for a good and faithful woman to be murdered was the fact that she was also a caring and dutiful wife. A moment's compassion for a husband who had become a monster, and he killed her for it. Richard Sinclair would have to be found. The body of the man had to be laid to rest, and the demon that wore his face must be sent to Hell.

"Where exactly are we going?"

"My order keeps many safehouses throughout Europe. I am taking you to one."

The carriage made its way south of the Thames, eventually rolling to a stop on Lambeth Road, outside of a two-storey house which backed onto the green expanse of George's Fields. Although not terribly large, the house was grand in size compared to the typical slums of Whitechapel, and a modest stable was built onto the side of it, big enough for a handful of horses. One of Renard's companions paid the carriage driver, and the three men departed the vehicle with Arnold following after them. A knock at the door from Renard was answered with the opening of a narrow slot and a rapid exchange of words in French. Then the door was opened, and Arnold followed the others inside.

His eyes took in the spartan interior of the house, which appeared in ways more akin to a barracks than a home. As pleased as Arnold was to have found men who were fighting the vampiric threat, he did wonder which specific order of the Catholic Church was able to maintain a covert military presence like this on English soil. So much blood had been spilled over the conflict between the Protestant and Catholic faiths, and so Arnold found it hard to imagine that the British Crown would give consent to these assassins operating here, however righteous their cause. Of course, that did also raise the question of whether the good King George and his ministers were aware of the existence of vampires.

Waiting inside the house were another four of these men, similarly attired to Renard and his two companions, and bearing the same grim expressions of men whose duty was to confront the Devil's work. Arnold may not have spoken a word of French, but from the hurried conversation that was occurring between the men and their commander, Arnold would guess that they did not take kindly to his unexpected presence. If that were the case, however, it also seemed that Renard's authority was enough to command their deference.

"Come with me," he finally instructed Arnold, his men stepping aside to make room as he led the way upstairs. The young curate followed, his mind alight with unvoiced questions. He wondered where this secret order found its recruits; Renard had introduced himself with the title of an ordained priest, but were all of these vampire-hunters men of the cloth? From the looks of them, it seemed more likely that they had been soldiers or other such violent professionals, hardened by conflict before joining the ranks of this society.

As for Renard himself, somehow Arnold doubted that his career had ever been typical of the Catholic clergy. If this Frenchman had lived a different life in a time before he took up the sword, then Arnold could only imagine that any such life was now long forgotten. He wondered when the man had acquired that scar upon his neck, but he also imagined it was not a topic that Renard would wish to discuss with a virtual stranger, fellow man of God or otherwise.

"Many vampires are solitary killers, but others group together into covens," Renard told him as they ascended the staircase. "You are particularly unfortunate in that the strigoi who have moved into London of late hail from one of the largest and most dangerous covens in Europe. The House of Laskaris have their roots in Byzantine nobility, more than seven centuries ago. To this day they maintain the centre of their activities in Constantinople. We do not know their true numbers, but they have at least dozens of agents in Europe, perhaps hundreds. Their leaders are among the worst of Semjâzâ's monsters upon this Earth."

"Constantinople? I wondered where they had come from. The ones who attacked me did not look British."

"Most of the Laskaris in this age are Turks, but whenever they colonise a new city, they recruit footsoldiers from among the local populace. Your parishioner, Sinclair, will be among the latest to join them. A pity we did not find him before he murdered his wife."

"How... how exactly does it work?" Arnold asked, nervously.

"How do these creatures make good people into their evil kind?"

Renard came to a stop outside a door on the upstairs landing. He turned towards Arnold, meeting the younger man's gaze. Something about the look in those bright, piercing eyes was enough to fill Arnold with a creeping sensation of dread. He knew that Renard was speaking not with academic understanding, but from personal experience.

"When they feed upon us, their bite contaminates our blood," he explained. "When they bite a victim, and then feed upon the same victim again before the bite has healed, that is when infection sets in. Repeated feedings transform a human being into a thrall, a creature that is close to death, yet stronger for the curse that now flows in its veins, and with a mind plagued by evil thoughts and instincts."

A thrall. A slave. That was what Lisa Brennan had become, a slave to an undead abomination.

"A thrall's damnation is not absolute. They can regain their humanity, but only if the feedings stop and they are kept forcibly separated from the one who infected them. Eventually, the body and soul will recover from the disease. But more often a thrall will serve their master for a time, until the master no longer needs them and kills them, or the master allows the thrall to drink of their blood. With this exchange, the thrall's spirit finally dies, and their body becomes a puppet for a demon. They rise upon the next sundown as a vampire."

Hope – fierce, *dangerous* hope – burned within Arnold's breast. If what Renard said was true, then his mother was not yet fully damned. She could be saved, if only he could track down and kill the vampire who had bitten her. Part of him wanted to tell this to Renard, wanted to confess everything, but he stopped himself before the words left his mouth. As much as he wanted to align his cause with this hunter, he could only imagine the Frenchman's reaction if he found out that Arnold's own mother was infected. This man had the conviction of a fanatic, and that left little room for nuance. Arnold would likely not be safe from him, and Lisa certainly would not.

"So," Arnold finally asked, "in what ways do you kill a vampire?"

"That," Renard told him, "is what I intend to show you."

The heavy wooden door opened into a room that was more akin to a cell. All furniture and decoration had been stripped out of it, leaving only bare walls and floorboards, etched all over with signs of the crucifix. From floor to ceiling the room was covered with crosses, save for a single barred window through which the sunlight poured in. Laying at the centre of the room, with wrists and ankles restrained by leather straps, was a vampire. Arnold recognised the creature as having a similar Turkic skin tone and features to the three who had accosted him.

The vampire had the face of a young man, one which had once been blessed with remarkable handsomeness, but now marked with such a look of pain and suffering that Arnold averted his gaze after just a few seconds of looking at it. The creature's clothes were torn and tattered, reduced to hardly more than rags, and he could see that a great scar began at the vampire's shoulder and ran most of the way through its torso. The creature seemed barely able to move as it lay within the window's light, and as the two priests stepped into the room, its only response was to turn its head slowly towards them and give a weak moan of pain through torn lips.

"We retrieved this beast in Constantinople," Renard explained. "At that point it was severely wounded, its body had been cleaved almost in half and its face was so broken that it could barely speak. But these creatures heal fast, especially if they have fresh blood in them, so we gave it enough rats to let it recover to this wretched state. Outside of this room, after dark and with human blood in its belly, it should have the strength of ten men. But this is consecrated ground, watched over by my brothers of the Faith, and with only rats to sustain it, this demon's strength is gone."

The Frenchman took a step forward, and called back to one of the men who had followed him and Arnold from downstairs. The acolyte answered by passing Renard a heavy-looking mallet and a long stake of ash wood, its tip sharpened to a brutal point. Arnold was immediately reminded of the strigoi that he had seen slain by the mysterious woman, when she had driven a stake into its back and then cut off its head.

"We made it talk, eventually. It was on this beast's information that we sailed here to London. We know that the Laskaris are gathering here in numbers, but alas, this lowly cur did not know what purpose its masters had in mind. With nothing more to tell us, I was due to dispose of this creature. I am glad that you will get the chance to observe."

The tip of the stake touched upon the left of the vampire's chest, right above its heart, and Renard brought the mallet down hard. The sound that followed, of wood striking wood and piercing into flesh, and the scream of the terrified creature, was a sound which would never rid itself from Arnold's memory. Even in its weakened state, the vampire's body lashed and contorted, blood bursting from its mouth and nostrils.

Another blow of the mallet, and another still, drove the stake through the creature's ribcage with the awful sound of breaking, splintering bones. The first death of a strigoi that Arnold had witnessed had been relatively quick, over in seconds with the sweep of a sword, but by comparison this was agonising in its slowness. The creature continued to spasm, its exertions growing steadily fainter, eyes rolled up in its skull and fanged jaws snapping feebly. Finally it fell still, and Renard released his grip upon the stake.

"To slay the beast, impale its heart," the Frenchman coldly explained, drawing a handkerchief from his pocket to wipe the blood spray from his hand. "Metal implements work on the younger ones, but wood seems to be more effective. Then cut off the head, and cremate the carcass. Bury whatever is left in consecrated earth. The older a vampire gets, the more stubbornly they cling to their foul existence, but I have never yet found one which can rise from ashes. Understand that any lesser injury – gunshot, stab wound or the like – is merely an inconvenience to these demons. If the body is intact, then do not be fooled into thinking that they are dead."

Arnold was pale, his eyes wide. His train of thought careened back and forth between the battle he had witnessed on Saturday night and the execution he had just watched now. *This was the path he would have to walk*, he realised with horrible, crushing inevitability. In committing himself to this crusade against Satan's children, the life that God had ordained for Arnold Brennan would be one of seeing this awful slaughter over and over again. If he was to cast the demons from this world, then eventually it must be his hand upon the mallet.

"The danger is greater than you know," Renard continued, and Arnold shook his head in disbelief. How could this possibly get any worse? "You are facing not one threat, but two. I told you that the undead often turn upon one another, driven by their territorial bloodlust, and when they war among themselves, humans die in the crossfire. The vampire woman who attacked her own kind when last you faced them, you understand that she is not your ally. She is among the very worst of them, and her evil is not abated by the fact that she is an enemy of House Laskaris."

"Who is she?"

"She is known as Julie d'Aubigny or Mademoiselle Maupin, among other names, and she is Semjâzâ's own whore. She is a creature of corruption and duplicity that I have been hunting for years. She travels Europe, drawing good men and women into her web, leading them into utmost sin. She feeds upon blood, but what she truly thrives upon is moral depravity. Now that she has seen you, she will likely not forget you."

Maupin. The name from the letters. By God, Sir Hans Sloane had been corresponding with this creature. Sean Musgrave had known about this fact, perhaps been an active accomplice to it. For the second time Arnold wanted to tell Renard what he knew, but he feared for what the Frenchman's response would be. Arnold felt as though his own family, his very bloodline, had become utterly tainted by this business, but until he had enough information to allay any suspicion upon himself, he dare not unveil this secret. More than ever, he needed to know exactly what was in those damnable letters.

"Whatever this demon's tricks, I will resist," Arnold tried to assure Renard, all too aware that the conviction in his voice did not sound terribly convincing. "I will not be tempted from the path of God."

"Perhaps there is a warrior's spirit in you, *Monsieur.* Take heart. Your faith has saved you once from the demons. When you face them again, God will once more lead you to triumph, and this time you know that you can seek my aid. You *will* seek my aid, if you discover anything of relevance. I will not cease my hunt until every last strigoi has been purged from this city, of that I assure you."

Renard's hand grasped Arnold's shoulder, in what the

younger man hoped was a gesture of camaraderie. How greatly he wished to believe in this vampire-hunter, and to have dependable, knowledgeable allies in the battles to come. But truthfully, Michel Renard frightened him almost as much as the vampires did. The hunter had an intensity about him that burned like the touch of ice, and in this moment Arnold could not bring himself to place trust in a man whom he could so easily envision turning against him.

He did not linger at the house for long after that. Renard gave him money for a carriage back to St Mary's, and Arnold promised to keep close guard of the documents, until such a time as a scholar from Renard's order came to read them. In truth he would be counting the hours until tomorrow night, and his planned meeting with his brother at the Minories theatre. It was imperative now that he learn all he could of his father's relationship to La Maupin, and exactly what had drawn the attention of House Laskaris to his family.

~ Julie ~

Thursday October 14th, 1756

"You will remember nothing of this."

Julie's deep green eyes were fixed upon those of the trembling streetwalker on whom she had fed, her gaze pinning the young woman to the wall. Panicked as she was, her thoughts were malleable as wet clay beneath the vampire's voice.

"You will recall no bite," she whispered. "No surprise, and no pain. I came into this alley as your customer, you performed your trade, and then I departed. I was satisfied, and you found it pleasant."

A handful of coin was pressed into the palm of Rebecca's hand, her fingers closing around her payment. With it came the illusory recollection of tantalising caresses and sensual pleasures that went beyond her jaded expectations. A comforting lie was offered to erase the unnerving truth, and her frightened mind embraced the lie.

"Thank you for your service, Miss Grey."

The fear in the girl's eyes started to abate as her memories were reshaped in accordance with Julie's commands. Women made up only a small share of her custom, but as the vampire's words sculpted her thoughts, they brought with them some sense of fondness for this encounter. Gently she pulled the shoulder of her dress back into place, concealing the fresh marks of vampiric feeding. Her breathing slowed along with her heartbeat, the desperation that she had felt moments earlier giving way to calm assurance. The beginnings of a smile pulled at the corner of her mouth as she relived the false memory she had been given.

"Any time, Miss," Rebecca finally breathed, as Julie finalised the deception by flashing her a lascivious wink, and then strolling away onto the main street. As the warmth of the girl's blood coursed through Julie's body, it brought with it that euphoric surge of puissance and vitality that only came from feeding on a live vessel. There had been no carnal lust in her victim's bloodstream, no exquisite taste of desire; the girl made her living as a prostitute, but she took no enjoyment to speak of in her profession.

There was fear in the moment, however, the delicious reaction of fight-or-flight as her primal brain realised she was under attack by a predator. With the taste of that in her mouth, Julie's instincts were now up, the demon within her yearning to test her muscles against some enemy, to feel flesh and bone come apart beneath her claws. By all the Gods, she hoped that Eşref would show his face this night. The echoes of Rebecca's heartbeat were still in Julie's ears as she moved to rendezvous with her companions, ready to begin tonight's surveillance around the Queen Anne Stuart.

It had been at least three nights since Eşref had last visited his bed-ridden thrall, whom Julie now knew to be called Lisa Brennan. Interesting, that this poor barmaid should happen to be the mother of that priest whom she had saved from Eşref's minions on Saturday evening. But then, that was just one among many pieces of interesting information which Lawrence Clayton had supplied.

For her own part, Julie was in two minds about that boorish detective. Aida had explained her reasons for wanting to recruit the man to their cause, but Clayton had not taken well to the news that Julie was one of the same bloodsucking monsters that he was seeking to destroy. The man had drawn his firearm when Julie was finally stirred to action, plucking the weapon from his grip like a parent scolding a disobedient child, before forcing her will upon his mind. To his credit, Clayton did his best to fight her compulsion; the man's inherent stubbornness had given him more resistance than most mortals, but he had not been able to struggle against the vampire's power for long. Eventually the aggression within him had withered beneath her mental assault, and made him compliant enough to talk to her without trying to kill her. And when he did talk, he had proven to be something of a goldmine.

Thirty-seven years had passed since Julie's partnership with Sir Hans Sloane had come to its end. She had allowed her old mentor to believe that she was dead, and it should hardly surprise her that during that time he had sought out another pupil to join him in his occult investigations. Whoever Sean Musgrave was, Sir Hans had clearly trusted him enough to share with him the details of his studies into vampirism, and his joint endeavours with Julie d'Aubigny. Of course Julie had been more than just Sir Hans' student in matters paranormal; where he had been the academic mind of their operation, she had been the instrument of wrath, the hunter who brought down the most dangerous of game.

From what Clayton had told her of Musgrave, it seemed unlikely that the late physician had filled her vacant role, but perhaps Sir Hans had simply enjoyed having a fellow scholar with whom to discuss the occult mysteries. Certainly he was more willing to trust his pupil with those matters than his own children, since if Clayton's descriptions were correct, then the collection of letters, studies and vampiric samples had all been entrusted to the custody of Sean Musgrave rather than Sir Hans' own daughters. With all that Sir Hans knew about the monsters lurking just out of mankind's sight, Julie could perhaps understand why he may wish to allow his offspring to live in blissful ignorance.

Whatever the motivation, the letters had passed from Sir Hans to Sean and now to his bastard son, Arnold. While Sir Hans had clearly wished to keep his family out of humanity's fight against the immortals, it seemed more likely that Musgrave wanted his successor to take up arms in the struggle, for why else would he choose to bequeath that information to a man of God?

At some point, Julie was going to have to seek out contact with the priest if she wished to acquire those documents. The fact that he was keeping them on consecrated ground was certainly the only reason that House Laskaris had not simply seized them by force. Maybe she could make use of Clayton to obtain them for her, given that he had already spoken with Brennan once. Julie had no desire to keep any mortal under her control permanently, so she would have to assess whether he could be trusted to operate without those mental shackles.

The group had gathered in the mouth of the alleyway across from the pub, the very spot where Lawrence had begun his watch of the place on the night when he saw a vampire for the first time. The evening air was cold, almost freezing, with occasional light rain that seemed to come and go in patches, as though the clouds above were undecided as to what they should do. While her three companions had all attired themselves warmly, Julie looked distinctly underdressed in only a single shirt and breeches, her coat unbuttoned. To her physiology, the evening's cold was all but meaningless.

"Now begins the wait," she addressed the others. "Let us hope tonight is our night."

The twins were ready for the fight, of that she was certain. Eşref was a powerful individual, but Julie was confident that she could take him alone if need be. Against the four of them, he would stand little chance. The weakest link here was Clayton, for this would be his first actual combat with an immortal, and while Julie could see that he was a strong and skilled brawler, he was deeply lacking in experience compared to Saul and Aida.

Back in her breathing days, Julie had been among the most capable duellists in all of France when she first took up her sword against a strigoi. By the age of thirty she had a long list of kills to her name, each one a life taken in single combat, and she had wounded and humiliated many others. With a blade in her hand, she would engage one enemy or a dozen with neither fear nor hesitation. She was just as ferocious when using her fists and feet as with a sword, and had more than once beaten an opponent close to death. In life Julie had been infamous as a woman who could fight and kill as well as any man.

And yet, that first vampire-hunt had very nearly ended with her throat ripped out. No amount of combat experience against humans could quite prepare someone for doing battle with an immortal.

This much had been explained to Clayton. When Eşref appeared, the plan was that Julie would engage him head-on while the others were to surround him and grab onto him. Ideally they would force him to the ground and pin his arms, making it simpler for Julie to drive one of her stakes into his heart. Like any plan, it would be subject to change depending on circumstances.

Clayton had mentioned that when he last saw Eşref at the Queen Anne, the strigoi had come here unaccompanied.

If he did arrive here alone then that was to their favour, but it was likely that he had minions in the vicinity that Lawrence had simply not seen. If additional strigoi arrived, Aida would have cause to put her Lombard pistols to use before the enemy could get into close quarters.

An hour passed, then a second, and was into the third without any sign of their target. People came and went from the Queen Anne, though the streets grew steadily quieter. As the evening progressed, the prospect was raised as to whether the group should split up, in order to surveillance the area from more than one angle, in case Eşref should approach from a different direction. Since they had taken this same action on the previous two nights, if only to give themselves a reason to walk instead of standing still in the cold, Julie agreed to it while she held her current position.

Sundown had come at five, and it was nearing eight o'clock by Julie's pocket watch when she caught the scent on the night air of a vampire's approach. The road outside the pub was empty, devoid of people. A couple of minutes later she heard her lover's footsteps approaching from behind, as quickly as she could while remaining quiet.

"I spotted him down the street," Aida whispered. "He has two others with him."

Julie nodded and sniffed the air, focusing her senses. Among all the rancid odours of this city, she could indeed pick out three distinct scents of fellow predators. Clayton was the next to reconvene with the group, and finally Saul. By the time they were together, Eşref and his two attendants were visible on the street approaching the Queen Anne. Saul's hand moved to the hilt of his scimitar.

"You engage Eşref," he whispered to Julie, "we will deal with the others."

"I recognise that one," Clayton pointed out, peering through the gloom towards the nearing vampires. "That's

Marcus Whitfield, the son of the dead lawyer. I spoke to him just the other week."

"Then he is one of them now," Saul replied, "He is under Eşref's control. We cannot afford to offer any quarter."

"The other is the girl I fought on Saturday," Julie added, and then quickly raised one hand, gesturing for the others to stop.

"Wait…"

Their enemies were dividing. Eşref had stopped and spoken briefly to his followers, and now Whitfield and the female strigoi were peeling away from him, heading towards one of the many side-streets. Julie looked back to her three companions.

"Go, follow them. Find out whatever errand he's sent them on, and put an end to them. I'll deal with Eşref myself; I'm certain the three of you can handle this."

Saul gave a nod of agreement, followed shortly by Aida, though Julie could tell that dividing the group's efforts was not their preferred decision; they obeyed her only because now was not the time for an argument. As the twins started to head away down the alley, Clayton hesitated for just a few seconds, and then took off after them. He suddenly appeared rather concerned that his first clash with a vampire was going to happen without Julie's help, but he did not wish to appear a coward, and the twins seemed to be confident of the odds, so he followed with all haste, drawing his pistol and a stake as he moved.

Now alone in the alleyway, Julie's eyes reddened with anticipation. She told herself that it made sense for the twins and Clayton to pursue the two minions. It was a sensible move to destroy as many of them as possible. Every Laskaris footsoldier slain was another enemy pawn swept from the board. None of that changed the fact that she was relishing the prospect of facing Eşref one-on-one. If he was the vampire that killed Marie de Senneterre, then vengeance ought to be personal.

Eşref stopped still as he neared the front of the Queen Anne, his nostrils twitching. Although Julie's position was down-wind of his approach, there was only so much she could do to mask her scent from her own kind. Unlike the attack at his haven in Constantinople, the two vampires here did not have the overwhelming stench of a tannery district to hide their presence.

Julie emerged from the alleyway, scimitar in hand, moving with the unnatural grace of a vampire who was making not the slightest effort to blend in. Her crimson eyes glinted beneath the yellow streetlight, and Eşref's own pupils shifted in response, the demonic fury rising in his gaze. Julie gave him a broad, malicious smile, baring her pearl-white fangs.

"Bon soir, mon cher."

Eşref bolted. The strigoi sprinted away at blinding speed, his shape becoming little more than a blur in the darkness. Julie tore after him, her footsteps kicking up mud as she charged along the filthy street. Her target jinked to the side and scrambled up a building, scaling the wall in moments and landing atop the roof. She followed, barely a second behind him, closing the distance with every moment. Her mind raced, her passions wild, every instinct craving blood-shed. In this moment she craved a physical intercourse with Eşref that was as brutal as her trysts with Aida were affec-tionate, and which would certainly be no less intense.

Eşref leaped from one rooftop to the next, effortlessly clearing the distance between houses. Sensing her closing in behind him he whirled to face her, and Julie's sword lashed out for his neck. The strigoi ducked beneath the arc of Julie's attack, and delivered a vicious blow to her face which sent her crashing through a chimney stack, scattering roof slate as she landed hard.

Julie laughed like a child at play and rolled to her feet as Eşref came for her again, his razor claws swiping through the air and lacerating her flesh as she tried to evade their reach. Pain blossomed in her forearm where she sought to block one attack, and again in her abdomen as his talons raked at her stomach. The fire of her wounds only heightened her bloodlust, and as he came in again she headbutted him with all the force she could muster, shattering his nose and sending him reeling back.

The sword in Julie's hand spun before she brought it up in another swipe, forcing Eşref further backwards, the tip of the blade slashing across his chest. The strigoi growled deeply, his rage that of a wounded lion, and he lunged for her once more with frenzied abandon. One hand latched onto the wrist of her sword-arm, while the other grabbed her by the face, his clawed thumb stabbing right through her cheek. Julie responded by driving the toe of her boot sharply into Eşref's groin, eliciting a wet crunching sound and a cry of pain. She slipped back out of his grip, but her opponent's arm struck out and landed a back-hand blow to her face, cracking her jaw and swatting her down onto her back.

More roof slates shattered beneath the impact, and Julie felt her scimitar tumble out of her hand. She rolled to grab it, but Eşref kicked the weapon away, sending it clattering off the roof to the street below. Above her, his outline was changing, his body flowing from one shape to another as he took on his true form. His clothes stretched and ripped, and soon all pretence of the man was gone, and Julie was looking upon the black chiropteran horror that lay beneath Eşref's skin.

His clawed hands came down and Julie threw herself

aside to avoid them, her enemy's blows punching holes in the roof on which they stood. She lashed out with one leg and kicked him off his feet, but no sooner had she pulled herself upright than his talons locked around her shin and dragged her back down with him. The two vampires rolled, slashing and tearing at one another in ugly, desperate contest, until they finally broke apart and regained their feet. Both of them were a mess of shredded flesh and clothing, bleeding in a hundred different places.

Eşref leaped again, coming for her with a leonine pounce, and Julie moved to block him, his jaws snapping shut upon her raised forearm. She felt his fangs bite deep, tearing through muscle and puncturing bone, threatening to rip the arm in two. Forcing her way through the agony she grabbed a stake from her belt with her free hand and rammed it hard into the front of her enemy's ribs, just left of his sternum.

The strigoi yelped and recoiled, the length of ironwood embedded in his chest. It looked like her weapon had found its mark, but she had not driven it deep enough to impale his heart right through. She lunged towards him, looking to grab the stake and push it further in, but he knocked her back with another lightning-quick swipe of his arm. As Julie scrambled back to her feet, she saw Eşref pull the bloodied stake from his body and crush its point to splinters in his hand, only to then turn and go into full retreat, a trail of bloody footsteps in his wake.

She had wounded him badly, and they both knew it. A vampire's unearthly physiology could shrug off all manner of trauma, but the blood-organ always remained their greatest vulnerability. Julie drew her second stake, giving chase as Eşref sprinted away, making for a nearby cotton mill. She saw him leap and grab onto the side of the building, dragging himself up the brickwork and onto the roof. Muscles burning with exertion, she followed after him. Her body was hurting, and the hunger was roaring in her ears after expending so much blood in the fight, but her enemy was weaker still. This hunt was nearly at its end.

Julie's legs launched her upwards and she landed upon the roof of the mill, not far behind the bleeding form of Eşref. The strigoi staggered as he turned to face her, one hand clutching at the wound in his chest. His body was shifting again, returning to human form as his strength ebbed. He desperately needed to feed, and his broken flesh was struggling to sustain the demon within. Julie watched as he dropped to one knee, so weakened by blood loss that he could no longer stand. She moved towards him, the stake gripped tightly in her fingers. This vampire was old enough that she would not trust this weapon alone to keep him down for good, but there would be plenty of time to make sure he was never coming back.

"It'll all be over soon, Eşref."

"For you, Camazotz," the strigoi panted, his voice choked with his own blood. Painfully he lifted his head, meeting Julie's gaze with his own. "It shall soon be over for you."

Her eyes narrowed. In all the years since her return from the New World, she had never once spoken of her bloodline to another immortal. No vampire on this side of the Atlantic had seen her true form and lived to tell of it.

"How do you know what I am?"

"She knows all about you. She's going to rip you limb from limb."

Anger flared, hot and red within Julie's breast, but that rage was only a veneer over something far worse. At its core there was fear, and a dreadful realisation. Somewhere there was a powerful vampire with information about her that they should not be able to know. If House Laskaris was aware of her bloodline, then there were all manner of other things which they might have discovered. Julie's anonymity, the very thing she most relied upon to conceal herself from her own kind, could be nothing more than an illusion. If her secrecy was compromised, it meant that her companions, her lover, were at greater risk than they ever realised. Eşref sensed her mounting dread, and a cruel, strangled laugh escaped his lips.

"You're dancing to her tune, you stupid whore. I wish I could see it when my Mistress pulls you apart in her hands."

Julie's eyes flashed and she struck Eşref *hard*, feeling her own knuckles fracture as she knocked him across the rooftop. He landed face-down and she sprinted after him, kicking him onto his back and bringing her stake down upon his open wound. A final gasp of laughter rose up as the stake rammed into Eşref's heart, piercing it through and bursting out of his back. His body shook and spasmed, fingers clawing wildly at the air as Julie stood back and watched him die.

"That was for Marie, you bastard."

Eşref fell still, his face still locked in a horrible, rictus smile.

You're dancing to her tune, you stupid whore.

They knew what she was. If they knew *what* she was, then to some degree they must know *who* she was. There were only two ways that such a thing was possible. Either House Laskaris had been watching Julie for a long time, and had deduced her nature while she remained blind to their machinations for all these years, even as she had hunted down several of their members… or they were receiving aid from the Americas, from one of the very few vampires in the world who knew her personally. From one of the Nine.

~ Arnold ~

Thursday October 14th, 1756

Within the rectory of St Mary's church, papers were spread across the floor of Arnold's room. The chest stood open, its contents scattered, as the clergyman had done all he could to organise the documents despite his complete inability to understand the majority of them. He had looked for and set aside every piece of writing which bore the signature of *Mlle. Maupin*, hoping that between them those letters should cast some light on exactly what had transpired between Sir Hans Sloane and this vampire for whom Father Renard held such a deep antipathy.

At the bottom the chest, hidden away from his previous cursory readings, he had found a leather fold containing the only series of letters in this collection which were written in English. They were, as far as he could tell, among the most recent of the documents, all of them dated from within the last four to seven years. They appeared to have been exchanged between Sir Hans and a fellow academic named István Rozgonyi, seemingly based at the Eötvös Loránd University in Buda-Pest, and their correspondence had continued until a mere few months before Sir Hans' death.

This man, Rozgonyi, appeared to be something of an

authority on mythology and folklore, and the letters contained a good deal of discussion on the nature of vampirism and documented cases of vampire 'outbreaks' in rural Balkan villages. The letters made mention of books and articles which had been posted back and forth, along with references to supernatural topics which seemed unconnected to vampirism, such as various sunken civilisations from different European legends. What drew Arnold's curiosity in the most recently-dated of the documents were the plans being discussed for Mr Rozgonyi to make an extended visit to London, perhaps even relocating entirely to England from Hungary. It seemed as though Rozgonyi had sent a substantial sum of money to Sir Hans, who had used those funds to purchase two houses; one here in London and one on St Martin's island, off the coast of Cornwall.

The last letter was from Sir Hans confirming the purchase of the properties, and arrangements with a lawyer – a Mr Garside – from whom Rozgonyi could collect the keys upon his arrival in London. Arnold wondered if this Rozgonyi had ever made good upon his wish to come here. The address given in the letters would be one worth visiting at some point, if only to determine whether Rozgonyi was another potential ally, or if Sir Hans had kept more than one undead monster among his list of contacts.

Even now, Arnold found it exceedingly difficult to imagine that the prestigious Physician Royal of Great Britain would knowingly consort with bloodsucking demons, or that Sean Musgrave would be a party to such associations. Surely any contact between Sir Hans and 'La Maupin' had to be the result of some deception on her part, one of those twisted games of depravity which Renard had mentioned? Perhaps Sir Hans had discovered her duplicity, and it was this very fact which had led him to begin his studies into her evil kind. To Arnold that seemed as reasonable an explanation as there could be, but it was all just conjecture until he could actually have the letters translated for him.

The light from his single small window was fading as the evening drew in, and the young clergyman lit some candles before he gathered up each set of documents and laid them back in the chest, packing away all of them except for those which pertained to La Maupin. As he did so he could not help but glance once more at all those framed teeth, feeling a shiver creep through him at the thought that they all belonged to real creatures. His eyes lingered on the pair of long canines which were labelled *'Strigoi, Roumanie'*, and this time he could very much confirm that they were genuine. He had now seen fangs just like those in the mouths of four separate individuals.

We do not know their true numbers, but they have at least dozens of agents in Europe, perhaps hundreds. Their leaders are among the worst of Semjâzâ's monsters upon this Earth.

Father Renard's words echoed in Arnold's thoughts. There truly was an army of horrors lurking in the night, but he knew that they were not unstoppable. For all their terrible powers, they could be fought and they could be slain. He could only pray that God grant him the courage and resolve to fight the coming battles. When the time came for him to hammer a stake through the heart of the beast which had infected his mother, he would be ready to do it.

Until then, however, the time was fast approaching for him to acquire some more answers about his father's role in this unholy business. God willing, tonight he would discover the missing pieces of this puzzle. He was not yet sure how he would convince Nathaniel that it was all real, however. His half-brother may have understood that their family was in danger, but it was a far cry from accepting that they were being hunted by literal monsters.

After several days of fasting, it was only since yesterday's meeting with Renard that Arnold realised just how weak and exhausted he had become, so he had made sure to begin eating again. He found time for a bowl of soup and a crust of bread, before he set out to the theatre with the letters tucked inside a worn leather satchel.

The Minories ran southwards from Whitechapel Street as far as Little Tower Hill, where the Tower of London stood. Although the name now belonged primarily to that single road, the Minories more widely encompassed an old parish of this city, one originally named for an abbey of Franciscan nuns founded in 1294. A couple of the original buildings still endured, now property of the Ordnance Office, and they had not been used for religious purposes since the dissolution of the monasteries under King Henry VIII. The Abbey of the Minoresses of St. Clare without Aldgate was functionally gone, but the title of the Minoresses lived on in the name of the Minories.

The theatre which bore that name was a popular playhouse, the kind of venue which dealt primarily in bawdy comedy and pantomime, with the occasional foray into higher culture. Tickets for the cheap seats and standing room tended to sell out for every performance, and yet despite this the theatre's income barely seemed to cover its annual running costs, leaving some parts of the building in dire need of maintenance.

The crowds of people that gathered to watch productions here could be described as 'jovial', 'enthusiastic' and often in some state of inebriation. It was the sort of entertainment that was a very long way from Arnold Brennan's idea of an enjoyable evening, and the curate felt as out of place here as he would at a fighting pit. When he saw his half-brother waiting for him in the lobby he was relieved, but that relief evaporated almost instantly when he saw who else was present. Why in the name of God above did Nathaniel bring his younger sister here?

Fifteen-year-old Imogen Musgrave stood at her brother's side, dressed up for the evening like the demure young society lady that she was, and watching her surroundings with politely concealed fascination. She had likely not been out of the house very much since her father's death, and she would almost never have come to somewhere as common as this. Her presence here tonight was a rare chance for her to skirt the boundaries of social class and partake of the same entertainments as the lower orders. At the best of times Arnold would probably have deemed it morally inappropriate for a girl like Imogen to be here, but with all that transpired right now, it seemed like madness for her to be anywhere other than safe at home.

"Arnold, good to see you," Nathaniel greeted him, beckoning him over with a wave of his hand. "I know this establishment seems a little rough around the edges, but Tom Ashford is an excellent manager and a good-hearted man. Rest assured, we shall be in warm and trustworthy company tonight."

"Yes, good evening, Nathaniel." He looked towards Imogen and gave her a nervous half-bow, "and to yourself, Sister. It has been some time. Nathaniel, I didn't know that Miss Imogen should be joining us tonight? I thought, after our previous discussion, that it would have been wiser for her to remain in safety?"

"Why ever should I not be safe here?" Imogen asked. "I have my brother here with me, and as he said, we shall be personal guests of the manager. I should not expect any danger in a theatre."

Schooled in etiquette and manners from an early age, her tone was the epitome of polite concern, though there was perhaps just the merest hint of mocking nonchalance.

Arnold realised that she likely viewed him as the archetypal overbearing man of the cloth, concerned with shielding her moral virtue from the sinful realities of the world. He did not at all relish the thought of trying to explain to her the nature of the threat that they all faced.

"It's quite alright," Nathaniel assured her, before leaning closer to Arnold. "Don't worry, old boy, we're quite safe. I don't expect any trouble here, and we're travelling by carriage rather than walking, so we shan't encounter any bother on the streets. But I do have my pistol with me, if it puts your mind at ease."

Of course it did not put him at ease in the slightest. Along with the documents, the satchel that he carried also contained the firearm that had belonged to the dead strigoi on Saturday night, but in truth he had only brought it with him because he felt responsible for it. After what Renard had told him, he had no faith in such weapons to protect his family from the enemies that hunted them. All the same, he gave a nervous nod of acceptance; all he could do was uphold some pretence of normalcy until he had an opportunity to present the truth.

However, Arnold's definition of 'normalcy' was not one he would apply to the elderly gentleman now striding towards them, whose peacockish clothing would have looked more at home on one of the previous century's aristocrats. From the beaming smile upon his face, he was evidently pleased to see the Musgrave siblings here. As he drew close he grasped Nathaniel's hand in an eager handshake, greeting him warmly. This must surely be Mr Tom Ashford.

"And you must be the charming Miss Imogen," he said to their younger sister, taking her offered hand and planting a kiss upon it. "Your brother has spoken most fondly of you, my dear. It is a pleasure to finally make your introduction."

"He has told me many kind things about yourself, Sir,"

she replied. "By his account you are a most worldly gentle-man of great wit and jest."

"The boy flatters me with such praise, though I do con-fess to being an old joker. As for worldly… well, maybe I shall share a few stories later this evening, but I leave it to your good judgement as to which among them are true."

Finally, Ashford looked towards the clergyman in the group. Compared to his far more cultured and refined half-siblings, Arnold could only imagine that he must look rather drab, and perhaps something of a disappointment. If that were the case, however, the elderly manager was making no sign of it.

"Arnold, I assume? It's a pleasure to finally meet you as well. You just happen to be the entire reason why Nathaniel received my special invitation to attend tonight. Well, per-haps not the *entire* reason, but certainly a major factor. I'm told that you have in your possession some most curious papers which you should like me to read for you."

"Yes, a number of letters written in French. I have them here with me. It's rather important that I learn of their contents."

"Of course, of course. When Nathaniel related to me your situation, I told him that I'd be more than happy to assist. From what he's told me, it all sounds rather fun and mysterious."

Increasingly Arnold was beginning to regret this course of action. Thomas had an air of kindliness about him, but if he considered this affair to be 'fun', then he was woefully innocent of the danger that it involved. Arnold was doubt-ful of the wisdom of bringing another poor bystander into the line of fire, but the only other translator that he knew of was Michel Renard. Nothing in the last twenty-four hours had made him any more inclined to entrust Renard with something which could potentially cast a shade upon the Musgraves, or on Arnold himself.

"Mysterious, certainly. Given that it is a matter between myself and my brother, however, I shall appreciate your discretion, Mister Ashford."

"Oh, do call me Tom, dear boy. And naturally, you can count on my confidence as a gentleman in this and all other matters. Your brother will attest to my ability to keep a secret or two. But all of this must wait until after the evening's performance, yes? *Twelfth Night* may have been written as a Christmastide play, but we're awfully fortunate to be hosting a production of it here this evening. Our seats await, so do come follow me."

Imogen had stayed quiet while Arnold and Tom spoke briefly on the topic of the letters, but a certain degree of curiosity was evident as she accompanied the men upstairs to their box. Either Nathaniel had made no mention to her of those documents, or he had only told her very little. If Arnold had known that Nathaniel intended to bring her along to this gathering, he would have insisted in the utmost terms that she be left out of it. His half-sister was a refined young lady of society, after all. He did not wish to draw her interest towards the horrible business of the Devil's creatures, or reveal the fact that her father had known of such things and kept the truth concealed from his family.

In all likelihood, she would consider it nothing more than wild fancy and think that Arnold's mind was addled by superstition. A worse outcome would be that she took an active interest and developed a morbid fascination for the subject. To learn that it was actual truth would undoubtedly rob her of her innocence, and it would be wildly unfair to expect a mere girl of her age to handle such revelations. Even with all that Arnold had witnessed, however, it was far from certain that his testimony would persuade Nathaniel to accept it as real, let alone Imogen.

On stage the play got underway, presenting William Shakespeare's story of the shipwrecked young woman, Viola, who took advantage of her resemblance to her twin brother Sebastian in order to disguise herself as a man and survive in the foreign land where she was stranded. Along the way she fell in love with the melancholy Duke Orsino, and unintentionally drew the affections of the grieving Countess Olivia. Nathaniel, Imogen and Tom watched the play with great enjoyment, laughing along with its comedic absurdities, its joking portrayal of mistaken identity and unrequited love, the confusion of the sexes and the cruel pranks of Olivia's uncle, Sir Toby Belch.

Arnold, by contrast, was far too distracted to pay it any great attention; he was not fond of stage performance at the best of times, and on this occasion the events of the play seemed of far less importance than the other matters weighing upon his mind. He kept polite silence throughout, gave his barest contribution to the applause at the end, and was rather gladdened when the final curtain fell.

The audience on the ground floor began to depart, but Tom seemed to be in no hurry to leave the box. When the call-boy came up to ask if the manager would be joining the rest of the staff backstage, Tom informed him that he would be busy entertaining friends for a while, but he would appreciate the lad bringing up a bottle of Syrah and some goblets. The wine arrived in short order, and Tom poured a drink for each of his guests, despite Arnold's attempts to decline. Along with the bottle was a small ceramic pot and a spoon, and after the old man removed the lid, he helped himself to a mouthful of the sweet, amber-coloured syrup within.

"Royal jelly," Tom mused with a sly grin. "One of my many vices. Sometimes I simply cannot get through a day without it. Do have some for yourselves."

The Musgrave siblings both laughed genially, and Arnold

had to remind himself that they could afford to be light-hearted because their thoughts were not plagued by the things that he knew. They felt safe here, and this was possibly the first occasion on which they had gone out and allowed themselves some simple happiness since their father's murder. As was expected of a society lady, Imogen had been in a state of mourning for the past month, and the pretty lilac dress that she wore tonight would be her first outfit in weeks that was not black.

Despite the unseen danger that loomed over them, Arnold considered the idea of not actually telling his half-siblings about the threat of vampires and House Laskaris. Maybe he should just let Tom read the letters and let the others think that it was all fairy-tales. It was a firm part of his faith that a stark truth was better than blissful ignorance, but in this moment it seemed almost cruel that he should snatch happiness away from Nathaniel and Imogen when they so clearly needed it. While the others talked and joked, Arnold's hand found the buckle of his satchel, opened it, and reached inside to bring out the fold of pages.

"Ah, I see your brother wishes to get down to business," Tom remarked to the others, upon seeing the papers. "Sombre lad, aren't you, Arnold? A priest doesn't have to be so dour, you know."

"I am just a curate," he replied, and in spite of everything, he could imagine some momentary glimmer of humour in his voice. Ashford's indomitable sense of cheer was perhaps a little contagious; "But with all respect, I very much want to know what these letters have to say. I shall greatly appreciate you reading them for me, though I'm not sure if their contents would be… wholly proper for an unmarried young lady to hear."

Imogen arched one eyebrow. If she had been interested in Arnold's discussion with Nathaniel earlier, she was doubly so now.

"Why on Earth should they be improper?" she enquired.

"Well, well," Thomas laughed, and began to pour some tobacco into his smoking-pipe, "I'd like to say this is the first time that a man of God has invited me to partake of something a little risqué, but that would of course be a lie."

"Not so much risqué, as macabre, morbid," Arnold clarified, though he sensed this did nothing to dissuade Imogen's curiosity. A hint of a mischievous smile tugged at the corner of the girl's mouth.

"Whatever is in them, I'm quite certain that my delicate ears can bear to hear it," she told him. "Has my brother not told you of my fondness for literature? If I can endure the depravities of the Greek and Roman myths, or some of the scandalous language of the Song of Songs, then I'm quite certain I can endure this."

"I… I simply feel that for the sake of civility, there may be things in those letters which may not be suitable for your company."

Imogen looked at him exactly the way that he expected her to. Just as he predicted, his behaviour was slipping into that of the overbearing moral guardian. It would have been a little less embarrassing if she did not appear so amused by it.

"Well I'm not going to leave you men alone to your discussion," she made clear. "I came here tonight with my brother and I have no other chaperone. Since it shall be *improper* for me to leave his side, if this conversation involves the three of you, then it must also oblige me to stay. Would you have me cover my ears?"

"Come on old chap, I think you're worrying a little too much about this," Nathaniel added. "Let's hear what they have to say, Tom."

Feeling just a little abashed, Arnold handed the bundle of papers over. Ashford took them with relish, before retrieving a pair of spectacles from his pocket and perusing the first of the letters. He had barely glanced over each of the pages when he saw the signature at the end, and his elderly eyes lit up with unexpected delight.

"My word... *Mademoiselle Maupin*. Now there's a name I haven't heard in many a year."

"The name is familiar to you?" Arnold ventured, concerned about what the implications may be. Renard's words of warning were ever upon his thoughts, and he could only speculate at how far this demon's web may spread.

"Familiar? My dear boy, did Nathaniel not tell you of my time in Paris when I was young? I went to work for the Paris Opéra when I was sixteen years old. That was back in 1699, and I was overjoyed to be a mere stage-rat. But Mademoiselle Maupin... Julie d'Aubigny, she was the Diva, the title act! She was an angel of the stage, beloved by many and hated by more than a few. What a life she led."

"I see. I did not know that she was a singer."

"Oh, that and so much more. Singer, dancer, artiste and adventurer, she was a fighter and a lover, of men and women alike. Her many romantic entanglements were the stuff of quite salacious gossip. But before she found fame at the Opéra, she made her living with demonstrations of swordplay. She was a devil with a rapier, I tell you that. Never one to back down from a fight, she would happily cross swords with male opponents. Stories say that ten men died upon her blade, in duels of honour. She would always dress in men's clothing when she gave performances, and her skill was such that she was often accused by her audience of being a man. More than once, she opened her shirt and bared her breasts to prove them wrong."

Arnold was beginning to see why Renard had called this woman 'Semjâzâ's own whore'. God had ordained that the role of woman was submissive to that of man, but she did more than simply disregard that mandate, she openly defied it, and embraced a life of sin. Arnold wondered if she was already a vampire during the time that Tom had known her, but if that were the case, she would surely have to be very adept at concealing her nature. Perhaps she had simply been this wantonly immoral even in her human life. Nathaniel was listening to this story with an amused smile, while Imogen was giving Tom's words her full attention.

"Tell me what salacious gossip had to say of her," Imogen asked, prompting Arnold to once again wish that his half-sister had not been brought here.

"I don't think that's the subject to discuss—" he began, but Ashford simply continued unabated.

"Oh, she cultivated no end of paramours," he explained. "She once told me personally of a brash young man who made a rather crude remark to her during one of her fencing displays. She challenged him to a duel there and then, and when two of his friends stepped up with swords drawn, she engaged all three of them, and ran her blade through the brash young man's shoulder. It later became apparent that the boy's name was Louis-Joseph, and he was the son of the Duke de Luynes. He sent her a note of apology for his remark, and she responded by visiting him in his recovery bed. They became lovers for a while, and at the time she told me this tale, she claimed that they were still firm friends."

"That all sounds rather exciting," Imogen remarked, now making no effort at all to conceal her enthusiasm for the topic.

"That was but one romance among many. Long before I met her, she had an affair with a pretty young merchant's daughter by the name of Cécilia, if my memory serves. Cécilia's family did not want the scandal of their daughter having a woman for a lover, so they packed her off to a convent to live as a nun. Julie was quite undeterred by this, and took Holy Orders herself in order to dwell at the convent and maintain their affair under the very noses of the Sisters. I recall one evening, after a truly dazzling performance of *Omphale* and a sinful amount of absinthe, she told me how during her time with Cécilia one of the elderly nuns died, and in this the two lovers saw their chance to escape.

"Julie took the body of the deceased Sister from its resting place, laid it in Cécilia's bed, and then departed with her lover and set the convent on fire! Afterwards, the burned body was presumed to be that of Cécilia, and Julie's absence was simply put down to her growing bored with the life of a nun and fleeing. The deception did not last too long, of course. Julie was later found, arrested, convicted of seducing Cécilia through witchcraft – among her many other crimes – and sentenced to be burned. She would have met her end then, had she not written to her old lover the Count of Armagnac and persuaded him to intervene and secure her a pardon."

Arnold listened to the tale with silent revulsion. Was there any blasphemy on God's own Earth that this harlot had not at some point committed? Even Nathaniel bore a mildly uncomfortable expression at the tale his friend had just related. Imogen, by contrast, had drawn a lace handkerchief, and was holding it to her mouth in an effort to conceal her grin. She evidently found considerable hilarity in this story. If Arnold thought that Sybil Musgrave would ever take the time to listen to him, he would have had stern words with her about the poor state of her daughter's morality.

"This awful woman sounds like the Devil made flesh," he finally proclaimed. "How can anyone of conscience do such vile things?"

"My dear boy, if you heard her sing you should swear that her voice was that of an angel from Heaven," Tom told him bluntly. "And believe me when I say that there was kindness in her. She had a mighty sense of justice too, wherever she saw the strong seeking to prey upon the weak. She would defend any actress or singer at the Opéra who was being troubled by the advances of an unwanted suitor. Men who sought to take advantage of vulnerable young women would suffer her wrath. Julie's precipitous heeding of her own passions often put her at odds with people of power and entitlement, but in the years that I knew her, I never once considered her to be an ill-hearted woman."

"Please, Tom," Nathaniel intervened. "Perhaps we could get back to the contents of the letter? I too shall like to know what she was writing about."

"Very well," the old man replied, and looked back towards the document in his hands. As he read, he began to mouth the words quietly, translating them into English.

"My dearest Hans,

Please forgive the lengthy duration since my last correspondence to you, though such is only to be expected given the remoteness of my current location. By way of an apology I have included with this missive a considerable number of samples, taken from the dangerous new forms that I have encountered here. I presently write to you from a Jesuit Mission on the Yucatán peninsula of New Spain, where I am recovering from wounds sustained in my most recent hunt. How vast this continent is; I feel I must have travelled twice the length of Europe to get here from where I first arrived in Newfoundland, if not more. What I write to you now is of the utmost importance, for I believe that I have uncovered a deep and terrible truth about our enemy."

Tom looked up from the page, a somewhat bemused expression upon his face. "Are you quite certain as to the providence of this letter? I am quite certain that Mademoiselle Maupin never once visited the New World. I know that when he married, Sir Hans acquired ownership of a plantation on one of the Caribbean colonies… Jamaica or Barbados, I don't recall which. But even if he and Julie had secret correspondence with one another, he could never have facilitated her travel there."

"What makes you so certain of this?" Arnold asked.

"Because Julie lived in Paris from the time I first met her right up until her death in 1707. I can say quite safely that during those years she did not find time for long excursions to alien climes."

"Her death in 1707?"

"Yes," Tom sighed, a deep sadness creeping into his voice, and very much reflected in his eyes. "For all her many affairs, it was towards the end of her life that she truly fell in love. She lost her heart to the Lady Marie de Senneterre, the Marquis de Florensac, the most beautiful woman in all of France. The pair of them shared such happiness together, and they kept their love remarkably discreet, but it was short-lived. Marie died of a sudden fever in 1705, and Julie was devastated. She departed from the stage and, for the second time in her life, retired to a convent. On that occasion her reasons were genuine, and she stayed there for two years until the announcement of her death. The Sisters never gave any word of what it was that killed her. If it is truly possible to die of a broken heart, then I believe that she did."

Wheels turned in Arnold's mind. Things were beginning to make more sense. Julie d'Aubigny had been a mortal woman throughout the time that Tom recalled, but if Arnold were a betting man, he would wager highly that the fever which took her lover Marie was no simple disease.

"Please, if you could continue?"

Ashford read the remainder of the letter, though he now did so in silence. He gave a sad little smile when he reached the end, seemingly appreciative – on some personal level – of what it said.

"An interesting work of fiction, to be sure," he told his three guests. "I could certainly imagine Sir Hans devising something like this in private, for his own enjoyment. This seems to be her report of a hunt for a creature called a 'camazotz', in the jungles of the Central Americas. She claims to have encountered the beast when it was preying upon a Jesuit missionary. The creature is described as some kind of demonic blood-drinking bat, of great size and terrible ferocity. Apparently it wounded her grievously in the fight, but she slew it with a dagger made of orichalcum, and afterwards the Jesuit Brothers nursed her back to health.

"The letter goes on to tell of her travels to a heathen village and her conversation with a Brujá – that is to say, a witch – who told her that the camazotz are the children of 'Nine Lords'. Supposedly these Nine Lords are at fault for unleashing a plague of vampirism upon the world, and the letter ends with Julie resolving to hunt them down and bring about their destruction. All rather fantastical, but I'm certain that if Julie herself read this tale, she should find it most amusing."

So what does this all mean? Arnold found himself wondering. The letter indicated that Julie was hunting vampires in partnership with Sir Hans, and that her pursuit of the undead took her as far as the New World. When it spoke of her 'considerable number of samples', taken from 'dangerous new forms', that must surely be referring to the teeth, especially the pair which bore the label, 'camazotz'. Those fangs could have been torn from the very creature which this document claimed she fought and killed.

What if the Nine Lords that she spoke of really were the progenitors of their kind? Could they be the foul ancients which – as Father Renard suggested – had survived the Great Flood? Perhaps she had thought to destroy them, but in the end she had been found wanting. Perhaps it was one of these very Lords who infected her, made her into a monster like them. Or perhaps at the time she sent this letter, she had already been turned, and this was just some twisted game, toying with Sir Hans for her pleasure?

"Orichalcum," Imogen remarked. "I recognise that word. It's a metal, I believe. An extremely valuable metal that was commonplace in legendary Atlantis, according to Plato."

"Very astute of you, Miss," said Tom with an affectionate smile.

"But orichalcum is entirely mythical, is it not?" she continued. "Just like the lost Atlantis, and camazotz, and vampires."

"There are more things in Heaven and Earth, Horatio, than are dreamt of in your philosophy," Tom replied with a laugh, quoting Hamlet.

And you are more correct in that than you dare realise, Arnold thought to himself. He would have so many answers, if only he could bring himself to trust what the letter said. He would have to find Renard, and ask him about orichalcum and its supposed effectiveness as a weapon against the undead. He would have to ask him if he knew anything about Nine Lords who ruled over the vampires.

As potentially useful as all this information was, however, none of it thus far pertained to House Laskaris, or indicated what had drawn their interest to Sir Hans. Renard had said that Julie was an enemy to them. Perhaps they had discovered her partnership with Sir Hans, and wished to know more about it?

"Thank you very much, Tom," Arnold said at last. "There are more letters. Would you be good enough to read the rest of them?"

Despite their earlier difference of opinion regarding Mademoiselle Maupin, Ashford did as asked and went through each of the letters in turn. It seemed that the one he had read first was in fact the last one chronologically, and the others told a story in reverse of how the distraught Julie d'Aubigny had suspected foul play in the death of her beloved Marie, and had reached out to various scholars and occultists in search of answers during her two years in the convent.

Sir Hans Sloane had been the only one to take her request for information seriously, and he had replied to her asking for more details about how Marie had died, stating his suspicion that she had been fed upon by a vampire. With Sir Hans' guidance Julie had learned all that she could about the undead, training and arming herself for the purpose of hunting them. She had sought out and killed a vampire in Paris – a strigoi – but she remained unsure if it was the same one who murdered her lover.

Sir Hans had agreed to finance her new lifestyle if she provided him with material samples of the creatures that she destroyed. And so she had faked her death, convincing the Sisters at the convent to let the world think she had passed, so that she could take on a new identity, travel in secret and wage war upon the vampiric threat. By the time he was finished reading it all, Thomas Ashford looked exhausted.

"I sincerely thank you for coming here this evening, my friends," he told them. "This has all been rather a stirring experience. But this fantasy in letters has brought back keen memories of a remarkable woman whom I should rather allow to rest in peace, so if you will all excuse me, for this evening I shall bid you *adieu*."

After the warmth of the theatre, and the hours spent amid the pervasive odour of red wine and Tom's tobacco smoke, Arnold found the cold night air of London to be pleasantly bracing. They had not long stepped out onto the street, however, when Nathaniel made his displeasure known.

"You were unnecessarily rude to him in there, Arnold. Tom is a very good friend, and he was a good friend to Father for many years. His story about that woman's life may have offended your moral sensibilities, but you could have been far more gracious about it."

"My *sensibilities*?" Arnold protested. "Brother, have you no sense of propriety? He should not have been saying such things in front of our sister!"

"Oh, for certain I am simply far too innocent and fragile to hear such talk!" Imogen declared, her expression a scowl of disdain. "We may share a father, but you barely know me, Mister Brennan. In two months' time I shall be sixteen, a grown woman, and Mother has made it quite clear that she intends to find me a husband shortly thereafter. Marriage will confer duties upon me, not least of which is the bearing of children. Given how your own life began, do you think I should be incapable of conversing about the unpleasantries of adulthood?"

"Marriage and childbirth are a woman's duties, which you should be honoured to accept, Sister. We all must face unpleasant challenges in life, but what Mister Ashford was speaking of in there was a descent into decadence and fornication! It should have been better for us all if your thoughts were never tainted with knowledge of such things."

"Why, you sanctimonious—"

"Please, let us all be calm," Nathaniel demanded, his tone making it clear that he would brook no dissent. "Imogen, as a clergyman it is Arnold's job to worry about the sanctity of your soul. Even I have to concede that some of what Tom said in there went a little too far for polite company. But likewise, Arnold, it was *just* a conversation. Knowing that this Julie d'Aubigny lived a scandalous life does not compel anyone here to follow her example."

It is all real, Arnold wanted to tell them. How desperately he wished to reveal to them that Julie d'Aubigny still walked the Earth as a bloodsucking demon, and that she was here, now, in London. He wanted to tell them that a legion of vampires lurked in the night, and that the Musgrave family had become a target for the foul undead. But he knew with all his heart that he had no evidence with which to convince them. He could swear by God and all that was Holy that his testimony was true, and they would simply think he had gone mad. Belief in monsters may still hold sway in the backwaters of the world, but not here in civilised London.

"I… I do apologise," he conceded. "I do not mean to give offence. Perhaps I have been a little overzealous, but a lot has been weighing on my mind of late. It is my mandate to confront evil, and… with certain recent events, I have been seeing a great deal more of it in this city."

"Thank you, Arnold," Nathaniel told him, and then looked towards his sister.

"I accept your apology," she said after a moment's hesitation. "And I was rather impolite myself, for which I am sorry. I'm sure that the burdens of a man of God must weigh heavily."

Perhaps she was being just a little facetious, but Arnold chose to take her words at face value. They were not waiting long before a Hackney carriage came clattering by, and Nathaniel hailed it down. He instructed the driver to take them to the Musgrave family home on the west end of Thames Street, and held the door for Imogen as she climbed aboard.

"Would you care to ride with us?" Nathaniel asked. "St Mary's is not far out of the way."

"I thank you for the offer, but I shall be quite fine walking."

"Very well, Brother, then I shall bid you a good night."

Nathaniel began to step up into the carriage, and had

one foot inside when he stopped for a moment, peering over his shoulder towards something which had just caught his notice.

"I say, is that not Marcus Whitfield over there?"

Arnold's blood ran cold. He followed his half-brother's gaze to the far side of the street, where a bespectacled man stood, watching; he was a good deal younger than the late Kenneth Whitfield, but the familial resemblance was undeniable. Not far behind him was the swarthy young Turkish woman whom Arnold recognised instantly, for last time he had seen her, she had transformed into the dreadful visage of a strigoi. He looked towards their feet, and although the light about them was meagre, he saw that neither of them cast a shadow. Nathaniel tipped his hat to the lawyer, and Marcus returned the gesture. Arnold deeply desired to get his two half-siblings away from here.

"It has been good to see you tonight, Brother. Have a safe journey home."

"But wait, I–"

"You should go home," he looked up towards the carriage driver. "Go, *now*."

The driver spurred on the horse and the carriage began to rattle forward, forcing Nathaniel to clamber into his seat and pull the door closed behind him. There was a look of confusion upon his face, and Arnold could only imagine that he did not take kindly to being dismissed in such a fashion, but he had more important concerns right now than any insult that Nathaniel might be feeling.

The clergyman turned his gaze upon the two vampires, seeing them shrink away into the alley from which they had emerged. He made no hesitation in moving after them, pausing only to untie the crucifix from around his neck and hold it firmly in his right hand. As he stepped off the main street and into the alleyway, his left hand reached into the satchel he carried and took hold of the loaded pistol. Faith was his sword and shield, but even if the flintlock were an inferior weapon, it could not hurt to have it.

Up ahead, he saw the two strigoi move. They leaped to the walls of the alley and clung to them, scuttling towards him like a pair of enormous predatory insects. Arnold hefted the pistol in the direction of Whitfield and raised his cross at the girl. Neither of them slowed in their advance, though they now bared their fangs as they came at him.

"In the name of the Lord Jesus Christ, I repel you," he began, and he was pleased to see that his proclamation did give them pause. "In the name of God the Father, and of the Son, and of the Holy Spirit, I command you begone from this place!"

The vampires shrank back, the bloodthirsty aggression on their faces now mixed with hateful fear. They dropped from the walls, twisting through the air to land on their feet. Their fingers curled into talons, but they dared not advance further as Arnold's admonitions clawed at their ears.

"I call upon you to leave here, I ask of this in the name of the Lord Emmanuel! And when He called unto Him His twelve disciples, He gave them power against unclean spirits to cast them out! And these twelve Jesus sent forth and commanded them, heal the sick, cleanse the lepers, raise the dead, cast out Devils!"

Whitfield and the girl both cried aloud as if stricken, the sound of the prayer causing them physical pain. Arnold could feel his zeal returning, the righteous fury burning in his muscles once more. This time, he knew what he was facing. This time, it would be his enemy on the run, for God was truly with him.

"You have one chance to save her!" Whitfield spat, and Arnold's eyes narrowed.

"I will not countenance your lies or your games, demon."

"I'm speaking of your mother, you bird-witted bastard," the undead lawyer snarled, and Arnold halted in his step.

"You know what I'm talking about," Whitfield continued. "You should have summoned up the courage to go to her, instead of hiding in your damned church. Our Master is with her right now, and if we don't return with what he sent us for, he will complete her metamorphosis tonight. She will become one of us, and you will be the first blood-sack that he sends her to kill."

Arnold faltered, his resolve wavering. He should not negotiate with the demon, he knew that much. The Devil's creatures could never be trusted or bargained with, for was Satan not the Father of Lies? And yet, Whitfield's assertion was not wrong. If Arnold had found his courage earlier, he would not have left Lisa alone in her room. His greatest hope in all of this was that his mother's humanity, her very soul, could still be saved. He could still feel the thrumming in his muscles, the power and the desire to smite these demons, but if he did so, he would lose her forever.

"What is it you want?" he finally asked.

"You know full well. The Master wants the chest that my father gave to you, and all of its contents. Everything that Hans Sloane left behind."

"That is all?"

"Yes, that is all!"

Don't do this, the voice of his conscience told him, *Don't make a deal with the Devil*. But he had the chance to accomplish here what he had wanted to do all his life, and bring salvation to Lisa Brennan. He could not simply abandon his mother to the whims of an undead monster.

"It's being kept at St Mary's church," he told Whitfield.

"You think we do not know that? You need to move it out of the building."

"Bring my mother there, alive, and I will hand it over."

"Not a chance, *Curate*. You will give the chest to us, and we will escort you back to the Queen Anne. Once our Master has what he wants, he'll be on his way and will leave your mother alone. Those are his only terms."

Arnold gritted his teeth, disgusted at the situation he was offered. The two vampires had inched closer as Whitfield spoke, and Arnold brandished the crucifix at them, causing them to recoil once more. So long as his faith in God remained, they could not hurt him. That meant that he could do this. All that was in the chest was just documents and teeth after all, far less important than a human soul; he could hand it to them, go with them to his mother, and as soon as he got there, he would turn upon these demons and banish them all in the name of the Lord. To take any other course would only ensure that she became one of them, and he simply could not allow it.

"*Fine*. I accept those terms."

Whitfield's fanged grimace gave way to a smile, one that was doubtless intended to convey assurance that he would uphold his end of the bargain, but the hellish redness in his eyes turned it into a horrible, leering expression. The girl had remained silent throughout, but the animal aggression in her posture abated just a little, now that a deal had been made. Claws and fangs withdrew, and bloody eyes returned to more human appearance. Had Arnold not already known what these two were, nothing in their looks would have suggested their inhumanity.

"You lead the way," he told them, unwilling to lower his crucifix, and certainly unwilling to turn his back on them, even for an instant. Whitfield gave a mocking bow, making it clear that he felt no such fear towards Arnold. The vampires turned away from him, at which point they and Arnold realised that they were no longer alone in this alley.

A pistol barked in the darkness, muzzle-flash lighting up

the surroundings as a bullet slammed into the face of the girl-vampire, catching her right between the eyes. Her head snapped backwards, blood and brains spattering from the back of her skull, and her body staggered back, yet incredibly did not fall. Arnold raised his own pistol, pointing it wildly, but his eyes widened as he caught sight of the familiar man who had just opened fire: Lawrence Clayton. If the Bow Street Runner did not know what he was dealing with, then the next few seconds could well be his last.

There was a second figure beside him, however, a woman dressed in a fine burgundy coat, her skin the darkest of any Negro that Arnold had ever seen. She too had a pistol in hand, which she pointed towards the snarling form of Marcus Whitfield. Arnold threw himself to the ground as she squeezed the trigger, and he was glad that he did so, for what erupted from her weapon was not a single bullet, but an immense gout of white-hot fire, which engulfed the vampire in a blazing inferno.

The inhuman shriek of pain which tore from Whitfield's lips was a sound which Arnold had heard before, and his mind was filled with yesterday's awful vision of Michel Renard pounding a stake through a strigoi's heart. The burning vampire clawed at the brickwork, trying desperately to drag himself away up the wall, but his agonised muscles could not coordinate themselves, and Whitfield only made it a short way up before losing his grip and tumbling to the ground. Arnold scrambled backwards, flourishing his crucifix, but Whitfield was paying him no attention. In moments the vampire collapsed to the ground, writhing and thrashing, his body a charred mess of blackened bone and sinew, still tortuously clinging to life.

Despite the bullet which had punched through her head, the female vampire was only momentarily stunned. Her gleaming red eyes fixed upon Clayton and she charged for him, darting forward in a blur. Yet a third assailant now made himself known, a tall and powerful-looking male dressed in deep green finery, and every bit as dark of complexion as the pistol-wielding woman. Arnold saw the gleam of a curved sword sweep upwards in his hand, and in the narrow alleyway, the strigoi had little room to evade it.

The blade struck her across the midsection, slicing her belly and spilling stringy entrails, along with a torrent of stolen blood. Clayton dashed forward and grabbed one of the vampire's arms, pinning the limb against the wall with all his weight. The Negro woman did the same, trapping the second limb while the sword-wielding man raised his weapon in both hands, pointing its tip towards the strigoi's chest.

Despite her wounds, the vampire did not remain trapped for long. Her right arm threw off Clayton's grip, and with a show of horrific force she grabbed the burly man by the front of his jacket, lifting him off the ground and hurling him sideways, casting him and her other two attackers to the ground. Now free of their grip, her gaze flickered towards Arnold, and – apparently deciding that the situation was unfavourable – she began to flee. She made it most of the way down the alley before there came the click of another pistol being cocked, and the flash and report of its shot.

The African woman had fired again, seemingly just an ordinary bullet this time, which caught the vampire in the back of the leg and caused her to trip forward, knocking her off her feet. Clayton and the Negro man were both upright once more, sprinting after her, and as Arnold pulled himself back off the ground, he saw Clayton using both hands to drive a wooden stake into the wounded strigoi's back, while his companion brought the scimitar down in a lethal blow. The vampire's head rolled away from her stricken body.

For a time Arnold watched in stunned silence. Although victorious, Clayton was clearly not uninjured, for the detective's hands were grasping at his lower back, and he was breathing deeply, wincing in pain. His two companions seemed to be faring better, though Arnold wished he knew just who these people were. A boorish brute of a Bow Street Runner and two Negroes dressed like aristocrats had come out of nowhere and slain a pair of strigoi, and from the looks upon their faces, this bloody encounter was nought but a routine occurrence.

"Clayton," the curate found his voice, "and... whoever you two are. Who are you? What in God's name just happened?"

Now that the Negroes had come closer, Arnold could see them a little more clearly, and it struck him that they were wildly unlike anyone he had seen before. There were never many slaves in Whitechapel, for very few of the residents could afford to buy one. He had occasionally seen slaves on his rare visits to more affluent parts of London, such as when he took coffee at Lloyd's with Nathaniel, and he expected that the Musgrave household had at least one. But not even the most well-groomed slave that Arnold had seen, nor even the few free Negroes that he had ever met, looked anything like these two.

There was not a hint of ingrained submissiveness about this man and woman; no bowing of the head, nor behavioural deference instilled by the lash of a master's whip or the stigma of being a 'foreigner'. Their clothes were rich, and their hair quite short, but nonetheless elaborately braided. Their features were strong, fiercely beautiful, their dark eyes both sharp and unyielding. The pair looked strikingly similar, so much so that they must surely be brother and sister. Arnold glanced towards the scimitar in the man's hand, and he could not fail to notice its keen resemblance to the one which Julie d'Aubigny had carried.

"You are Arnold Brennan," the man spoke.

"You know who I am?" Arnold replied, then realised that of course they must, for if they were working with Clayton, he would have told them.

"Calm yourself, boy," the detective said, moving towards him with a noticeable limp. "We're hunting down these devils. These two know a lot about what's happening."

"No," Arnold replied, shaking his head. "No, you shouldn't have done this, not yet! I needed them. I needed to get them to stay away from my mother, their master is going to-"

"No, he is not," the Black woman spoke. "Their master was going to your mother tonight, but he will not succeed. Our ally was waiting to stop him. By now he is most certainly dead."

Our ally? Arnold looked once again at the man's sword. As far as he could tell, its design really was identical to Julie's. They had to be working with her. And if that were true, these people were anything but his allies.

"Your mother was very weak," the woman added. "You should go to her. We will deal with these remains."

She turned away from him, and Arnold realised that he was still clutching his cross and pistol. He had kept the crucifix raised throughout the whole encounter, but none of these people had flinched away from it. Whether they were serving Mademoiselle Maupin or not, it was clear that they were very much human, not thralls and certainly not vampires. But any further questions could wait until later. Arnold took off at a run towards the Queen Anne Stuart, hoping against all hope that his mother was still alive.

His mind was still racing by the time he arrived at the pub. The evening was in full swing, and the Queen Anne was packed with drinkers. Behind the bar, Robert Darby was rather surprised to see Arnold come crashing in at this hour, especially with such a panic-stricken look upon his face.

"Fuck me, Arnold, what the blazes has gotten into you–"

"I need to see her!" he replied, not pausing for a moment as he sprinted up the stairs to his mother's room. He flung the door open as he drew near, racing to her bedside, his foot kicking against a bowl of cold, uneaten stew which spilled across the floorboards. He looked upon Lisa Brennan; weak, pale and painfully thin upon her bed, and the bite of grief in the back of his throat brought tears to his eyes. Falling to his knees, he grabbed her frail hand and cried. Her fingertips, cold and blackened with necrosis, pressed against his cheek.

When he forced his eyes open, however, he saw something through the blur of pain that caught him by bitter and joyful surprise. His mother was smiling faintly; not the spiteful, predatory grin that he had seen on his last visit, but a tender smile of loving recognition. Her fading eyes looked at him with as much affection as he had ever seen in them.

"My son... my beautiful son."

He choked back another sob, gripping her hand tightly.

"I'm sorry, Mum," he gasped, trying to keep his voice level and failing utterly. "I'm so sorry. I've been trying to save you, I swear I have. I wish I'd been braver."

"You are brave," she breathed, her voice barely a whisper. "I'm proud of you, my boy."

The grief bit even deeper, and Arnold could not stop his tears. He soon stopped trying at all, instead simply clutching his mother's hand in both of his, staying by her side as her life ebbed. He continued to hold her, cried for her, prayed for her not with words, but with all the feeling in his heart. He did not know how many hours had elapsed when she breathed her last, but there came a time when he realised that she was gone, and the body which lay on the bed was an empty vessel.

He remained a while longer, whispered some final words to her and to God, and forced himself back to his feet. He would have to tell Robert that Lisa had passed. He would have to get back to St Mary's and start making arrangements for the funeral. He did not have the funds to buy her a grave, but he was sure that Reverend Lowther would make arrangements for one. Space could be found in the church yard. After tonight, he would not see his mother buried anonymously in a poor-man's-hole.

A prickling on the back of his neck told him that he was not alone. Arnold turned slowly, floorboards creaking beneath his shoes as he looked towards the door, and the lithe woman with a sword on her belt who stood in the room with him, watching him. Her clothes were slashed and bloodstained from battle, yet she bore no fresh wounds; only the livid pink scars of fading injuries. *Julie d'Aubigny.* His hand trembled, a surge of fury running through him. On reflex he grabbed his crucifix, thrusting it towards her.

"Get behind me, Satan!"

Her eyes flashed red and she took a step back, lips pursed, her hands clenching into fists.

"In the name of God, I banish you!"

"Lower that thing…"

"In the name of the Father, and of the Son, and of the Holy–"

"Lower it! I've been standing here all this time, if I wanted you dead I would already have killed you!"

"– of the Holy Spirit, I command you begone from this place!"

"I saved her!"

Arnold blinked.

"What?" he stammered.

"Did you not know? Eşref was going to make your mother into one of his Progeny *tonight*. I killed him. Then I came here to wait for my friends to return, and I decided to come up to this room. I saw how weak your mother was. Eşref took a *lot* of blood when he last fed from her, he barely left enough for her to survive. The infection has been keeping her alive for the past three nights, but her body was failing, and her mind was breaking for him. So I removed her memories of him. I let her think that she had just grown sick. I made it so that her last thoughts could be of love for her son, and not yearning for her master. Do you understand me?"

"You… you did *what*?"

"I altered her memories. I undid the damage that Eşref had done. I could not save her life, but I made it so that she could die in peace."

Arnold felt fresh tears run down his face. Julie's eyes looked human again, and he searched them for any hint of deception, but he could find none. This woman was a vampire, and she could never be trusted, but in this moment his instincts told him that she was not lying. Somehow, that made things worse. To be the recipient of a demon's kindness only added to his sense of defeat. He had not the slightest wish for her to be here, but she must have reasons for what she had done, and he was already forming questions of his own.

"Before I came here… Lawrence Clayton, those two Negroes, they killed two vampires. They are working for you?"

"The twins are my companions," she affirmed, "and Mister Clayton is new to my efforts, but he has proven to have his uses."

"Tell me what you want."

"You have some property of mine. Some letters."

"They were property of my late father."

"They were written to Sir Hans Sloane, by *me*. I do not care what claim anyone else feels they have upon them."

Fumbling for his satchel, Arnold managed to undo the buckle, and pulled out the bundle of papers with one hand. More than anything he just wanted her gone, wanted this to be over. If giving her the letters would make her go away and leave him to his grief, then so be it. He finally lowered the crucifix, offering her the documents. The vampire moved cautiously towards him, reached out, and took them from his hand.

"There should be more than this," she remarked, her eyes darting as she looked over them. "I sent him samples from my kills along with these. Teeth, mostly."

"I still have them."

"Where?"

"St Mary's church. It's the safest sanctuary I know."

"I'll need to see everything you have that belonged to Sir Hans."

"Why?"

"Because the House of Laskaris wants it, and that makes it dangerous, to you and everyone who comes into contact with it."

"If this 'Eşref' is dead, then is there still a threat?"

"Most definitely."

"Then I should not let the collection leave the church grounds. It's safest on consecrated earth."

"Then I will come and view it there. Setting foot in the church will weaken me, but that should not be a problem, since I have no hostile intentions towards you. I simply want to see what has become of my property."

Arnold breathed. A storm of conflicting thoughts and feelings raged in his head, and he could not find the right words to speak.

"I'll leave you for now," she told him. "Take tomorrow to grieve. Make arrangements for your mother. But on Saturday, my friends and I will come to St Mary's at sundown. With good fortune, that will be the last time we ever have to cross paths."

With nothing more for her to say, Arnold watched Julie turn and leave. For all the horrors of these recent weeks, for all the death and madness that had gathered about him, there might finally be a glimmer of dawn to end this darkness. After Saturday, this nightmare might finally be over. He would trust in God, and in his allies, to help him do what needed to be done.

~ Michel ~

Saturday October 16th, 1756

Father Renard steadied himself against the wall, his lungs burning like a fire with each ragged breath he took. Each fresh jolt of agony was another reminder of last night's failure. He had failed to anticipate an attack by House Laskaris. He had failed to accurately gauge the strength and determination of this enemy. He had failed to protect his men, and now they were all dead. He himself had only barely escaped with his life. His exhausted body trembled with pain and blood-loss, much to the consternation of the Brother-Surgeon kneeling beside him.

"Keep still," the man reminded him, as his fingers carefully applied needle and thread to Michel's wounds. The hunter took another deep breath, gritted his teeth, and steeled himself against the blistering protestations of his nerves. This would be the sixth laceration stitched; beyond that, another two awaited treatment. Those eight deep cuts were the result of just two glancing blows he had taken from a strigoi who got close enough to strike him. If he had been an inch nearer to the beast when those talons connected with his flesh, or an instant slower in his efforts to dodge, he would undoubtedly have been eviscerated. Just as his loyal Brothers had been.

The neglected house in which he now stood lay near High Holbourn, in the north-west quarter of the city. This small residence, with its faded décor, had once been owned by Don Diego Sarmiento de Acuña, the Count of Gondomar and Spain's ambassador to England more than one hundred years previous. In this decade, the deed belonged to a Spanish sympathiser to La Compagnie du Saint-Sacrement, and so the building served as an emergency safehouse for the Company's operatives in London. Michel had fled here in the early hours of the morning, limping and bleeding after his narrow escape from the attack on the Lambeth safehouse.

After cleaning his wounds with brandy and bandaging them as best he could, he went on to hastily pen and seal a letter, and then pay a far greater than usual sum of coin to a messenger, to have them go to the docks and await the arrival of a ship that morning called the *Cleopatra*. The messenger was to hand the letter to the first men to come off that ship, and say that it was for the important passenger. That passenger would then reimburse the messenger a further generous sum of coin. The letter, written in Latin, had told the passenger not to proceed to Lambeth or to await escort, but to instead come directly to High Holbourn.

Naturally, Michel would rather have been present at the dock with his men for the arrival of Brother Fabian Devereaux, the envoy of His Eminence the Bishop of Meaux. Instead he had to wait here, alone and wounded, for the envoy to arrive. When the knock at the door had finally come, he was grateful to see that Brother Fabian had made the journey here safely, along with his assistant, Brother Sardis, and his bodyguard, the towering monolith of a man called Brother Jacques. It turned out that Brother Fabian was a man ever mindful of danger – one might go so far as to suggest paranoid – to the point where he travelled with a personal physician whenever he left France. Brother Sardis filled that role, and he had immediately set about the task of suturing Michel's wounds.

For his part, Brother Jacques had not said a single word since his arrival, which made Renard wonder if the man was bound by a Holy vow of silence, or had perhaps had his tongue cut out. Neither would be unheard of within the Company, though it was quite possible that Jacques was just a quiet man by nature. Michel was of course grateful for the medical assistance, and his loyalty to the Company remained absolute. Long had he been willing to kill or die for his Brothers, but in this moment he was feeling a distinct lack of fraternal support from Brother Fabian.

"Your last report to His Eminence was met with enthusiasm," the envoy told him, his voice cold and reed-thin in its tone. "The bishop's own words were 'very promising'. Such was his interest, that he dispatched me directly to oversee the next steps in your mission. So please, do tell me why I find you in this state, with not one of your men standing by your side?"

Wincing as he felt the needle stab into his side once more, Michel looked his Brother up and down. Fabian was a tall and lanky fellow, his features aquiline, his eyes as deep brown as Renard's were piercing blue. Slender of build, he certainly did not have a warrior's physique, and Michel could not imagine that this man had ever hunted many vampires, or drawn his sword against the forces of Semjâzâ. That was not the role of every acolyte of the Company, of course; the organisation had need of scholars, spies, diplomats and administrators as well as hunters, and doubtless if Brother Fabian ever found himself in a combative situation, Brother Jacques would be on hand to deal with it.

"I underestimated how quickly House Laskaris would deduce our presence in this city," Michel began. "I thought that God had granted us good fortune, when the Company's contacts in this city were quick to inform us of cases of vampiric infection in the Whitechapel district. I praised our spies for their vigilance. But now I wonder whether House Laskaris had deliberately cast its net wide, infecting more people than they normally would, in order to draw our attention and lead us into a trap. I think they made some of their thralls and activities obvious to us, so that more subtle eyes could keep watch, identify our agents and follow us."

Brother Sardis finished his work, placing the final stitches on Michel's left side and tying off the thread. Renard winced again as he felt the sutures pull tight, but when Sardis offered him the bottle of brandy, he gratefully accepted and took a swig. The fiery liquid coursed down his throat, bringing a blissful numbness in its wake.

"They attacked our safehouse in Lambeth last night. They came in numbers, I cannot be sure of exactly how many, but I think there were at least eight. They did not try to invade the building. Instead they set fire to it in order to force us out. They were led by a very powerful strigoi, one of the strongest I've ever seen. It exhibited a degree of power over the elements, which few vampires wield. It showed very little fear of the Holy cross, and I watched it rip three of my men to pieces like they were made of rags. It was a Master, I am certain of it."

"Do go on," Fabian urged him.

"As I tried to repel their leader, one of the lessers approached my blind side and wounded me. I ran my sword through its heart, but even as it fell, our situation had become hopeless. The surviving Brothers rallied to me and told me that they would fight to the last, to cover my retreat. I blessed them as they made their final stand. There were enough strigoi that they could have overwhelmed my men and still pursued me, but when I fled into the burning stables, their fear of the flames stayed them. I was able to mount a horse and break through their lines to make my escape."

In truth, his men's final stand had been over in moments, and his blessing had felt distinctly empty. Their bravery succeeded in drawing the vampires' attention, but the beasts were simply too numerous, and their Master's will suffused them, making them heedless of their own survival. Fearing neither cross nor sword, the strigoi came at them from all sides and tore them apart.

Michel could still hear their cries as he gave voice to the events. The only mercy was that in such a brutal death they were spared all risk of infection, and their souls would now be at peace in the hereafter. Fabian appeared to consider Michel's words. Given his long record of service to God and the Company, Renard did not appreciate the feeling of being interrogated by his own order.

"Their numbers were great enough that they could have easily surrounded the stable, yet you were able to break through them?"

"They had spread out to encircle the area when I charged them. In numbers they could have overrun me, but I rode straight and only one of them blocked my path. I trampled it beneath my horse... would that I could have stopped to remove its head."

"And the Master who led them; she did not pursue you, despite her greater resistance to your faith?"

Michel paused, eyes narrowing in suspicion; "No, she did not. But, Brother, when did I say that it was female? I never saw their leader's human guise. The hour was late when they struck, the night was dark, and the city's smog was very thick. Once they took us by surprise, they felt no need to hide their nature. By the time we became aware of the attack, the demons all wore their true forms."

Fabian eased himself into a chair, his long limbs folding as he sat down. His eyes were coldly appraising as he looked at Michel over steepled fingers, and it was clear that he had something he wished to say, but had not yet decided if his Brother could be trusted with the information. Either that, or he was simply drawing out the moment to please his own sense of ego. If that were the case, Michel's next letter to the bishop would make mention of Fabian's unbecoming pride.

"While you were sailing here from Istanbul, His Eminence received a different letter, from a Brother in Vienna," the envoy finally revealed. "The missive described the capture of a strigoi there, and its confession under torture of having arranged transportation to Hamburg for a powerful member of its kind. It claimed to have been working for Serena Laskaris."

Michel blinked in surprise.

"Serena the Byzantine?"

"Yes," Fabian confirmed. "In light of the more recent information that you have provided, we do not believe that Hamburg was her intended destination at all. His Eminence suspects that with House Laskaris gathering here in London, she may have come to take charge of their efforts directly."

Renard fell silent as he processed Fabian's words. In the hidden libraries of the Company of the Holy Sacrament, there were texts which spoke of a vampire by that name dating as far back as eleventh-century Byzantium. What was known about her for certain was limited, but she was believed to be among the most powerful of the strigoi Masters who ruled over that coven.

Normally ensconced within their own territory, protected by layers of secrecy as well as cohorts of living and undead servants, those Masters were all but impossible to hunt. Opportunities to eliminate such a vampire came few and far between.

"This obviously raises questions," Fabian continued. "Firstly, if Serena was the Master who led the attack upon you last night, then what is it that House Laskaris desires to achieve in this city, which is of such great importance to them? And secondly, if one of its oldest Masters is prepared to risk vulnerability to accomplish this goal, then why did she kill your men and burn your house, only to allow you to escape?"

So that's why this feels like an interrogation, Michel realised. Of course Fabian had to consider the possibility that Renard had become in some way corrupted, or was being used to serve the vampire's ends.

"I do not know her motives for letting me flee," he confessed. "In the fog, the strigoi might have pursued me along Lambeth Road, but I am certain that I was not followed north of the Thames. But I do have some understanding of what the Laskaris may be seeking in London. My report to His Eminence mentioned an Anglican curate, which I am sure you know of."

"Monsieur Brennan and his curious documents, indeed. Your letter said that he had already come under attack once, and yet survived. You indicated that you were quite willing to keep watch on him, and let him serve as bait for House Laskaris."

"To a degree, yes. I think it is the documents which are the bait, more than Monsieur Brennan himself. He told me that they originated from his father, and ultimately from Sir Hans Sloane. For that reason I believed that my primary target, La Maupin, would be seeking them."

"That is likely true," Fabian agreed, "though at this moment you are in no condition to be hunting her. The bishop was, however, most interested in these documents that you spoke of. Sir Hans was the only human that we know to have had regular contact with La Maupin in the years following her public death. His papers may contain vital insights of which we have been unaware. For that reason, as well as them being of interest to House Laskaris, I will be taking them into my custody. All the same, I find it hard to believe that Serena the Byzantine would come out of the shadows for the sake of some old papers, however illustrious their author."

"I have no doubt that a vampire of her great age has other schemes afoot, Brother, which remain hidden from us. I merely share what I do know. Monsieur Brennan believes me to be his ally. He may be a follower of the false church, but he is still a devout man, and I believe it heartened him to find committed crusaders against the undead. I told him that I would send for a scholar to examine his papers. I expect he'll be quite willing to let us view them."

"Am I to care for the consent of an ill-educated Protestant? I will examine those papers quite carefully myself, once I have possession of them. The cooperation of this Anglican heretic is of no concern. And given the state of your wounds, Brother, I am of a mind to order you to stay here and rest. You may accompany me when I move to acquire them, but only as a courtesy to your efforts thus far. If we meet any resistance, I will take whatever action I see fit."

As much as Michel wanted to protest, he bit his tongue and kept his silence. That 'ill-educated Protestant' had demonstrated his value when he warded off three strigoi by faith alone, and Fabian knew it. He knew, but did not appear to care, however, and within the hierarchy of the Company, Renard had no grounds to refuse an order from the bishop's envoy. He could only hope to voice his displeasure next time that the bishop deigned to grant him an audience.

"I will do as you ask," he relented. "I pray that our Lord grant me swift recovery, but it will take some time for me to heal these wounds. In the meantime, what is your plan?"

"Your testimony of the attack does confirm that a powerful Master strigoi is here in London," Fabian replied, dispassionately, "and that it may indeed be Serena Laskaris. The prospect of her destruction is enough to warrant the allocation of additional resources. I will send a missive to His Eminence with all haste, requesting in the strongest terms that he send additional men, weapons and funds. We will hold fast here until they arrive, and then we will scour this hideous city for the one who burned your safehouse and slaughtered our Brothers."

"And what of La Maupin? I know that she is also here."

Fabian reclined in his seat, once more peering at Michel with that unpleasant, clinical gaze that he would typically reserve for a captive under interrogation.

"Mademoiselle Maupin is an agent of the Adversary, and should she cross our path, we must destroy her as any other. These letters of Sir Hans Sloane may aid us in anticipating her movements. But beyond that, this Master strigoi must be the primary focus of our efforts. La Maupin is a lone, nomadic vampire; Serena Laskaris commands a coven of dozens, at least."

Michel shook his head and averted his eyes from the envoy, doing his best to contain his frustration. It was not his place to question the wisdom of his superiors, but sometimes he felt as though he alone, among all of his order, understood just what insidious a threat Julie d'Aubigny represented.

"La Maupin may have no coven that we know of, but her strength is considerable, as is her talent for manipulation. She exploits the best intentions of mortals, and transforms noble virtue into hedonism and vice. I will not underestimate her."

"And nor should you," Fabian told him. "But ask yourself, Brother, is your hunt for her motivated by righteous zeal, or by the fact that she has humiliated you in the past? Hatred for the enemies of God is a good and just thing, but be careful that your personal feelings do not occlude your judgement. As soldiers, we must obey the commands we are given, and my command to you is that until this Master vampire is found and slain, La Maupin is not your primary target. Do you understand me, Brother Michel?"

Defeated, for now, he lowered his head.

"I understand you, Brother Fabian, and I obey."

~ Julie ~

Sunset was almost upon the city, and in her room at the Devil's Tavern, Julie's companions had gathered. As promised, she had left Arnold Brennan to his own devices throughout Friday. Tonight was the night to uphold the second part of that promise, but while she had kept her own distance until now, she had not left him without observation. After all, she had not survived thirty-seven years as a vampire by being generous in her estimations towards men of faith. That was a mistake she had made once, and vowed not to repeat. Saul, Aida and Clayton had shared the task of keeping a discreet eye upon his movements, and Julie wanted to hear today's report.

"I told that Gypsy boy, Manfri, to keep watch on St Mary's this morning," Clayton informed her. "When I found him at lunchtime he said that Brennan had left the church once that morning, and he'd followed him south of the river, down onto Lambeth Road. He told me that Brennan got as far as some burned-down house by George's Fields, then made a quick-sharp turnabout and headed back home. I hadn't heard about any recent fire in that part of town, so I asked him which house. He said it looked very

244

recent, still smouldering in places, so it must have only caught fire last night."

"So we decided to investigate," Saul added. "A local constable was already in the area, but Mister Clayton quickly convinced him to let us take a look around the scene."

"What did you find in there?" Julie asked, though her list of expected answers was a short one. She had a feeling that there were only a few directions this conversation could take.

"Nine bodies, badly burned. Little more than skeletons, but many of their bones were snapped, or bore marks consistent with the claws of a strigoi. We also recovered a few items which had survived the blaze."

Saul looked towards his sister. Aida stepped forward, placing down a roll of cloth upon the bedside table, which she carefully unwrapped. Nestled inside were a soot-blackened silver crucifix, made in the French Catholic style, along with a slender Italian dagger of fine quality, and a carved hardwood stake engraved with a cross, badly charred but still recognisable.

"La Compagnie du Saint-Sacrement is here in London," Aida said, giving voice to what Julie was thinking. "We knew that they were likely to follow us from Constantinople."

"We knew that Renard would pick up our trail, sooner or later. But I should have torn the head off that damned strigoi that we questioned, rather than hand them a captive."

"Listen you're going to have to tell me who this Company is," Clayton interceded, "because I haven't got the first idea who this Renard or any of these people are."

"The Company of the Holy Sacrament is a sect of Catholic war-dogs," Saul told him. "Murderers for Holy Mother Church. They hunt vampires, and are quite effective at it, but as you might guess, they are no friends of ours."

"If Brennan knew them well enough to be visiting their

safehouse, then he probably intended to betray me to them," Julie remarked, her fingers drumming rhythmically upon the table as she fought to keep her anger in check. The redness briefly crept into her eyes, but she forced it to recede. "We should have arrived at St Mary's and found Renard's men waiting for us. But this also means that he likely has no idea who they truly are. As a Protestant, he's almost as much an enemy in their eyes as I am. And from what you've told me, it sounds like House Laskaris may have gotten to them first."

"It is possible that Renard was one of those bodies," Aida ventured, "though we could find nothing to identify them."

"Maybe. But that bastard is a resilient one. He's cheated death plenty of times before. It shall not surprise me if he escaped."

"So what do we do about Brennan?" Clayton asked. "Is he a threat now?"

Julie looked intently at the detective. Despite his initial resistance to her, over the past several days there had been remarkably little cause for her to reinforce her influence upon his mind. Wilful though he was, Clayton was ultimately a creature of hierarchy, and he had quickly found his place within hers.

"We shall visit him now, as planned. Even if Brennan somehow got a message to Renard on Friday, the Company is not going to be able to mount an effective ambush if they've just lost nine men. Outside of France, they only ever operate in small cells."

"If Brennan turns on you, you will be weak on consecrated ground," Saul warned her.

"Then I shall be relying upon you to protect me. Let us make sure from the start that he has no opportunity."

In her night-to-night existence, Julie was quite happy to give the edifices of religion a wide berth. Aside from the two sorrowful years she had spent in the convent after Marie's death, she had never held much truck with faith in her mortal life, and now as a vampire it was largely anathema to her. Faith was the weapon of those who hunted her, and as such it felt rather strange for her to approach the white chapel of St Mary Matfelon with the intention of setting foot inside.

As she drew close to the front door she could already feel a prickling discomfort beneath her skin. The sight of it brought an unbidden clamour of formless whispers into the back of her mind, dredging up every half-forgotten memory of shame and regret, sapping her resolve. She took a deep, unnecessary breath, bracing herself for what lay ahead. Coming to a halt, she turned towards her two male companions.

"Circle the building", she told them, and Saul and Clayton set off in opposite directions, checking the exterior for any sign of hostile intent. Aida remained by her lover's side, one hand inside her coat, resting on the hilt of a pistol. As the two men were returning from their reconnoitre, the sound of an opening door drew Julie's attention. The noise came not from the church in front of her, but from the small rectory building adjacent to the main chapel.

Illuminated by the light of a solitary candle, Arnold Brennan stood in the doorway. The vampire began to approach, her three companions in tow, but she stopped a respectful distance from the entrance. With one hand Arnold held the candlestick, and she could see that the other was clutching his crucifix.

"Are you alone?" she enquired.

"The Reverend is not here. I persuaded one of the parishioners to invite him to dine with them this evening. He will not return for a few hours. I thought it best that he not become involved in this."

"A wise choice. May I come inside?"

Arnold did not answer. Clearly the young curate was not at ease with the notion of inviting a demon into the house of God, even if it was just into the rectory. Whatever his internal conflicts, however, Aida was not prepared to wait for him to resolve them. She drew one of her duelling pistols and cocked it with a loud click, stepping close to Arnold and pointing it at his chest. That was enough to make the boy back away, and Saul and Clayton wasted no time in taking advantage, muscling him inside and leaving the doorway open.

"You'd best stay quiet, lad, let's not make a fuss," Clayton told him, as Saul plucked the cross from Arnold's hand.

"Come inside," Aida told Julie, after stepping across the threshold. Julie advanced, making her way indoors, feeling an unwelcome shiver crawl through her as she set foot upon the blessed ground. Even with two strong men gripping his arms firmly, Arnold met her with a look of utmost loathing. She stepped close to him, breathing in his scent, her face only inches from his.

"You were awfully quick to turn to treachery, *Monsieur*. Not terribly becoming, for a man of God."

"You burned that house, didn't you?" he accused her, his voice laden with anger and spite. "You slaughtered all of those men."

"No, I did not. Until earlier today, I was not even sure that the Company had yet reached London. I learned of them only because you went to visit them."

"You've had me followed."

"Of course I have. I do not want to be your enemy, but I could hardly afford to trust you, could I? You had every intention of betraying me to Michel Renard."

"It is no betrayal. Betrayal applies to men and women, not to the Devil's monsters. You are a monster."

His voice was cold, but the rage in the boy's eyes was fierce, causing Saul and Clayton to tighten their grip upon him.

"This monster enabled you to say goodbye to your mother in peace, rather than watch her die screaming and raving."

"Nothing but a trick, to gain my trust. Duplicity is second nature to you. I know all about who you are. You were remorseless in your sin and depravity while you lived, it is no surprise that you are the Devil's own undead now. You are—"

"Go on," she told him, "call me a harlot. Call me the Whore of Babylon. Call me a murderess, and a corrupter of innocence. Men like you tried to burn me alive, even when I was human. Call me whatever you must, to sooth your anguish towards a woman who will never fear men."

"You are *not* a woman. You are an abomination."

"And I have saved more people than you have met. You think yourself a soldier for God? I watched you piss yourself, the night that House Laskaris came for you. What do you think should have happened, had I not intervened? Or two nights ago, when you thought you could save your mother by making a deal with Eşref's dogs? He was going to turn her no matter what you did. And then he would have killed you, or worse."

"How can I believe a single word that you speak?"

"Release him," Julie said, after a few seconds of icy silence. Saul and Clayton shared a wary look, a moment of hesitation, but they did as asked. Arnold felt his captors' hands relinquish their grip.

"Where did you learn about my life? Who told you what little you know of vampires? I imagine it was Michel Renard, but are you even aware of who he serves? That man and his Company are not your allies."

The curate looked at her warily. Although no longer

restrained, he was still heavily outnumbered here. And yet, for all that he had plotted to kill her, Julie had not ordered her companions to put an end to him, even though he suspected they would have done so quite readily.

"If you know him, then you know that he works for the Vatican," he told her.

"He works for the Company of the Holy Sacrament. You will find that they are not any recognised part of the Catholic Church today. They were formed early last century, in France, to protect Mother Church from all threats, the greatest of which they deemed to be the growing popularity of your Protestant faith. They were officially disbanded in 1665, after their antipathy towards their fellow Christians had grown so great, that King Louis the Fourteenth renounced all support of them.

"But by that point, a small number within the Company had discovered the truth of the existence of vampires, and had dedicated themselves to hunting them. With the support of a few sympathetic bishops, the Company continues to operate covertly to this day. Tell me, Monsieur Brennan, do you believe that to men such as these, you are anything more than a disposable asset? They will use you, and discard you the moment it suits their purposes. I am already certain that they have told you more lies than I have."

"Whatever their past sins, they are still human. They are not demons like you." Arnold was trying to sound firm, but Julie could hear a note of uncertainty that had crept into his voice.

"If that was all it took for you to trust them, you would have told them that your mother was infected. You would have told them about everything that has happened to your family."

"And how should you know that I did not?"

"Because if Renard knew that, he would have killed your mother himself. He has no mercy for thralls. He would then use your brother and sister as bait for House Laskaris. Whatever my sins, Monsieur Brennan, I have no intention of harm towards you or your family."

"He did warn me of you. He told me to be wary of you, above all other vampires."

"Of course he did. He has never forgiven me for that scar on his throat."

"*You* did that to him?"

"I first met Michel Renard seven years ago, near Limoges. We were both tracking a vukodlak which had left a trail of butchered victims through several villages. I observed him for a time as he investigated, and then approached him with an offer to combine our efforts. He was not receptive to discussion, and he attacked me. He gave me quite a fight, but alone he was unable to best me. I dealt him a severe beating, and then to replenish myself, I fed from him. I was not gentle. I held back from killing him, but I gave him a bite that he would not forget."

"If you had him at your mercy, why not finish him? He is dedicated to hunting you, and all your kind."

"You said it yourself. Whatever his sins, he is still human. I try not to kill humans, unless they give me no choice."

There was now confusion upon the curate's face. Whatever he had expected to happen this evening, this conversation was clearly not it.

"You don't kill humans?" he repeated. "But how do you feed your hunger? Your undead nature condemns you to drink blood."

"*Undead*," Julie scoffed. "I am not a walking corpse, whatever the folklore may say, though the mechanisms of my body are... rather *alien*, to those of mortal creatures. I do require blood to sustain myself, but I need only take small amounts at a time, from a wide number of vessels. Like many vampires, I do not drain my prey dry. A successful parasite does not kill its host."

"But you still have to keep yourself hidden, or else the whole world would hunt you. So what you did to my mother, altering her memories, do you do that to everyone you feed upon?"

"Everyone who is not a willing donor. All vampires have the power to manipulate human thoughts to some degree, though it is not always easy. People who have been recently bitten are much more susceptible to that power. After feeding, I can remove or reconstruct someone's entire recollection of an encounter."

Julie did not have to look deeply into Arnold's eyes to see how unnerved he was by that information. She could hear the increase in the boy's heart rate, and smell the subtle change in his sweat. But rather than recoiling from the truth, he was questing for answers, and she considered that a good thing.

"If all vampires can do that, why do they kill at all?" he asked.

"Because it is not easy to constrain oneself to the life of a parasite, when you are surrounded by prey who can so easily be deceived or killed. There is a demon within me, and in its hunger it constantly tells me how fragile mortals are, how easily I could become a remorseless predator. This is one reason why I uphold relationships with human companions, to remind myself of the value of their lives. Love and loyalty are a bulwark; the demon's urges would be far harder to resist if I tried to do so alone. And if I were part of a coven, keeping the company of other vampires, all resistance would become pointless. When immortals cluster together, they amplify the worst in each other, and invariably speed their descent into cruelty."

"I feel that there is a great deal I do not know," Arnold conceded.

"Maybe you can find some answers in your collection," Julie told him.

Within the cramped confines of Arnold's room, they emptied out the chest and separated out each bundle of documents, and each frame of mounted teeth, spreading them out over the narrow bed.

"I remember each one of these kills," Julie mused, looking over the preserved fangs. "Normally when a vampire is slain, the remains return to human form, and all traces of their condition fade within hours. Sir Hans developed a chemical treatment which stops the process. He was only ever able to compound small amounts of his formula, but it was enough for me to preserve these teeth for him."

Some of those kills had been hard fights. Most had come about from traps or ambushes, or daylight raids upon vampire lairs. After almost dying in her first hunt, Julie had swiftly learned how to stack the odds in her favour.

"Was he eager to work with you?" Arnold enquired.

"Extremely. Sir Hans loved nothing more than a bit of secret knowledge. He liked to know things that others did not, and I was offering to supply him with real physical samples of creatures thought to be myth. His enthusiasm was considerable."

"So he financed your lifestyle, as you travelled the world in search of monsters."

"He did. Whenever possible, I sent him reports of my activities, and trophies from my kills."

"Your last letter was sent from the Americas. It spoke of you discovering Nine Lords, ancient progenitors, and your desire to hunt them down. What happened there?"

The question caused Julie's expression to grow distant.

The memories of those events were painful, and it had been some time since she had related them to anyone. The twins had heard the story, of course, and they were the only people alive who knew it in detail. She was dubious about sharing it with Arnold, but she had watched him endure painful events of his own, and she could sense his enmity towards her diminishing as they conversed. Perhaps she could afford him some degree of trust. Clayton was also present, but she was quite confident of his ability to keep this story silent.

"What happened is that I was a fool," she began. "In the religion of the Maya and the Aztec, the cycle of the night is ruled over by Nine Lords. These Lords govern the calendar of yearly rituals, determining when human sacrifice is to be performed. In the stories their purpose is to ensure that the sun and moon perform their journeys across the sky, and that the cycle of the cosmos continues. But I assure you that the truth is far less altruistic. The Lords are not some distant gods in the heavens, but are here, in this world, and they are responsible for the existence of all vampires. They are also much, much older than the Maya, though at the time I did not grasp the sheer scope of their age, and their strength.

"I went hunting for one of them, who was named Tloque Nahuaque. The Maya call him Tohil, and the Aztec know him as Tezcatlipoca, among his many other names. I was as prepared as any mortal could be to face a powerful vampire. My guns were loaded with bullets of consecrated silver. My neck and wrists were tattooed with crucifixes. I carried occult amulets to protect me from mental control. My sword had been consecrated, and even my coat was lined with passages from scripture, each one individually written and blessed by the Jesuit monks who had sheltered me. I have never been a good Christian, but *their* faith was formidable. Lastly, I had my orichalcum dagger, and a strike to the heart from that weapon had never failed to kill a vampire."

Julie sighed, remembering the crushing futility of what transpired next.

"None of it mattered. In the forest I found and set fire to a whole nest of camazotz, to draw out their Master. Tloque Nahuaque came before me, and all my protections proved worthless. He was ancient before the time of Abraham, what did He care for petty icons of a foreign deity? In His mind, He and the other Lords were the only true divinity on this Earth. My bullets did not slow Him. He caught my sword in His hand and snapped it like kindling. I struck at Him with the dagger, but He was too fast for me to land a blow. He grabbed hold of me, and my tattoos did nothing to repel Him as he sank his teeth into me. But when He threw me to the ground, I grabbed the dagger from where it had fallen, and stabbed it into His leg. I heard him cry out in pain."

The memory of that particular moment brought a smile to her lips, but it was short-lived.

"The fact that I hurt Him at all is the only reason I'm not dead. It had been centuries since a mortal warrior had last risen to challenge Him, and in ages past, He had 'collected' those who gave Him good sport. So He chose to collect me. He kept me alive, fed upon me several times until I became His thrall, then He gave me a taste of His blood. That is how Julie the hunter finally died, and how Julie the camazotz came to be."

Silence hung in the air for a time, as Arnold absorbed what Julie had told him. For all of his initial mistrust of her, she could tell that he understood her tale to be sincere, however terrifying its implications. Eventually he managed to speak.

"And what happened after that?"

"For years afterwards, I was entirely under his control. Any vampire can exert influence over their own Progeny, but among the Nine Lords, that power is almost absolute. I was his trophy, his plaything, and his every whim was my command. I served for his amusement in ways that I have no wish to describe. And then one night, his control began to slip. He would still give me orders, but my thoughts were able to stray from the path of obedience. Over the span of a year, I reached the point where if I wanted to disobey him, I could. But I continued to feign compliance, gave him no reason to suspect that my will was my own. I noticed that he was growing bored with me, that some nights he would pay me little attention.

"I planned my escape carefully, waited for a ship that was to sail back to Europe, and when the time came, I slipped aboard that ship and left. The journey was hellish, trapped on a long voyage, hungry and constantly surrounded by the beating hearts of the crew. I hid among the cargo, not daring to expose myself, feeding only very little. But the greater the distance grew between myself and my Maker, the more surely I knew that He would not be able to summon me back to Him. When the ship finally docked in Lisbon, I was free."

Julie looked Arnold in the eye. The account she had given was an honest one, as best he could judge, even if he preferred to believe that a vampire could only speak in deception. Clayton predictably said nothing, maintaining his stoic demeanour, though even he had a distant look in his eye, as though unsettled by something that his mind did not quite wish to comprehend.

"Every word of those letters to Sir Hans is genuine," she added. "Did you read all of them?"

"Yes," Arnold affirmed, causing Julie to raise one eyebrow.

"You read French? You're better educated than I thought."

"Well, I didn't read them *myself*, exactly," he admitted, soon realising that he'd said more than he meant to, and confirming what Julie suspected.

"So who read them for you?" she asked.

"Is it better to not leave them out of this? They don't know the full truth of it all."

"Who read them? Whoever it is could already be in danger."

"A local gentleman, if you must know. He manages the Minories theatre, his name is Thomas Ashford. He claimed to have known you, from his time in Paris. My brother introduced me to him, as a man who is fluent in French."

The name caught Julie off guard. After a moment of recollection she began to smile, this time with gentle fondness. She remembered a sweet, awkward and relentlessly energetic boy in his middle teenage years, starry-eyed amid the magnificence of the Paris Opéra, rushing to and fro backstage as he heeded the demands of every performer, and of every stagehand with the barest seniority. She remembered his eagerness to please, an eagerness which she had rewarded once or twice, when the mood took her. His inexperience had been charming, in its own way.

"*Petit Tom* is still alive?" she mused gaily. "And running his own theatre now? That boy always did love the stage. I shall have to pay him a discreet visit, to ensure his safety."

"He seemed to rather admire you," Arnold told her. "He told me with great relish about the adventures of your life. He remains, however, convinced that those letters were a fiction concocted by Sir Hans, given that they pertain to events after your apparent death. I don't think it should do him any good to believe otherwise."

"Then he need not know otherwise. But all the same, I shall prefer to make certain that the Laskaris are not watching him."

Arnold nodded in agreement, and took a step back, giving Julie and her companions space to examine the collection without further interruption. She began to leaf through one of the Latin discourses on the nature of vampires, somewhat impressed at the level of detail which Sir Hans had recorded. A good deal of it was speculation based upon the reports she had given him, postulating explanations for the capabilities and limitations observed among the blood-drinkers, and the strigoi in particular. As she read, she became aware of Clayton shuffling nearer.

"What happened to your tattoos?" he asked, when she looked his way. "Those cross tattoos that you talked about?"

"I flayed my own wrists and throat," she answered bluntly. "The skin grew back, but of course the ink did not. My Maker wasn't happy about it. He'd never forbidden me to remove them, but He was displeased that I never sought His permission. Just one of the many transgressions for which He punished me harshly, during those early years."

The answer was enough to make the detective ask nothing further of her. He did turn his attention towards Arnold, however.

"These letters in English, do you know who they're from? They're signed by an István Rozgonyi, does that name mean anything?"

"I only know what is in them," Arnold replied. "Rozgonyi is some manner of scholar from Buda-Pest. He seems like someone very learned in East European folklore. It does not surprise me that Sir Hans should have corresponded with a man like that, given his studies into vampires."

"Not just vampires, is it?" Clayton remarked. "This here mentions him sending a parcel of books on sunken cities. Atlantis, Kêr-Ys, Lyonesse… I've only heard of one of those, and it doesn't say much about why these places should be of interest. If vampires are real, do lost civilisations exist as well?"

"For all mankind's explorations, there are still a lot of blank spaces on the map" Julie considered. "I don't know if Atlantis was ever real, but I know that orichalcum is."

"An extremely rare and arcane metal?" Arnold ventured, recalling what Imogen had said two nights previous.

"Indeed. I doubt it was ever common, and there's barely any of it left in the world now. Sir Hans spent a number of years, and went to great personal expense, just to acquire enough to forge that one knife. The metal is lethally poisonous to vampires, though. That blade was the most effective weapon I ever wielded, until Tloque Nahuaque claimed it. Maybe Sir Hans was looking for more of it."

Throughout the entire discussion, the twins had remained quiet. Saul and Aida were poring over a fold of pages written in Arabic, only occasionally exchanging whispered words with one another. Sensing that they had discovered something of interest, Julie glanced in their direction. Saul met her gaze, and addressed her in French.

"This curate is sitting upon far more than he knows."

"What have you found?"

"These pages are part of an exegesis, and copies of fragments of an original text. But I cannot fathom from where he acquired them."

"What text are you talking about?"

"The *Kitab Al-Azif*," Aida answered, and even Julie could not fully conceal her sense of surprise.

"Might I ask what it is you're discussing?" Arnold enquired. "Since you are in my home, I surely have a right to know."

A silent look passed between the three companions. Saul would happily have kept this to himself, but after a moment's hesitation Julie gave a shrug and spoke in English;

"These are his documents, not mine. He may as well know."

"You have pages here from the *Kitab Al-Azif*," Saul explained to Arnold. "Do you know what that is?"

"No, I don't."

"In my country I grew up speaking both Arabic and French. *Azif* means something that is fraudulent or forged, but it is also an archaic term describing a sound of nocturnal insects, presaging the coming of evil. Sometimes it is compared to the howling of demons. *Kitab Al-Azif* is the Scripture of the Howling of Demons. It is a forbidden text, an occult grimoire of tremendous rarity and insight."

"A book of devilry, then."

"Far more than that. There is a Latin copy in the library at the Sorbonne in Paris, one of very few that are known to exist. But even that is regarded as an inferior translation of earlier work. I was never permitted to read it in any great depth, but I have seen some of its pages. It speaks of mighty and unknowable beings from ancient aeons, and rituals for invoking their power. Not mere superstition, but actual magic."

"The original text is believed to have been written in the Yemen, around one thousand years ago," Aida said. "It was considered heretical among scholars even then, and was never widely circulated. But in the tenth century, a copy arrived in Constantinople, where Theodorus Philetas transcribed it into Greek. The Latin translations stem from his work."

"And some years ago, I learned that among the many patrons of Theodorus Philetas was a Byzantine noblewoman by the name of Serena Laskaris," Julie continued, "who just happens to be one of the most powerful strigoi in Europe today. She may well be the Master who first infected her household, and made it into a vampire coven."

"A Master? You mean like Eşref?" Arnold ventured.

"Eşref's Progeny called him by that title, but he was not a Master. He was infected with vampirism like most others, he just survived long enough to become quite powerful in his own right. A Master vampire is one who *chose* immortality when they were human, and gained it by undergoing one of the Rites of Blood, the sacrificial rituals originally written by the Nine Lords. The camazotz were the first and only bloodline sired directly by the Nine. Every other form of the vampiric disease has its origins in their Rites of Blood."

"You're not honestly suggesting that Sir Hans Sloane was looking into these Satanic rites, are you?"

"I don't know," Julie admitted. "I don't think that he would ever want to *become* a vampire, not even to have the power of a Master. But do I think that intellectual curiosity alone might drive him to seek out that knowledge? That, I cannot rule out. What I do know, is that if this István Rozgonyi had access to an original *Al-Azif*, then it's possible that he had already crossed paths with House Laskaris when he wrote his letters. Since before I arrived in London, I've been wondering how the Laskaris had learned of Sir Hans. We need to find out more about Rozgonyi."

"We may have a lead to follow for that one," Clayton offered. "This letter says that Rozgonyi sent money to Sir Hans and asked him to use it to buy two houses for him. One of them's on Dover Street, over by Piccadilly."

"Then we have to investigate."

Julie turned back to Arnold. She had told him that this may be the last time they need see one another, and she was quite willing to uphold that much. Perhaps their conversation had lessened his antipathy towards her, but from here on in, she would happily go about her business and let him be about his.

"Thank you, Monsieur Brennan, for your time, and for letting us view these items. You have been of help. Now with that, I think it is time we bid you goodbye. I doubt that you will be saddened to see us leave."

Arnold, however, did not seem to share her opinion.

"No, wait," the boy began. "I really should come with you."

"Why?"

"Because there's so much I don't yet know! What you've told me this evening gives me some answers, but it also raises more questions. I'm involved in all of this now, I cannot just step back from it!"

Julie certainly wasn't going to question his motives. Arnold's desire, his *need* for more understanding was written plainly upon his face. Beneath that, however, there burned a fire with which she was all too familiar; the need for revenge. He had been robbed of his mother just as Julie had once been robbed of Marie, and he wanted to strike back at those responsible. She understood that feeling intimately, but all the same, she could not help but harbour some scepticism about his willingness to work alongside her.

"Why should you wish to go anywhere with a demon like me? I am no different now, than when you called me an abomination. Has merely learning about my past changed your views so greatly?"

"Please," he asked, and the undercurrent of his voice, although lessened, was the same as that which Julie had heard in Lisa Brennan's bedroom; that of a stoic and pious man facing desperation.

"Please, with Renard and his people gone, I have nowhere else to turn. You four are the only organised opposition to House Laskaris that remains in London. I have to be a part of this."

A look passed between Julie, Aida, Saul and finally Clayton. Her companions would accept her word on the matter, she knew. If she left Arnold to his own devices, then he was bound to try something by himself, which would likely end in disaster. Aida had made that very same judgement with regards to Clayton. But while allies were certainly useful, their group could not afford to take in every stray who had survived a brush with a vampire.

The only meaningful question was whether this foolishly naïve, fiercely devout young clergyman would prove to be a greater asset than a liability. Despite all of his earlier vitriol towards her, Julie found herself believing that he deserved a chance. Maybe after four years with Aida, she was growing a little *too* much like her lover.

"You had better get these items locked away safely," she finally relented. "We will wait for you outside."

~ Arnold ~

Saturday October 16th, 1756

What in God's name am I doing? The thought gnawed at
Arnold as he walked, crawling upon the inside of his head
like a swarm of ants on a summer's day. He was a man of the
cloth, a soldier of Christ, and yet here he was, for the second
time in a rather short span of his life, having negotiated
with a creature of Satan. Every word that Julie d'Aubigny
had spoken to him this evening might have been true, but
none of it made her a human being. Even if she did not kill
to sate her thirst, she was still a vampire, a walking perver-
sion of nature. God could not want for such a creature to
exist upon His good Earth. *And yet here you are, walking
beside her,* Arnold's tormented mind told itself.

The group would be walking for some time, to reach
Piccadilly. A Hackney carriage would have been quicker,
but they would need more than one to carry all five of them.
The night was dark and bitterly cold, and yet Arnold was
not sure that he had ever felt safer on London's nocturnal
streets. Even a man of God had to be wary of thieves and

maniacs in a place like Whitechapel, but Julie walked these alleyways without a hint of fear. She was stronger, quicker, a thousand times more dangerous than any poor bastard chancing his luck with a knife or a garotte, and on this occasion, her protection extended to Arnold Brennan. Even that much was enough to further feed his guilt.

Few people passed them by as they moved. Even those who were out at this hour sensed that Julie and her odd mix of companions were best not trifled with. A vampiric woman in men's clothing, with a scimitar on her belt; a pair of richly-attired and well-armed Negro twins; an imposing Bow Street Runner, and a rather fraught young clergyman: Arnold struggled to imagine any stranger group out in London this evening. As they walked, he felt the need to make some conversation.

"The Nine must be extremely ancient," he remarked in hushed tones as he walked beside Julie, "for how else could their knowledge have spread so far? If Serena Laskaris was able to perform the Rite of Blood in the tenth century, then that knowledge could not have come from the New World, for civilised men had not yet discovered it. Perhaps the Nine Lords only went to the Americas after the Great Flood. Renard told me that some in his order believed the first vampires to be creations of the Devil, Semjâzâ. Maybe they wrote down their Rites of Blood, carved them into stone tablets or some such, in the time before the Flood."

Julie scoffed, and Arnold wondered what he had said that she found so risible.

"*Civilised men*," she repeated. "I have seen the American frontier and its conflicts. Some night I shall tell you of the behaviour of civilised men, and those whom you might call savages. But yes, I've heard the theory you speak of. Semjâzâ, the Prince of the Fallen, the son of God who took a daughter of man for his wife and fathered the first of the

Nephilim. There are some apocryphal texts which say that it was the proliferation of the Nephilim, and not the sins of mortals, which caused God to smite the world with the Flood."

"There were Giants upon the Earth in those days," he mused, referencing the book of Genesis. "Do you think that is what the Nine Lords are? Nephilim who survived the great deluge?"

"I do not think so. Even the Nine were human, once. But they remember a time when the New World and the Old were not as separate as they are now. They recall land joining the two, in the place where the Strait of Anián lies."

"The strait of what?"

"Bering's Strait, I think it's called now."

"But the only time that land could have joined those continents would be before the Flood."

"Honestly, I'm not sure if there ever was a global flood. Tloque Nahuaque never told me of surviving one, and he often bragged about his exploits. I met each of the other Lords when He was parading me around as his pet, and out of those which found it amusing enough to converse with me, none of them spoke of the deluge. A great flood happened long ago, but maybe it never covered the whole world. It didn't cover theirs."

After that, Arnold chose to walk in silence. The pillars of his understanding had been shaken to their foundations enough times in recent weeks, without a discussion of the historical recollections of ancient monsters. On such matters he decided that he would cleave solidly to the Biblical truth of the world, over any tales that the bloodthirsty Nine Lords and their children might have to tell. For the sake of his sanity, he had to believe in the word of God over the word of demons.

To Arnold's eyes, the City of Westminster could have been a world away from the crushing poverty of Whitechapel. Here in the West End of London, the houses were larger and sturdier of build, not nearly so ramshackle as those of their poorer neighbours. The streets were still filthy and the gutters still brimming over, but the district felt more developed, more urbane, and entirely lacking the air of desperation which Arnold was so accustomed to in his home neighbourhood.

The signs of poverty were still present here, of course, but they contrasted with a level of prosperity which the young curate glimpsed only rarely in his life, and typically from afar. Arnold's idea of well-to-do people might include the sea captains and merchant venturers who drank coffee alongside Nathaniel at Lloyd's, but this district of London was home to aristocrats, members of parliament and wealthy entrepreneurs, the upper crust of society with whom he would never expect to rub shoulders.

Portugal Street – more commonly known as Piccadilly for the past ten years or so – was among the busiest thoroughfares in London, a place of commerce and enterprise, as well as grand houses where learned men gathered to discuss matters of import. Dover Street branched off of it to the north, close to the corner of the Green Park. Among these looming stone buildings, Arnold felt uncomfortably out of place.

He realised that it was to some degree a ridiculous notion, to be anxious about the feudal propriety of class boundaries when he was crusading against the forces of Satan, but deference to wealth and status was a behaviour that had been ingrained in him all his life. The rich man in his castle, and the poor man at his gate; this hierarchy was so fundamental to English society, that to Arnold it was just another attribute of the divine order of the world.

Upon reaching the address detailed in Rozgonyi's letter, the group came to a stop and appraised the sizeable townhouse. The place appeared neglected and ill-cared for, a once-beautiful property now seemingly abandoned to decay. No candlelight illuminated its windows, and no sense of warmth or homeliness emanated from it. Cautiously, Saul took the lead and made his way up the steps of the front porch. Arnold watched him approach the front door, raise one hand to give it a gentle tap, only to stop before making contact. It took the curate a moment to realise what Saul had seen, but when the man gestured towards the door handle, he saw that the lock was in fact broken.

A gentle push from Saul caused the door to swing inwards, and Arnold could hear a chorus of squeaks and the skittering of tiny feet as the building's rodent occupiers scurried for cover. This house was evidently abandoned, and might have been for quite some time. Saul proceeded inside and waited for the others to follow. When Julie reached the doorway she paused for a moment, but then stepped across the threshold with no apparent difficulty. Curiosity furrowed Arnold's brow.

"Do you not require an invitation?" he asked her.

"Only for a place of residence," she told him. "Nobody calls this place home. If anyone lived here, I should feel it."

"The Queen Anne was my mother's home. Did you need an invitation to enter there?"

"The Queen Anne is also a public house. A place of business cannot keep me out. I should have had difficulty crossing the threshold into her personal room, which is why I persuaded the landlord to let me visit her. His permission was all the invitation I required."

"You looked like you'd just walked in off a battlefield that night, and he still told you to go on up?"

"It's not hard for a vampire to be very convincing."

"And if a given invitation were to be withdrawn?"

"It would not matter. Once a vampire is invited in, they can return as often as they please."

Arnold had more questions in mind. He wanted to ask what would happen if she tried to force her way into a home uninvited, but a shift in Julie's mien suggested that her attention was on more important matters than his education. Her nostrils twitched as she sniffed the air.

"I think the Laskaris have already been here," she informed the others. "I can smell traces of strigoi, but they're old, and faint. Any clues we might find here could already be long gone."

"But we have nothing to lose by looking," Saul replied.

"You're right. Search every room, we might find something that they missed."

The group began to spread out, moving warily through the house. Arnold had never carried out an investigation such as this, and felt somewhat out of his depth as the others began their search. Aida had a lantern, but had also brought several candles, and Arnold thanked her when she handed one to him and lit it. The twins began to move upstairs while Clayton explored the sitting room.

Thinking of no better option, Arnold chose to stay close to Julie and observe her at work. Unlike the others, he noted, she had no need of candlelight to aid her in the dark. She made a rapid survey of the kitchen and its pantry. Any food that was being stored there had already been claimed by the rats; a few well-gnawed bones betrayed where a collection of hams had hung upon meat-hooks.

"What are you hoping to find?" Arnold ventured.

"Anything out of the ordinary."

The search of the downstairs rooms found little of use. Julie and her companions were not the first to investigate this place, and those who had come before had not been subtle. Drawers and cabinets had been rifled through and emptied, and furniture left overturned. From above, there came the thumping noise of something heavy being moved across the floor. Julie moved back to the hallway and the main staircase, with Arnold following after. Clayton was already on his way up.

As the three of them emerged onto the landing, they joined with the twins in what looked to be the guest bedroom. Like the other rooms, this one bore signs of having been ransacked; a toppled wardrobe lay upon the floor, but Saul and Aida had pushed it towards the bed, and seemed more interested in the wood-panelled wall behind it.

"You found something?" Clayton asked them.

"These panels," Aida indicated, tracing her fingertips along the edge of one. "I think they are intended to be removable. They conceal a hollow space. If we can just find the way to loosen them…"

Julie knocked idly against the wood with her knuckles, confirming that the space was indeed hollow. A moment later Arnold winced as the air filled with the sound of snapping, splintering wood. The vampire's arm moved in a blur, driving her fist through the panel in a single shattering blow, before tearing it free of the wall. The twins stepped back, giving her space as she ripped away the adjacent panels. Despite having witnessed her lethality in combat before, Arnold could not help but be a little shaken at this display of horrible, unnatural strength. To see Julie punching cleanly through solid oak panels left him in little doubt that she could tear a human body apart with her bare hands, if she so desired.

With the hollow space broken wide open, the vampire stepped aside to reveal what lay within: a German-made strongbox of sheet iron, secured with a heavy-looking padlock. Arnold had very occasionally seen such items before, used as cash boxes in shops which could afford them. As Aida shone her lantern upon it, he saw that there were letters painted all around the edges of the box, in some foreign alphabet that he could not begin to recognise. It did remind him, however, of the way that the verses of the Psalm had been carved into the chest which held his inheritance.

"Are those words a prayer?" he asked Julie. "Some countermeasure against your kind?"

"It is a spell from *Al-Azif*," Saul answered him, crouching down to take hold of the box and drag it out into the open.

"I can't touch it," Julie confirmed. "I can feel its resistance from here. If I try to open it, I expect it will cause me a great deal of pain."

Arnold watched as Saul hefted the iron box up, and placed it atop the fallen wardrobe with a heavy thud. Even if Arnold had never seen him fight, the size and build of Saul N'Dour would leave little doubt that he was a man of great physical prowess, but the way that he lifted the box showed his strength to be truly impressive. Reaching down to his belt, he retrieved his mallet and chisel.

"Hold up," Clayton interjected, "it's just a screw-key lock. Give me a moment, I reckon I can open it."

The detective moved in, pulling a small roll of leather from his pocket and opening it to reveal a set of delicate metal picks. Arnold watched in fascination as he inserted two of them into the padlock, his meaty fingers carefully manipulating the components until, with a series of clicks, the lock popped open. Clayton gave a satisfied smile and opened the lid, lifting out the box's contents one by one. There were several leatherbound books, and stacks of papers, carefully tied with string.

"More documents," Arnold sighed. Part of him wondered if Michel Renard's vampire-hunts had involved following this many paper trails.

"Perhaps they will contain some answers," Aida replied, placing her lantern down so that she could begin to read. Saul and Julie clustered around her, eager to see what information could be gleaned. Arnold's eyes caught the title of one of the books.

"*The Folly of King Gradlon and the Demise of Kêr-Ys,*" he mused. "Was Kêr-Ys not one of the sunken cities mentioned in Sir Hans' letters?"

"The City of Ys is an old Breton legend," Julie replied as she read through a handful of pages. "A great and prosperous city, built upon land reclaimed from the sea in the Baie de Douarnenez, and protected from the tide by an embankment with a single gate. It is said that in a state of a drunken revelry, the king's daughter, Dahut, stole the key from her father and opened the floodgate, letting the waters in and drowning the city. The legends typically paint Dahut as an unrepentant sinner. They vary as to whether King Gradlon was a virtuous man, or a decadent and debauched ruler. In some versions, Dahut survived the drowning and lived on as a mermaid."

"I see."

Arnold wondered what importance this legend might have to Sir Hans and his father's studies. Were they really just looking into any and all stories of sunken lands in hopes of finding some more orichalcum? He could not shake the feeling that there was more to this, and as strange as it sounded, the idea of the mythical Dahut becoming a mermaid seemed to fit the idea all too neatly. In his room, Julie had described the Rites of Blood as sacrificial in nature, and Arnold found himself imagining that a depraved and ambitious princess, bent on gaining immortality, might sacrifice her entire city in order to facilitate her transition into an immortal creature. Maybe the tale was more allegorical than literal, but it seemed to have some direct relevance to the process of becoming a Master vampire. He picked up another book and began to leaf through it.

"*Critias*, by Plato. I imagine this is a source on Atlantis."

He picked another.

"*The Prose Tristan*. This is Arthurian legend."

"That will be referring to Lyonesse," Aida remarked. "The lost British kingdom still existed during the time those stories were written."

"Lyonesse is a lost British kingdom? I'm not very much of a mythologist, I'm afraid."

Aida smiled.

"You should diversify your reading, Monsieur Brennan. Lyonesse was a part of old Kernow, what you call Cornwall. Stories say that it was a beautiful land, but sometime towards the end of the eleventh century, it was broken up and sunk into the sea by a great storm. Of course they claim that this disaster was a punishment from God, for some great sin that the people of Lyonesse committed."

"St Martin's island," Arnold realised. "The Isles of Scilly, off the Cornish coast. That's where the second house is, that Sir Hans bought for Mister Rozgonyi. Are those islands what is left of Lyonesse?"

"They very likely are, or at least were very close to it."

"Then we need to find out why he was so interested in going there. He should not have gone to the trouble of buying property there if it wasn't for some important reason."

"Ruins," Saul interjected, only adding to Arnold's confusion.

"What?"

"According to this letter, Sir Hans and István Rozgonyi made plans to search for some very ancient ruins in the Isles of Scilly. Ruins older than the Flood. Older, perhaps, than mankind."

After his earlier discussion with Julie about the Nine, Saul's words were almost enough to make Arnold shudder. He was talking about relics from an earlier aeon of creation, a time when all manner of demons and foul creatures walked the Earth, preying upon the fledgling race of mankind with impunity. If the Nine Lords had survived from such a time, what else might still endure?

"How can such a thing be so?"

"*Kitab Al-Azif* makes mention of a race of sea-dwelling demigods that lived in ancient times; creatures both piscine and amphibian, but which walk upright like men. Pagan mythologies remember them by various different names. The Dogon call them Nommo. To the Babylonians, they were Apkallu. The old Irish legends called them Fomorians, and in this letter, Sir Hans names them Gargouilles de la Mer.

"He speculated that they built temples and strongholds in coastal regions long ago, and although this claims that the Gargouilles are now extinct, it also says that their legacy lingers on. Their knowledge of the elements, their magics, could still be exploited in areas where their ruins stand. In this letter he wonders if the fall of Lyonesse, of Kêr-Ys, even of mythic Atlantis, could be connected to the power of these creatures."

Arnold wanted to believe that this was preposterous, superstitious nonsense, but with all that he had discovered in the past week alone, how could he even begin to dismiss such claims? If demons could infect the blood of mortals and create vampires, then the servants of Semjâzâ could exist in other forms, too.

"How did they get onto any of this business, from looking into vampires?" Clayton asked, sounding even more at a loss than Arnold had been.

"By looking into their origins," Julie told him. Several

papers were spread out in front of her upon the wardrobe, mostly pages of text in Latin, but one of them bore a strange, nine-pointed diagram, marked with symbols that were completely alien to Arnold.

"Sir Hans knew about the Nine Lords from my last letter to him. It seems that Rozgonyi knew about them too. They had been investigating all kinds of forbidden texts, trying to learn what they could about the first vampires."

Julie looked up from the pages. There was a distant, haunted look in her eyes which Arnold did not like in the slightest.

"When I served Tloque Nahuaque, he once took me swimming in a cenote," she began. "There are no rivers on the Yucatán peninsula. All the water is in these pools, and their underground tunnels. Deep down, he led me to a cavern which held a pocket of rancid air. Inside there were the remains of stone structures, a shrine to dead, forgotten Gods. It was older than I can imagine, but I could feel the power of the place, resonating in my veins like a song. He told me that it was in a place like this where the Nine transcended their humanity, and became the Teeth of the Gods."

Julie's fingertip slowly traced its way along the lines of the diagram, visiting each of its nine points in turn. Each one was marked with the name of a Lord.

"*Tohil. Awilix. Kukulkan. Ix-tab... Through blood, all things,*" she breathed, and then met the eyes of her companions. "I don't know the truth behind those ruins in the New World, but if these Gargouilles de la Mer that Sir Hans speaks of are real, then they could be their builders. And if their magic was powerful enough to make the Nine Lords out of simple mortals, then I'd wager it was also sufficient to smite whole nations beneath the waves."

"Do you think this is what House Laskaris is really

looking for?" Arnold questioned, though he felt that he already knew the answer. It seemed like a tremendous stroke of fortune, that although the enemy had gotten here before them, the strigoi had missed this vital clue. Maybe, in some way, God was still smiling upon his own.

"I think so," Julie confirmed. "If a vampire as formidable as Serena Laskaris has learned about the origins of the Nine Lords, then she could also have discovered that there are Gargouille ruins outside of Yucatán. They will be looking to find those sites, and harness whatever magic remains within them. I should not want to see what House Laskaris wishes to accomplish with that kind of power. If there is a shrine on the Isles of Scilly, it is vital we get there first and make sure that they have no chance to claim it."

After discussion of the documents, the remaining rooms of the house were carefully examined, but the search yielded no further leads. With nothing more to be found, the books and papers from the strongbox were distributed among the group to be carried. Arnold suggested that St Mary's was the safest place to hold them, and to his mild surprise, neither Julie nor any of her companions objected to his reasoning.

The box itself was left behind for the time being, having been deemed impractical to carry through London's streets without the aid of a wagon, though Arnold had every intention of returning with the proper equipment to collect it. An iron chest which was protected from the touch of vampires seemed like far too useful an asset to simply abandon, even if that protection stemmed from heathen magic.

The group moved with purpose back to Whitechapel, towards the church. Along the way, they quietly discussed preparations for their journey to Cornwall. In the morning, the twins would purchase four draft horses and a suitable carriage for their travels. They would be on the road for a few days after leaving London, and upon reaching Penzance they would hire a ferry to St Martin's.

Clayton would have little difficulty in accompanying the group, for the nature of his employment was not dependent upon him attending regular hours at the Bow Street office. His income was primarily based upon each wanted criminal he apprehended, and if he informed the magistrates that they would not see him for a week or two, they were unlikely to raise any great objection.

That only left Arnold, and he wondered what reason he could give to the Reverend Lowther as to why he would be departing St Mary's for a time. He could tell him that he felt the call to undertake a spiritual pilgrimage, though he did not wish to directly lie to the kindly old man. Maybe he could simply state that the vicar had been right, and that God had shown Arnold the path he needed to walk. Leaving the church would result in the suspension of his meagre wages, but he had enough money stored away to provide for his upkeep during the journey. Somehow he doubted that he would have to pay for many of his own meals, however; it seemed clear to him that Saul and Aida had wealth and generosity to spare.

As the Church of St Mary Matfelon came into view, however, Arnold's thoughts soon turned away from journeys to Cornwall. He could see that the front door of the chapel was ajar, and he was quite certain that he had left it locked when the group set off. Reverend Lowther had almost certainly returned from his evening meal by now, but it was not at all like the vicar to leave the door open at night, especially during this frigid time of year.

The curate began to pick up his pace, a dreadful sense of unease gripping his belly, and soon he broke into a full run. He burst in through the door, fearing the worst, his eyes searching the darkened chapel for any sign of foul play. To his horror, he could see an alabaster-haired form, splayed limp upon the cold stone floor. The books that he carried tumbled from his hands, forgotten as Arnold sprinted to the fallen vicar's side, all his thoughts consumed with the hope that the old man was still alive.

"Charles! Vicar, please! Please say something!"

He scrambled to roll the old man onto his back, and was aghast at the sight of the horrible purple contusion upon his cheek and jaw, where someone had brutally struck the vicar across the face.

"Please, God. Please, Charles, don't be dead!"

Panic was setting in. He had already lost his mother, and Reverend Lowther was more of a father to him than Sean Musgrave had ever been. He could not bear to lose this man in such a fashion, to see him die broken and bleeding in his own church. Desperately, he began to shake him by the shoulders, wishing to elicit some response, *any* response. He fought back a sob as the vicar's eyes remained steadfastly closed. At first he was only distantly aware of the feeling of strong hands grabbing him, hauling him back. He cried out for them to release him, but Saul held him tight, his arms immovable as a vault door.

"He is breathing."

Aida's voice cut through Arnold's despair, her words reaching his ears like the proclamation of an angel. *Charles Lowther was not dead.* His struggles ceased as the woman crouched over the vicar, examining him.

"But he is badly hurt," she said. "There is nothing that we can do for him here. We need to get him a physician."

"The London Hospital," Arnold gasped. "It's not far from here, just on Prescot Street. We can carry him there."

Saul released his grip, and Arnold staggered forward. In spite of his elation at Aida's news, in his near-hysterical state he was angry at being manhandled in such a fashion. It was almost maddening how calm the twins were right now, how detached they seemed from the immediacy of the situation, but clearly their experience with life-threatening wounds far outweighed his own. He fought down his sense of outrage, stepping back to give space as Clayton moved in to lift the stricken old man in his arms.

"I'll take him," the detective assured them. "Trust me, it'll raise far fewer questions if I turn up with an unconscious priest, rather than you two."

"I'll come with you," Arnold began, but no sooner had the words left his throat than Julie's voice cut through the air like a knife.

"No. Not yet. You stay here."

Her presumption incensed him, and in a fury he rounded on her. It was one thing for him to defer to her two Negroes, but he could not stomach this vampire bitch giving him *orders*, while the good and kind man who had mentored him for the past six years may be dying.

"You do *not* tell me what to–"

"Renard was here," Julie snapped. She was crouching close to the doorway, her fingertips scraping over the stone-work, before she sniffed at the dirt upon her nails. Fixing Arnold in her gaze, she rose to her feet.

"Renard was here, and three others that I can smell. No more than an hour ago. You failed to sell me to them, but they came here anyway. They attacked your old priest. You are culpable."

Clayton was gone, carrying the reverend away into the night. Arnold wanted to follow, but he could barely move a muscle as Julie's eyes pierced into his.

"I… I gave them no reason to…"

"You told the Company about your inheritance, didn't you?"

"I thought they were my allies. Catholic or Protestant, we were all Christian men against the hordes of the Devil!"

"You are dreadfully naïve."

She turned and set off towards the rectory with the twins in tow, and as Arnold felt the paralysis lift from him, he hurried after them. They soon arrived at the door to his room, and it was no surprise that the chest and all its contents were gone. The sight of his ransacked living quarters felt like a lead weight in the curate's stomach. He had been neglected, belittled and lied to many times in his life, by many different people, but never before had he been betrayed like this. Never had he been turned upon by men who professed devotion to God. Now, everything that his father had left him was in the hands of men callous enough to brutalise the good Reverend Lowther.

"We can… we can get them back," he muttered, though he knew that he did not believe his own words.

"We cannot," Julie told him, her voice cold. "The Company will be holding that chest under guard, on consecrated ground. I won't be able to fight my way in, and I'm not risking the lives of my companions for your collection. You put your trust in the wrong people, and now you're paying for it."

The vampire left him, striding away without a further word. Aida followed after her, but Saul lingered for a moment, looking Arnold in the eye.

"Despair will not serve you," he said. "Tomorrow we prepare for our journey. On Monday we leave. Come with us, or stay here. You do whatever you must."

Arnold gave a hesitant nod, agreeing with the sentiment of Saul's words even if he struggled to muster their sense of resolve. He did not wish to abandon the hunt. Whatever awaited them on St Martin's, he still wished to be involved, and to confront it head-on. He wanted to do his part in thwarting House Laskaris' schemes, and confronting the horrors of the antediluvian past.

Whatever his mistakes and shortcomings, Arnold Brennan was still a soldier for the Lord. He could not just step back from his duty. But right now, the most important thing was that he be at the side of Charles Lowther. Whatever else may happen, in this hour he needed to be there for him. Left alone in St Mary's, Arnold locked up the church, barred the front door, and set off to the London Hospital.

Part III

~ Julie ~

Sunday October 17ᵗʰ, 1756

The waters of the Thames were black and sluggish beneath the evening's cloud-filled sky, and from the window of her room, Julie watched the lights of the docklands going about their business. The shutters were open just a little, the night-time breeze cool on her skin after the heat of passion. From behind her, she felt the inviting softness of her lover's body press against her back. Warm arms encircled her, and Aida's gentle lips caressed her bare shoulders. She let her eyes drift closed for a time as she enjoyed the sensation, and then turned within her lover's embrace, to gift her with a kiss.

"I am glad to have visited this city with you," Aida whispered when their mouths parted. "But I cannot say that I will miss it. London so far has not been to my liking."

The vampire laughed softly, losing herself in the dark and amorous depths of Aida's eyes.

"We shall make certain to return here under different circumstances," Julie assured her. "And it will be a far more pleasant trip."

"Or after this, we could go somewhere far away. The Orient? The Americas? Or you might even come to Africa with me. Perhaps you would visit my home in Saint-Louis."

"You think that your father would appreciate that?"

"I am sure that he should love to meet the dashing French noblewoman with whom his children have been adventuring."

"Then I shall have to work on my pretence of nobility. It's been some time since I wore an expensive dress."

"And I shall take great delight in having one made for you. I will hire the finest seamstresses in Paris."

Julie smiled and the two women kissed again, slow and tactile. Playfully, she pushed Aida back down onto the bed. For a moment she looked ready to mount her again, but to her lover's disappointment, Julie instead looked towards the bedside table, where her bundle of old letters to Sir Hans lay. Carefully, she picked up the documents.

"Everything is ready for us to leave in the morning?"

"It is."

"Good. Even if the Laskaris know of our presence, they are unlikely to pursue us by day. We shall make the best of that advantage."

Aida looked at her with concern.

"You think that they will be coming for us? If they knew who was hunting them, surely they should have retaliated by now?"

"I think that for some time now, they have known more about us than we realise. When I killed Eşref, he knew who and what I was. He called me a camazotz. No vampire on this continent should be aware of my bloodline. Until last night, you and Saul were the only two people who had that information."

"Eşref was more than two centuries old, was he not? Perhaps he had visited the New World in that time, and encountered a camazotz there. He might simply have recognised the scent of your blood."

"No, it is more than that. Before I killed him, he told me

that I was 'dancing to her tune'. After what we found yesterday, I truly think he could have been talking about Serena Laskaris. If we have drawn the attention of a strigoi such as that… I do not know how long she might have been playing games with us. I do not know what end she could have in mind."

"If she comes for us, then we will kill her. We have beaten Master vampires before. My love, you are the direct Progeny of one of the Nine. I do not care how old she is, you are stronger than her."

"We've beaten Master vampires when we were hunting them. We've never had to deal with one of them hunting us. Outside of London we have a better chance of seeing them coming, but we will have to tread carefully. And I don't want to leave any traces."

Julie gave one last look to the letters in her hand, and then tossed them unceremoniously into the fireplace. She watched the papers curl and blacken as the flames licked at them, the fire soon beginning to consume them.

"Those were the last conversations you had with Sir Hans…" Aida remarked, her surprise evident.

"Sir Hans believed me dead for the last thirty years of his life. Perhaps I should also let him rest in peace."

Julie climbed onto the bed, sitting down beside her lover as they watched the letters burn. The back of her hand gently brushed along Aida's forearm.

"You have something more that you wish to do, before we leave tomorrow?"

"I do need to pay a visit to Tom Ashford tonight," the vampire confessed. "There are very few left, who knew me in my first life. I want to know that he is alright."

Aida nodded, and softly pressed her face to her lover's shoulder once more.

"Then you should see him. Saul and I will remain here tonight. I will be waiting, when you return."

"I look forward to that."

Julie sank back into the bedsheets, pulling her lover down with her. Tenderly she kissed her way down Aida's cheek, her neck, to the base of her throat. She stopped at the spot where she had last fed from her, a month ago in Constantinople. The scar had healed entirely, her ebon skin unblemished. Aida purred softly, her fingers grasping Julie's hair as hot sanguine nectar pulsed beneath her skin. Rolling Aida onto her back, the vampire continued to kiss her way downward, choosing a spot just above the dark bud of her lover's nipple.

Gently she caressed the sensitive flesh with her tongue, tasting the copper-and-salt of human sweat, before allowing her fangs to descend in hungry anticipation. Aida's body tensed, gasping aloud, her back arching as Julie inflicted the very shallowest of bites, her needle teeth pricking the skin. A scarlet trickle began to flow, and the vampire lowered her mouth to drink.

The heady piquancy of Aida's lust remained hot in Julie's belly as she made the journey from the Devil's Tavern to the Minories. Wary of being observed, she clung to the shadows, traversing the streets with silent, animalistic stealth. Senses heightened, she had circled the tavern's vicinity twice over after leaving it, making certain that the building was not being watched. Her alertness did not ebb even as she arrived within sight of the theatre, though her apprehension was growing as she wondered how she might react to seeing Tom again after five decades. It was true what she had said to Aida; those who knew her in her mortal days were now few and far between, so the chance to glimpse one whom she had once called a friend was a rare opportunity.

This being the Sabbath day, the theatre was naturally not open for business. Julie suspected that Tom must live somewhere nearby, and her intention was to slip inside the building, have a sniff around the manager's office and hopefully find a scent that she could track to his home. As she drew closer to the theatre she noticed that a carriage was parked just across the street, its driver leafing through a copy of *The Gentlemen's Magazine* by the light of a lantern. Immediately her suspicions were raised, but as she passed by the vehicle she could sense nothing of any vampire about it, so she continued on her way without incident.

Avoiding the front entrance of the theatre, she made her way around the side to the staff door. In truth she expected to have to climb in through a window, but to her surprise, the door yielded when she turned the handle. Her eyes narrowed, curious as to whether Tom had simply forgotten to lock the place up last night, or if someone was actually in the building. Silently she made her way inside, finding herself in a short corridor which led into the main dressing room.

Her eyes wandered over the chairs, the dressing tables, the stage-costumes hanging upon the racks. She could smell the lingering traces of perfume and wine in the air from those who had occupied this space last night. She walked past the mirrors, seeing the familiar absence of her own reflection, feeling as though she were haunting the backstage like a ghost.

Simply being here was enough to stir her recollections of the Paris Opéra. Alone in the dark, her mind was reliving the frantic preparations in the hours leading up to each production; the catty rivalries between performers and writers jostling for prestige, the desperate scurrying of the stagehands from one job to the next, and the bacchanalian revelries that followed a successful show. She remembered standing before a full-length mirror in the days when she could still see herself in the glass, giving her songs one final rehearsal even as a team of girls fitted her into her dress, styled her hair and applied her makeup. Back then, she had sung for the ears of royalty, even at the grand palace of Versailles itself.

The sound of laughter from further down the hall caught her attention, snapping Julie out of her contemplation. She could discern two voices in merriment. One belonged to a man; deep, strong and clearly trained for the stage, albeit weakened by age and weariness. The other was the sweet, high voice of a girl, one on the verge of womanhood. The vampire did not have to listen for long to be sure that the male voice belonged to Thomas Ashford, and it brought a smile to Julie's lips to know that he was here and happy, even now. But he must now be in his seventies, and while veterans of the theatre often enjoyed the attentions of younger ladies, the female voice sounded a little too young to be a mistress of his.

Feeling curious, Julie slipped through the door of the dressing room and into the hallway. A number of candles had been lit in here, casting their flickering illumination upon the walls. Several closed doors belonged to private dressing rooms, for those eminent performers who had earned the privilege of such. Beyond those, Julie could see another door standing slightly ajar at the far end of the hall, with additional candlelight spilling from within. She made her way towards it, feeling ever more like the theatre ghost as she drew nearer. As the laughter faded, she could hear the girl talking.

"What I really came to see you for, Mister Ashford, was this. I wasn't sure who else to turn to, but after our first meeting, I thought you might be someone who could help me. You see, when Father died he left almost the entire estate to Nathaniel, as expected, but there were certain items that his will specifically bequeathed to Mother and to myself."

Julie came to a stop outside the door. Her ears could detect two beating hearts on the far side; one old and tired, the other young and excited.

"He left me this," the girl's voice continued. "I really did not know what to make of it. Such an ugly thing, barely fit to be called jewellery. I don't know what kind of metal it is made of, nor can I find any reference to the markings upon it. But you seem like a man who may have knowledge of esoteric things, and I wondered if it meant anything to you."

"My word, what a frightfully unusual little trinket. Do let me take a closer look, my eyes aren't quite what they were, you know."

Tom's voice. It was changed by the years, undoubtedly, but Julie could tell without question that it was Thomas Ashford's voice. To hear it again after all this time was a delight; a living, breathing connection to a life that she had long left behind.

"You know, I may just have something that could help. I met a fascinating French-Algerian once, and he claimed to be something of an alchemist. He sold me some books, which I still have lying around here somewhere. I told myself that someday they might come in useful as props or some such, but in truth it was just my own damnable curiosity which drove me to buy them. Just wait here a moment, I'll find where I put them."

Julie could hear the man pulling himself to his feet. As he came towards the door she slipped away to the side, scaling the wall in a flash and clinging to the ceiling. Thomas emerged, passing beneath her, his head covered by a powdered wig as snowy-white as the old vicar's hair had been at St Mary's. She saw that he now walked with a cane, but in spite of that, his posture was still strong for a man of his age, and vitality had not abandoned him yet. He made his way into the main dressing room, where the stage props were stored, and Julie followed him, dropping to the floor as silently as a shadow.

She observed him fondly as he opened a large cabinet, rooting around among the various theatrical paraphernalia inside. She knew that she ought to remove herself from the situation, to withdraw and leave him be now that she had seen him, but the temptation to reconnect with her past was simply too great to be ignored. This was the last chance she would ever likely get to speak to anyone from that life. Easing the door closed behind her, she kept a respectful distance behind him as she announced her presence.

"*Petit Tom*. How long it has been."

She heard something tumble from his hands as the old man stood bolt upright. Slowly, he turned towards her. His eyes were wide as they met hers, and his hands trembled visibly.

"My God…" he breathed.

"No," Julie returned with a smile, "it's just me."

Seconds passed as her gazed at her in silence. For a little while Julie worried that he was not going to speak at all, but relief warmed her as his mouth crept into a broad smile.

"I knew it," Tom finally said. "I knew it, when I read those letters, that they were real! Even after fifty years, I recognised your writing."

"Every word was true," she confirmed.

He glanced over her shoulder, towards the mirror that stood behind her, seeing his reflection and his alone. She made no effort to stop him.

"By God in Heaven… you really are one of them. You started hunting vampires for what they did to your Marie, but they made you one of theirs. I hope you're not here to kill me, my dear, because that would be most unfair to the young guest I'm entertaining."

"I'm not here for blood, Tom," she told him with a chuckle. "My hunger is quite sated for tonight. I was told that you were alive in London and... I just couldn't stay away. It's been many, many years since I last spoke to anyone from the Opéra days."

Julie wanted so desperately for some light-hearted cheer in this moment, but while Tom's face was smiling, his joviality did not mask the primal fear in his eyes. Of course he was afraid. He was terrified. When he had last known Julie he had been barely a man, but while he was now elderly, she had scarcely aged at all. It was one thing for him to read about bloodsucking demons in her letters, but another thing entirely to be suddenly standing in a room with one.

"Tom," she assured him, "you and your guest are quite safe."

"Forgive me," he replied. "This is all rather a shock, I'm sure you can tell. For the past forty-nine years I'd believed you dead. And now you stand here, striking as ever, alive and seemingly eternal. I must ask you, am I in fact dreaming?"

"I promise you, you are very much awake."

"So I'm not dreaming, and I'm not mad?"

"Not at all. Well, perhaps no more than you ever were."

Tom laughed. The horror in his pale eyes had abated a little, but there was something more than a touch manic in his gaze... again, not unexpected, given his situation. As he looked her up and down in awe, Julie spied the motif upon the cuff of his jacket: three interlinked golden rings, the symbol of the secret brotherhood with whom Sir Hans had become involved.

"I'm happy to see you running your own theatre," she told him. "You've come a long way from that sixteen-year-old stage-rat I once knew."

"The course of life turned out rather fortuitously for me, it is true. In its way, this place is my own little kingdom, and

I do love it so. I live my life for the art, just as passionately as you did. Although, maybe I haven't gotten into quite so many swordfights as yourself. And I fear that the passage of years has not been so kind to me as it has to you."

"Don't assume that time has been kind to me, Tom. This life of mine is not one I should wish upon anyone."

Tom shook his head, as though disbelieving in spite of what stood before his eyes. And yet with each passing moment, his mind accepted a little more that he was looking at Julie d'Aubigny, the same Julie d'Aubigny that he had known and admired all those years ago. It was her face, her voice, still speaking to him now the way she had spoken in Paris.

"For a woman of eighty-two, I'd say you're doing rather well. Just how long ago did you receive this gift of endless youth?"

"1719, was the year that it happened."

"Twelve years after all of France thought that you'd died. I must say, those years have not dimmed your beauty in the slightest. If anything, you are lovelier than ever."

"It's easy for a vampire to look youthful when we've recently fed. Take a look at me when I've gone a week or two without blood, and things would be different. See me when I'm in the throes of hunger, and my beauty would be the last thing on your mind."

"Whatever is it like, to live with such a need? How does one come to terms with preying upon your fellow human beings like animals?"

"It's not easy. The temptation to indulge, to take more than I need, is always there. But I find my ways of keeping the demon at bay. I'm not a murderer."

Julie wondered if she said those words to convince Tom, or herself. Gingerly he reached out one hand towards her, and she stepped forth to take it in hers, letting him feel that she was real, solid, not merely an apparition.

"Does your heart still beat?" he asked.

"Yes," she whispered, laying his aged palm upon her chest. For a time he held it there, waiting, until he felt a single quiet *thump* from beneath her sternum, and his expression softened. The smile upon his lips was more genuine now, less a mask for his terror, and his eyes looked upon her with more wonderment than fear.

"I felt it."

"It's slow," she told him. "Slower than it ever was. It works differently now, to how it used to. But it does still beat, and it does still feel."

"So what brings you back to me now, after all these years?"

Julie paused. What was she to say to him, truly? *It's lovely to see you after so long, Tom, but you may be in danger from Europe's most powerful vampire coven?* He was clearly happy in his life, but if the Laskaris had noticed him, surely she had a duty to tell him as much. She would not be able to protect him by herself, after all, certainly not once she had left London. But first, she had a question of her own to ask him. Her hand moved to the cuff of his jacket, the tip of her thumb caressing the three-ringed motif.

"How did you come to know Sir Hans, Tom?"

"So you know of my acquaintance with him, do you?" he mused. "I met him through a shared fraternity of ours, the Order of Patriotic Oddfellows. We're a group of men devoted to charity and philanthropy. There are some among us with a few... radical ideas about how the social order of Britain could be reshaped, for the benefit of the common folk. Though there are plenty of other reasons why we embrace the moniker of *odd* fellows, of course. There are those in our brotherhood who take an interest in occult matters. I tell you all this in confidence, of course. We are a *secret* society, you know."

"Oh, I'm quite accustomed to keeping secrets."

"Well, there were none among us who took such a keen interest in obscure and esoteric knowledge as old Sir Hans. If only I had known that you and he were correspondents! If only I had known that my old friend Julie lived beyond her death, an immortal vampire."

"Tom, I'm not the only vampire in this city…"

"Mister Ashford?" that sweet, high, feminine voice echoed down the hall from the manager's office. Footsteps were coming this way. "Mister Ashford, are you quite alright?"

Julie looked at Tom.

"Who exactly is your guest?" she mouthed.

"A friend," he told her hurriedly. "Imogen Musgrave."

"*Musgrave*?"

The dressing room door opened.

The girl was a pretty young thing, by Julie's reckoning. In her mid-teens by the look of her, the flower of adult-hood was only just beginning to bloom. If this were the same Imogen Musgrave whom Clayton had mentioned as Arnold's half-sister, then she had clearly lived a far more privileged life than he had. She bore no callouses or pock-marks to tell of childhood diseases and hardships, and her dress was of the fine, fashionable variety. She might not have been true aristocracy, but hers was clearly a life of comfort, compared to so many in this city.

Imogen looked at Julie with confusion, wondering at the identity of this strange, masculine-attired woman who had just appeared in the dressing room. Clearly she had not expected Tom to have other guests this night. Then her eyes caught sight of the row of dressing mirrors, where Tom's reflection was present and Julie's, notably, was not. Imogen's mouth fell open, shocked, but not uncomprehending.

Indeed, she seemed to comprehend just enough to be deeply afraid.

The girl picked up her skirts and ran, sprinting for the room from which she had come. She did not scream. There was not blind panic in her flight, but clear purpose. Whatever she hoped to achieve, however, it availed her nothing. Julie darted after her with impossible swiftness, leaping up to the ceiling and scrambling above Imogen's head, before dropping back down in front of her, cutting off her path. The girl skidded to a halt, coming just short of crashing headlong into the vampire, and in an instant she found her shoulders in the steely grip of Julie's fingers. Behind her, Tom came running and panting, his body rebelling at this unaccustomed exertion.

"She's rather young for you, is she not?" Julie called out playfully to Ashford, before looking Imogen in the eye. "I was but fourteen when the Comte d'Armagnac made me his mistress, you know. So easy to be swayed by older men, is it not? But even he was not in his seventies at the time. Has sly old Tom charmed you so much, at your tender years?"

Imogen's face could certainly be described as horrified, though perhaps less at the accusation and more at the fact that she was staring eye-to-eye with an inhuman predator. The girl's heart was thumping at a mile a minute, her breast heaving and her skin flush with blood, and the demon within Julie was all but salivating at the prospect of such tender prey. She blinked, fighting to keep the red hunger out of her eyes.

"There is nothing so untoward going on here!" Tom protested, between gasping breaths. "And I'm certainly not sleeping with her! Imogen, it's quite alright. You're safe, I promise you. I have the very great honour of introducing you to my old friend, Mademoiselle Maupin."

Julie's hands relinquished their grip. Imogen scurried

backwards, eager to put some distance between herself and the bloodsucker, and she soon found herself backing into Tom. The old man did his best to reassure her, to keep her steady.

"Julie d'Aubigny," Imogen breathed, her eyes wide. "By Heavens, it's all real. Vampires are real."

"Very clever. So you have read the letters as well?" Julie ventured.

"She was here when I translated them for Arnold and Nathaniel," Tom explained. "She never sought out any of this herself. She's an innocent here."

"I am quite capable of speaking for myself!" Imogen snapped, stepping away from Tom. Julie smiled a little, gladdened by the display of the girl's wilfulness. Even in the face of a demon, it seemed she was not willing to let anyone presume on her behalf.

"I did hear the contents of those letters," Imogen asserted. "So if there was truth in them, I know your story."

"You know *part* of my story. Don't assume too much."

"My half-brother knows, doesn't he? Arnold has known all along. That's why he did not want me involved."

"He did not tell me that you knew of this. So I suspect that he does indeed not want you involved. How disappointing for him."

"*Did not tell you?* You mean to say that he has met and conversed with you?"

"I spoke with him on Thursday night, if it pleases you to know. And again yesterday."

Imogen's horror had given way to outrage. Julie could not help but find her suppressed, ladylike furore somewhat adorable.

"It does not please me to know that Arnold chose to involve his father's family in a dangerous affair when he needed help, yet refused to disclose the full details. He allowed us to think that those letters were part of some elaborate fiction, when their author is now standing before me, forty-nine years after her apparent death."

The vampire laughed, gaily. Imogen did not appear to see the humour in the situation.

"Julie," Tom interceded, "just before, you were telling me that you're not the only one in London?"

"You're right," she responded, her momentary levity giving way to seriousness in light of his question. "There are other immortals here. They are looking for those letters. They are looking for every written document that Sir Hans Sloane possessed on the topic of vampires. The fact that you have handled those papers means that they might cross your path. I assure you, they will be far less cordial with you than I."

A look passed between Imogen and Tom. The past few minutes had been a whirling tempest of emotions for the both of them, but now they were confronting the perilousness of their own situation, and they had precious little to hold to beyond Julie's words.

"Whatever can we do to protect ourselves?" Imogen asked. "Surely there must be something."

"Stay indoors after sundown," she told them. "Do not invite strangers into your home, for any reason. If you have any faith that God cares for the lives of mortals, then carry a cross or a Bible with you. Most vampires recoil from displays of piety. And there are some herbs which we find repulsive; garlic, verbena and wild rose can deter us."

It felt like feeble advice. She was telling them to burrow down and ride out the storm, when clearly Imogen wanted to know how to bring the storm to an end.

"Your half-brother has been of some assistance to me," Julie continued. "With his help I believe I have identified exactly what the other vampires want here in England.

Tomorrow I will be moving to ensure that they cannot have it. I think that Arnold may be coming with me. Once that is done and I make sure they learn of it, I think they will retreat to more familiar territories than this one."

"If Arnold is coming with you, then I should also. My brother Nathaniel, too. Arnold's antics, and his insistence upon secrecy, have put us all in the line of fire. We should have a part in resolving this threat to us all."

Imogen's voice and eyes were filled with nothing but determination, for sure. Tom looked deeply uncomfortable. Julie, however, was not going to entertain this notion.

"Oh, I think not."

"Why ever not?"

"Tell me, girl, are you well-schooled in the lore and vul-nerabilities of the creatures of the night?"

"No, but you are, and I am a very quick study."

"Are you a woman of devout faith?"

"I am as faithful as any good Englishwoman."

"Do you know your way about a sword or flintlock?"

"…I do not. I should need to learn, and practice."

"The first time I encountered Arnold, I saw him hold off three vampires through the force of his faith. But you are not him. If I put a cross in your hand right now and allowed you to recite chapter and verse, I think you would struggle to drive me back even a step. And I promise you, there will not be the hours for you to become a proficient combatant during the time in which I intend to act. In a fight you shall be nothing but a liability. You are not coming with me."

"Then I am simply to stay here and hope that you and Arnold can solve this problem by yourselves?"

Again, Julie laughed.

"I am not by myself. I have plenty of other allies. But you are not ready for battle, *ma cheri*. If I were to let you come along, I should only be forcing myself and my companions to protect you. It is an obligation we cannot afford."

Imogen looked sullen, defeated. Her frustration was palpable, caught in the desire to act, but lacking the tools to do so. All that she wanted to do was protect those dearest to her, but Julie was not going to relent. She was not going to take a completely untrained and ill-equipped mortal on a journey to a site of ancient, unholy power. Though admittedly, part of her was tempted to do so, just to see the look on Arnold's face.

"So is there nothing I can do?" the girl asked.

"You can stay here, and stay safe. Keep watch on your family. Make sure they are not being followed. Be alert for any strange alterations to their behaviour. But you must keep all of this secret. This is civilised London. If you try to tell people that creatures from backwards foreign folklore are real, they will think you hysterical. Keep what you know to yourselves, and before this coming week is through, I will bring an end to this business."

It was not a satisfying answer, but the satisfaction of Imogen Musgrave was a very long way down the list of Julie's concerns.

"I should go. It was good to see you, Tom."

She began to make for the exit. Revealing herself here had not been a wise decision. She had enjoyed speaking with Ashford again, but this encounter carried the potential to cause too much trouble. She wondered if she ought to simply feed upon them both, and erase their memories of the past half hour altogether. But in her way she was still fond of Tom, and doing that to him would feel like an act of violation. She could not envision him as a threat to her, and in this instance, she felt more at ease with the risk of trusting him and his young guest.

"Julie, wait."

She stopped, glancing back. Tom was coming after her.

"I have to ask something of you," he began. "Just one small favour."

Julie raised one eyebrow quizzically.

"I know that I ask this with little time to prepare, and a very limited audience to appreciate your efforts, but you should do my humble theatre a great honour if you were to sing upon my stage before you leave."

His request took her by the utmost surprise. For a few seconds she was speechless, unsure if this was his idea of a jest.

"Are you quite serious?"

"I am entirely serious, *Mademoiselle*."

"Tom… I haven't performed on stage since I was mortal. I am decades out of practice."

"And I cannot say how many years I have left in me, Julie. But what I know for certain is that if La Maupin herself visited my theatre, and I did not ask her to sing for me, then I should regret that missed opportunity for the rest of my days. Let me hear your voice one more time."

Singing opera was not something that one could simply step into on a whim. It was a skill that had to be maintained through regular reinforcement. The last time that Julie had sung professionally was in 1705; more time had passed since her last stage performance than the entire length of her mortal lifespan. It seemed ludicrous to think that she could just resume her former role so easily. And yet, there was such exhilarating temptation in thought of doing so. How incredible it would feel to relive the life she once had, even for just one song, for just the ears of her old friend Tom and his young guest, whose bright, clever eyes were still so bitter with disappointment.

"Very well. Give me some time to warm up."

As her audience went to their seats, she chose a dress from among those on the costume rack. It was of laughably poor quality compared to those which she had once worn for the Paris Opéra, but it would suffice. Her mind reached back to her past performances, and as she stood in the dressing room she practised verses from several different songs, trying to find one which she was most comfortable with.

Her contralto voice came back to her more quickly than she expected; much more quickly. It seemed that with every line she practised, her vocal cords fluidly recalled their old movements, summoning up the sounds which had so thrilled and impressed the Parisian nobility some five decades previous. There was no orchestra to support her, no instruments to set the melody; she would be singing a capella, yet the thought of doing so did not intimidate her in the slightest.

She settled upon a song from a part which had once been written specifically for her; the role of the Saracen princess, Clorinde, in André Campra's tragedy Tancrède, set during the first crusade. In 1702, Julie had sang that part during Tancrède's debut performance, to great acclaim. The dress that she wore now did not exactly look the part of a Saracen warrior, but she took the sword-belt from her breeches and wore it atop the dress, so that she would at least have her scimitar by her side.

The theatre may have been silent, but she could hear the orchestra in her head as she made her way up onto the stage. The seats were empty, save for two in the front row where Tom and Imogen sat, yet all too vividly her eyes could recall the golden splendour of Versailles, and a packed audience of richly-dressed and lavishly-perfumed aristocrats. She let the illusion wash over her, consume her, until all that surrounded her were the trappings of the life she had once known. She strode to the front of the stage and bowed deeply to her two viewers, as though they were no less than royalty.

Then she stood straight, parted her lips, and let the music flow.

~ Arnold ~

Sunday October 17th, 1756

The curate awoke to the sound of incessant hammering upon the rectory door. He was in no mood for this. Yesterday afternoon, after giving the morning sermon, Arnold had buried his mother. The funeral had been a thoroughly miserable affair, with only a scant handful of mourners. He had led the ceremony in all its bitter sorrow, his heart heavy with blame for the fact that Reverend Lowther was lying unconscious in a hospital bed. The surgeons had done what they could, and the vicar was still alive for now, but even they were unsure that he would ever awaken.

Arnold knew that the alms collected by St Mary's would not last long in the face of physician's bills, but it seemed that God had delivered a reprieve in the form of the N'Dour twins, who had offered to cover all costs of the reverend's treatment. Arnold had accepted their overture, acknowledging their generosity, but it brought him little comfort to do so. He could not escape the fact that death and suffering had come to everyone he cared for, and that he felt responsible.

Then had come the arduous task of writing to the bishop, announcing his immediate sabbatical from the role of curate of St Mary's. The bishop would in all likelihood take it as a resignation, an admittance that Arnold possessed neither the heart nor the stomach to continue in his position after the mysterious and brutal attack upon Charles Lowther. He fully expected that he would come back from Cornwall to find St Mary's under the leadership of a new vicar, with a new curate and no chance for Arnold to reclaim his old job. Every minute as he penned the letter, he wondered if he should just elect to stay here instead, keeping the church running and spending every free hour by the vicar's bedside, hoping that the old man would awaken from his ordeal. Nothing was forcing him to go along with that bloodsucking monster and her pack of miscreants, after all. Nothing, except for the unshakable feeling that this was the path that God wanted him to walk.

When Arnold had finally gone to bed for the evening, the only truly good thing he could say for this day was that at least his mother had a grave. Lisa Brennan's body had been given its own resting place beneath consecrated soil, and not dumped to rot in a pauper's grave as he had first feared. He had gone to sleep in the knowledge that he had accomplished that much, but now even his respite was being invaded by the frantic pounding of a hand upon his door.

With a groan he dragged himself from beneath his threadbare blankets, reaching first for a candle, but then thinking better of it. Instead he sat on the bed with his eyes open for a time, forcing his bleary vision to swim into focus. Fingers groped for the crucifix on his bedside table, and once he had that in his grasp, his other hand sought out the loaded pistol. Carefully he left his room, and proceeded towards the main door of the rectory, weapons in hand. If House Laskaris or the Company of the Holy Sacrament had come to finish him off at this hour, they would not take him without a fight. When he opened the door just a crack and peered outside, however, the face that he saw was the very last one he expected.

"Imogen?"

"Arnold, Brother, I need to speak to you. This is vitally important."

"Imogen, it's very late, and Whitechapel is hardly safe for a young lady. What are you even doing here?"

"It is very late. Mother will be furious with me for not letting Wilson drive me home sooner. But I shall accept her reprimands, because I *must* speak with you. If you think me unsafe out here, then will you please let me in?"

"Yes, yes, come inside. Just wait here in the hall. I'm in my nightshirt, I need to dress properly."

Imogen hurriedly made her way in, and looked him up and down.

"You answered the door with gun and crucifix in hand?" she observed, and then added –"Of course you did. That makes perfect sense."

"Just wait here a moment, please."

Arnold returned to his quarters, quickly changing into some daytime clothes. Once decent, he opened the bed-room door and invited his half-sister to join him.

"For what do you wish to see me?"

"Tonight I met Julie d'Aubigny," she stated bluntly, and Arnold felt a look of worry overtake him. Fear gripped his gut at the thought of Imogen being drawn into this unholy mess.

"I was visiting Mister Ashford at the Minories, and she came to see him," she continued. "I saw her standing before a mirror without reflection. I saw her move faster than mortals can move. She is more than eighty years old, yet her face looks barely half of that. I was left in no doubt as to what she is. But you knew this when you met Nathaniel and I on Thursday, did you not? You knew all along."

"Yes," Arnold said, seeing no point in lying at this stage. If she had already come face-to-face with the truth, then his breaking the Ninth Commandment would not spare her any further pain or danger. "Yes, I knew. I didn't want you to be involved, Imogen. I didn't know that Nathaniel was going to bring you along that night."

"You had no right to keep this from us, Arnold. Our family is being stalked by monsters. You're a man of God, is it not your job to protect people from the forces of evil?"

"It is my job, and it is an obligation I take extremely seriously, my sister. But had I approached Nathaniel or yourself a week ago, how might I have possibly convinced you of the threat? If I tried to explain what I had discovered, you'd think me an eccentric, lost in backwards superstition. If I pressed the issue, you'd think me mad. I'd have been locked up in Bedlam."

"But now you're working with her. She said as much."

"I am working *alongside* her. She happens to be fighting against the vampires who murdered our father. I am not her ally, we simply share a common enemy."

Imogen stopped, her eyes widening at Arnold's words. In the moment, it had not occurred to him that she was still unaware.

"It was they who killed Father?"

"Yes. Yes, I am sorry. They are responsible for our father's death, and my mother's."

He could see the rage boiling behind the girl's eyes. Her delicate frame was trembling, incandescent. The news had stirred up the grief that she had spent the past month laying to rest, and now it was all the more intense with the knowledge of the culprit.

"Why?" she stammered, her pained lips struggling to form the words. "Why did they kill him?"

"He had knowledge that they wanted. Documents.

Maybe they tried to force him to hand them over, but he would not comply. I don't know, exactly. But they killed him, and in his will, he left those papers to me."

"So you have them here, these papers that Father died for?"

"Not any longer. They were stolen from me, by another group of vampire-hunters. It is a… complicated issue. That robbery is the reason that Vicar Lowther is currently in the hospital."

"There is more," Imogen asserted. "I went to see Tom tonight because I wanted his help in identifying something. There was an item that was on Father's person when he died, and his will made it clear that it was left to me. It was a piece of jewellery, or something like one, an amulet of sorts. He also left me a sealed note, which told me to keep that item about me should I ever feel afraid or threatened. I have been trying for weeks to identify what it is. It's some unusual kind of metal, with strange markings carved upon it, in no language I have ever seen. It matches nothing in any of my books. But when Tom read those letters to us, they stirred a suspicion in me. I think it may be orichalcum. I think Father intended it to protect against vampires."

She extended her hand towards Arnold, showing the aged, lumpen disc of silver-bronze metal that she was holding. It might once have been a fine piece of work, but time and neglect had left it with a crude and weathered appearance, not the sort of thing that a fashionable lady or gentleman of this city would wear for jewellery. A cruciform sigil was engraved at its centre, and around it were circular markings of some alien script. Arnold's eyes widened as he recognised the nature of those markings, and gingerly he traced them with one finger.

"Do you recognise this?" Imogen asked him.

"Those markings… they are a form of writing. I don't

know the language, but I have seen something very similar, just recently."

"Do you know their purpose?"

"Yes. They were inscribed upon an iron strongbox. They were part of an occult spell, some kind of heathen magic. They made it impossible for vampires to touch the box."

"So this is a talisman to be used against them?"

"That seems certain, yes."

If his father had been carrying that item on the night that he was killed, Arnold wondered if it ought to have been sufficient to drive away his attackers. At Rozgonyi's house, Julie had said that she could feel the power of those inscriptions without touching them. Even if Sean was not a devout man, this sorcery by itself was enough to force a vampire to recoil. But perhaps, much like Arnold's cross, it would not stop a vampire from pulling a trigger.

"Imogen… I was told that Father was murdered when I was summoned to Whitfield's office, but there were certain details I never asked for. Were you ever informed of the exact nature of the wound that killed him?"

"I was told that he was shot, at very close range."

Arnold looked towards the pistol which lay upon his bedside table and immediately felt sick. His sense of nausea must have shown upon his face, for Imogen followed his gaze towards the weapon.

"I took that from a dead strigoi. I never realised…"

Imogen went pale.

"By God… by God, Arnold, is that the gun that killed our father?"

"I did not know! It might not be, but I don't know!"

"It doesn't matter," Imogen said, choking out the words, though Arnold was uncertain if she was assuring him or herself. "It's just a weapon. Wood and steel, nothing more. You said you took it from a dead *strigoi*?"

"Strigoi, yes. They're one kind of vampire, among many. He threatened me with that weapon, and then Julie arrived and cut off his head. It was the first time I saw her. I took the pistol from his body."

"Then at least justice for Father's murder is done."

Arnold looked at his half-sister. He had never imagined that her young face could hold such a look of cold resolve. She was fearful, terrified even, but there was more courage in her than he would have previously credited. She returned his gaze, and pressed the metal amulet into his hand.

"You take it," she told him. "It did not protect Father from a bullet, but it might be of more use to you. You are the one who is going hunting for these creatures."

"Imogen, this was left for your protection."

"And I am *giving* it to you. But I want you to tell me how they can be fought. They must have weaknesses, or they would have conquered us all long ago."

Arnold nodded.

"They do. They are strong in the night, but the daylight weakens them," he explained. "They cannot bear the signs of faith and piety. And they cannot enter a home unless invited in."

"Mademoiselle Maupin told me that there are also herbs which repel them. She mentioned garlic, verbena and wild rose."

"I have not been told of such, but it may be true. My knowledge of them is far from complete."

"Should I believe her word?"

"I would say that she is a creature born of evil, and is not to be trusted. But she has not lied to me, that I know of."

"Then I shall heed her advice along with yours. I will do what I can to proof my home against these devils. I expect that when I come home tonight, Mother will forbid me all excursions for a time, as punishment for my late return. In light of what I have learned, I shall be happy to oblige."

"See to it that you do, Sister. Vampires have already taken my father and my mother from me. I could not bear to lose any more kin to them. There is Communion wafer and blessed water here at St Mary's, I shall give you some to take with you. Keep it about you at all times."

"Thank you, Brother. I have every intention to survive this," she affirmed, "but you have to put an end to this evil business. Work with Julie d'Aubigny, or do whatever else you must, but do not stop until they have all been slain or driven out of London. Promise me as much."

Arnold took her hand.

"I promise. May God watch over and protect you."

He barely slept the rest of the night. As much as he wanted to rest, Arnold could not banish the demons from his thoughts, and by morning he was feeling quite exhausted. All the same, he had his meagre possessions packed for the journey, and he waited in the rectory without unlocking the church. He did not know when – or even if – he would deliver another sermon in the white chapel.

When he heard the sound of approaching hooves and the rattle of wheels, he moved to the door and locked it behind him, before turning to watch as a large carriage with shuttered windows rolled to a stop, drawn by four impressive horses. Saul N'Dour and Lawrence Clayton both sat up front in the driver's seats, while the carriage's remaining occupants were concealed within. Atop the roof were tied a couple of large travel chests, along with six wooden barrels, covered by a canvas tarpaulin.

"You have made your decision," Saul greeted him, his words a statement rather than a question.

"I have," Arnold replied. "I shall come with you."

"Then you can ride on the roof, or stay inside with the ladies."

"So long as the weather is dry, I will take the roof, thank you."

"A wise choice. I think that my sister and Julie should prefer to keep their privacy on this journey."

Arnold climbed atop the carriage, settling down with his back against one of the barrels. It was not an especially comfortable way to sit, but certainly no worse than the church pews at St Mary's. With Saul at the reins the carriage began to roll forward, and Arnold pulled the brim of his hat low over his face, hoping that as the trip progressed he might be able to make up for some of last night's lost sleep.

"What is in these barrels?" he asked, curious as to what cargo they were carrying.

"Gunpowder," Saul called up to him, causing Arnold to sit upright with a start.

"This man and his sister tell me the best way to deal with ancient demonic ruins is to blow them up," Clayton added. "But I'm sure once that's done you can say some prayers over the smoking crater. That ought to keep both man and God happy, wouldn't you say?"

But knowing that he was riding with six barrels of explosive powder made the young curate far from happy. Somehow he doubted that he would find much rest on this trip after all.

Before leaving London, the group stopped on Dover Street and retrieved the strongbox from Rozgonyi's house. Arnold aided Saul and Clayton in carrying the hefty box and adding it to their existing luggage, though he felt somewhat superfluous next to the two far stronger men. Heathen magic or no, he was glad to have the item with him, for it gave him a chance to examine the strange letters painted along its edges. They were definitely the same arcane language as the markings upon the amulet which now rested in his pocket, though he could not even begin to guess at what the words might say, or how the incantations should be pronounced.

The carriage made its way down Piccadilly, westward as far as Knight's Bridge and then beyond, leaving the grey urban sprawl of London behind as their surroundings gave way to farmers' fields. The sky above was heavy with clouds, but no rain was yet falling, so in spite of himself, Arnold lowered his hat once more and made another attempt to sleep.

The road journey from London to Penzance was some three hundred miles, or thereabouts, so under typical conditions their travelling time would be expected to be around nine or ten days, accounting for the poorer-quality roads that they would have to deal with once they went west of Exeter. The weight of the carriage meant that they would have to change horses relatively frequently at coaching inns, and while this was an expense, it was one which the twins were quite capable of paying. The expected rigours of travel were explained to Arnold by Clayton during their first day on the road, but they soon found that the conditions of travelling with a vampire were far from typical.

Most carriages only travelled in daylight, stopping at inns or by the roadside after dark, but by nightfall it seemed that Julie was quite willing to take the reins. Much as she could manipulate the minds of humans, so too did it seem that she could subject beasts to her will, and with her power driving them, the horses would push on tirelessly, seemingly untroubled by fatigue.

Arnold did not see Julie feed during this time, even when he tried to stay awake through the night to watch her. He imagined that she must sustain herself upon sleeping travellers that they encountered in the dark, but if that were the case, she clearly had no intention of letting him see it happen. Although Arnold was morbidly curious, he could not bring himself to ask her.

At dawn of each day they would take a few hours to rest, and then the journey would continue with Saul or Clayton at the reins, on to the next inn to trade their exhausted animals for new ones, and for the group's human members to buy food and drink. For Arnold this was all new experience, for he had never before travelled beyond the city of his birth.

By Wednesday they had passed the town of Yeovil in Somerset, which Aida said lay roughly halfway to Penzance. It was a crisp and clear October day, cold but exquisitely bright, and Arnold sat upon the carriage roof with Saul as Clayton drove the horses. His gaze took in the green expanse of the countryside, its rolling fields and trees that were a blaze of gold and red autumnal leaves. It was a world away from the smog and soot that had surrounded him all his life.

"I never knew that the world held such beauty," he mused, glancing upwards to watch birds wheeling in the sky above. He breathed deeply, inhaling not the noisome stink of the city, but air that was clean and fresh.

"The world is a big place," Saul replied. "Full of beauty, and ugliness, and strangeness. You would do well to see more of it."

"Perhaps I would. Perhaps when all of this is over, I will find a new calling as a missionary."

Saul laughed, for the first time that Arnold had heard. It was an irresistible sound, both deep and gentle, like velvet upon the ears. The curate found himself smiling.

"Is that really so funny?" he asked.

"I find it easy to envisage you as a missionary," Saul replied. "You seem exactly the sort."

Arnold was unsure if that was a compliment, but the man's words had drawn his curiosity.

"I take it that you have met a number of missionaries, then?"

"Growing up in Saint-Louis, of course I have. In the past, missionaries proved quite fortuitous to my family."

"Tell me about it, if you would. Tell me where you came from, and how you came to be here, with Mademoiselle Maupin."

Saul turned his head to observe him. There was something deeply, penetratingly intelligent about the Black man's eyes, and Arnold could not escape the unsettling feeling that he was being studied. Saul looked back towards the road ahead as he began his story.

"My family have been wealthy merchants for many generations. My ancestors built their trade in gold, salt, ivory and slaves. When Europeans first came, we traded with them and grew all the richer for it, even when the foreigners started to war among themselves. But when the French came to Ndar island and built the port of Saint-Louis in 1659, my great-great-grandfathers were quick to realise the direction of the wind. They had previously followed the teachings of Mohammed, but to gain favour with the French they renounced Islam and adopted the ways of the Holy Cross. My family soon grew close to the colonial authorities."

"You're Catholic? I have not seen you wearing a cross."

"My sister and I were raised Catholic. Our time spent with Julie has changed our outlook somewhat."

"I see."

"My father wanted his eldest children to benefit from a French education. He had many friends and business partners among the French, so he was able to secure places for us in Paris. I went to university at the Sorbonne. My sister went to finishing school. It was an important time for us both, and it was where we met Julie."

"How did it happen?"

"A friend of mine, a fellow student, fell suddenly ill. I did not believe that his sickness, nor his death soon afterwards, were entirely natural. I made it my business to investigate, and my sister aided me. We did not know what to expect, but we learned that my friend had become prey to an upyr who was passing through Paris at the time. A creature by the name of Piotr Kovalevsky. In our efforts to find him, we crossed paths with Julie d'Aubigny. After we helped her to destroy him, she asked us to become her companions."

"That's quite remarkable. And your father back home had no objections to this?"

"Our father believes that we are travelling with an adventurous French noblewoman, meeting many important people and becoming experienced in the refined ways of European society. My sister writes very persuasive letters to him, telling him of the valuable things we have learned, and why he should continue to send us credit notes to finance our travels. Someday, when I return home, I may tell him the truth."

"Do you look forward to returning home? Must be nice to have a life of wealth and comfort to return to."

The question caused Saul's demeanour to shift. The change was subtle, and while the conversation thus far had been genial, Arnold perceived rather less cheer in the man's voice when he replied.

"You are of Irish descent, yes?"

"Yes, I am. My mother and father, both."

"I am told that the Irish are not held in high regard in England. You are Christian subjects of the British Empire, and among England's closest neighbours, yet many view you as no better than savages."

"Well, as a clergyman I–"

"But Sir Hans Sloane was also an Irishman, and he became personal physician to your Royal family."

"He did indeed."

"So tell me, do you think that wealth and comfort would taste as sweet to you, when they are dependent upon capitulation to a foreign interloper?"

Saul became quiet after that, and sensing that he did not wish to continue the discussion, Arnold did not press him further. The N'Dour twins were surely among the most unusual people he had ever met, but he was glad that some part of their mystery had been revealed to him. In his three days on the road with them he could not fail to notice that a great deal of affection existed between Aida and Julie, and given what he knew of the vampire's past, he could only assume that the two women were lovers.

It was not a notion which sat comfortably with him, but he did his best to pay them no mind. He was, after all, travelling with an ageless semi-demon who drank the blood of mortals and possessed an array of unearthly capabilities; compared to those things, her predilection towards female paramours seemed like a minor footnote.

The group made it to Penzance in six days, arriving on the afternoon of Saturday the 23rd of October. When Julie disembarked from the carriage, she did so under Aida's parasol, and Arnold was struck by just how different she now seemed, compared to how he had seen her previously. He had witnessed the vampire's strength and power many times now, and the terrible things that she could do were seared into his memory, but none of that power looked to be in her now.

Beneath the sunlight her movements were so much weaker, her bearing so much more fragile, that she could have been a completely different woman. She looked older to his eyes, her usual pallor having grown to the point of unhealthiness. Her skin appeared thin and parched, with dark veins faintly visible in places, and even her hair was dry and discoloured, devoid of its typical lustre. She kept her eyes hidden behind a pair of smoked-glass lenses.

At the Penzance docks they wasted no time looking for a ship to take them and their belongings to St Martin's, though the captain looked at Julie with unease. The boisterous old sailor voiced his concern that the seas could be rough at this time of year, and that the journey may be hard upon a lady who looked to be in a delicate state of constitution. Repeated assurances were given until he agreed to sail them to the island, however, and the offer of additional coin was enough to waylay his worries for Julie's health.

The ship carried the five passengers, four horses and their cargo across the surging waters, over what had once been the glorious kingdom of Lyonesse. Arnold could not help but peer into the murk and the salty spray, wondering what relics of that fallen nation might still endure beneath those waves. At one point he journeyed up to the helm and asked the captain if he knew anything of the ancient land that had once stood here, and the sailor spun him a tale of how on certain days, when the tides and the currents were right, one could hear the bells of Lyonesse's sunken cathedral ringing from within the water.

None of the others on deck commented on the matter, though Arnold found it haunting to contemplate that a Christian cathedral might still be found upon the seabed. Saul had said that the Gargouilles de la Mer were an extinct race, but in Arnold's mind it was all too easy to envision the coldly graceful silhouettes of piscine demons, gliding silently through ruins which had once been a house of God. If any among Satan's creatures were capable of surviving the Great Flood, it would surely be devils who made their home in the sea.

Arnold kept his thoughts to himself, however, as the

ship negotiated its way past the rugged outcroppings of the Chimney Rocks, Great Ganilly and English Island, finally arriving at St Martin's and docking near the golden sands of Higher Town Bay.

The white shapes of guillemots squawked and screeched overhead, calling to one another, clustering around the vessel in hopes that it was a fishing boat landing with a feast, but the hungry birds would be disappointed. For Arnold, their cawing shrieks almost felt like a war-cry, a challenge from the lips of Semjâzâ himself. Here he was, far from home for the first time in his life, in the company of dangerous people and a far more dangerous vampire, as they set out to find an ancient place where the darkest of powers still tainted the Earth.

In London, Arnold had spent his life looking upon the evils that lay within the human soul, and doing whatever he could to fight them. But now, in this strange and beautiful place, he was seeking out a purer, more primal force of malice than any he had known. He should rightly have been scared, but in truth he was trembling with anticipation. Now that he was here, he was ready to face evil, to fight the good fight, and he would do so with the same fervent righteousness that had filled him before. At last, the hunt was afoot.

~ Julie ~

Saturday October 23ʳᵈ, 1756

At barely two miles from end to end, St Martin's was tiny, and taverns were rather scarce. Fortunately there were none too many travellers here at this time of year, and Julie and her companions were able to acquire lodgings at an inn called The Rock of Priscillian without any great difficulty. The lodgings were far from sumptuous, but they would serve their purpose. The horses were stabled and the carriage was tied up outside, while their travel cases were moved to the upstairs rooms. The twins had certainly drawn their share of curious stares from the locals drinking at their tables; a couple of Black-skinned strangers dressed in aristocratic finery were a rare enough sight in London, but in a place such as this, Julie suspected that most of the residents had never seen – or perhaps never even imagined – such a thing.

Following their arrival, Saul and Aida ordered food from the kitchen downstairs with Arnold and Clayton, while Julie retreated to her room in order to wait out the rest of the daylight hours. Given the choice, it was her preference to leave no more than two nights between her meals. Feeding little and often was the best way to keep the demon in check, and ensure that she did not succumb to the killing urge.

The six days she had spent on the road here had only permitted her to feed very sparingly, however, and by sundown she was hungry. The stable boy tending the horses served to slake her thirst, the poor lad not even sensing her approach until her hand slipped over his mouth and her teeth pierced his throat.

In the ecstasy of feeding, her self-control had faltered and she took more from him than she intended, but the boy was strong and he would live. Afterwards she coaxed away his memories of the attack, and left him unconscious atop a pile of straw as the horses snorted and whinnied nervously. On her way back up to the bedroom she contemplated upon the way that the blood of country-folk was different to that of city-dwellers. There was typically far less variety to be tasted in remote places such as this, the flavour and texture of her prey was much more uniform than in a diverse metropolis, but their blood often seemed healthier, less contaminated with illness and industrial filth.

She chided herself for indulging such thoughts; drinking blood was both the greatest of pleasures and the vital crux of her existence, but she did not wish to think in the manner of those vampires who viewed humans as nothing but walking meals, their lives brief and inconsequential.

Arriving at her guest room door, Julie paused and glanced along the landing towards the room where the men of their party were staying. She had walked past Aida and her brother downstairs at the bar, and Clayton had been nearby, but the curate was not among them. He was up here now, however; she could smell him on the far side of his door. The thought struck her that maybe now was a fitting opportunity to converse with him alone. There were some discussions that were better had one-on-one, with no twins or Clayton to intimidate him, no Michel Renard whispering in his ear and no recently-deceased mother to stir his grief. She opened the door to Arnold's room and slipped inside.

Although her footsteps may be silent, the door hinges were not. The boy's head turned in her direction as he heard the squeaking of neglected metal. He was kneeling before the open window at the far end of the room, his little crucifix clutched in one hand. Julie closed the door behind her, and she saw his fingers tighten around the cross. He rose to his feet and his eyes met hers. For a moment she saw the same pitiless hostility that had filled his gaze in Lisa Brennan's room, and again when she had confronted him at St Mary's, but with some clear effort on his part, his look softened.

"I did not intend to interrupt you at prayer," she began, "but I thought it best that we talk."

"I was just finishing, actually," he replied. "and I expected that sooner or later you would wish to converse. So let us talk, Miss d'Aubigny. Or do you prefer Miss Maupin? Since we are joining forces, I should really adopt a more civil term of address for you than 'demon'."

The vampire's lips twitched into a hint of a smile.

"Just 'Julie' will suffice from you, Monsieur Brennan. I find that my surname is rarely pronounced correctly by English-speaking tongues. And 'Maupin' is for the stage only, and besides, it was my husband's name."

For all the terrible truths that he had learned in recent weeks, it seemed that there were some revelations which could still take Arnold by surprise. For a second or two, the young curate looked positively shocked.

"You're *married?*"

Deeply amused by his expression, Julie let out a girlish laugh. Arnold was swift to regain his composure, but she was not going to forget the fleeting look on his face.

"Do you find that so unlikely?"

"I… well, I suppose… with all I'd heard of your life, I never imagined that you would have much interest in Holy matrimony."

"It was arranged for me," she admitted. "When I came of age, my lover wished to ensure that I would be provided for, so he found me a suitable husband. Jean Maupin was a tax official, a dependable sort, but we were hardly a love-match. When he was sent to work in Toulouse, I did not follow. I did see him again, towards the very end of his life."

Arnold shook his head.

"A young woman enters a marriage arranged for her by her lover. It is… it's not how things are done where I come from."

"Common enough in France," Julie told him with a shrug. "And I suspect it is far more common than a pious man like you would think, among the upper echelons of English society."

Her whimsical demeanour grew more serious.

"But I think you know what I really came here to discuss."

Arnold nodded, fully understanding. He had not let go of his crucifix.

"You wish to be certain that I am not going to turn on you."

"You already tried to betray me once."

"And I don't regret it for myself, nor for you," he told her, his gaze not flinching from hers even when a spark of red fury flashed in her eyes. "Only for what they did to Charles Lowther. I believed that I was doing the right thing. Renard and his men are violent, dangerous, and I was wrong to trust them. But given the opportunity, I would still prefer to conduct this hunt alongside fellow men of God, than align myself with a vampire. Make no mistake, I am here only because I see no other way to join this fight."

"And when this is over?" she asked him. "When we have

found and destroyed the Gargouille ruins, and denied the Laskaris their prize? What happens between us then?"

"Then I will return to London, repent of my sins before God, and find whatever life will best allow me to serve him. I did tell Saul that I may take up missionary work in the colonies."

"So you will not seek to destroy me, once we no longer have a common goal?"

"No, I won't. I don't believe that a vampire can ever be a part of God's kingdom, but in hunting your own kind I think you are serving His purpose. I don't understand why the Lord would choose an instrument such as yourself to do His will, but... He does work His works in mysterious ways. Though forgive me, I shall pray fervently that God prevents our paths from crossing ever again."

"I am glad to hear that. Whatever your failings, and your unbearable sanctimony, there is good in your heart, Monsieur Brennan. I should hate for the two of us to come to blows."

She turned away, about to leave him alone, but as she took hold of the door handle, she found that playfully vindictive urge rising within her once more. Julie glanced back over her shoulder towards Arnold.

"The Church of England permits its clergy to marry, does it not?"

"It does," the boy replied, uncertain of where this question was leading. Julie turned to face him fully.

"But you have no wife."

"I do not," he told her. "In my commitment to God I have never found myself with the time to pursue such things."

"And before you joined the Church, you never laid with a woman?"

Arnold had stared her dead in the eye a moment ago, but now he was looking anywhere else, his cheeks reddening with discomfort. This was clearly a topic he was not accustomed to discussing, least of all with a woman.

"To lay with another outside of matrimony is adultery, and that is a sin which I have thus far not committed."

"Thus far."

Julie stepped towards him, one hand moving to gently touch the boy's chest. She did not have to press her palm to him to feel the rising thunder of his heartbeat; in this moment, her ears could have detected that from down the hall.

"With all the danger that surrounds you, there is no guarantee you will survive this hunt of ours," she whispered. "If you do not wish to face death as a virgin, I could initiate you right now."

She tilted her head towards his throat, her lips mere inches from him. His fingers gripped his cross, and yet, he had not raised it to force her back. Tortuous seconds passed in which he wrestled with temptation. On some level it felt cruel to play with him like this, but Julie was loving every moment of it.

"Would Miss N'Dour not consider this a betrayal?"

"She would happily join in, if I invite her. Your first time could be with both of us. Just imagine that."

He was certainly imagining that. She could all but see the images that danced through his thoughts, conjured by her words. Her hand rose to softly caress his cheek as she moved to kiss him.

"I would thank you to leave me alone," he finally gasped. Her fingertips tightened upon the front of his shirt, and for a moment she considered reaching down between his legs, just to see if his resistance would crumble, but she decided against. She had tormented the poor boy quite enough for now. Stepping back, she gave him some room to breathe.

"Hold on to that faith of yours, Arnold. We're going to

need it. And make yourself ready, we're having a strategy meeting soon."

With a nod of respect, she opened the door and complied with his request.

An hour after sundown, the five hunters convened in one guest room. The arsenal chest was open, and Saul was busying himself with checking and preparing their weapons. The papers recovered from the house on Dover Street were piled upon a table, along with pages of hand-scrawled notes made during the journey here, and a sailor's map of the Isles of Scilly which Aida had purchased. Julie folded her arms across her chest and leaned back against the wall. Aida was addressing the group, and the proud hint of a smile formed upon the vampire's lips as she watched her protégé explain the situation to the gathered men.

"We had ample time to examine Rozgonyi's documents while we were on the road," Aida began. "We know that Sir Hans and his friend from Buda-Pest planned to come here looking for Gargouille de la Mer ruins. We also know what they believed those ruins to be. It seems that they conducted a good deal of research, examining fragments of the *Kitab Al-Azif* and other occult scriptures, and they learned that sea-dwellers worshipped Gods of their own. Sir Hans referred to these deities as the Qlippothic Ones, ancient forces of evil which dwell in the Outer Darkness."

"And I say unto you, That many shall come from the east and west, and shall sit down with Abraham, and Isaac, and Jacob, in the kingdom of heaven," Arnold said, quoting the Book of Matthew. *"But the children of the kingdom shall be cast out into outer darkness: there shall be weeping and gnashing of teeth."*

"Yes," Aida confirmed, "that is the Outer Darkness of which they speak. A place beyond Creation, beyond hope, beyond light. The Qlippothic Ones are the denizens of that realm, terrible forms that are hateful and powerful beyond measure. The Gargouilles revered them, and once performed great rituals of sacrifice to them. They built shrines and temples in which to commune with their Gods. Most of these places are deep beneath the ocean, but in times long past, some of them were built upon the land. Sir Hans was searching for the last remnants of these shrines. They are places in which the Outer Darkness touches upon the world of mortals, and where the power of the Qlippothic Ones can be invoked with the correct rituals."

"We cannot allow any such place to endure."

"And we shall not. Now that we are here, we can investigate the house that Sir Hans purchased for István Rozgonyi. Hopefully we will find clues there, to where exactly they believed these ruins to be found. If not, we will simply have to scout every island in this archipelago until we find them ourselves. Fortunately, when I spoke to one of the sailors on the boat from Penzance, he told me that the tides are very low here in the autumn. I suspect that the ruins will be in one of the coastal caves."

"And once we find them, we can roll those barrels of gunpowder down there and blow them to smithereens," Clayton added, clearly reiterating his enthusiasm for this solution.

"Will that be enough?" Arnold questioned.

"From what Sir Hans believed, the ruins of the original shrine should be an essential component to any works of magic that are performed there," Aida replied. "Destroying them will make it impossible for any outsider to exploit the site's power easily. But in theory, the area could be rebuilt, or repurposed by someone with the correct mystic knowledge. You may not be an ordained priest, Mister Brennan, but you are the only man of the Church that we have. It would be worth you doing what you can to bless or sanctify the area afterwards. If the surrounding land can be made Holy, it will only further discourage House Laskaris from going there."

"I am not ordained, Miss N'Dour, but if I pray, I do believe that God will hear my plea. I will do all that I can."

"And what is the likelihood of us meeting resistance?" Saul asked, placing Arnold and Clayton's respective pistols upon the table. The weapons were cleaned and freshly loaded, and the two men took the flintlocks with a nod of thanks.

"Of that we cannot be certain," Aida said, a rare note of unease in her usually calm voice. "All the information we have tells us that the Gargouilles perished from the Earth long ago. Sir Hans certainly did not expect to encounter any alive in his searches. But we are looking for a place that is tainted by the Outer Darkness, a place set apart from God's kingdom. We cannot truly know what may dwell there."

"The one that you saw in the Yucatán," Arnold said to Julie. "What was it like? Was it defended?"

"It was deep beneath a cenote, far underground," the vampire told him. "No air-breathing creature could hold its breath long enough to reach that place. And anyone who came searching for it must intrude upon the territory of the Nine Lords themselves. I think that the shrine needed no greater defences than that. But if I had tried to destroy it, I cannot say what might have happened. With the power that I felt in that place, it could have possessed any number of arcane protections. True magic is rare in the world, and my understanding of it is far from expert. I have no way of knowing."

"Whatever we may face, I trust in the Lord to see us through. We are doing His will."

Arnold's remark caused Julie to meet his eyes with a look, recalling their exchange in his room. She was pleased that his conviction had not faltered, despite his discomfort towards her earlier behaviour.

"Then let us begin our search," Aida concluded. "The house that we need overlooks Scilly Point, at the northern tip of the island. We shall proceed there."

The sailor with whom Aida had spoken was not wrong about the tides. As the group made their way along the clifftop path on the island's western coast, they could see that the waters beneath them were in distant retreat, leaving exposed stretches of sandy beach and rocky shore alike. Tonight was the night of the new moon; if the skies had been overcast then the evening would have been as black as pitch, but the night was clear and the white swathe of the milky way gleamed above with millions of twinkling lights.

The starlight was sufficient to see by, even for Arnold, who of all the group was the least accustomed to working in the darkness. To Julie's inhuman senses the night was as clear as a summer's afternoon, and whenever she glanced upwards with her keen eyes, she felt as though she could count each individual star. Her thoughts echoed back to her journey to England aboard the *Agueda*. She recalled the taste of that young deckhand, Christiano... she recalled how he too had been contemplating the stars, before she sunk her fangs into him.

At Scilly Point, the tide had withdrawn far enough that it would be a simple matter to cross over the rocks from St Martin's to the uninhabited White Island further north. The five hunters had no reason to go that far, of course, for the house that they sought was quite obvious. The two-storey construction of weather-beaten granite stood alone upon barren, rocky ground, its front windows peering eastwards over the bay, towards the large protruding rocks of Little Ledge and Great Merrick Ledge.

The building looked neglected to the point of dilapidation; the house on Dover Street may have been abandoned, but this one looked as though nobody had lived here for years. Whole patches of roof slates were broken or missing, and the windows had been shuttered for so long that the hinges had rusted closed. If Sir Hans had indeed purchased it for Rozgonyi, it seemed that his Hungarian friend had long ago ceased to pay the place any mind.

Julie approached the front door cautiously, sniffing the air. There was a musty scent from the interior of the house, but nothing more than would be expected from such an ill-cared for building, and nothing to suggest that any blood-sucker had set foot here. All the same, she could not shake off a feeling of apprehension, a sense that something was deeply amiss. She tried the front door and found it locked, so she gestured to Clayton and quietly stepped aside for the detective to perform his work. Unlike the shutter hinges, the interior of the lock had thankfully not rusted solid, and after a short period of attention from Clayton and his lockpicks, the door opened with a *clunk*.

A look of trepidation passed between the group as the heavy wooden door swung outward, revealing the house's murky hallway. Blades were drawn and pistols cocked, just in case they should become necessary. Aida took out her tinderbox and struck a flame, using it to light a pair of lanterns. One was handed across to Clayton and Arnold; the other she kept for herself and Saul. With the way open, Julie took a step towards the threshold. A house that had been uninhabited for so long should pose no hindrance to her, for who could possibly call this place home?

And yet her instincts still revolted at the thought of proceeding, and she paused as she made ready to step through the door, unable to shake off the sense of deterrence that it presented. Her eyes fixed upon the interior of the jamb, where a familiar style of writing had been carved into the wood. Aida lifted her lantern to illuminate the inscriptions. They appeared to run right around the door frame, and the carving looked to be quite recent.

"What do you think it is for?" she asked.

"I don't know," Julie replied. Warily, she extended one hand until her fingers almost touched the letters. Her arm began to shake with muscular tremors, straining with the effort of forcing her way in uninvited. But no sudden pain struck her, and she felt no prickle of her skin or thrumming in her veins to suggest the presence of active magic.

"I don't think it's a protection ritual," she ventured, "or at least not one against my kind. Perhaps it is a spell which has not yet been completed. I could understand Rozgonyi wanting to ward this place against dark powers, but these marks are not years-old. Someone has been here very recently. Whoever it was, they might have been making preparations for something."

"Shall we proceed?" Saul enquired, appraising the markings for himself. Julie saw him reach into his pocket and retrieve his iron medallion, holding the item up to compare the engravings upon it with those of the door frame. Much like the sigils painted upon Rozgonyi's strongbox, the form of the occult language appeared identical, albeit in different combinations of letters. Of course, that did not make its exact meaning any less of a mystery.

"Let's go," Julie confirmed. Aida stepped inside without further hesitation, and invited her lover to follow. With those words, the revulsion that weighed upon Julie's shoulders dissipated, and the threshold presented no resistance. Behind her, she could hear Arnold begin to converse with Saul.

"What do you have there?"

"A protective talisman."

"A magical thing?"

"Yes, bought from a witch in Damascus."

"And what exactly does it do?"

"Perhaps I shall explain another time. For now keep to your cross, Mister Brennan."

The group advanced into the house, carefully opening each door that branched out of the hallway. A large oak staircase, its timbers stained with damp and riddled with woodworm, led to the floor above. Aida soon found a door which revealed a much narrower stone stairway, vanishing down into utter darkness.

"Spread out and search, just as on Dover Street," Julie instructed the others. "The four of you check the ground floor rooms and the cellar. I'll look upstairs."

Leaving the others to set about their work, the vampire ascended the rotten stairs to the upper floor. Even under her catlike steps, the ill-maintained woodwork creaked more than once. Surely the five hunters were alone in this carcass of a building. Surely nobody could be squatting in a place as unfit as this, not on an island with such a small population, yet her instincts were screaming at her to beware. If there was another vampire here, she would smell them a mile away. So why the intense unease? Unlike the others, Julie had not drawn any weapon, but her hand rested upon the hilt of her sword all the same.

She made her way along the landing, checking each door in turn. It seemed to her that not only had Rozgonyi failed to make use of this house after Sir Hans' purchase, but it had never even been refurnished after the previous occupants had moved out. Rooms stood bare, devoid of any sign of human habitation. On the floors, only rats and insects scurried to avoid Julie's gaze when she disturbed each chamber, while irritated bats flapped and squeaked in the rafters above. Then she came to the master bedroom.

The room itself was in no better state than any other in this place. The floorboards were soiled and the walls mouldering, yet a goose-feather mattress and clean linen sheets lay upon the otherwise-neglected bed. Julie moved closer to investigate, her eyes wandering over the luxurious material.

A small wooden bookcase had been moved in here, and it was in poor enough condition to have belonged to the house, yet the modest collection of books upon it bore no accumulated dust or degradation of their pages. Eyes narrowing in confusion, she lowered herself to the bedsheets and inhaled deeply. The bed was not perfectly made; clearly someone had slept here, and yet she could detect nothing beyond the vermin-ridden scent of the house itself.

A movement in the periphery of her eye caught Julie's attention, and she spun to face it, drawing her scimitar in a fluid motion. Some form of thick, dark mist, akin to a coal-fire's smoke, was creeping in through the doorway, moving by itself in the absence of any breeze, and instantly she knew what she was facing.

Master vampires often displayed a talent for metamorphosis, hiding in the forms of beasts just as easily as their human guises, but even among their ranks it was a rare gift to become entirely incorporeal. Very few vampires had the skill to abandon physical form and travel as mist or shadow, and yet here was one who could do so.

The dark cloud began to gather upon itself and rise, billowing together and congealing, solidifying into the shape of a woman. This new arrival was not tall of stature, but her baring was regal, her Byzantine features aquiline and sharply patrician. Like Julie she had dressed in the fashion of a man, but her clothing was of the utmost finery, comprised of jet-black silk breeches, waistcoat and evening-cloak, over a pristine white shirt. A dainty black bergère hat decorated with white ostrich feathers sat atop her russet-red hair, which hung in a thick braid from the back of her head. About her was an air of cold and merciless authority, her icy blue eyes hardened by seven centuries of cruelty, intrigue and betrayal.

"Julie d'Aubigny, Progeny of Tloque Nahuaque. It is an honour at last."

The woman addressed her in perfect English, though Julie suspected that she could have conversed in a hundred different tongues with equal fluency. There was a trace of an accent, albeit one that was lost to the ears of this century, but beyond all of that, her voice carried the weight of her power. Julie had no doubt that dominating the will of mortals was an effortless thing to her, coming so easily that she commanded absolute obedience with her every word. Even Julie felt her instincts recoiling, the demon within her steeling itself at the presence of such a formidable rival.

"Serena Laskaris, I presume. However did I not sense your approach–?" She faltered, a moment of realisation dawning. "Of course. The inscriptions downstairs."

The Master vampire smiled, a mechanical gesture that was as joyless as a shark's hungry gape.

"Yes. A simple spell of concealment. Enough to mask our presence from your senses."

"*Our* presence?"

From downstairs, there came sudden cries of warning. The sounds of a skirmish began to erupt, and the hallways echoed with the crack of a discharging pistol. Anger surged within Julie, fingers tightening around the hilt of her weapon. In a blink her eyes reddened in fury, her fangs lengthening behind her lips. Serena had set an ambush, and like a fool she had led her own people into it. Arnold and Clayton could die for her mistake. Aida and Saul, the most beloved and loyal companions she had ever known, could die for *her* mistake.

"How long have you been waiting here?" she snarled.

"Not long at all," Serena responded with a dismissive laugh. "My dear girl, you followed every breadcrumb that I laid for you. Michel Renard and his band of imbeciles might have disrupted the proceedings if they were allowed to continue, but once I slaughtered them, it was certain that you should come here. All of the clues were planted to draw you to this place."

"Is that so? I expect that István Rozgonyi was also working for you in this entire charade?"

"Who would have thought that the learned Sir Hans Sloane would be so easy to fool with a few letters? He thought he had found a staunch ally, a fellow scholar of great expertise. But no, *Mademoiselle*. I *am* István Rozgonyi."

More gunfire could be heard from below, along with the bloodthirsty shrieks of attacking vampires. Clawed feet were ascending the stairs rapidly, and a second later the inhuman shapes of four strigoi loomed into Julie's vision, filling the doorway behind their Master.

"Take her," Serena uttered, slipping away like a shadow as her servants advanced into the bedroom.

Julie screamed in rage. The strigoi had her outnumbered and cornered, and she did not care. Serena Laskaris could well have her outmatched, and she still did not care. Her companions, her lover, were fighting for their lives downstairs, and so long as there was any chance that the twins still drew breath, Julie would let nothing keep her from them. She hurled her blade at the nearest of the oncoming vampires, and within the close confines of the bedroom, the creature had little space to dodge. It raised its arm in an effort to block the thrown scimitar, but did not move quickly enough, and it roared like a beast when the hefty weapon bit deep into its chest.

In the wake of her sword, Julie launched herself forward, abandoning all pretence of finesse. Rarely did she ever reveal the monstrous form that lay within her. It was very much her preference to maintain the guise of the woman she had once been, even when in battle, but there were occasions when the capabilities of her true shape proved useful. There were also occasions where she simply felt no desire to hold back. As Julie charged, her skin began to stretch and tear, her mortal shape splitting apart like the caul of a newborn. In a space of moments the visage of the lithe woman disintegrated, and her vampiric self emerged in all its hellish grotesquery.

The thing was huge; a loathsome, alien amalgamation of gigantic bat and unadulterated nightmare. Its immense chiropteran wing-arms stretched more than twelve feet from tip to tip, and their hands bore curving black talons as long as daggers. Coarse, oily fur covered the monster's horrible, flabby body, which was larger than that of any strigoi. The bat-horror's hideous face carried jaws filled with rows of demonic fangs, and from within its mouth there protruded a snaking, prehensile tongue. Not without reason did the K'iche' Mayan language name this creature camazotz, the *death-bat*.

Julie crashed headlong into the wounded strigoi, forcing her enemy to the ground. Her claws descended in a flurry of brutal strikes, breaking open the creature's skull and scattering its brain matter across the floorboards. The force of the blows was more than the rotten timbers could take, and the floor gave way beneath Julie and her victim, sending both of them plummeting into the room beneath. The mostly-decapitated strigoi hit the ground, its body still writhing wildly as Julie released it from her grip. She landed not far away, her bulky frame moving on all fours, as the other three vampires came leaping down in pursuit.

No sooner had one of them landed than she swiped the legs out from under it, dragging it down and ripping furiously at its throat with her teeth. The remaining two strigoi descended upon her, tearing deeply into her flanks with their claws, and she welcomed the pain of their blows, letting it add to her rage. With another shuddering bite her jaws broke through the downed vampire's spinal vertebrae, and she swatted the creature's head away from its body.

As she rounded upon her other two foes, the strigoi leaped back from her reach, trying desperately to put some distance between themselves and her. In their crimson eyes there was now more fear than rage, each bloodsucker terrified that they were the next to face her wrath.

The report of a nearby gunshot briefly drowned out all other noise, and in that moment Julie attacked. At random she chose the strigoi to her right and threw herself upon it, overwhelming it with her strength. The panicked creature thrashed and struck out with a fury born of pure survival, slashing and biting at her, but this fight was only going to end one way. Her talons punched into her enemy's ribcage and her arms heaved, the room filling with the ghastly snapping of ribs and the tearing of muscle as she split its torso wide open.

The strigoi tried to howl in agony, but it could no longer force air through its larynx as Julie lunged into its open chest cavity, seizing its heart in her jaws and crushing it with a bite. The creature's muscles spasmed for the last time, and then fell still.

Julie raised her bloodied head to survey the room, seeing that her fourth enemy had fled. With an ungodly snarl she forced her body to reassert its mortal shape, her great wings and monstrous physique shrinking away, disappearing beneath the womanly guise which spun itself around her form and cocooned her. It defied all reason for such a hellish creature to hide within human skin, and yet as the camazotz returned to the shape of Julie d'Aubigny, only her bloody eyes and predator's fangs made clear her true nature.

The remnants of her shredded clothes hung upon her in tatters, matted with blood from her open wounds, but there were not words to describe just how little this concerned her. She moved towards the dead strigoi which was still impaled upon her scimitar, and she tore the blade free with a wrench of her hand, determined that Serena Laskaris would be next.

The sound of all other fighting had stopped, but the place was saturated with the stink of mortal blood and bowels, and she moved directly towards the source. Emerging into the living room, relief washed over her as she saw Saul and Aida both alive, although badly beaten, disarmed and on their knees. Arnold was there too, lying stricken upon the floor, cradling the bleeding mess that was his right hand.

His bloodstained crucifix lay where it had fallen, and Serena stood not far away with a pistol still smoking in her hand. Julie realised that the last gunshot she heard must have come from that weapon. In desperation Arnold lunged for the wooden cross, his fingers reaching towards it, but Serena moved in a blur and kicked the icon away from his grasp. Her boot came down and pinned Arnold's head to the floor, threatening to crush his skull at a moment's notice.

Finally there was Lawrence Clayton, the poor man whimpering in pain as he looked upon his split open belly, coils of pink intestine spilled out across the floor in front of him. It was the smell of his shit that pervaded the air. Surrounding Julie's companions were six more of Serena's war-dogs, some in human form, others openly displaying their monstrous selves.

Six bloodsuckers still standing, three that Julie had

brought down, and the venerable Serena Laskaris herself. The group had faced ten strigoi this night, and in this place of their enemy's choosing, such odds were hopeless from the start. There was no way that they could have prevailed, being ambushed by so many.

Julie met Serena's gaze, her sword still in hand, as if there were any way that this battle could be won. The Master vampire tilted her head towards Clayton, or rather, towards the strigoi who was standing over his maimed body.

"That one is of no use," she stated bluntly, and her minion responded by sinking its fangs into the Bow Street Runner's fleshy neck, biting deep and drinking hungrily. Julie started as if to intervene, but he was already far too wounded to be saved, and a single look from Serena told her that if she took even one step, more deaths would swiftly come. Clayton gave a final, strangled cry as the last embers of his life were snuffed out. His body slumped, its strength spent, and the vampire who killed him lifted its head, blood still dripping from its bestial jaws.

"Are you quite ready to give up?" The Master enquired of Julie. "Or would you prefer to watch all of your allies be killed before your eyes?"

At first Julie struggled to reply, and for the briefest of moments her eyes made contact with those of Aida. She immediately cursed herself for it, for the glance did not escape Serena's notice.

"Rest assured, your little harlot will be next. And I will make her final moments more exquisite than your worst imaginings."

This was how defeat truly felt, Julie realised. It had been so long since she had last tasted its bitter sting. But this was far worse than simply being bested by an enemy. Aida was going to die this night, she was certain of it. Serena had not an ounce of mercy in her soul, and the only reason that Julie's lover was alive at all, was because Serena clearly wished to force her compliance.

Julie could not begin to guess what insane scheme made her compliance necessary, but right now all she could do was cling to every chance, and buy more time for Aida to stay alive.

"I surrender," she forced the words from her mouth.

"Again," Serena demanded, and Julie threw her sword to the ground in a show of despair.

"I surrender! Please, do not kill her."

"Very good."

The Master vampire lifted her foot off of Arnold's head, stepping away from the young clergyman, and two of her underlings immediately moved to keep the boy pinned down, even as he clutched at his bloodied and enfeebled hand. Serena glided towards Julie with casual nonchalance, as though the two women were simply a pair of old acquaintances, or even friends. Her expression was sanguine, but her cold eyes were filled with nought but cruel triumph. Then her hand darted to her wrist, drawing a slender stiletto dagger from its hidden sheath in her sleeve. Julie spied the glimmer of the blade, immediately recognising the strange, silver-bronze metal of which it was forged.

Orichalcum.

Serena plunged the weapon into her belly, twisting *hard*, and Julie's world exploded into crippling torment.

~ Arnold ~

Saturday October 23rd, 1756

Everything had happened so fast. Arnold had begun to search the living room with Clayton, when Saul's voice had declared that they were under attack. The twins came bursting into the room in a fighting retreat, a whole pack of strigoi bearing down upon them. The vile creatures must have been lurking in the cellar, but it was clear that they were not surprised by the intrusion into this house; if anything, they had been waiting for it.

For all their martial skills and fine weapons, Saul and Aida were swiftly overwhelmed. Clayton and Arnold both fired shots with their pistols, but bullets alone were scarcely an inconvenience to the bloodthirsty demons. The clergyman had watched in horror as one of them gutted Clayton with a swipe of its claws, but the sight of the detective's evisceration had awakened his zeal. He drove the monsters back, forcing them to retreat as he held his crucifix aloft and proclaimed words of divine admonition.

Then that terrible woman had arrived, appearing as though out of nothingness. With wordless obedience her minions parted to make way for her, and while she did not approach nearer to Arnold, neither did she flinch in pain from the sight of the cross or the sound of his voice. She raised a pistol of her own, and before he could react, she used it with brutal precision to relieve Arnold of his weapon.

He had stumbled, tripping to the floor, his reason lost in the hot pain of the gunshot and the sight of his bleeding wound. Then Julie was there, and the dreadful woman's boot was upon his face. That moment had felt like an eternity, the sheer imminence of his death pressing down upon him. In truth, the entire exchange had been over in barely a minute.

Now Arnold felt himself being dragged to his feet, the savage grip of the two strigoi upon his arms, hauling him up from the floor. Julie had fallen; a dozen different wounds marked her flesh, the deep slashes of vampires' talons, and yet she was clutching at her stomach as though the stab of Serena's knife was the only pain she could truly feel. Arnold stared about the room wildly, seeing that Saul and Aida had likewise been pulled upright, manhandled by captors who were taking no chances. Swords, stakes, hammer and firearms were seized from them and thrown into the middle of the room.

Arnold tried to get a look at the two who were restraining him, and the face that he glimpsed to his left was one that kindled a horrible recognition; the face of his own parishioner, Richard Sinclair. He recalled Renard's visit to St Mary's, the news of Helen Sinclair's brutal death, and in that moment he truly hated Serena Laskaris. What burned within his breast was not the righteous anger of a devout Christian towards the Devil's soldiers. She was the instigator of all this misery, and what he felt for her was hatred, pure and personal.

His loathing was written plainly upon his face as he met her eyes, but in her pitiless blue gaze there was not the slightest care. She looked upon him with such disdain that his courage withered beneath it, his fierce conviction eclipsed by a smothering sense of utter powerlessness. In her long life this creature had faced hundreds of pious men like him, perhaps thousands, and not one had been able to bring her low. He could feel her power crawling into his mind, growing in his psyche like some malignant weed, sapping his will. This Master vampire had matched wits with the heroes of old, with great warriors and knights of Christendom in ancient Byzantium. What hope was there for a poor bastard like him, to best her where such mighty men had failed?

In the grip of his captors, Arnold's body slumped. Yet even as his legs gave out, he moved barely an inch; to their great strength he was as weightless as a ragdoll. Behind him, the remaining vampires helped themselves to the group's piled weapons, greedily laying claim to whatever they pleased. Distantly, Arnold was aware of Imogen's talisman still in his pocket, undiscovered by their foes. He had not shown the orichalcum disc to anyone, even though he had been struck by the similarity of its design to Saul's rough-hewn iron amulet. Having seen how easily Serena's dagger had crippled Julie, he wondered if he could use the talisman to do the same to her, but to go on the attack now would be folly; he knew that the monsters could kill him in a heartbeat.

"Time to go," Serena announced, and her servants began to muscle their prisoners outside, two strigoi holding each of Julie's companions by their arms. The twins were first out the door, and as they were hauled past him Arnold saw just how ferociously they had been mauled in the fight. Saul's face was swollen and purple with bruises, his cheek and scalp marked by the grip of a vampire's claws, his nose broken and left eye hidden among the mass of battered flesh where his skull had been beaten against the floor. Similar marks blotched Aida's throat where one of the beasts had almost strangled her, and she was walking with a painful limp, her leg having twisted badly when the strigoi threw her to the ground.

Serena herself took care of Julie, grabbing the fallen woman by one leg and dragging her along the ground like an animal pulling a carcass back to its den. Julie groaned in pain, and Arnold wanted to believe that it was merely a ruse. He imagined that at any moment she may leap up and turn the tables, falling upon Serena from behind and tearing into her, but no such thing happened. Instead the whole group was marched outside and roughly conveyed eastward from the house, down to the beach of Little Bay, where a large tarpaulin awaited them, weighed down with rocks. The canvas was pulled aside to reveal two dinghies beneath, each around sixteen feet in length. The captives were unceremoniously shoved aboard one of them, with Julie being dumped upon the deck at their feet, and the vampires began pushing the boat out into the gently lapping sea.

The journey that followed was as grim as it was quiet. Arnold, Saul and Aida huddled in the boat, clustered above their stricken leader. Two of the strigoi manned the oars while the others kept watch, crimson eyes fixated, lengthened talons trembling as they anticipated Serena giving them the order to kill. The Master herself sat at the prow of the boat, her back to the sea and stiletto in hand as she observed her captives, almost daring them to try anything.

Nobody spoke a word. Only a fool or lunatic would think that escape or mutiny could possibly succeed here, and so they sat in silence. For much of the trip the only sound was Julie's agonised whimpering. Aida reached down to take hold of her hand, tears rolling down her cheeks at the sight of her lover's suffering. She looked down at the deep puncture in Julie's gut; the flesh around it was blackened and necrotic, the edges of the wound horribly mangled. When the boat rounded the north-east corner of the island, and began heading south towards the Eastern Isles, Aida finally spoke up, addressing Serena directly.

"Is this going to kill her?"

She struggled to keep her voice level, but the undercurrent of grief and rage was impossible to hide. The Master vampire looked at her with the same infuriatingly calm, entirely contemptuous expression that she had worn from the beginning. Despite her feigned disinterest, Arnold sensed that she was finding Aida's anguish to be rather entertaining.

"The orichalcum is slowly poisoning her," Serena remarked, dismissively. "Her body cannot heal it without fresh blood. But it will take some time for her to die from a little scratch like that one. She'll last long enough, for what I need."

"And what is it that you need?" Saul spat the question. Serena shot a glance towards the vampire Richard Sinclair, who responded with a malicious smile before driving his fist into Saul's gut, doubling him over and leaving him gasping for air.

"Speak like that again, *slave*, and you will not live to find out."

Arnold met Sinclair's eyes as the strigoi returned to his seat. He hoped to find some trace in there of the man that he used to be; the faithful parishioner, the loyal husband and father. But all that he saw was Serena's bloodthirsty puppet, a demon that gleefully served her will. Perhaps Julie had once been like this, when she was her Maker's plaything, before she regained some sliver of her lost humanity. Perhaps Sinclair could in time do the same, if he were removed from Serena's control. But somehow, Arnold doubted that the option to save him would present itself.

The boat proceeded along its course into the craggy rocks of the Eastern Isles, the uninhabited outcroppings that lay between the larger islands of St Martin's and St Mary's. The long, flat-topped ridge of Great Ganilly was the biggest of them, with waves breaking in a spray of white foam along its base. East of its southern tip was the much smaller isle of Great Innisvouls, and it seemed to be this particular rock which the dinghy was approaching. As the boat drew near, Arnold could see that the low seasonal tide had exposed a narrow opening in the granite, just barely wide enough for their vessel to enter. Judging by the black mass of seaweed which stretched all around it, this cave was far below the normal waterline.

Arnold steeled himself, digging deep to find his faith, wordlessly battling to resist Serena's influence upon his mind. What lay within there was the place he had come here to find, the place where the Outer Darkness tainted God's Earth. He may not have been going there with gunpowder as the others had planned, but he was still going there as the Lord's devoted soldier. When the time came, he would find it in himself to act. The closer they came, the more the weight of the amulet in his pocket began to feel comforting, a secret weapon that he could still utilise. He gave silent thanks that the monsters appeared to consider him less of a physical threat than the twins. After disarming him of his pistol and his cross, they had not bothered to search him further.

The dinghy glided silently into the sea-cave, its wooden sides nudging upon the rocks. As the cave roof loomed up ahead, the light of the stars vanished, and all around them was plunged into deepest blackness. Arnold floundered, unable to see, though the dark presented no hindrance to the strigoi. Once again he felt their hands lock upon him in an unbreakable grip, the boat rocking beneath him as he was hauled over the side and up onto a hard, cold granite surface. He could hear the cries of protest from the twins as they were likewise pulled ashore, just as blind to their surroundings as he was. The air down here was rank with the smell of salt and seaweed, and Arnold was sure he could hear the crawling of unspeakable things on the walls about him.

Roughly he was manhandled to the ground, and although he could no longer feel taloned fingers holding him, an all-too-familiar inhuman snarl confirmed that there was a vampire close by, ready to end him at any moment of the Master's choosing. Serena's voice cut through the dark, no longer haughty and disinterested, but now supremely cold and commanding, speaking not in English but in some guttural tongue that was surely not made for human mouths.

Arnold thought of the alien inscriptions upon the strongbox back at the inn, upon the jamb of the doorway at the house, and on the amulets that he and Saul carried. Was this how that strange, unknowable language sounded, in its spoken form? Its syllables gnawed at the ears, their meaning unintelligible, yet somehow the mind tried to assign meaning to them, conjuring up a sense of things twisted and impossible. Arnold felt his stomach clench with nausea, the bite of acid scalding his throat. Then a ripple of tension enveloped the area, a sensation akin to passing through the surface of water, and hundreds of tiny flames ignited amidst the Stygian gloom. A sprawling array of candles burst into life, their glow illuminating a scene that had no right to exist beneath God's sky.

As Arnold blinked the stars out of his vision, his eyes adjusting to the new light, he perceived the cave which surrounded him. The mouth may have been narrow, but its granite belly was almost as large as the rectory of St Mary's Church, though to him it felt more like a tomb. The walls hung thick with weed, and it was clear that the sea would normally fill this place, save for the few times each year when the tide fell this low. The seaweed had been cleared away from the central area of the cave, however, where a series of tall, lumpen menhir presided around the great flat slab of an altar.

The stones were deeply weathered, eroded by time and tide, but Arnold could see that they had once been fashioned by a sapient will. Their ugly, antediluvian forms bore the imitation of a strange anatomy; bipedal like a human, but with hunched bodies, long ape-like limbs and grisly piscine heads. These ruins were the legacy of the scions of the deep, the gargoyles of the sea, and as he looked upon these perverted mockeries of Creation, Arnold had no doubt that he stood before the truest enemies of his faith. This world was fashioned by God to be the home of man, and there was no space within it for Semjâzâ's monsters.

Candles surrounded the altar and its guardian monoliths in a rough circle, bathing the area in their smoky, yellow light. Their smell was rancid, enough to compete with the already foul air of the sea-cave, and Arnold did not wish to speculate on what creature's fat they were made from. By the look of things they had been placed here recently, so the strigoi must have prepared this cave in advance. If the candles had been here for any length of time, the tide would have covered them at least once, and by rights they should have been too wet to burn. But then again, Arnold had witnessed them be lit by nothing more than Serena's spoken words. This was magic; real, actual devil-craft in action.

The curate lowered his head and began to pray, hands clasped tightly, but he looked up in surprise when the sound of choking, coughing laughter touched his ears. Julie was laughing, even as her hand still grasped at her dreadful wound. Serena moved to stand over her, looking down upon her fellow bloodsucker without confusion or concern at her behaviour, but perhaps with a glimmer of curiosity.

"Whatever you do here, you're wasting your time," Julie forced out the words. "These ruins are *dead*. When I last saw a shrine like this, I could feel its power running through me, but I feel nothing here. The magic in this place is spent. You'll achieve *nothing*."

A look passed between the twins that Arnold could not fully read. For a moment he felt a breath of hope, the sense that even if he died here tonight, at least this devil-woman would not be able to accomplish her goals. That hope died when the corner of Serena's mouth twitched into a smile.

"You presume far more than you know."

The Master grabbed Julie by the throat, dragging her up from the ground and carrying her, one-handed, towards the waiting altar. A heavy thud filled the chamber as Julie was thrown face-down onto the slab, a lamb to be sacrificed. Blood from her belly-wound began to spread across the rock, running in weathered channels upon its surface, gathering in a shallow gutter at its base. She bled profusely, as though the altar itself were pulling the stolen life from her body. She tried to struggle free, but Serena's hand upon her spine kept her pinned in place.

Arnold felt himself being muscled forward; Richard was now behind him, pushing him towards the awful ritual about to unfold. Other strigoi were likewise shoving the twins ahead, bringing them to the edge of the candles, forcing them all to their knees.

"The power here is not dead," Serena told her, cruel pleasure dripping from every word. "It is merely dormant, as were the ruins at Yucatán, when the Nine first found them. When they came to Mexico, they spilled their own blood to awaken the shrine there, and so they made the land their own."

"So you are… working for the Nine…" Julie hissed, her voice horribly weak.

"Only for one of them," Serena smiled. "This is the bargain, for my House's expansion into the American continent. When the shrine in Yucatán was awakened, the sacrifice almost killed the Nine, it took so much from them. My Lady wants to come to Europe, but she is not prepared to risk her own blood to do so. So she offered yours, and through it, your direct connection to Tloque Nahuaque. The Nine are stronger now, than they were then. The blood of just one should suffice."

Serena grabbed a fistful of Julie's hair and wrenched her head upright, gazing down into her dying eyes.

"My dear girl, do you really think that you slipped free of your Maker's control by yourself? You escaped because my Lady willed that you escape. Ix-Tab sends her gratitude, for delivering this land to her. And know that once you are gone, your pet priest is going to be mine. I always enjoy adding men of faith to my ranks. Your pretty twins shall be the first to slake his hunger."

No. As Julie lay bleeding, Arnold had wondered why it was that Serena had kept himself and the twins alive for this long. The knowledge that she planned to infect him, to make him into one of her demons, was more than he could stomach. His hand dived into his pocket, fingers closing upon the orichalcum disc. Sinclair spotted the movement and growled with fangs bared, one hand reaching for him, but Arnold thrust the talisman towards the strigoi, who yelped in pain where the metal touched his fingers. All eyes turned towards him as he rose to his feet, rounding upon Sinclair and grabbing hold of him, pressing the disc onto the vampire's forehead. The words came to him, the same words he had used before, in the alley outside the Minories theatre:

"When He called unto Him His twelve disciples, He gave them power against unclean spirits to cast them out! And these twelve Jesus sent forth and commanded them, heal the sick, cleanse the lepers, raise the dead, cast out Devils!"

Richard Sinclair screamed, his animal shriek echoing through the cavern. The vampire tried to pull free, but all his great strength had faded to nothing, and Arnold's grip remained unbroken. The skin of his face was discolouring, poisoned by the metal's touch, weakened by Arnold's indomitable faith. Blood began to pour in rivulets from his eyes, nose and lips. The strigoi fell to the ground, his blackened tongue lolling from his mouth, muscles twitching weakly.

Arnold turned towards the rest of them, his whole body aflame with righteous zeal. He raised the talisman, presenting its cruciform symbol to the gathered vampires, who shrank back from it, snarling wildly, unable to look upon it. Even Serena now gave him her full attention, releasing Julie from her grip. She stepped towards him, drawing her stiletto blade, but even she faltered, unable to advance as he focused upon her. Behind her, Julie forced herself off the altar, rolling feebly and dropping onto her back.

Again Arnold began to speak, this time reciting the words inscribed upon the chest that held his inheritance, the words of Psalm 23.

"The Lord is my shepherd. I shall not want. He maketh me to lie down in green pastures: He leadeth me beside the still waters. He restoreth my soul: He leadeth me in the paths of righteousness for his name's sake. Yea, though I walk through the valley of the shadow of death, I will fear no evil: for Thou art with me."

The twins saw their opportunity, and did not waste it. In a single fluid movement Saul was on his feet, pulling his scimitar from the belt of a vampire who had claimed it, and hacking the head from the creature with a vicious, two-handed sweep of the blade. As he launched himself upon the next foe, Aida grabbed a familiar pistol from the fallen vampire and pointed it towards Serena, thumbing back the hammer and squeezing the trigger. Arnold realised what was happening and screwed his eyes shut, just before a cloud of white-hot magnesium blazed in the darkness.

A chorus of bestial cries went up from the remaining vampires, their vision scorched by the flare of light. Saul stumbled, disoriented, one arm thrown across his face. But even as the blinding whiteness died away, it became clear that their enemy had not. With impossible speed Serena had thrown herself clear of the fire, and was now leaping back to her feet. With a cry of rage Aida seized a fallen stake and sprinted towards Serena, her eyes alight with fury, every fibre of her will bent upon avenging the wrong done to her lover. The sharpened length of ironwood thrust forward, striking out for the Master's heart. Serena's arm moved far quicker, her fist pummelling into Aida's jaw and sending the young woman reeling. Heavily she crashed into the stone altar, ribs crunching, and she collapsed to the floor with blood spilling from her mouth.

Her fall struck Arnold like a punch to the gut. Sean Musgrave. Lisa Brennan. The Whitfields, the Sinclairs, Charles Lowther, Lawrence Clayton and now Aida N'Dour. Too many people had been hurt and killed by all of this, too much death and carnage had surrounded him, ever since Serena Laskaris set her sights upon England. His knuckles were white as he gripped the talisman, his feet carrying him towards the Master with Holy resolution in every step.

"Go back to Hell, demon!" he commanded her, and for all of her power she still retreated in fear, her blue eyes wide, even a vampire of her mighty strength unable to withstand his fervour. "You are banished! I consecrate this place in the name of the Lord Almighty! I declare this ground sanctified in the name of God the Father, and of the Son, and of the Holy Spi–"

Serena's hand moved in a flash, darting in his direction. Arnold staggered, his words catching in his throat. He tried to draw breath, and could not. He tasted his own blood, his hand moving to his neck, fingertips touching upon the hilt of the stiletto which protruded from his flesh. The thrown blade had struck him in the windpipe, piercing through him, its razor tip emerging from the back of his neck. Realisation hit him even harder than the pain.

Please, God, save them. The words passed through his mind as his legs gave way beneath him, and then he knew no more.

~ Julie ~

Saturday October 23rd, 1756

Trapped upon the altar beneath Serena's grasp, feeling the blood draining from her belly, Julie had been certain that her eternity was about to end. That ancient shrine was consuming her, drawing the life from her just as she had done to countless others since her vampiric transformation, and she knew that it was not going to stop until she had nothing more to give. The last thing she would see as she died was Serena's face, a sneer of mockery upon her lips as she revealed that Julie's treasured freedom had all this time been a lie. Her life was no more than a puppet for one of the Nine, a pawn on the chessboard of Ix-Tab, the Suicide Goddess. And now, Julie's sacrifice was going to unleash that monster upon this corner of the world.

Her vision grew dark as the stone altar drank deeply, the world fading from her sight. The table beneath her was far more than simple carved rock; these ruins were a conduit to a malignant intelligence, ancient and endlessly hungry. With each drop of blood the veil of reality was fraying, growing so thin that she could reach her hand across it, and in the howling darkness beyond, the timeless Qlippothic Ones awaited. She was Theirs for the taking.

Just as the altar was a conduit to them, so too was her blood a conduit to that of her Maker. By herself, Julie could not have been a great enough sacrifice to awaken the power of this place, but the godlike strength of Tloque Nahuaque was more than sufficient. What the darkness had given, so too could it take, and even though thousands of miles lay between Julie and her Maker, she felt His sudden reaction as He realised that He was under attack. His immortal life was draining through her, feeding the same hungry Gods which had once bestowed it upon Him.

Not in millennia had the great Tloque Nahuaque felt fear. Not in millennia had He perceived Himself as anything other than Lord and Master of all He surveyed. But in this moment He felt it, intimately understanding the nature of the sword that was speeding toward His throat. As Julie stood on the precipice of the abyss, the knowledge of her Maker's terror brought her some bitter sliver of vindication. *I will die, but at least I get to drag you with me, you evil old bastard.* It was cold comfort, compared to the knowledge that she was leaving Aida, Saul and Arnold to the mercies of Serena Laskaris.

Reality slipped away and her mind tumbled into the void. Visions assailed her; memories of her Maker, memories of this place, memories of the hungry shadows that reached for her with strangling black tendrils. She perceived a time before time, an aeon where the race of humanity was but a glimmer of a distant future. She saw the stones of this shrine pushed into place, and carved with bizarre tools wielded by slick, crocodile-green hands. She heard the croaking, gurgling cries of the builders, piranha-toothed jaws uttering prayers and incantations to their Qlippothic deities. They made sacrifices of sea-beasts and of their own kind, spilling blood to honour the hungry Gods who lurked in the darkness. Through their terrible rituals, some of those

Gods clawed Their way into the world, to feast upon the life that dwelt here. Julie glimpsed the awful, blasted realm from which They came.

She saw the scions of the deep grow mighty in their worship of the Qlippothic Ones, building immense coral cities upon the ocean floor. She witnessed their ageless, cruel and coldly beautiful lives. She beheld the fall of their Eden, their civilisation shattered by plague and war. The survivors dispersed, to hide away and scratch out what living they could in a world they had squandered. All that they had once accomplished was forgotten, scraps of their existence remembered only in the myths of the fledgling land-dwellers who inherited the Earth.

She saw a tribe of those land-dwellers, those early men and women, in a time when the world was frozen, trudging their way across the ice as they sought a better and easier life. She saw their arrival in a new and bountiful place, a place like none they had imagined. They found tall forests rich with game and fruit, streams and coastlines brimming with fish, more food than they thought possible. She saw the night when nine of the tribe's members, after a day's foraging along the shore, took shelter in a coastal cave from a wild storm. She saw them stumble unwittingly across the ruins that the Gargouilles de la Mer had built, and she saw them rouse the attention of the last Qlippothic One who lurked within, their intrusion disturbing Its long slumber.

She saw them fall to their knees in terror before the great winged shadow, knowing that their presence had provoked a terrible spirit. She saw Its burning trilobite eye look upon them, Its life-hunger stirring. It longed to devour them, but in those nine It saw more than just food. It reached into their minds and offered them a bargain; nevermore would they fear the beasts of the wild, nor the elements, nor the passage of years. It would share Its nature with their own, and make of them immortal spirits like Itself. In their fear, the nine men and women accepted. It led them in the first Rite of Blood, allowing them to partake of Its essence. Afterwards they became mighty, for the power of the Outer Darkness was in them. But so too, they discovered, would they share in Its hunger, condemned to slake their thirst upon the blood of those they had called kin. And when they took life to feed themselves, so did they feed It. They had become Its mouth, Its teeth.

She saw them rule over their former people, unchallenged in their power at first. She saw them feed upon those they had loved. As the Qlippothic One had mixed its essence with theirs, they experimented by mixing their blood with that of mortals, creating the first of their lesser Progeny, those which the Maya would call camazotz. She witnessed them try to replicate the Rite of Blood, to make more with power like unto themselves, but they lacked the knowledge to succeed fully, instead creating 'Master' offspring who spawned new and different bloodlines.

She saw the rule of the Nine grow intolerable for the people. The tribe realised that while their Lords were strong at night, under the daylight they could be fought. She saw the humans come for them with fire and spears and axes, driving them away at great cost in lives. The Nine fled, and the Masters they had spawned were slain or scattered, with some escaping back across the ice to the Old World.

She saw the exiled Lords come to a place far south of where they had originated, into a land of lush, steaming forests. They had travelled long, and they had grown weak, unable to find respite so far from the ruins that were their birthplace. But something in this land called to them, a place where the Outer Darkness touched the world. Heeding the call they swam deep into a cenote, uncovering another derelict shrine of the sea-dwellers. With the spilling of blood they consecrated it for themselves, and the land became theirs. In millennia ahead they would feast upon the people who came to dwell there, raising themselves upon thrones of deceit. The people built great cities and temples, and blood would flow to the Nine Lords like rivers; immortal parasites glutting themselves upon religions that venerated human sacrifice.

Julie saw all of this endure for an age, until mysterious pale-skinned foreigners arrived in their ships, and soon after, came strange vampires who were the distant Progeny of the lesser Rites of Blood. For so long their attention had never wandered beyond their own borders, but now, some among the Nine were gazing with hungry interest towards the world across the Atlantic. They were coming, and Julie's death was paving their way.

Her fingers pressed upon the stone altar. She was so very weak, her senses swimming, yet she could no longer feel Serena's hands pinning her down. It took all the will that she could muster, but with a shove she forced herself away, removing her body from the insatiable shrine and breaking the connection. She hit the ground hard, but was too depleted to even cry out. She needed blood, she craved it desperately, and her nostrils flared as she could smell it so close by. A living body, a beating heart, injured lungs fighting for breath, so very near to her.

By her fingernails she dragged herself across the ground, instinct pulling her towards the warm flesh that promised relief from her torment. Lips pulled back, fangs bared, and she bit down to drink, the precious, delectable blood of Aida N'Dour rushing to fill her mouth. In her yearning she barely registered that it was her own lover she was feeding on, for although the taste of her victim was unmistakably familiar, all else was lost in the sheer voracity that gripped her. Hot blood coursed through Julie, muscle fibres burning as the vital fluid restored her enfeebled strength. The pain in her belly was still there, the poisoned wound unwilling to recede, yet even now it felt more distant, less crippling than it had been. Her body was starting to heal, and having sated its hunger for blood, the darkness within her was now howling for retribution.

She raised her head, her bloodied teeth withdrawing, and she was met by Aida's unblinking gaze. Her heart, slow as it was, seemed to stop altogether. The faintest gasp arose from her lover's throat, her body's desperate attempt to cling to life in spite of all it had suffered. But Aida was broken. She was breathing her last, and Julie knew that she had killed her.

"Aida... no, my love, please no."

Carefully she held her lover's face, fingertips searching her skin for warmth, for vitality, willing her to endure. Aida's head tilted, her unresponsive eyes now staring past Julie, and the immortal woman bit down upon the tide of grief and remorse that threatened to overwhelm her. In her mind she was back in France, fifty-one years ago, watching the love of her life slowly succumb to a vampire's bite. To watch Marie's life fade away had been the greatest anguish Julie had ever known, driving her to the edge of madness, and setting the stage for all that was to come. And yet this was worse, far worse, for it was her own inescapable hunger which had done the deed. Gently she pressed a kiss to her lover's forehead, and then turned away, averting her eyes.

In the near distance she caught sight of Serena Laskaris. The Master vampire was standing above Arnold Brennan's unmoving body, looking down upon him with the detached curiosity of a taxidermist evaluating a dead animal. Serena sank into a crouch, her slender fingers reaching down to pluck her stiletto blade from the corpse's neck. Fury rose within Julie, swallowing her guilt, sharpening her all-consuming grief into utmost hate. Her hand closed upon a nearby rock, and she staggered towards her enemy with hellfire in her eyes. Julie swung her arm, and Serena looked up just in time for the sea-worn hunk of granite to smash into her temple, sending her expensive ostrich-feathered hat flying, and striking her to the ground in a spray of blood.

The sea-cave echoed with the infernal screams of Julie's vengeance. Her fists hammered down upon Serena like a blizzard, pummelling the elder vampire with relentless blows. The dagger fell from Serena's grip and Julie scrambled to snatch it up, rounding upon her enemy and thrusting it deep into her side. Serena howled, and for the first time Julie saw the icy blue of the Master's eyes vanish, eclipsed by the crimson rage that filled her growing pupils. Serena's fist barrelled into Julie's chest, forcing her up and back, and then a vicious kick to the side sent Julie flying through the air, slamming into the cave wall. The orichalcum dagger slipped from her hand and tumbled into a narrow crevice.

All around her, the panicked strigoi were beginning to flee. Their Master was wounded, Arnold's faith and his bizarre talisman had terrified them, and despite the curate's death, the effect of his prayers had not ceased. Julie could feel the same keening sensation that had plagued her at St Mary's, the feverish whispering of her sins, and with it the dreadful sense of divine judgement. Perhaps his consecration of this place was permanent, perhaps it was only temporary, but it was nonetheless palpable to the vampires. Saul was fighting with a hero's valour, a second decapitated corpse now lying in his wake, and the remaining strigoi soon went into full retreat, leaping into the sea to get away.

Only Serena stood her ground, upright once more despite the poisoned wound that she had taken, and she looked ready to add Saul to the list of the dead. But there was no way on Earth or Heaven that Julie was going to let another one of her companions be murdered by this bitch. She pounced towards Serena, her body tearing out of its human guise as she once more took her true shape, and she tackled the Master into the water. Serena struggled wildly, throwing off her attacker and scrambling out of the cave entrance, but Julie pursued her and grabbed onto her with taloned feet.

Powerful wingbeats launched the camazotz into the air, dragging her foe beneath her, but Serena seized hold of Julie's leg and wrung with all of her strength, brutally shattering the thigh-bone. Julie shrieked aloud and the two vampires plummeted from the air, crashing hard into the rocky surface of Great Innisvouls, rolling apart from one another. The camazotz pulled herself up onto all fours, her crippled leg dragging behind her, as Serena's body warped and shifted into its own true, monstrous shape.

Even through the fog of rage, Julie knew that by rights Serena should have her outclassed. Julie may have hailed from a stronger bloodline, but Serena was a Master vampire with seven centuries of experience, and it ought to have been suicidal to face her head-on in single combat. But with Aida's last sacrifice fresh inside her, Julie's body was healing, fighting off the worst of the orichalcum poisoning. By contrast, each passing moment caused Serena to weaken a little further, and while she had thus far resisted her wound far better than Julie could, the baneful metal was taking its toll. Unless she was able to feed, her strength and her reflexes would continue ebbing.

The pair of inhuman predators clashed in a tempest of fang and talon. They tore at one another in a frenzy, gouging flesh and splintering bone with every blow. Their struggle was desperate, hideous, a ferocious battle of survival between demons who could afford one another no quarter, no shred of honour. But attrition was on Julie's side, and as Serena's muscles began to slow, Julie forced her to the ground, seizing her and dashing her head again and again upon the unforgiving rocks. The Master's struggles grew weaker, the fight robbed from her with each successive blow, the punishment too great for even a body such as hers. For a moment Julie relented and Serena rolled away from her grasp, her demonic visage fading as she withered back into her human form.

Exhausted, brutalised, but victorious, the camazotz returned to her own mortal guise, once more displaying the shape of Julie d'Aubigny. Now it was her turn to stand above her shattered and helpless enemy. Now it was Serena's turn to lay broken upon her back, her flesh torn to ribbons, her innards aching from the toxic bite of the orichalcum blade. Now, after seven hundred years, the death that she so richly deserved was finally about to catch up with her.

And now, just as Julie herself had done, it was Serena's turn to laugh. The fallen Master looked up into Julie's eyes, her torn lips grinning widely, her voice lively with infuriating cheer even as she coughed out the words:

"I have not had this much fun… in *decades*."

Julie's fists clenched, and her mouth snarled. Her beloved Aida was dead. Arnold and Clayton were dead. Julie herself had almost died, all at Serena's hand, and all of this to her was no more than a jolly amusement. Julie's claws lengthened, ready to rip Serena's heart from her breast. She hoped that this monster would stay conscious long enough to watch Julie devour it in front of her.

"Your lover could still be saved, down there. Are you just going to let her die?"

What?

In spite of herself, Julie hesitated. The words were surely

a distraction, a subterfuge, just a final desperate gambit to achieve... *what*, exactly? And yet, Serena was not wrong. It had been less than a week since Julie had last tasted Aida's blood. The scars of her last feeding were still upon her skin. In that cold moment, Julie realised that in taking Aida's blood down in that cave, she would have begun the process of vampiric infection. Aida would have become her thrall, and that meant that some tiny, tenacious sliver of life might still be within her. It meant that there was a means by which she could be saved.

The pause only lasted for a second, but Serena did not waste her chance. The Master vampire's body unravelled before Julie's eyes, her ravaged flesh dissipating into smoke and shade.

"No!"

With a scream of cheated fury, Julie threw herself at the ground where Serena had lain, her claws carving grooves into the very rock. But her enemy had gone, slipping into the night, and beneath the light of the stars the only thing that could be seen of her was a patch of dark mist, drifting away over the waves.

The darkness within Julie was howling, wanting nothing more than to give pursuit, to chase Serena down and rip her apart when the morning sun forced her back into physical form. But to do so would have been to abandon Aida. Limping badly upon her wounded leg, Julie moved with all haste that she could muster, throwing herself down the cliff into the waters below, and scrambling for the entrance to the sea-cave. Frigid water dripped from her bare skin, only a few sodden shreds of clothing still clinging to her.

Saul was sitting with his back to the cave wall, his head in his hands as Julie passed by. Wounds and exhaustion had finally taken their toll on him, but Julie was certain that he would live. Instead she limped straight towards Aida, towards her fallen lover, whose life yet hung by the narrowest of threads. The girl was not breathing, and Julie's ears could detect no heartbeat, but she was not so far gone as to be beyond reviving.

So many times, Aida had asked her what it would mean, to join her lover in immortality. So many times had she raised the possibility, and so many times had Julie always refused. But now, after all that had transpired, Julie did not want to let this woman die. The vampire's body was covered in wounds. She positioned her arm above Aida's face, right where a deep slash from Serena's claws would drip its blood between her lover's lips. She watched some of the vital fluid spill forth, droplets staining Aida's mouth, trickling onto her tongue, running down her throat. From behind her came the sound of Saul's voice, calling to her weakly as his one good eye peered through the gloom.

"Julie? Julie, are you there? Aida? What is happening?"

She ignored him, cradling his sister as the blood continued to flow. Movement stirred in Aida's lips, the taste of it calling out to her, rousing her. Julie pressed the open wound to her mouth.

"It's alright, my love. Come back to me."

Unconsciously, Aida began to suckle hungrily.

"Come back to me."

~ Epilogue: Michel ~

Monday October 25th, 1756

After the cold and filth of London, being at home in Paris felt like nothing less than a return to civilisation. Michel Renard stood beneath the vaulted ceiling of the Cathedral of Saint-Étienne, gladdened to be back within its magnificence after receiving the letter of summons two days previous. His heart, however, was still weighted with the burden of failure. His mission in England had not been a success. Aside from his wounds, all he had to show for his time there was a stolen chest full of papers and teeth, and memories of unpleasant brutality that his Brothers had inflicted upon a fellow Christian, even if he was a misguided Protestant. Michel's body was at least healing, well tended by the skills of Brother-Surgeon Guillaume Sardis, but it would be a while yet before he was back to his best. He had taken to walking with a cane until his leg fully repaired, which he entirely despised.

The hour was late, night had long since fallen and the cathedral had been closed to visitors, save for any who should come here seeking sanctuary. Renard did not stand alone, however. Brother Fabian and Brother Jacques were making their way towards him, flanking between them the richly-attired figure of His Eminence Antoine-René de la Roche de Fontenille, the Bishop of Meaux. If he were any ordinary Catholic, Renard would have shown the utmost honour and deference to the bishop, but within the clandestine hierarchy of the Company of the Holy Sacrament, this man was the Commander whom he had sworn before God to obey, even unto death or worse.

Painfully he descended to one knee, clutching his cane for support as he bowed his head. The bishop extended one portly hand, and Renard leaned forward to plant a kiss upon the ornate golden ring which adorned his finger.

"God bless you, my Son."

"God bless and protect you, Your Eminence."

"Stand. Let us talk."

The hunter obeyed, though rising to his feet brought him a fresh wave of pain, worse than the kneeling had. The bishop began to walk slowly through the cathedral, and Renard fell into step beside him. Brothers Fabian and Jacques kept a polite distance behind, though it soon became clear that His Eminence had no intention of asking them for privacy. Renard wondered if he was going to be assigned penance for the deaths of his men at the hands of House Laskaris.

"I am told that the enemy's trail in London has gone cold, my Son," the bishop began.

"Alas, it seems to have done so," Renard replied. "Ever since you sent me more men I have had them combing London's streets in earnest, but we have found nothing, save for a handful of abandoned strigoi nests and a few lowly bloodsuckers who were beneath the notice of House Laskaris, or of La Maupin. We despatched them, but it is a trivial victory."

"God smiles upon the banishment of every demon, no matter how lowly. Each vampire slain is one more evil removed from the world."

"Of course, Your Eminence. But I failed to accomplish our more pressing goals. I am no closer now to finding Serena Laskaris or Julie d'Aubigny. These devils are still free to run the night."

"You are confident that they are no longer present in London?"

"For the past week we have found no further signs of undead feeding or infection among the people, even in the filthiest districts. We have tracked no lairs, save for those which are abandoned, and found no indication of organised vampire activity. I think that House Laskaris is gone from that city. Whatever drew them there, they have either achieved their objective or cut their losses."

"And of the documents that you acquired from the Protestant, do you still believe that they were the enemy's objective?"

"I do not know, Your Eminence. I am certain that the Laskaris wanted them, but I do not think we know all of the details. Their schemes ran deeper than we could discern, I am sure of it."

The bishop came to a stop, turning to face Renard directly.

"Those documents are far more valuable than you may realise, my Son. You did not read them?"

"Brother Fabian took charge of that, Your Eminence. He examined them after we took them, and became most keen to deliver them to you in person."

"Indeed he did, and he was right to do so. Much of the information in those papers is nothing that does not already exist in our libraries, though perhaps some of it was framed by a more modern, scientific eye. But in amongst them were some very rare pages, original Arabic fragments of the *Kitab Al-Azif*. Does this name mean anything to you?"

Michel's brow furrowed. The title was not unknown to

him, but it was a subject on which his personal knowledge was limited.

"A book of diabolism, is it not? I thought that no original copies existed anymore. Only Greek and Latin translations, such as the Book of Dead–"

"The Book of Dead Names, yes," the bishop cut him off. "I too believed that no original copies of this foul manuscript remained in circulation. The copy at the Sorbonne is tolerated solely because much of the knowledge within it is diluted and mistranslated. Even the pages that have been brought to me this past week are only a fraction of the complete grimoire. But all the same, they are direct copies of the pure text, and that makes them dangerous."

"What do you ask of me, Your Eminence?"

"From all I have read of those papers, it seems that the fragments of *Al-Azif* were sent to Sir Hans Sloane by a Hungarian scholar by the name of István Rozgonyi. I will be despatching agents to Buda-Pest to begin investigating this name. The fragments are recently written, so the text from which they were copied must likely still exist. Beyond that, we must begin looking into any and all surviving associates of Sir Hans. We knew of his previous relationship with La Maupin, but this is our first evidence that he continued to make meaningful study of vampires after she broke contact with him. We must know what other secrets he may have uncovered."

"Does this mean that I will be returning to England?"

"It does, my Son. I need you to discover for me the full extent of Sir Hans Sloane's occult researches, especially with regards to *Al-Azif.* That text contains secrets that are the stuff of damnation. It poses a tremendous threat in any hands but our own, and especially in the hands of the undead."

"Of course, Your Eminence. Whatever devilry that man

has unearthed, I will pursue every lead. I will unravel every strand of this web."

"See to it that you do. Knowledge of this kind is perilous to the soul, but in the hands of we who are truly faithful, it offers valuable insights into the motives of our enemies. I find it hard to believe that in the years after La Maupin's disappearance, Sir Hans never considered the possibility that his protégé had joined the ranks of the demons. I expect that he planned and gathered the means necessary to destroy her, in case he should ever need to. Perhaps, among all his secrets, you may find a weapon that will help you to accomplish that which vexes you most."

"I do as commanded, Your Eminence. I will see that demon destroyed, by whatever means that the Lord Almighty should present to me."

~ Epilogue: Aida ~

Tuesday October 26th, 1756

In the rocky bay of Porth Seal on St Martin's, Aida stood alongside her brother and her Maker. Saul had been incapacitated for a full day after the clash with House Laskaris beneath Great Innisvouls, and even after Julie had conveyed him back to his room at the Rock of Priscillian, it had taken a further day's rest before he was back in possession of his faculties. When he had discovered what became of his sister, his reaction had been far from appreciative. But he knew that Aida had wanted this fiercely, and so despite his misgivings he bit his tongue, accepting the new reality for what it was.

At nightfall on Sunday, while Saul still lay in recovery, Aida had awoken to her new life. How beautiful the world had seemed to her in that moment. She walked outside and could smell each of the myriad scents upon the night air, a smorgasbord of intriguing sensations. Her ears could hear the subtlest of sounds, from the splashing of the waves upon the shore to the scuttling of mice beneath the floorboards of the inn, and the beating heart of every mortal who passed her by. When she looked up at the sky above, her newborn eyes fixed upon the slender white crescent of the moon, and she could pick out every bright ridge and shadowed crater upon its distant surface. It made her feel that she had never, even in her most blissful moments, truly perceived the splendour of existence until then.

But with these gifts came the sense of something else; an emptiness within her, and the dreadful certainty that this emptiness could never truly be filled. As Julie's lover, she was intimately familiar with what the act of feeding entailed. Her Maker had kept watch as Aida selected a young lad wandering drunkenly at the Lower Town Quay, and lured him away into her clutches. That first taste of his blood upon her tongue was simply divine, and all that she craved was to drink and drink until his veins were spent, his life consumed. Julie had not allowed her to indulge such impulses, however, and had pulled her off of him when she judged that the feeding had gone on too long.

Aida understood why, of course. She had seen how hard Julie had to fight her own instincts, simply to avoid becoming a careless murderer. It would not do for Aida to sink into depravity when her own Maker was so adamantly against it. When the time came to cover her tracks by altering the boy's memories, the deed came so naturally to her that she felt as though she had done it a hundred times before. His thoughts were exquisitely malleable beneath the force of her will, and all he would remember was passing out in a haze after too much ale. Even Julie's eyes betrayed a flicker of concern at just how readily Aida played with his mind.

Afterwards, Aida had spent some time imagining how delectable it might be to share a meal with her lover, to have both of them feeding upon the same victim simultaneously, feeling the same heartbeat, but she did not voice those thoughts aloud.

Later that same night, they went on to demolish the ruins and collapse the sea-cave entrance on Great Innisvouls.

Although they had debated waiting until Saul was ready to be involved, they had in the end decided not to delay, if only for fear that Serena Laskaris might come slinking back with some contingency plan in mind. They saw no sign of the Master vampire, however, and Arnold's body still lay where he had fallen. They wrapped him in a canvass and placed it upon the dinghy, and took time to recover both his talisman and Serena's orichalcum blade.

Once the barrels of gunpowder had been positioned within the cave, they poured a trail, set a torch to it, and then made a swift departure before it detonated behind them. Some of the barrels had been placed to destroy the stone altar and the menhir that stood watch around it, blasting those evil structures to rubble. The rest made certain that nobody would ever again stumble across that cave. Then the two vampires had returned to the house overlooking Little Ledge and Great Merrick Ledge, recovered the body of Lawrence Clayton, and wrapped him alongside that of Arnold Brennan.

The Monday passed quietly, but now that Saul had regained his senses, the time had come to pay their respects to the departed. In the narrow cove of Porth Seal they built a pyre out of driftwood, along with timbers ripped from the derelict house. Then they retrieved the bodies from where they lay, carried them down to the shore, placed them atop the pyre and doused it with whale oil. None of them knew any last rites for the Church of England, so they simply thanked the dead for their service, before Saul picked up a torch and set the pyre ablaze.

For a time they stood and watched the fires burn, the flames dancing in the eyes of the two women. Saul looked uncomfortable, shooting furtive glances at his sister and her Maker. In his hand he held the talisman that had belonged to Arnold. As the only one of the three who was human, he was the only one who dared touch the orichalcum disc with his bare skin. Aida noticed her brother's behaviour, but while previously she might have asked him to speak with her of the cause of his upset, she knew that his willingness to confide in her was diminished, perhaps forever. She was still his sister, and perhaps he still considered himself her brother, but ultimately he was still human, while she and Julie were not.

As they watched the flames consume their fallen allies, it was Julie who eventually broke the silence. Her words did not come as a surprise to either of the twins. They knew that things could not simply go back to how they were.

"It has been an honour to have you by my side, Saul. I thank you for all your help. Live the best life that you can, for me."

He nodded, his expression stoic, but there was sorrow in his dark eyes which he could not conceal.

"It has been an honour to travel with you these past years. I have learned a great deal from you."

"What will you do now?" Aida asked of him.

"I shall return to London for a time. Arnold's family – those that are left – deserve to know that he is dead, and that he died fighting for what is good."

"That thing you hold belongs to his sister," Julie added. "The night I visited Tom at the theatre, Imogen Musgrave was there, asking him to identify some artefact that her father had left her. I didn't realise it would be anything as valuable as orichalcum."

Saul turned the disc in his hand, examining it. The design upon it was almost identical to that on his own iron medallion, a spell of protection against vampiric influence upon the mind, but this was far superior in its quality and craftsmanship. It also looked to be a great deal older. For all that he knew, this thing hailed from mythic Atlantis itself.

"Then I shall return her property to her," he affirmed, "and I shall tell her how Arnold used it. I feel that she may need its protection, one of these nights. After that I will sail back to Saint-Louis. I think that Father and I will have a lot to discuss. What will be your next move?"

Julie turned to look at him, heartened by the news that he was ready to rejoin his family. In response to his question, she reached down to the stiletto dagger on her hip, and drew it from its sheath. She spun the weapon once in her hand, its orichalcum blade gleaming like quicksilver in the firelight.

"I'm going to track down Serena Laskaris and plant this in her heart," she stated. "And then I shall start planning for the longer game. When I was bleeding upon that altar, I saw how the Nine Lords came to be. It showed me the Thing that they struck a bargain with, and I saw the place that It came from. There is a legion of hungry shadows, waiting in the Outer Darkness. They merge themselves with humans in order to feed upon the life here. That's what vampires are, what our power and our hunger come from. It's why we don't reflect or cast shadows of our own, because joining with them removes us in part from this world. Each bloodline is simply a different manifestation of that union. But now that I know how the Nine were made, I think it's time I start looking for ways that they can be unmade."

Aida felt her admiration rising at the resolve in her lover's voice. She was quite accustomed to Julie's fierce devotion to the hunt of her own kind, but the way she spoke now was different, rooted in something greater than personal vengeance. When Julie had taken up arms against the Nine in the last days of her mortal life, it was because she had wanted them to face justice for unleashing the vampiric plague upon the Earth. Maybe, she even believed at the time that defeating the Lords could bring an end to that plague. Perhaps the things she had seen upon the altar had rekindled that belief, or perhaps they had not. Maybe she was simply ready to go to war with the blood-gods because war was what they deserved.

"I will have your back, my love," Aida told her. "I will be with you every step of the way."

She took her lover's face in her hands and kissed her, her passion blazing like the flames that roared behind them. But Julie did not return the gesture. Instead she backed away, her mouth parting from Aida's, a look of pain in her emerald eyes. Gently, she shook her head.

"I'm sorry, my love. But you shan't be coming with me."

The words hurt, deeply. Aida stared, uncomprehending, at the woman who had changed her life so much. After four years, Julie had finally shared that which Aida had most wanted. Vistas of potential lay before them now, possibilities spanning beyond anything mortals could experience. How could she turn her back upon all of that?

"Why?" she stammered.

"Because you are my Progeny," Julie's voice wavered, her heartbreak colouring every word that fell from her lips. "The darkness in you listens to the darkness in me. If I told you to kill your brother for me right now, you would do it. You might hate me for it afterwards, but you would still obey me. However hard we try to resist, in time all we can do is feed the very worst of what we are. I cannot ask you to be my conscience any longer, Aida. And I know I cannot be yours."

Julie related the very sentiment that her brother had spoken to her, not three weeks previous in London. Aida knew the words to be true, but that knowledge did not lessen the feeling of betrayal. Poisonous anger welled up inside her, eclipsing even her grief. The fledgling darkness within her growled hungrily, tasting this bitter emotion for the first time, and liking it.

"You turned me and now you wish to *abandon* me?"

"I turned you so that you didn't have to die. And now I'm leaving you for the exact same reason. If you want to hold on to what is good, find people that you care about, and surround yourself with them. Their love will keep you on the path, and their shame will hurt you when you stray from it. Please take care of your brother for me, my love."

Julie looked past her, towards Saul.

"Please take care of your sister."

Like that, Aida watched the woman she loved turn and walk away from her. She wanted to pursue her. Her hands clenched into fists. She wanted to grab her, and hold her, and punch her and kiss her and tear her into bloody pieces. The sheer flood of horrible, conflicting desires stopped her in her tracks, eyes wide in shock at the things she was feeling. Never in her life had she so wished to do such harm to her lover, and the fact that she could feel this way at all frightened her to her core. She forced her fingers to uncurl, willed her fangs to recede. She had to let Julie go.

Tenderly, she felt Saul's hand touch upon her shoulder.

"She has to go her own way, Aida. We have to go ours."

The vampire closed her eyes and nodded, a cold tear streaming its way down her cheek. She followed after her brother as he began to make his way back up the shore, heading inland. In the distance behind her, she heard the rush of chiropteran wings as her Maker took off skyward. Of course Julie would not be travelling back to the mainland with them. Very few of their possessions were hers, after all, and she could fly faster than any ship. Aida could too, she supposed, but she thought it preferable to travel back to London with Saul. It would be better for him not to be on his own in such a dangerous city. And then perhaps she too would sail back to the Senegambia, back home to Saint-Louis and their family.

She thought about the plans for her future that awaited her there. She was quite certain that Father would already have made arrangements for her to find a husband, one who would advance both his business and the family's social standing. She could already envision him talking about the matter over quiet drinks with Saul, deciding which future brother-in-law would be the most profitable. Her expression hardened at the thought of it.

Perhaps, when Aida returned home, she and Father would have some quiet discussions of their own.

About the Author

James Frost grew up in the north of England, where he earned a BSc in Applied Biology and an MSc in Wildlife Conservation, before going into laboratory work. While the natural world was always his great passion, he developed a keen interest in both history and the macabre ever since reading *Dracula* in his school years.

From university onwards, much of his leisure time revolved around the hobby of tabletop and live action role-playing games, where he developed a taste for crafting stories. While always an avid reader, this book is his first foray into writing novels.

Lightning Source UK Ltd.
Milton Keynes UK
UKHW011154130622
404347UK00002B/132

9 781914 498749